Master of the Sweet Trade

Master of the Sweet Trade

A Story of the Pirate Samuel Bellamy, Mariah Hallett, And the Whydah

Elizabeth Moisan

FMC Press, Inc.
Dennis, Massachusetts

Master of the Sweet Trade:

A Story of the Pirate Samuel Bellamy, Mariah Hallett, and the *Whydah*

Second edition.

ISBN: 978-0-9794324-5-3

Printed in the United States of America

In memory of my husband Peter

and

In honor of our son Andrew

also

In memory of my father, and in honor of my mother

William and Frances Geberth

"No, a merry life, but a short one shall be my motto."
Attributed to Bartholomew Roberts, 1682?-1722
From *A General History of the Robberies and Murders of the Most Notorious Pyrates*
By Captain Charles Johnson (Daniel Defoe)

✠ ✠ ✠

"What's past is prologue."
The Tempest, II, i, 261
William Shakespeare

Author's Notes

Whydah*, Samuel Bellamy's famous ship, is pronounced ***whī*-dah. She was a three-masted, square-rigged gally built in London in 1715 specifically for the slave trade, and carried about 600 captives. At approximately 300 tons, she could also be powered by long oars called sweeps. She was a "separate trader," which meant her owners paid a fee to the Royal Africa Company for the right to engage in slave trade on the West African Coast.

*Until the nineteenth century, the word *larboard* was used to define the left side of a ship or boat, and anything associated with it. But because of the confusion caused by its similarity in sound with *starboard* (the word for the right side), it was eventually changed to *port*, and remains so today. Sam Bellamy and his contemporaries would have said larboard in their lifetime, and so it is in this book.

*Mariah (mah-***rye***-ah) is the old-fashioned English spelling and pronunciation of Maria, which is Latin for Mary. I am using this spelling because it is unlikely the Latin pronunciation would have been used three hundred years ago in Protestant New England.

*In the September 19, 2008 issue of *Forbes Magazine*, an article by Matt Woolsey entitled "Top-Earning Pirates" reported the wealth of twenty pirates from the seventeenth and eighteenth centuries calculated in 2008 dollars. In first place, with plunder equaling $120 million is Samuel Bellamy. His short career lasted approximately eighteen months, and his greatest success came from seizing the *Whydah* and her treasure.

Acknowledgements

No book, as they say, is written alone. This is my chance to thank the many people who helped, supported, contributed, advised, guided, listened, soothed, relieved, praised, critiqued, corrected, discussed, analyzed, asked, answered, did a favor or two, came to the rescue, came in handy, threw in their two cents, asked if the end was insight, opened conversations with, "So, how're the pirates?", and who read, read, read, and read again.

Thanks to Barry Clifford for following his dream and finding the *Whydah*;

Thanks to *The Whydah Project* in Provincetown, Massachusetts, for basic research, answers by the dozen, and their terrific museum;

Thanks to my parents, William and Frances Geberth, who are there for *everything*—always, always, *always*;

Thanks to everyone in my writing groups: the Brooks Free Library Writing Group in Harwich, Massachusetts, and the Heatherwood Writer's Group in Yarmouth, Massachusetts;

Thanks to those who edited different chapters, drafts, and revisions: John Prophet, Linda Foley, Andrew Moisan, Charles Strauss, and Marge Frith;

Thanks to The Readers who gave their time and thoughts freely, right from the very beginning: Mom, Dad, Deb, Andrew, Jim, Tom, Dave and Marilyn, Linda C., Linda M., Ilse, Rick, K, Desiree, David, Gayle, Ed and Sylvia, and John and Ellen. If I forgot someone, I do apologize;

Thanks to the Cape Cod National Seashore Salt Pond Visitor's Center; the Cape Cod Museum of Natural History; the Warren

Anatomical Museum, Harvard Medical School in Cambridge, Massachusetts; the Department of Fish and Game of the Commonwealth of Massachusetts; and the United States Coast Guard;

And a very special thanks to my three favorite pirates: John, Jim, Charles. This book would not have sailed without them.

✠ ✠ ✠

Since I began work on the second edition of this book, the world of historical pirates lost a champion with the sudden death of Kenneth J. Kinkor in June of 2013. Nearly thirty years ago he brought his love of pirates and history from his landlocked home state in the mid-west to maritime Cape Cod to work with Barry Clifford and *The Whydah Project.* During that time, as the dive team brought long-buried artifacts to the water's surface and daylight for the first time in almost three hundred years, Ken brought the objects back to life with careful research and close attention to detail. He was willing to share his knowledge with people interested in historical pirates, and I am not the only author whose work benefited from that generosity.

We're glad Ken had pirate wallpaper when he was a kid, and he followed his youthful pirate dreams to adulthood. Barry Clifford followed his dreams and found Sam Bellamy's gold. And Sam? He dreamed, too, at least in my book, of bigger and better things. That the lives of these three men crossed in our time is a gift to all who love history.

Those of us who knew Ken, even a little, will miss a smart man with a wicked dry sense of humor. And we thank him very much.

Contents

The Third Part

Gathering Clouds – April 26, 1717

THE CRAWLING MIST THREADED ITS GHOST-LIKE FINGERS THROUGH THE *Whydah's* rigging, pulling her in hand over hand until it reached her stern and swallowed her whole. Water lapped against her hull in small rhythmic splashes as she floated nearly motionless on the calm sea. She groaned and creaked, adding her own dark whispers and shadowy noises to the watery concerto.

The ship's bronze bell tolled out its warning, its clear, purposeful voice cutting through the menacing silence like a double-edged sword. Announcing their presence in the fog kept the *Whydah* safe from colliding with another ship, but also left them vulnerable to discovery. The edgy crew, willing to fight to the death to save themselves and their rich cargo, kept a silent watch. Bound together in this enterprise by an oath, each man was alone in his vigil and in his thoughts.

It was all in Sam Bellamy's hands, and never had he felt as exposed as he did here, deep inside this dense, soul-draining fog. His crew was loyal, and in exchange for that fidelity, he'd given them his best. They followed his orders knowing his plans to be square and true. Every day for a year and a half they risked capture and the hellish blackness of the gallows and gibbet, to be with him at the end of their journey. And now, so close to Maine and the safe haven on Green Island that they might be there within a few days, Sam charted a new course to Cape Cod, their rendezvous with the *Marianne* postponed so he could follow his heart to Mariah.

They'd been trapped in the murky sea-smoke northeast of Nantucket for close to twelve hours, and with each passing minute their chances of remaining unseen and unchallenged decreased.

Everything was at stake: their prize ship, their golden plunder stored in the dark belly of the *Whydah*, their dreams of ease and abundance—and their lives. Their luck couldn't hold out much longer.

Sam stood aft, his breath shaking slightly as he exhaled. He hated fog and always had. It was peculiar and close, blurring the past, present, and future, setting men off their stride. The measured stroke of the bell's iron tongue became hypnotic and he began to relax. He lifted the bottle of Madeira wine and drank eeply. An echo rang in counterpoint to the deeper voice of the *Whydah's* bell, and he closed his eyes, listening to the music of the song that would be their death knell—or their salvation.

Suddenly alert, Sam stiffened. This was no echo. It was a second bell. An unknown ship had pierced the wall of fog that surrounded them, violating their small patch of visible ocean.

They were no longer alone.

The First Part

Morning Watch: 1701 – 1715

A Different Road

SAM BELLAMY SLOWLY PULLED OFF HIS HAT AND COAT AND HUNG THEM on pegs, aware of the subdued atmosphere in the great room. He'd jogged the last few yards through the fog to his family's home imagining the boisterous welcome from his siblings, followed by the somber, well deserved dressing down from his father that he would take like a man. His explanation for breaking an important work rule, and for being late to supper, would so astound his family with its utter brilliance that all would be forgiven and the sun would shine on his future forever. This vision pleased him, and he opened the door with a big smile already on his face. The unexpected silence that greeted him blocked his path like brick wall, and for the second time that evening he felt alone in a dark, foggy maze.

Lizzie stirred the contents of a pot that warmed by the fire, studying the simmering liquid with unusual concentration. The second of six children, she'd been nine when Sam was born, and was the only mother he'd ever known. Despite stepping into her role as substitute mother at that tender age, she managed her troop of younger siblings with natural ease and grace. It was her serious expression that worried him the most.

"Come away from the door," she said, "an' have your supper."

"Where's pa?" Sam asked, looking around the room.

"He come home from work madder'n I ever saw him, an' took his supper in there." She nodded toward their father's bedchamber and ladled stew into Sam's bowl. "He ain't come out, nor said a word. He wants you in there when you're done eatin'."

Sam picked up a spoon and stared into his bowl of stew. He'd been famished only a few minutes ago. The heavenly aroma, drifting up on the steam, tantalized his nose—but he'd lost his appetite. He cast a worried glance across the long trestle table at Margaret and Anne, his two middle sisters. They were less than a year apart in age, and oneseldom did anything without the other. They gave him encouraging half smiles—tinged with pity, he wondered?—before turning back to stitching their samplers, heads close together, whispering and watching.

"Well, go ahead. Eat!" It was Charlie. The next youngest, he was always first to speak, usually without thinking. He seemed determined to make teasing Sam his life's work despite what he might choose to do for his living. "Pa's goin' to tan your hide," he added gleefully, "an' use the rest for fish bait."

"That's enough, Charlie," Jack said. He was the oldest, and assistant to their father who was foreman at the ropewalk. "Tend to your business an' study your next move. You're goin' to lose men." They were playing draughts, and Charlie turned back to the game board.

"What's this all about?" Jack asked Sam. "Where've you been?"

"I tell you he's been down to Billy's," Charlie said. "He's so daft, he got lost in the fog, is all. Eh, Cap'n Bellamy?" He snickered. "Lost for hours an' hours, wanderin' 'round in circles, is my wager. How're you goin' to navigate at sea if you can't find your way on land right here at home—in Plymouth; in England."

Sam flushed. "Shut up. Just shut up."

Lizzie stopped Charlie's retort with a light cuff to his shoulder and he fell silent. Jack studied Sam's worried face. "Thought you liked it, workin' with us. What happened?"

"Sammy don't want to make rope no more. That's what happened."

"Charlie, you keep out of this. It don't concern you."

"Does so, Jack. If I have to work there, so does he!"

"I'm talkin' to Sam, not you. You settle down."

"I ain't! Pa's the one to do the talkin', an' you ain't pa!"

"But I am." Stephen Bellamy's quiet words stopped the commotion in mid flow. He spoke only to his youngest child. "Sam." Sam put down the spoon and went to his father, who ushered him into his bedchamber and closed the door.

✠ ✠ ✠

They sat before the small fireplace for some moments, and Sam, on a low stool, leaned closer to the hearth, hating the silence. Silence in the fog. Silence in the great room. And silence here. He wanted to shout just to fill the emptiness with sound. He stole a glance at his father who sat in the only upholstered chair in the house with his legs stretched out before him. His face, half hidden by the muffler he wore against the chill, glowed red from the fire, and looked restful—almost sleepy—and not cross at all.

Sam knew he was expected to speak first, and he searched the flames for words. "I'm sorry for bein' late to supper, Pa," he said after a while. "An' for leavin' work before quittin' time."

"One of my other 'prentices had to do your work as well as his own."

"I know. I'm sorry."

"Bein' sorry ain't enough, Sam. You walked away from somethin' you agreed to do, without sayin' a word. An' I don't like you bein' down to the waterfront alone at night, especially in a bad fog like this one. Or daylight neither, now there's war. A good deal more dangerous than it was."

"I can take care of myself."

"So you think."

"I been down there lots of times."

"There's been talk of press-gangs coming ashore takin' men—an' sometimes lads your age an' younger. How was I to know where you got to? You didn't do no thinkin' except about yourself."

No, Sam thought ruefully, I didn't.

"Where'd you go?"

Sam bent to study his shoe and fingered the leather strap. His head, once filled with his simple plan and its glorious outcome, was suddenly crammed with details and issues he'd never once considered.

"I was to Billy's. But you already know that, Pa. Everyone knows."

"Ain't up to 'everyone' to tell me where you been, it's up to you. Doin' somethin' on the sly don't work out too well, does it? Someone always knows if you're lyin' an' cheatin'." He paused. "You get lost in the fog?"

"Some. Over by the warehouses. Wasn't scared, though. Much."

"I see." Stephen unwound his muffler. "Now what's this all about? You had a long face ever since you started workin' at the ropewalk."

"I know you want me to work there, but I can't, not no more. Billy says now I'm twelve it's time I started thinkin' like a man an' I was to tell you, so I'm sayin' it." Sam bit his bottom lip. He'd been holding in his feelings for a long time now, and he finally let them out.

"I hate it! I hate the work an' I hate the place! How can you do it, day after day?" He threw his arms open wide, as if taking in the whole ropewalk. "It's all you do. You an' Jack—you walk for miles an' miles, an' you never leave the buildin'. Never." He swallowed hard and took a deep breath. "I go in the warehouse to look at all the rope, Pa, an' there's mountains of it. An' what's it used for? It's for ships an' riggin'. You an' Jack make it all, an' you don't travel nowhere. It's the rope that goes to sea!" He stopped. His father sat silent, waiting. "I don't want to do this," Sam continued. "I just don't. No more. I ain't got a head for it. All I want is to go where the rope goes. I want to go to sea."

"A hard life."

"I know. I can do it."

"So you reckoned it out, an' talked to Billy, did you?" Sam nodded, and Stephen was quiet a moment. "I see. An' if I was to forbid it?"

"But why? It's a honest trade same as rope makin', riggin' is."

"How'd riggin' get into it?"

"Billy says I should 'prentice with him to learn the trade of riggin' first, so's I could get a good berth when I go to sign on. An' I want to go work for Billy, Pa. I do."

"Ain't no fault in riggin' or sail makin' that I ever seen. If it's the work you want to turn your hand to, that's well an' good. But I'm forbiddin' you to go to sea."

"Why?"

"It ain't the life I want for you."

"But I want it."

"How can you know such a thing? You're too young to know what you want."

"No I ain't. Billy says he's seen it in me. He says you'd know."

"Seems like Billy White got more'n enough to say on Bellamy matters," Stephen observed.

"It ain't like I'd be goin' off to sea now," Sam said, "though some does as cabin boys an' powder monkeys." The wisdom of the words Billy had spoken only a short while ago suddenly came to him, and he played his trump card. "I got it all worked out. I reckon on bein' at Billy's place for a few years 'til I come to the end of my 'prenticeship. Then when I got my full growth, I can sign on any ship when it suits me."

"But it don't suit me."

"Why're you so dead set against it, Pa?

"I don't want my sons at sea."

Sam's face clouded with frustration. "That ain't a reason!"

"You keep a civil tongue when you talk to me, boy! If it's my blessin' you want, then it's reason enough if I say it is." Stephen gave a great sigh and shook his head. "I knew I'd face this one day. You was always the different one: head in the clouds most times, dreamin' of foreign parts." He studied his son's face in the firelight. "You favor your ma in more'n just her looks. Some in her family didn't fit the farmin' life in Devon an' went to sea. Some walked a different road an' went to the colonies. None ever come back, Sam. Not a one. Broke her ma's heart thinkin' on them loved ones, gone for good, an' it ain't goin' to happen now." He shifted uncomfortably in his chair. "God took your ma before you could walk, an' I promised her. She died, holdin' you, you know." Sam nodded solemnly. "I promised her none of our sons would be lost—" His voice trailed off and he coughed back the catch in his throat. "It's reason enough, what I told you, an' there it stays."

They sat quietly for a long moment, Stephen remembering Elizabeth, the pretty young woman he'd married so long ago, and Sam imagining the mother he had never known.

"I'm sorry," Sam said after a while. "An' I'm sorry it'd make ma sad. But rope makin'— I tried, I really did, but it just don't suit me. I got another year in the hemp loft, an' when I get to move on, it's just downstairs. It ain' t enough, Pa, it just ain't. The ropewalk's good for Jack an' Charlie, but not me."

The fire snapped and crackled. Sam picked up the poker and pushed at a log. It broke in two, sending a spray of sparks up the blackened chimney.

"You played at seafarin' when you was younger," Stephen said. "Turnin' a child's game into a man's dream is a mighty big step, an' it took a man to talk to me the way you did. You spoke out your thoughts in a honest way. I ain't goin' to say it sits well with me, but it's your nature, then you ought to have your chance. You finish out the month with me an' I'll talk to Billy."

"Thanks Pa."

"One more thing. I'm givin' young Dick Wilkins some time off from work. He done his work today, an' yours, and tomorrow, you'll do his. An' Sam, there's ways of gettin' what you want in this world that's fair. What you did ain't one of them."

"Yes, Pa."

Sam cupped his face in his hands and dreamed of sailing before the wind, toward an ever-moving horizon. Stephen watched him for a while, and worried.

2

Sam went to work for Billy White at his rigging and sail making business in 1701 when he was twelve, and stayed four years. On the first day he discovered his tasks were the same as some of the ones he'd done at the ropewalk, but he didn't care. He swept, cleaned, and carefully put tools away at the end of the day's work, never once taking his eyes off the activity around him. He was waiting at the shop door when Billy, or his oldest boy, Alf, came with the keys early in the morning, and because he helped tidy the workroom for the next day, he was one of the last to leave at closing time. Everything was different. He was different.

The building Sam worked in was square and chunky instead of long and narrow like the ropewalk. The sail loft, taking up the whole second story, was wide open and uncluttered, almost large enough to spread an entire sail on the floor. Daylight flooding in through the four big windows made the polished floor shine brighter than any he had seen before. When it wasn't covered with canvas, Sam swept it clean as a whistle.

He took particular care washing the windows, for each one provided a different bird's eye view of the waterfront. Allowing extra time with cloth and vinegar-water on the south window, he studied the horizon. It had never looked so clear, so close, or so beckoning.

The rope Billy stored in his warehouse had been made in the ropewalk, and Sam went in to look at the heavy coils. Had the twin been spun from hemp bales he'd cut open? He touched the rope. It felt the same, but how different it looked in here, waiting to go to sea. Like me, he thought.

Billy kept a close eye on Sam, who went about the business of learning with such spirit that one day Billy said to Stephen and Jack: "He's bright an' brisk, that lad o' yours. Damn near wears me out. Full o' questions an' wants his answers right smart."

For the first time in his life, Sam was sorry when work stopped for the night. Then, on one very bright, brilliant morning, it happened.

"Sammy!" Billy called to him. "We got a brig down t' the yard wantin' her halyards, sheets, an' braces refitted. Grab that box o' tools, an' come give me an' the lads a hand." The clerk who handled Billy's accounts stepped aside deftly as Sam picked up the heavy box and bolted out into the street.

Sam put his feet on the deck of the two-masted vessel and breathed in the glorious earthy smells of tar, wet wood, wet hemp, low tide, and salt air. Finally, he was here. He was sure everything he would become in the rest of his life started right now. His heart thumped and his blood raced. It was all he could do to keep from skipping around the deck shouting with sheer joy.

There were too many things to look at and no time to see any of it because work started right away. All day long, Sam fetched and carried. He jumped out of the way when a length of rope fell to the deck from high above him, and he helped hold things steady when one of the lads needed an extra hand. He ran a few errands back to the shop, to the chandlery, and once to the counting house. He let the immense activity sweep over him as he hurried along, looking at it as if he'd never seen it before.

The Plymouth waterfront was full to bursting. Merchant ships from all over the world lay side by side along the wharfs and in the harbor, and now, because England was at war, the great fighting ships of the Royal Navy were there, too. The men who worked these ships swarmed all over them—loading and unloading, aloft in the rigging, down below in the holds, over the sides painting, repairing, scraping, cleaning. The work was endless. On the docks, sailors, merchants, ships' owners, travelers, insurance men, ships' masters and mates, carpenters, chandlers, riggers and sail makers shouted and jostled one another, intent on the business of the day. Officers and seamen of the navy, marines, soldiers, and press-gangs muscled in, each claiming his place in the crowd. Innkeepers, shopkeepers, tavern landlords, and the women who hawked their wares down on the docks, all did a brisk trade.

Sam was part of it now, with business to attend to and a job to do. As the weeks sped by, he no longer thought a ship's rigging looked like a huge, broken spider's web. Patterns slowly began to emerge from what he'd first seen as a jumbled mess, and as Alf coached him, he began to understand—just a little—the elaborate, precise system of ropes and pulleys that made sailing possible. An unexpected pride washed over him when he finally understood the importance of the ropewalk and the work his family did there.

One evening, after the shutters were put up and the shop doors were locked, Sam went to the Broken Bell to have supper with Billy and the lads for the very first time. The tavern was so close to the docks it was nearly in the water, and on many a morning he'd hare right past it on his way to the ropewalk without noticing it at all. Inside, Sam sat at a long trestle table sandwiched between Billy and Alf, his stomach growling impatiently. One of the lads handed him some bread and cheese, and as he munched he looked around the crowded, noisy room. Sailors from the merchant and the naval services were crammed in cheek-to-jowl, merry in their drink, squabbles and differences forgotten for the night. Someone was singing a sea chantey about a saucy young girl that drew laughter

fromthose sitting close enough to hear all the words. And Alf pointed out
the two toothless old salts, sitting in the far corner, who had once sailed with the famous pirate, Henry Avery.

A steaming bowl of stew was put before him, and he breathed in the delicious aroma. Sighing, he glanced around. Everyone in the tavern belonged to the sea in one way or another, and with a tremendous burst of pride, he knew he did, too. This was the way of life he'd wanted, and here it was, laid out before him. If he'd learned anything at all in the past few months, it was when you want something badly enough, the thing to do was reach right out and take it. He grabbed his spoon and tucked in.

3

By the summer of 1709, Sam had been at sea four years, and now, at twenty, he was shipping out as bosun on the *Bonnie Celeste.* She was at wharf-side in Plymouth taking on cargo, and supplies for their next voyage were piled on deck. He and his mate were checking the deliveries from Billy's warehouse and from the chandlery, when he was hailed from the gangway.

"Ahoy, Sam! Sam! There's news!"

Sam looked up from his work. "Davy!" He turned back to his mate. "Aye, Jim. You an' the others get this lot stowed away, then." He joined Davy Turner at the deck rail. "What news?"

"The master! Slipped his cable! Keeled over right after his breakfast, so's I heard, down t' the Broken Bell. 'Twere his heart, Sam. Stopped just like that!" He snapped his fingers.

"Dead? Higgins? Sorry to hear that. He ran a tight ship. Who's takin' his place?"

"Devil's own spawn—Caleb Jones an' none other."

"Bloody hell," Sam said. "Well, we're in for it. Someone'll run afoul of him on this voyage, an' that ain't no lie. If you're smart, Davy you'll keep close quarters. He'll not be takin' your talk in the loose, easy way Higgins did, rest his soul."

"Amen t' that. An' them's right words, true enough, but they's worse."

"Worse?"

"Aye," Davy said. "Seems when you get Jones, you get his mate right along with him."

"Martin Hale? He was struck dead off Gibraltar a couple of years back, as I heard it."

"Well, he didn't stay dead for long. Just like him t' come back alive from Davy Jones an' snarl a man's line."

"So, that's why I ain't seen Burns all day," Sam said, thinking of the first mate. "I wondered where he was. Another good man, Duncan Burns, an' fair, too."

"The owners was goin' t' bump him down t' second," Davy said, "but he takes his papers an' walks."

"Jones an' Hale," Sam said, shaking his head. "There's more honest seamen bringin' grievances against them, but nothin' don't ever come of it. They bring the cargo in an' that's all the owners care about. When Jones is feelin' crossed, somebody pays. An' Hale—he walks the decks holdin' that bloody cat-o'-nine tails like its growin' right out of his hand. Many's the foremast-jack who knows the touch of Hale's whip for nothin' more'n movin' too slow." He paused and caught Davy's eye. "There's too many that's kissed the gunner's daughter under Hale's cat that ain't lived to tell about it."

Davy snorted. "Aye, they're foul enough, them two. Hard t' say who gets the deepest pit in hell—the black-hearted maggot what dreams up a whip with nine lashes, or the stinkin' scupperlout what uses it."

Sam looked aft to the poop deck where the ship's wheel stood waiting for Davy's hands, and then back at his friend. "Mark my words an' steer the bloody ship, bein' mindful of your tongue. Maybe this cruise'll be clear sailin'."

✠ ✠ ✠

The *Bonnie Celeste* set sail for Africa's Ivory Coast, with the crew resigned to dealing with Martin Hale and his cat-o'-nine-tails as best they could. Caleb Jones kept to his quarters seeing no one but Hale. He appeared only at four o'clock in the afternoon for the first Dog Watch when he would stand on the poop deck and stare forward, barely moving for the full two hours without saying a word.

Hale, the first mate, ran the ship carrying the cat much as he always had. With the nine knotted cords wrapped around the foot long handle, he'd take a poke at a shoulder or two to hurry the men along. Watching from the poop deck, or moving among the working men, he'd play with the cat, keeping it moving, sending its tails through the air with a sharp snap or slapping them against his right leg. He'd threaten, curse, and growl, lashing the cat-o'-nine-tails across the ship's fittings, woodwork, or the deck—but never once on human skin. Every man aboard the *Bonnie Celeste* knew his reputation, and Jones', too—and the master and his mate were not running true to form. The voyage, which had started out as uneventful, soon became unnerving.

They'd put to sea again, and were heading for Portugal. Davy sat at mess with seven others of the off-duty crew at a long table below decks. "This voyage ain't natural," he said. "How can Jones know his ship if he don't never go amongst his crew?"

"Don't got to," Jim, the bosun's mate, replied. "Jones is got Hale, an' Hale is got the cat."

"Now why, I asks." Davy put down his spoon. "Why? We go all the way t' Africa, an' now we're a day out o' Lisbon, an' he's still carryin' that thing, 'cept he ain't bloody used it! Not once! Why the hell not? It's like them two is darin' us t' step wrong. Gives me the bloody jumps, waitin'. What's wrong with Hale, then, that he ain't actin' natural? Is he ailin'?"

Jim chuckled. "Davy got a nursery-maid's concern for Mr. Hale an' his pet cat. He ain't flogged nobody, an' we're nigh to raisin' Lisbon. Don't matter how come. Luck's comin' our way."

"Aye. 'Tis true as true, for it ain't no lie," one seaman put in.

"'Course, it may just be he likes the way it feels on his leg when he swishes 'em nine tails 'round, as he does." All but Davy laughed.

"Why've you got yourself tied in such a big knot over Hale, eh?" Jim asked, looking at Davy's tense face. "You feel his cat before?"

"No, I ain't," Davy said. "But I ask you! Why's the lot o' you so becalmed, then, eh? I ain't the only man-jack aboard this ship sweatin' cold over this."

"No, but you're the only one who can't talk o' nothin' else," Jim replied.

"We knows their ways, Davy," another sailor put in. "No point in worryin' till I got somethin' to worry about, is my motto. Nobody ships with Jones an' Hale but what somethin' big happens. It just ain't happened yet, is all."

"When's it going t', then?" Davy asked. "Can't take the waitin' no bloody more."

The next morning, Davy stood at the wheel holding the ship on course, his mind on Jones and Hale. He'd been reckoning the days left in the voyage against the odds that Hale would run true to form before they raised England, but determined to keep his mind on his job he tried to jettison his negative thoughts. He'd just glanced at the compass when he heard a voice behind him. "Steady as she goes, Mr. Turner."

"Aye," Davy snapped, "steady as she bloody goes, like I got a bloody choice. What bleedin' sack o' fish-bait thinks I got nothin' else t' do but keep her steady?"

"Mr. Hale," the voice continued, "remove this man from his station and give him over to Mr. Bellamy for proper discipline. Mark this insubordination at six bells, Morning Watch."

Davy spun around and looked into the face of Caleb Jones.

"Bellamy!" the first mate shouted.

Sam came aft. "Aye, Mr. Hale."

"Secure this man to the main pinrail and prepare him to receive the captain's justice."

Davy gripped the wheel with one hand; his knuckles were white.

"Get on with it, Bellamy," Hale said, seeing Sam hesitate.

"Assemble the ship's company, Mr. Hale," Jones said.

Sam had a firm grip on Davy's arm as they walked away. "What happened?" he asked, his voice low.

"What's the old man doin' on deck now, for? It ain't no Dog Watch," Davy groused.

Sam and his mate, Jim, stripped Davy's shirt off and lashed him in place. "Sorry, Davy," Sam said, tightening the cords. "I don't want to do this."

"Don't matter now, do it Sammy? It were goin' t' happen, an' I get the short straw."

"That'll do, Bellamy," interrupted Hale, getting a good grip on the cat-o'-nine-tails. "Captain's order is for Moses' Law. Count aloud. Now."

"Moses' Law?" Sam glanced up at Jones who had not moved; his face still unreadable. He turned back to Hale. "This don't warrant Moses' Law."

The crew and officers on deck to witness the flogging grew quiet, watching closely as this twist in the drama played out.

Hale glared savagely at Sam and, grabbing him by the front of his shirt, rammed the handle of the cat up hard under Sam's chin. He was tall enough to look Sam square in the eye. "It don't matter to me who I flog, or why, or where, for I'll take as much pleasure from flogging you, Bellamy, as I do this scum-of-a-helmsman. You toe the mark when I give you captain's orders, and it's captain's orders for you to count out Moses' Law—forty strokes, less one!" Hale shoved Sam hard enough to knock him off balance and he tripped on the corner of a hatch cover, landing hard the deck. But he was on his feet in an instant, every muscle tight, his fists clenched.

Davy heard it all. Fear clutched his throat. His shallow breathing couldn't fill his lungs fast enough and his mouth was bone dry. His arms were stretched out, tied high above his head.

A bar of wood, the ends lashed to the inside of each ankle, forced his legs apart. He couldn't bend his knees or shift his weight. When he peered under his left arm he could see Hale standing at the ready, the cat in his hand. From under his other arm he could see Sam, red-faced and angry. He passed his tongue over his teeth and lips in an effort to wet them. Each long, ponderous second dragged on like a heavy load. Why didn't they begin? He closed his eyes and thought of the pain. He thought of his shipmates, gathered to watch Hale inflict the captain's justice. When he opened his eyes, he saw a belaying pin so close to his nose he could study the grain of the wood. He'd never noticed the dark swirls in the golden oak before. Good English oak: the mainstay of—

The whip struck hard. Davy's tensed body twitched. The long tails lay across his back for what seemed to him an unusual length of time. He felt each knot. He knew where each of the nine leather cords, stiffened with dried blood, lay. The tails slowly crawled over his skin, and the cat lifted off his body. He heard Sam say, "One." Thirty-eight to go.

"Again, Bellamy!" Hale called out, leaning back the full way to deliver the second blow.

"One!" Sam repeated, loud and clear. "Two!" Hale brought his body forward, his arm out straight as the cat's tails whistled through the air and clawed Davy's back again. "Three!"

Hale's body picked up a rhythm, and Sam counted time.

Davy waited for the fourth lash. It came as a jolt, and his bladder let go. A warm stream of urine ran down his leg, pooling on the deck. He looked up along the mast as it disappeared in the sails and rigging. For a while, all he heard was the buzzing in his head; then he heard Sam. "Eight! Nine!" He clenched his teeth, and the long cords in his neck stood out like knife blades. The searing pain pulsed in every part of his body.

"Ten! Eleven!" The sound of the lashes hitting naked skin grew louder, and Sam no longer heard his own voice. He kept his eyes on the whip as it pulled away from the pulpy mess that was Davy's back. Its tails traced an arc of blood through the air.

Davy lost count, but turned his head toward Sam when he heard "Fourteen!" He bit down into his bottom lip—he was past crying out. The blood ran down his chin, mixing with the sweat that dropped from his face.

"Sixteen! Seventeen!" They were killing him. Sam wanted to stop the assault, but was tied to the spot where he stood as surely as Davy was tied to the mast.

"Eighteen!" Davy's body sagged—dead weight suspended by the rope around his wrists. "Nineteen!" His slashed back exposed raw, bleeding muscle. "Twenty!" He's dead, Sam thought. We're beatin' a dead man.

"Twenty-one! Twenty-two! Twenty-three—"

The cat was silent.

The scene stopped; the players motionless in the grim tableau. Sam had grabbed Hale's powerful right arm before he could bring the whip down on Davy again, and the cat's tails swayed lightly in the soft breeze.

"Cut him down!" Sam's grip on Hale was tight. No one moved. He took a quick glance at the poop deck; Jones was gone. "Cut him down, I say!" His face was inches from Hale's. They pushed away from each other with a force that sent them both staggering backward. The spell was broken.

"Belay that!" Hale shouted, rushing toward the men cutting Davy loose. "Get him up! Tie him back up! It's Moses' Law, and it's not finished."

"It is finished." Sam shoved Hale aside. "You killed him, you bastard. He's dead."

"No, he ain't!" Jim called out. "He's alive!"

They lay Davy face down on the deck and someone doused him with a bucket of cold seawater to wash off the blood. His scream ripped the air, his back arching as the salt stung his open wounds.

"Bring fresh water," Sam said to Jim, and knelt by Davy. "An' somethin' to bind him with."

"Get away from him, Bellamy," Hale said, and turning to the seamen standing near by, pointed the bloodied whip at Sam. "Lash him to the eight-pounder. He'll soon learn who gives orders here."

"Stay your hands, mates," Sam said, standing. The men who approached him stopped. Hale's face was crimson, and he shouted orders again, but no one moved.

Jim waited, uncertain. "Get the water," Sam said over his shoulder, without taking his eyes off Hale.

"I gave orders to leave him!" Hale yelled. "Get back to work, you bilge water low-lifes! Ship's company is dismissed! Bellamy, you'll pay for this." He gripped the cat.

Sam faced Hale, Davy's blood on his shirt. "There ain't been no crime here that fits this punishment."

"It was the captain's judgment."

"The captain's—or the devil's."

The men were tense and still.

"You're out of line, Bellamy. On this ship you either agree with the captain or keep your mouth shut."

"My shipmates bear witness to what happened here today, an' they mark what you do now." He turned and squatted by Davy. Hale raised his arm and with a grunt, laid the whip hard across Sam's back. Sam dropped to his knees, his head swimming from the force of the blow. But before he could stand, Hale struck again.

Sam pitched forward, his head and arms on the deck. He was very still. With a groan, he struggled to his feet. Then, in one swift, fluid movement, he twisted the cat from Hale's hand and threw it overboard.

Two shipmates seized Hale and held the struggling man between them. "What'd we do with him?" one of them asked Sam.

"Is it mutiny or murder, Bellamy?" Hale demanded. "Either way, you'll swing for this."

"Let him go lads, this ain't the way."

Hale laughed and roughly shook the men's hands off his arms.

"You're a stinking coward, Bellamy. A hen-hearted, scurvy, son-of-a whore coward. And you interfered with the running of this ship for the last time."

Sam's challenge was clear.

"Remember the day you made a enemy of me, *Mr.* Hale, 'cause I ain't never goin' to forget. When this voyage is over, pray to whatever god watches over scum like you, for if it ever comes my way to pass judgment on you—you'll burn in hell."

4

"So," Charlie asked, "what happened? Did you meet them again, this Jones, an' Hale?"

In late-January 1715, Sam sat with his two brothers, Jack and Charlie, in Plymouth, in the Broken Bell. The roaring fire in the great room made the tavern snug and warm against the winter's biting wind, and Sam's story held their close attention.

"It's been more'n five years since that voyage, an' I never saw Jones again, nor Hale. Fact is, no one ever saw Jones again after that floggin', not even in the Dog Watches." Sam took a long drink from his tankard. "Hale did his job without no word but to work the ship, an' when we got back to Plymouth, he collected his pay an' disappeared."

"What happened to Davy, then?" asked Jack.

"He got put ashore in Lisbon. Can't think how he survived that beatin', but he did. Never saw him again, neither. Best helmsman afloat." Sam shook his head. "No, never saw the like, a man beat like that, before or since."

They sat in silence for a while. Then Sam drew deeply on a clay pipe, his eyes narrowed against the rising smoke. "Did hear about Jones, though, two years or so past. Hale wasn't with him no more, so he took to usin ' the cat himself. Well, it seems he had a cabin boy, about eleven years of age, an' he took issue with somethin' the lad did. They were carryin' two eight-pounders, so he had the boy lashed to one of the guns an' he flogged him to death with his own hand. The crew cut him down, what was left of him anyway, an' they buried him at sea, with nary a word from Jones."

The wind, blowing hard outside the tavern, rushed in when the door opened to admit a shivering customer. Sam pulled his collar close and looked across at Jack and Charlie.

"Justice is hard to come by when you're a foremast hand an' all the power belongs to one man, especially a devil like Jones. But there was true justice aboard that ship, after all.

"Now the crew, they were fond of that boy, an' to a man, they took a mighty objection to Jones. It happened they were runnin' through a squall, with heavy seas an' the deck all awash, an' Jones, well, he just happened to slip somehow, an' went right overboard. It was a real mystery as to how nobody seen him go, or how nobody was there to throw him a line. The mate took the ship home fine, an' all the whole way no one spoke of Jones, almost as if he was never there. The owners, well, Jones' loss didn't sit well with them, but they took the story of the accident as gospel." Sam looked at his brothers. "I tell you there ain't one man-jack of us who ever walked a deck that don't know what really happened to Jones, nor one who don't understand."

Jack and Charlie sat in silence, their minds full of the images Sam had painted for them with his words. After a while, Charlie spoke. "But life at sea ain't always like that, is it? You had good voyages, travelin' to different places, seein' all manner of things."

"Aye, true enough, but don't everythin' come with a price? You remember when the *Carolina* was sunk durin' the war? She went down with all hands, but the big commotion was over the loss of the cargo, not the crew. No, the sea ain't like other masters, nor other work. A man's at the mercy of too many things comin' together to make life real hard. Greedy owners, foul weather, an' foul men like Jones an' Hale. No, it ain't worth it no more."

"You quittin', Sam? What'll you do?" Jack asked. Then he chuckled, adding, "Ain't comin' back to the ropewalk, are you?"

"No. No, I'm headed for America—Boston."

"What?"

"You mean to visit," Charlie said. "You'll come back, like you always do."

Sam shrugged. "Can't say for sure. I talked to pa a while back. He says ma had a cousin over there, Isaac—or Israel—Cole, on Cape Cod in Massachusetts Colony, an' I'm goin' to find him. See what kind of life I can make for myself."

"But why not stay here? You're away more'n you're home, so why not give Plymouth—or England—a chance?"

"It ain't enough, Jack. It ain't never been enough, not from when I was a lad, you know that. I was always reachin' for somethin' that was beyond what I could get easy. No, I got to do this. Stayin' here's the wrong future for me. Everything's all laid out here like it's been for—" he shrugged, "a thousand years. Ain't nothin' new here, ever. Even the future's old."

Charlie leaned back in his chair. "That don't make no sense, Sam. Future ain't happened yet. How could it be old?"

"Don't you see, Charlie?" Sam asked. "The more things stay the same, the older the future gets 'cause it don't change none, either. You started workin' at the ropewalk with pa when you were a lad, you're still there, an' you'll be there next year, 'cause now you got a family. Same as Jack. It's a old future. You know how it'll work out. On board a ship you don't know how it'll work out, 'cause you may be fightin' for your life in the next hour. The future's always new."

"That don't make no bit o' sense neither," Charlie put in, a cross look spreading over his face.

Sam began his retort, when once again Jack stepped between the brothers. "Stay home with us."

"You helped me leave," Sam replied, smiling fondly at Jack, and then at Charlie. "I ain't never felt settled since leavin' Billy's, an' I ain't never felt like I belonged anywhere since leavin' home. Maybe in the colonies I'll find the things you have. All I know is I can't find them here."

✠ ✠ ✠

His ship, a galley, was to sail for Boston on the early morning tide. That evening, as he sat in the house where he'd grown up, surrounded by his siblings, their spouses and children, he realized how much leaving them would hurt. They had all come to share the mountains of food and drink, and they had all come to say goodbye.

He knew he would have to leave for the dock soon after the household was asleep, so when he had a chance, he found a quiet corner and spoke to his father. "I ain't never really counted—how many nieces an' nephews have I got?"

His father laughed. "I got seventeen grandchildren, eighteen come May. An' half of them belong to Lizzie." He glanced sideways at Sam. "Don't suppose I'll ever be seein' your children, will I? Maybe you'll write an' tell me about them."

"Aye, Pa, I will."

They were silent for a moment.

"You been at sea—ten years, now?—an' you always come home. Leastways for a short stay." Stephen's face was solemn. "Ain't the same, this time, is it?"

"I can't say how it'll work out. I wish I could."

"I know, son, I know." He sighed and studied Sam's face in the soft light. "Of all my children, you're the one who favors your ma the most. I see her every time I look at you, especially now you're older. She was a good woman. When you take a wife, I hope you find the same happiness I had with her."

Then Stephen Bellamy took his youngest child in his arms and blessed him. Sam remembered the reluctance with which his father had first allowed him to choose his own life, and how, after time had passed, the reluctance had become encouragement. Never again would he question Sam's choices, and here was the same understanding.

They stepped apart, and Sam said, "Thank you, Pa."

The old man's eyes glistened with unshed tears. "You're welcome, Sam."

✠ ✠ ✠

The next morning at about five o'clock, when the tide turned, Sam Bellamy left Plymouth confident in his decision. He was sailing to a new life in the New World.

Forenoon Watch: 1699 – 1711
As God Ordained

"MARIAH HALLETT, I BAPTIZE THEE IN THE NAME OF THE FATHER, and of the son, and..."

The Reverend Mr. Samuel Treat stopped speaking the holy words and caught his breath. His hand was still. Drops of water trickled from his fingers into the silver, shell-shaped bowl that sat on the plain table, in the plain church. He looked into the face of the tiny child cradled in her mother's arms, and the newly born Mariah, swaddled snuggly against the chilly day, looked back with an expression in her eyes that unnerved him. Had she mocked him? It was fleeting, and had disappeared almost as soon as he'd seen it. He glanced at the faces of the people standing nearby; no one else was disturbed. Had they not seen as he had? Had he seen anything at all? His heart thumped fiercely as he dipped his shaking hand into the water, and for the third time, anointed her head. "...and of the Holy Ghost. Amen."

Her unusually focused gaze held him, never leaving his face. He laid his wet hand on Mariah's head and felt her pulse through the soft spot. The birth hair was downy and fine. Forcing himself to close his eyes, he murmured softly, "Let us pray."

The solemn act of bringing a human soul into the Kingdom of God is also a joyful one. This time, though, Mr. Treat was upset, and it blotted out the happiness he always felt when administering this sacrament. From the doorway of the small building he watched Matthew Hallett load his young family into the farm wagon and accept warm wishes from other parishioners. Mary Hallett, looking strong and healthy for having given birth three days before, held her baby and spoke quietly to the two-year-old Lydia.

Just what sort of conversation the new parents would have when Matthew repeated the minister's words of concern to his wife, Mr. Treat could only guess. He hadn't meant to speak so strongly, but the disturbing memory of the 1692 witch trials in Salem, only seven years before, weighed on his mind and guided his thoughts.

He'd stopped the farmer as he was leaving the church. "I didn't hear or see nothin'," Matthew had said, surprised by the minister's description of his experience. "Nor did Mary. No one did, that I know of, leastways. Child's newly born, Parson. A babe just from the womb don't laugh, nor look particular ways with its eyes. You know that."

"Yes, I do, which is why I'm—" He had hesitated. "Matthew, Holy Baptism creates a covenant with God, and for the briefest of moments I felt the making of that covenant had been interrupted. It was as if something had violated the sanctity of the place and the moment."

"Violated?" Matthew had repeated the word, struggling with the implication until he looked into the minister's troubled eyes. "You tellin' me Mariah ain't baptized?"

"No! No!" Mr. Treat had hastily reassured the farmer. "No, I read the words, and you and Mary answered for her, just as it should be. Only, I thought— Perhaps after all, it was nothing more than an illusion of my own." He had been quiet for a moment. "But if it wasn't—"

"Well?"

"Mariah must learn to walk in God's path," Treat had said. "She must be prepared to resist the devil and all his works. Satan is wily, choosing his servants carefully by finding a foothold in a free and open soul."

"I ain't listenin' to this!"

"You must! Together we will protect her soul and prevent that from happening! I know you and Mary will teach both your daughters to be faithful, virtuous women, but you must take special care with this child! Above all, she must learn to fear God and bring Him glory in her daily life as well as in her devotions." As the farmer tried to leave the church, Mr. Treat had restrained him. "Hear me out, please! Mariah can only benefit from your—our—strict guidance, and that guidance can only come from being informed. We cannot let down our guard. I'll speak with your wife—"

"No more of this, Parson!" Matthew had interrupted. "This ain't right, what you're sayin'! Devil ain't in my child! Nothin' happened inside there," he pointed toward the church, "an' nothin's goin' to happen to Mariah. She ain't your concern. An' don't you go an' say anythin' to Mary, neither. I'll not have her upset, what with her just givin' birth."

"Since I baptized your baby, her spiritual life and well being are my concern. I would be remiss if I didn't caution you to be watchful. If you won't heed my warning, I can only pray for God's intervention for Mariah's sake, and for your family."

Matthew had climbed into his wagon feeling at odds with his anger at Mr. Treat. He'd allowed it to rise up when he'd roughly brushed the minister's hand off his arm and shouted "No more!" before joining his family. He snapped the reins with more vigor than usual and drove home, urging his horse to a brisk trot.

Watching the farm wagon roll away, Samuel Treat wondered if his reaction to the events in the last hour had been out of proportion. Although he was more liberal in his theology than the few Puritans who lived in the small Cape Cod community of Eastham and the many who lived up Boston and Salem way, he could not deny the ease with which the devil slipped into the hearts and minds of his fellow humans. With second-guessing and self-doubt in his heart, he went back into his church to pray.

During the months after her baptism, Matthew closely watched Mariah for the signs Mr. Treat had seen. His heart had skipped a beat at her first laugh, and when she first focused on the things around her, he had worried while following her gaze. When he felt sure all was well, he forgot his anger and fear. His pointed conversations with Mr. Treat— "And how is young Mariah today, Matthew?" "Just as God ordained, Parson." — lost their double edge and became simple pleasantries. Twelve years passed quickly and quietly, and in that time he never once repeated the minister's words to his wife.

2

Ned Winslow, cutting through a corner of the Hallett farm on his way back to his own place, stopped to speak to Matthew. "Hard, clearin' this land. Ought to be easier, considerin' all the sand in the soil," he observed wryly. "Pine needles don't help none, neither. You an' Mary ought t' have had boys. Better on the land."

Although it was a cool spring day, Matthew took a cloth from his pocket and wiped his damp forehead. "Well," he said, leaning on his pitchfork, glad for the rest, "you can only take what the Lord provides. Girls're good workers in their own way. Lydia's easy-tempered an' a beauty. She'll make a good marriage one day, now she's nearin' the age. Mariah—" He paused.

Winslow chuckled. "Mariah's a rare one, that's for sure. Funny how she an' John Knowles' girl, Thankful, took to bein' such good friends. I mean, what with them bein' so different, an' all."

Matthew studied the pile of brush he'd made and shook his head. "John Knowles—"

The friends stood in silent understanding for a moment, then Winslow chuckled again. "Your Mariah mayn't be the womanly kind, as is Lydia, but she's smart as a whip."

"Too much so, for a girl," Matthew muttered, kicking at a clod of earth. "Head-strong."

"Maybe, maybe. But I heard my wife talkin' t' the ladies 'bout her weavin', when we was out t' church t'other Sunday. Admirin' her skill, they were, an' shakin' their heads with wonder over it all. A man'll go mighty far an' fare worse afore he finds someone t' take t' wife who's got the healin' skill with animals as she does. Can't deny that."

"Got her place, it's true," Matthew agreed, smiling, "but she's too young to be thought of in a wifely way—not even for your older boy. She's just twelve years."

"Ain't goin' t' be stayin' twelve, if you take my point. Good match t' plan on one day, my boy an' your Mariah," Winslow said happily. "Oh, an' don't know if you been hearin', but there's a poacher in our midst stealin' fresh kill. Opened two o' my traps, an' cut snares on George Burgess' land, an' Henry Thomkins', too, down t'other way."

"I heard 'bout them empty traps," Matthew said. "But springin' traps an' cuttin' snares don't make much sense if we're talkin' 'bout poachers. A poacher'd be wantin' the fresh kill."

"That's what's so puzzlin'," Winslow mused, scratching his head. "Been keepin' my eyes skinned, but ain't seen nothin' yet. Criminal, t' be stealin' a man's catch. Saw Mariah t'other day, walkin' across my land with that basket she always totes. She might o' seen somethin'. Worth askin'." He shook his head and shouldered his canvas bags. "Well, time to be headin' on. Best to Mary."

Winslow walked away and Matthew, suddenly chilly, put on his coat. He worked steadily for a while, thinking about the unknown poacher and the trapped animals, and then, quite unexpectedly, remembered Samuel Treat's concerned words about Mariah from the long-ago day of her baptism. Worry and fear began to grow slowly in his mind as the image of his daughter, with her box of healing salves and potions, became impossible to ignore.

✠ ✠ ✠

The injured rabbit lay on the straw in the brightest corner of the shed. Humming softly, Mariah stroked its ears and fur while examining the terrible wound. "There's somethin' that'll make you better," she whispered, working with a rag and fresh water, "but I got to clean you up first." Her patient lay still and she looked at the fox, with a bandaged leg, and the pheasant, flightless forever, that rested closeby. "This rabbit'll be stayin' with you for a time," she remarked as she worked. "I took him from a trap, too, so you know how he feels. I know you'll leave him be while he gets well."

Inside a wooden box were the potions, poultices, and salves she'd made from plants and herbs growing in the area. Like most girls, Mariah had learned healing skills from her mother, but these recipes were her own. Her unusual ability with animals had become so important on the farm, and occasionally to neighbors, that her parents tended to overlook the wild creatures she cared for, allowing her rations of feed and fresh straw for bedding. The firm understanding was that livestock always came first.

The rabbit, its leg neatly bandaged, nestled into the straw and fell instantly asleep. "That'll do you the most good," she said softly. She tended to the fox and pheasant, leaving them food and water, then picking up the box, headed back to the house.

A few hours later, Matthew left the field early and stood alone in the shed. The fox lifted its head and looked at him, then, moving slightly, went back to sleep with a little sigh. Fresh blood soaked the rabbit's bandage. Squatting to study Mariah's patients more closely, he passed a calloused hand over his face and swore.

✠ ✠ ✠

Mariah sat on the bench by the loom, winding her shuttles. The shawl she'd made for herself from scrap lengths of different colored worsted and linen thread was draped over the back of the settle. She squinted at it, admiring its intricate pattern and enjoying the full effect of the afternoon sunlight falling directly on the fabric. The smooth, shiny linen seemed to sparkle.

"Where's your mama?"

She jumped at the unexpected sound of her father's voice and stood politely to speak to him. "Mama's in the garden with Lydia. Do you want me to call her?"

"No. I want you to tell me 'bout the animals in the shed. Where'd they come from?"

"Where—?"

Mary appeared at the door. "Matthew? I saw you come home. Is somethin' wrong?"

He ignored his wife and spoke again to Mariah. "You know what I mean. Ned Winslow said he saw you on his land yesterday carryin' that big basket o' yours. Are you stealin' game from our neighbors?"

"Mariah!" Mary looked at her daughter with wide eyes, then turned to her husband. "Matthew—?"

"Are you? Answer me!"

"They were just there, in the grass, an' the woods," she said in a small voice. "Different places—"

"Don't lie to me! I just come from the shed. Those animals look like they been cut up by traps. Do you do this, Mariah? Do you?"

"The animals are hurt an' scared when I find them. I can't leave them to die," she said in a small voice. "Why's it stealin' if I help them?"

"You admit this?"

"Yes. But Papa! If I leave them, they'll die! I can't do that, I can't!"

"Don't back-talk me, girl, I'll not have it! Animals are here to serve us, an' it's their fate to serve us this way. When you steal from a man's trap, you're deprivin' his family of meat for the stewpot. From now on in, when you come on a trap that's been set, you leave it be! You hear me?"

"But they're hurt in traps! Aren't I doing right by helpin' them? By helpin' God's creatures? Aren't I? Mama?"

"Listen to me, child," Matthew insisted, more gently this time. "When you go onto a man's land to steal his game—for whatever reason—you're breakin' God's commandment, an' the law. Do you understand?"

Tears brimmed over and ran down her checks. She bowed her head. "Yes, Papa."

"I'll have no more o' this. You'll keep your word an' obey me."

"Yes, Papa. But Papa—"

"That is enough!"

✠ ✠ ✠

"There's no accountin' for this," Matthew said, a little while later. He and Mary stood in the shed, considering Mariah's patients. "The fox ain't bad hurt, an' it can walk. There ain't no reason for it not preyin' on the pheasant or the rabbit, but it don't. It lies quiet, an' them others show no fear havin' it close by, no fear at all. It ain't God's way. It's as if—" He stopped and cleared his throat. When he spoke again, his voice was tight. "It ain't just the poachin'. There's more. Somethin' I ain't never talked of." He told her about his conversation with their minister on the day Mariah was baptized.

"What?" Mary gave a short laugh of disbelief. "That doesn't sound like Mr. Treat. It sounds like John Knowles an' his foolish Puritan talk. Nothin' happened durin' her baptism, Matthew. I never took my eyes off her!"

"I watched real careful in those first weeks, an' after, while she was very young. Waitin' and wonderin'—lookin' for signs."

Mary stared at him, surprised by the gravity in his voice. "Signs of what?"

"Her soul bein' too free an' open. Like Parson's warnin'."

"He never said anythin' to me."

"I told him not to."

"Why?"

"'Cause I thought it was—foolish. Puritan talk. Like you said."

"No!" Mary cried. "No! You believed it! You believed it an' you kept it from me for all these years! Why?"

"I don't know." He bowed his head to avoid her eyes while he searched for the words. "I was scared—wanted to be sure." He took a deep breath and let it out slowly. "After a while, when I saw her growin' as she should, with nothin' unusual 'bout her ways, I decided there was nothin' to tell, an' Treat'd been wrong. 'Til now. Look around you! How do you explain this?"

Mary studied the resting animals. "Well, her healin' skills—she's always had the gift—"

"No," Matthew said, "no. This is different. This ain't natural. Think, Mary. You ever seen the like of this before? I ain't."

"But—but she cares for our livestock—for our neighbor's—"

The fox yawned, and on shaky legs limped to the dish of water where it drank its fill. It gently nosed the rabbit, then sat in the shaft of sunlight that came in through the open door. The pheasant, roused from its sleep, went to sit near the fox to feel the afternoon's warmth.

"How's this possible?" Mary whispered.

"I don't know." Matthew rubbed his hand over the coarse stubble on his face.

"But how can this be wrong? Mariah must be touched by God to have such skill." Mary caught her breath. "You still believe Parson's warnin' don't you." He turned away from her and she grabbed his arm. "Don't you?!"

His deeply tanned face had a sickly gray pallor, and his silence stretched on as he struggled to give voice to his fears. "He warned me. Parson warned me to watch out for Mariah bein' easy prey for the devil—" His voice trailed away. "How can anyone do this without—without—"

"Say it, Matthew! Say what you fear! Without what?"

He held her frightened eyes with his own, and she saw his mouth harden to a tight line. When he spoke his words were flat and she barely heard them. "Castin' spells."

"You believe this—of your own child? How can you?"

"How can I? How? You tell me how she does this, then, 'cause I can't see the answer!"

They'd gone outside and she faced him, hands on her hips. "Matthew, you must tell Parson about this."

"No."

"Well, if you won't I will."

"No! I forbid it!"

"Why?"

"There's more hurt done by talkin' of things best kept private even in the church. You will do as I say, an' keep this to ourselves." He looked up at the sky. "Still some daylight left," he muttered. "I'm goin' back to the field." Mary watched him walk away until he was out of sight.

When she returned to the house, late afternoon sunshine streamed though the window, drenching the room in rich, golden light. Mariah sat at the table copying out the Bible verses her parents had put before her, her pen scratching across the paper. Mary's heart beat wildly as she watched her daughter. Then, sick with worry, she prepared the evening meal.

3

Josiah Barrett had been the town jailer for almost as long as there had been a jail. He was a gentle man who didn't talk much, so people didn't know a lot about him. When the jail was empty he did odd jobs at Israel Cole's boatyard. Sometimes, he spent time at the Great Island Tavern where he was known to quaff a few and give out a good song.

He had been to sea as a young man and had sailed for many years with his good friend, William "Old Bill" Lee. He'd been pleased when Old Bill had come to settle on the Cape and open his chandlery. The two old men had stories to tell of their grand old days and Mariah was an eager audience. She often sat listening with her arm around Samson, Josiah's big dog, who sometimes laid his head in her lap as she stroked his silky black fur.

Josiah enjoyed Mariah's company. She was bright and cheerful, asking questions that showed she'd been listening, and more importantly, thinking, and because of this, he encouraged her independence. He was a bachelor, and he liked to believe that if he'd had a granddaughter she'd be very much like this young friend of his. For her part, Mariah discovered very quickly that talking with Josiah but she knew, even at twelve years, that she could speak more freely was different than talking with her parents. She couldn't say why, with her friend than she could at home.

On the day after she'd been scolded by her father, Mariah walked to the jail with her mind full of worrisome thoughts. She found Josiah standing with Old Bill in the field behind the stone building, where he had a small garden patch. They were watching Samson.

In the distance, Samson hobbled back and forth, tethered by a thick rope to an iron ring in the side of the building. His right forepaw was covered with dried blood, and he held it off the ground. The hackles on the back of his neck were raised; foaming saliva dripped from his snarling mouth.

Mariah crossed the field and the frenzied Samson ran at her. She backed away, falling as the rope snapped taut, yanking him hard by his neck. His legs gave way, and he dropped to the ground near her, his full weight on his injured paw. Loud yelps of pain gave way to savage growling as he gripped the slack rope with his teeth and shook it, sending snaky waves down its length. His wound opened and blood spurted across the sandy soil.

Josiah rushed forward just as Mariah scrambled to her feet and he lifted her with one arm, carrying her to safety.

"What's wrong with Samson?" she cried when he'd put her down. "Why's he like this?"

"Can't say. Been like this best part o' three days. Don't know how he hurt his foot. Won't eat or drink. Last time I tried t' get near he went for me, just like now. He's been gettin' worse an' worse. Can't leave him like this."

"What d'you mean?" Mariah asked. "We have to help him! What're you goin' to do?"

"Only one way t' help him." Josiah went indoors.

The once gentle dog strained hard at the rope, his vicious growls breaking Mariah's heart.

"Mariah! Go 'round t'other side of the buildin'," Josiah insisted as he came outside with a gun in his hands.

"No! No, you can't!" Mariah yelled, running to him and pulling on his arm.

"Get off me, girl! Do as I say!"

"No!"

"Come with me, Mariah," Old Bill said, guiding her along, his hand on her shoulder.

"No!" She shook him off. "I can help him! Please, Josiah! Please let me try!"

"You can't do nothin', nobody can. This is best for him." He lifted his gun and took aim.

"No!" She lunged at him, pushing on his arm as the gun fired.

"God A'mighty! Mariah!"

"Let me *do* this!" She moved toward Samson, holding her arms out before her, her fingers pointed at his dark eyes. Her young voice calm and firm. "Samson. Samson." He crouched to attack, his teeth bared. She ignored him and walked on.

"Stop!" Frightened, Josiah rushed to grab her.

Old Bill held him back. "Let her try. If she gets in trouble, shoot the dog."

Josiah picked up his gun and, again, aimed it at his pet.

"Samson. Samson." She started to hum a deep, throaty, droning sound, so soft and low the men could hardly hear it. But the big dog did, and he stood still, his three good legs shaking beneath his weight.

Her hands were inches from his sharp teeth.

"Down, Samson, down." Her whisper was as gentle as breathing. With a little whimper he collapsed. He lifted his head to look at her, then relaxed and closed his eyes.

Mariah knelt beside him, stroking his head and ears and touching his nose. She ran her practiced hands down his shoulder and leg, and examined his hurt foot, all the time speaking gentle words to him. After a while, she went to Josiah's rain barrel and fetched a dipper of water. "Get me a piece of cloth," she said, walking back to Samson. Josiah stood as if he had not heard her. Then, in a daze, he handed his gun to Old Bill and brought her a rag.

Mariah worked a bit longer with Samson and came back to where Josiah and Old Bill waited in quiet amazement. "It looks as if he was caught in a trap," she reported. "I don't know how he got away, but bones're broken in his foot an' skin's torn. He's been chewin' on it. It's festered, an' he's got fever, too. I'll bring you somethin' that'll draw the poison out, an' a poultice you can wrap 'round his foot. When the fever breaks, he'll start to eat. I'll be back soon. Leave him be for a while."

They watched her walk toward the woods. Old Bill looked at Samson. Josiah looked at his gun. His voice was husky. "I nearly killed him."

"Seen a lot in my time," Old Bill said, "but I ain't never seen nothin' like that."

Mariah's remedies worked well. On the third day, Samson was eating and drinking, and feeling like himself again. His first shaky steps grew stronger and he was soon limping gamely along on his three good legs.

Several mornings later as Josiah and Samson were walking together they met Mr. Treat as he rounded the corner of the church.

"G'day, Parson."

The minister carried a load of books, and shifting them, stretched his free arm out to Samson, who licked his hand. "Good morning,

Josiah! Well, look at Samson! He's a new dog! Why only a few days ago you were set to put him down! What happened?"

Although the story had been repeated many times, Josiah told it once more. Clouds hid the sun as the old man bent to caress his pet, and the pastor shivered, wondering if the chill he felt came from the sudden shadow or from what he was hearing.

"Heaven-sent miracle. That's what I say," Josiah said, finishing his tale with a happy sigh. He looked down at Samson who sat at his side. "Heaven-sent."

The sun came out again while Mr. Treat watched the two walk away. With thoughts as heavy as the books he carried, he went back to his church, unable to shake the cold.

Later, he sat in his study staring at his open Bible. He should have been writing Sunday's sermon, but the story about Mariah worried him and he couldn't concentrate. He'd heard about this sort of healing before, in his ministry to the local natives, and in their villages it seemed right. Of course, when he asked them to accept his God, and they had, in large numbers, he believed in their willingness to trade pagan magic for God's miracles. Had Mariah been to their villages? He thought not.

Samuel Treat got up and looked out the window. He believed the devil was real and evil could take many forms. He also knew there were things in this world he simply did not understand. Then kneeling, he folded his hands in prayer and placed his worried confusion before God.

As he made his way to the Hallett farm the next morning, his scrambled thoughts were still on Mariah. Every rational interpretation of Josiah's story led to unwanted and troubling questions. Had Mariah used magic to help Samson? Had Satan come to her, and preying on her innocence, taken her soul in exchange for this healing gift? He shook his head in an effort to dislodge these fears. Spurring his horse to a canter, the question he feared the most, the one that challenged his personal faith, dashed into his head and refused to be ignored.

Why was it so much easier to believe Mariah had been touched by Satan, than by God?

Matthew was in the barn sharpening a scythe when the minister found him and told him what Mariah had done. "There were witnesses, "Mr. Treat said, after describing the incident in detail, "and I've seen the dog." The farmer listened, his face pale. "You've seen evidence of this at home?"

Thinking of the rescued animals in the shed, Mathew spoke with a firmness that belied his worry. "No. She's good with animals. Helpful 'round the farm—'specially at lambin' time. But she ain't never done nothin' like that." He narrowed his eyes with suspicion. "What are you tryin' to say?"

"I'm trying to understand. Mariah's done something unusual and, perhaps, disturbing. I know she roams around the area a bit. Do you know to whom she speaks? Does she go to the native villages?"

"No."

"Are you sure? You didn't know she's been to the jail and is acquainted with Josiah. Don't you know where she goes and what she does when she's not at home?"

"Mariah ain't done nothin' wrong. Dog's better, ain't it?"

"The dog's better, but that's not the point. If she's come into contact with evil—"

"If she done right by the animal, how can it be evil? Eh, Parson? Tell me that, then!"

"You tell me how she comes by this other-worldly skill?" Mr. Treat challenged. "Where—and more importantly, from whom—did she learn this?"

"I don't know that she's learned anythin' from anyone, no more do you. You come 'round here askin' all these questions 'bout a thing you ain't even seen yourself! Mariah's no one's business, 'cept mine, an' I don't have to tell you nothin'!"

"If she's in trouble, then you do have to tell me everything. Not only to save her, but for the good of the community. I warned you about this at the time of her baptism."

Matthew threw down the scythe and anger flushed his face and neck. He ran both dirty hands though his hair. He'd known this would happen. He'd known he'd have to choose between keeping Mariah's extraordinary skill a secret and asking for the help and reassurance his pastor could provide. The strain of chosing was almost too much to bear. "Nothin' come o' that warnin'," he burst out, pointing his finger at Mr. Treat, "an' nothin' is wrong here! Take care how you accuse my daughter."

"Have a care yourself, Matthew. One way or another Mariah is slipping out of your control. I warned you many times that allowing your daughter to remain unchecked would lead to an ungodly end. She is young yet, but surely you can see where her behavior is taking her. If she remains thus, it may be impossible to save her from the devil's grasp." He fixed the other man with hard, steady eyes. "Perhaps in your failure to correct her, you are doing the devil's work. I will pray for her—and for you."

Matthew watched the minister walk away then covered his red face with his hands. "Oh, God!" he cried, wiping the sweat and unexpected tears from his eyes. He paced around the barn, his heavy stride muffled in the straw and his breath coming in gasps. Struggling to gather his thoughts, he went to the house.

"Mariah!" His angry voice thundered in the small room. "Come stand before me!"

She had been working at her loom when he burst through the door, and went obediently to him. "Yes, Papa?"

"I know 'bout the dog."

Mary looked up. "What dog? What happened?"

"Keep still!" he snapped at her. "How do you learn these things, Mariah? Who teaches you? Where'd you learn to treat animals the way you do? Answer me!"

"I— I—"

"Tell me!" he insisted. He took her by the shoulders and she winced in his firm grip. "Who talks to you 'bout this? Who taught you what to do?"

"No one!" Mariah said, sobbing. "No one tells me anythin'! Papa! It hurts!"

"How does it happen?" His big hands squeezed harder. "How? Tell me! How?"

"I don't know! I just do it! It just happens! Please, Papa, don't!"

"Matthew, stop! Matthew!" Mary pulled at his arm.

He stared wide-eyed at his terrified daughter and released her, turning away from her in shame. "Go to bed, an' stay there 'til I call you."

"Oh, Papa!" Mariah cried, and ran up the stairs.

✠ ✠ ✠

When Samuel Treat got back to his study he sank in his chair, his weary body aching in every bone. The room was quiet and his closed eyes shut out the light. But in his silent darkness there was no peace. No matter how many ways he looked at the problem, he couldn't find an easy answer. Was God working through this child? Had it been the miracle Josiah believed? It could be that simple. But the farmer had not been pleased—he'd been frightened. The story about the dog had been familiar to him. He was protecting his daughter. Something was wrong and Treat knew it. Matthew Hallett had lied.

4

Old Bill's undeniable talent for telling a good story came not only from remembering all the details, but from inventing new ones as well. On the day he told Mariah's story with a dark, mysterious twist, an indentured servant named Tom was in his shop on an errand. Things got out of hand when Tom repeated it as well as he could to his master, John Knowles, who knew his time had finally come.

John Knowles was a church elder, a town selectman and a man of property. The bright light he shone on himself cast a long shadow over the small community, and he liked to make sure the position he maintained was as clear to everyone as it was to him. He followed a strict Puritanical doctrine and believed the heat and force of "hellfire and brimstone" could solve most of life's problems. His concern that the devil would sooner or later come among the people of Eastham took up a lot of his time, and he looked for signs of this daily. When he heard that Mariah Hallett had been casting spells he saw a chance to test his resolve, and Old Bill's story was all the proof he needed to make his point. Very early the next morning he stood in the minister's study, angry and determined.

Samuel Treat had been trying once again to compose a sermon, but his mind kept sliding back to his conversation with Matthew Hallett the day before. He had no doubt John Knowles would make an issue of this story, were he to hear it, and was not at all surprised by his caller. He would have welcomed almost any other interruption.

"I have been vigilant, long expecting this to happen, and now it has!" Knowles exploded, pacing back and forth. "The devil has brought witchcraft into our midst through Mariah Hallett, and Eastham, like Salem, must be saved. I am as certain of this as I am sure that God calls me to lead the army of light into battle against eternal darkness."

"John," Mr. Treat said, "you must be reasonable. Mariah is a child."

"The possessed of Salem were children."

"So they were, but their stories were false. The names of the condemned have been cleared, and restitution is offered in shame and regret. Keep in mind that Mariah, herself, tells no story. People tell stories of her."

"That is of little consequence. The devil works in our midst, and in Salem he has made a mockery of the law. Had I been there, sir," Knowles continued, striking his fist on the minister's desk, "God's justice would have been sure and swift. The trials would have been brought to a firm and unquestioned end."

As Knowles talked on, Reverend Treat thought about Salem's dark days only nineteen years before. He knew just how easily misunderstood feelings and mysterious events could get out of hand. "John, Eastham is not Salem; we do not have that problem here."

"I know Mariah Hallett has been casting spells and is a disciple of the devil. She is like a small fire that swiftly grows into a hellish inferno. We must quench that fire in God's name!"

"You know nothing of the kind. Your information is hearsay. I have spoken to Josiah and have seen the dog. If there's indeed a problem, we must approach it with care. We cannot assume—"

"Sir! I assume nothing about the power of evil! I put this problem before you because you represent the authority of the church. But if you do not deal with this matter immediately and handle it with the seriousness it deserves, I will! Your lack of action places us all in mortal danger. Remember, Mr. Treat, that I was influential in calling you to this pulpit, and I have the power to replace you!"

"Do not presume to threaten me," the pastor said, standing to face Knowles. "I intend to inquire into this matter thoroughly, and I will do it my way. Do not interfere."

"I shall watch—and wait. Good day, sir!" He marched out of the study and slammed the door.

Mr. Treat's headache pounded. He was certain Knowles was unaware that there might be a problem at the Hallett farm, and he was glad of it. Knowles' blustering bravado could usually be taken with a grain of salt, but what if this time he was right? Would he, Samuel Treat, minister of this parish, have the courage to face Satan should Knowles' words prove true?

Still, something was wrong and whatever it was, he would have to insist on wisdom and caution at all times. He sighed, feeling wretched and tired. Surely, he thought, even this self-appointed crusader would not lead a holy war against a twelve-year-old child.

He went back to the Hallett farm the following day, hoping for insight, but knowing full well that whatever Matthew knew to be true would remain a secret. Would he be more successful if he spoke to Mary?

He found Matthew in a field gathering stray sheep, his dog bounding on ahead controlling the flock. They walked together for a while in uncomfortable silence. "It's being said that Mariah has cast a spell over the dog," Mr. Treat said.

Matthew's face darkened with anger. "That ain't what you told me. Where'd you hear that?"

"John Knowles."

"He witnessed this?"

"No, he didn't. There's talk, Matthew. Some believe in the miracle Josiah saw, and others are taking the story Bill Lee told with more seriousness than it deserves."

"Old Bill's mouth runs on faster'n his brain." Matthew said. "If this is a miracle, then why do you accuse my daughter of—of—"

"I do not accuse her of anything. But consider, things are not always what they seem. The devil is a trickster, and is ready to quote scripture when it suits him. We must know what we're facing. Knowles may have a stubborn nature, but he's a powerful speaker. He's talking of Salem now, and people remember. Some are frightened and will believe his words if we don't do anything to prove otherwise."

"John Knowles is a fool."

"Well, yes," Mr. Treat agreed, "in a lot of ways he is, but his opinions are dangerous. Matthew, for Mariah's sake you must keep her under control. If nothing else happens, then in time people will forget." He paused. "Please, you must tell me the truth. Has Mariah done anything to remind you of this incident?"

"No." Matthew's grip tightened on his shepherd's crook and the veins in his temples pulsed, but he didn't flinch at the minister's steady gaze. He turned and walked away, whistling to his dog.

Mr. Treat realized he'd been holding his breath and let it out in a gusty sigh. He went home knowing he'd been lied to again.

The next morning, Mariah found she was to be kept under close watch inside and outside the house. She was to go nowhere alone, not even to the privy, and was to speak to no one unless a family member was with her. Out of necessity her farm chores kept her near the livestock, but she was not allowed to go to the shed. Even her favorite cat had been put out in the barn.

Mr. Treat came to visit with her almost daily, and while they sat together he'd ask the same questions her father had and her answers were never different. Sometimes they'd walk toward the sea speaking of the things that interested Mariah the most, and on one walk she showed him the shed.

"Papa says I'm not to come here anymore, or show this to anyone," Mariah said, shyly. "I think I can show you because God is with you all the time, isn't he?"

"He's with you, too, Mariah, all the time."

"I know. An' he's with these animals." She knelt by the rabbit and the pheasant, attending to them, while Mr. Treat watched intently. He didn' t see the fox until it came out of the shadows and nuzzled Mariah's hand. He caught his breath as she stroked its face and ears, and speaking gently, examined its healing paw.

Mr. Treat squatted beside her. "I've never seen anything like this. How do you do it, Mariah?"

"I don't know," she said, running her hands over the fox's sleek coat and bushy tail.

"Will he let me touch him?"

She shrugged. "You could try."

The minister put out his hand and touched the reddish-brown fur. The fox made a small sound and trotted away to watch from a safe distance.

"Thank you," Mr. Treat said. After a few moments he asked, "What does it feel like—to heal animals like this?" He saw her brows furrow as she tried to find an answer. "Does it hurt? Does it torment you?"

"What's torment?"

"It means terrible pain and misery in your heart and mind."

"No, it don't hurt. Do I have torment?"

He looked into her young, innocent face like a man who at last knows the truth. "No, Mariah," he said with a smile, "I don't believe you do. God has blessed you." On his way home, he wondered if John Knowles or Matthew Hallett had ever touched a living fox.

5

One day, not long after Samson's cure, John Knowles rode to the Hallett farm. "I've come to speak with Mariah," he said when challenged by Matthew. He dismounted, and fetched a book from the canvas sack he carried strapped across his chest. "There are tests, here," he held up the hand-sized volume, "that, when administered properly, make it possible to judge the extent to which the devil possesses a soul. Satan's ownership of Mariah may not be complete, and she may yet be saved. With—"

"Go home, John, an' take your devil-book with you. There ain't nothin' wrong here. Parson's been, an' says it's so."

"Samuel Treat has fine qualities, to be sure, but it is into my hand and mine alone that the Almighty has placed his sword, alight with the fires of the righteous! I've come to do battle for your girl, Matthew. For her soul!" He headed toward the house. "I will speak to Mary—"

Matthew blocked his way. "You done enough. Leave my family be."

"Mariah's soul will writhe in the pit of eternal damnation without deliverance. Let me go to her!" Knowles cried out. From inside the house, Mariah heard her name and went to the open window to watch and listen. "She must not gratify the devil, but confess and give glory to God!"

"Get off my land, John!" Matthew shouted. He picked up his pitchfork and advanced toward the other man. "Take your foolish, wicked notions an' get off my land! Stay away from my daughter!"

"The kingdom of God must come into her! Let me cast out her devils!"

"The only devil here is you! Go or I'll get my gun!"

"The day will come, Matthew Hallett, when the truth is known and I will be called 'deliverer'!"

"No, John, people'll call you 'mad'! Go! Now!"

Mary, hearing the shouting, looked up from her sewing to see Mariah listening at the window. "Come away, child," she said, guiding her back to the loom.

"Why's Mr. Knowles shoutin' at papa? What did I do wrong? Why's papa so angry?"

"Mr. Knowles is—is angry about the way you cured the dog. Papa doesn't want him to know about the animals in the shed."

"Why not? Why does everyone think it's wrong to help Samson? Wasn't I right?"

"Yes," her mother said, drawing the word out , "but people are worried about how you learned to do this, about the person who taught you. Why don't you tell me, Mariah?"

"I already told papa. I told Mr. Treat. Nobody taught me—it just happens."

Mary closed her eyes for a moment, then took her daughter's hands in hers. "Sometimes people are afraid of what they don't understand, an' of things that are different. Your skill—with animals—makes you different." She stroked Mariah's hair. "We thought—" she paused. "Well. You must be very, very good an' follow the rules papa's laid down for you. In time things'll change. You'll see."

Later, Mariah sat at her loom, the shuttles in her lap. The fire threw shadows of the frame against the wall and she stared at them, lost in thought. "Lydia pleases everyone so much more than I do," she whispered to herself. "No one's ever cross with her." She ran her hand over the long warp threads, neatly strung side by side. "Each single strand of yarn is waitin' for me to weave in the weft threads," she murmured. "One by one, I put all the threads together to make one piece of cloth."

A length of finished cloth lay folded on a bench nearby and Mariah picked it up. She'd woven an intricate pattern into the fabric and the warp and weft threads, which had come from the same hank of yarn, had been dyed the same color. "They all fit together like a family. Like mama, papa, an' Lydia. Each thread is different, but the same, too." The shawl she'd recently woven for herself was on the settle and she spread it open on her lap. Several complicated patterns made up this cloth, for she'd experimented as she worked on it. The warp and weft threads were different scrap lengths of wool and linen in such a variety of shades, it always reminded her of Joseph's coat-of-many-colors—the one in the Bible. "This one is mama, an' papa, an' Lydia," she said, folding the solid colored cloth first. Then she folded her brightly colored, odds-and-ends shawl. "An' this one is me."

Mariah had known instinctively she was unlike Lydia, and hadn't been woven into the pattern of her family in quite the same way. She didn't know why, and, until that day, she couldn't have found even the simplest words to explain something that felt natural to her. Studying the two fabrics didn't make the reason easier to understand, but she did see that being different wasn't necessarily the bad thing so many people told her it was. Was this why she often felt she was looking in at her family from the outside? She puzzled over this new idea for a while, then, feeling curiously comforted, picked up her shuttles and went back to work.

The heat of the summer had long since dissolved into a cool, crisp autumn before Mariah was once again allowed outside by herself. During her confinement she had promised to abide by the rules her parents had laid out for her and was as good as her word. Now and then she met Josiah and Samson as they crossed her father's land on their way to the boatyard, but she no longer went to the jail or the chandlery. The townsfolk, for the most part, put the devil-talk behind them. Practical and thrifty, they knew she could be of use to them and cautiously accepted her skill with animals, neither noticing, nor caring about, her odd ways or John Knowles' wild stories.

Mariah's parents no longer watched her every move and turned their attention to Lydia, who was now of marriageable age and beginning to attract attention. But they were grateful for the pity and sympathy from the friends who understood that Mariah, despite her many gifts and talents, was indeed a difficult child.

6

John Knowles had never liked the idea that Mariah was allowed to run free in the area, nor did he approve of her having made friends of Josiah and Old Bill. His oldest daughter, Thankful, was Mariah's closest, life-long friend, and the two girls were together as often as possible. He'd always worried about Mariah's influence on Thankful, and he seized the opportunity provided by Mariah's confinement to clamp down on his daughter who was, in his opinion, plucky enough on her own.

He also took advantage of the recent brush with witchcraft to insert his concerns into the family's evening devotions. Thankful, even at twelve years, had already learned to hear her father's sermons, prayers, and readings with her head bowed and her mind filled with other thoughts, but she listened carefully to his opinions about Mariah and the devil. She'd always admired her friend's cleverness and, especially after learning of her father's interference, secretly agreed with Josiah that Mariah's skill was heaven sent.

Rebellion entered Thankful's heart one evening, and as her father began another prayer she stole a glance at her mother. She was still too young to fully consider them as adult people outside their parental role, but for the very first time saw her mother as a woman who was not happy. She peered up at her father as he paced about the great room talking to God, and wondered why they had married. I won't ever marry someone like him, she thought, he's too grim and cross. Why does God talk to him? She instantly flushed with shame. Bowing her head deeply, Thankful pressed her folded hands to her forehead and asked God for mercy. And since he knew what was in her heart, to please not tell her father who always said everything he needed to know came directly from God, himself.

Thankful's mother never discussed Mariah's problem with her, and if her parents spoke to each other, their conversations were in private. So she was surprised and happy when, after life was once again quiet and peaceful in the village, she and Mariah were allowed to visit. How, or why, this had come about she never understood. In looking back over the stressful, upsetting summer months, the only changes in her family's routine were the nights her father slept in the barn after arguments with her mother. Whether this had anything to do with her seeing Mariah, she didn't know.

John Knowles, ultimately recognizing an immoveable force when he saw one, gave in to pressure from his wife and agreed that the long friendship between Mariah and Thankful should continue. But taking no chances, he watched closely and prayed often. He took credit for having been the first to recognize the possibility of real evil in their midst, and for having played the most important part in beating it back before it spread.

The Reverend Mr. Samuel Treat took time to relax and rejoiced in the beautiful colors of fall. He went about the business of ministering to his congregation knowing that credit for the peace and quiet in their community was due entirely to God.

Afternoon Watch: 1715
Spanish Gold

SAM ARRIVED IN BOSTON IN THE EARLY SPRING OF 1715 JUST AFTER HIS twenty-sixth birthday. He worked off his passage as a hand on a small sloop bound for Provincetown, an active fishing village at the very end—the hook—of Cape Cod.

"Israel Cole, then, eh?" The sloop's master gave a dry little chuckle as they cut through Cape Cod Bay. "Should've gone to Great Island, if you was lookin' to find that ol' skin-flint. Tighter'n a drum, is Israel, an' sharper'n a serpent's tooth, besides."

Nearly everyone Sam spoke to, as he walked south from Provincetown through Eastham, knew this distant cousin of his mother, and opinions were varied and plentiful. Sharp tongues gave sharp answers to his questions. "What'd you be wantin' the likes o' Israel for?" some people would ask. They'd eye Sam with curiosity, then dismiss him with a scornful laugh. "You don't look half smart enough t' take him on." Sam was intrigued. Bit by bit he put together an image of this sly, old, fox-of-a-man and began to look forward to meeting him, for if there was anything he liked best in the world, besides being at sea, it was a good challenge.

So when he finally found Israel's house, he stared at the plain, wooden building. Dark and unwelcoming, it was not at all what he'd come to expect considering all he'd heard about Israel's business successes. Sam wondered what he did with his money.

"Israel Cole?"

"Who asks?" The man who answered Sam's knock was as plain and severe as his home. A stern, tight-lipped man, Israel glared with suspicion while Sam explained their remote family connection. As they stood, silent, regarding each other with cautious interest over the threshold, Israel's eyes narrowed to slits. He distrusted Sam's sudden appearance and open, smiling way, and yet, there was something—

"Who was your grandfather?"

"Henry Paine."

"Huh." He looked Sam up and down. "Aye, might be you'll do." He moved aside, and Sam stepped over Israel's threshold and into his new life.

Israel, it turned out, was a canny businessman who had an interest in so many different concerns that his own farm was almost a sideline. Two of his businesses, a small boatyard and controlling interest in the tavern on Great Island, became part of Sam's life right away. Israel hired him to repair rigging and sails at the boatyard, and he didn't forget to take a coin from Sam as pre-payment for a week's lodging in the tavern starting that very night.

Sam, who had grown up in the busy port of Plymouth, England, and spent time in the exciting, colorful ports of the Mediterranean, Africa and Asia, was not prepared for the rugged, windswept lands of Cape Cod. The wide beaches and tall stands of trees that mixed with the sea-grass-covered dunes were almost as exotic in their simplicity as the ports of North Africa were in their activity. He wasn't sure if he didn't like this better. It was a new and pleasant experience to walk through the small villages, not always on the alert for trouble or needing to keep his sea knife close to hand. Settling into a new routine, he felt content to have firm land under his feet again instead of a wet, rolling deck. He relaxed. This was a good move—at least for the time being.

In the tavern Sam met Israel's partners, Palgrave (Paul) Williams and Will Brown, the innkeeper. Paul was from Rhode Island where his late father, a former attorney general, had educated his family and provided them with comforts Sam could only imagine. Now married with children of his own, Paul was a successful goldsmith and moneylender. When he listened to Sam's stories of sailing the trade routes in and out of exotic ports-of-call, his eyes glowed.

As they sat together at a table in the tavern one night, Sam took a deep drink from his tankard. "Sometimes I knew what we hauled," he said in answer to Paul's question, "but I never saw any of it. Well before the cargo's brought aboard an' stowed away, it's packed in crates an' barrels an' such like. We didn't always carry finery. But when we did, it'd be you an' others like you—rich men—who'd be the ones to know of it, in your grand house an' in your grand work, an' all. Not me. I just bring the goods to you to buy an' use. We come from different worlds, you an' me."

Paul drew on his pipe and the tobacco burned bright red in the dim light. "I wonder," he said.

"What's there to wonder about?" Sam asked, a slight edge coming into his voice. "It's as plain as plain, an' truth besides."

Paul pushed away his empty dinner plate. "You know, everything was handed to me. Family money and connections made it easy for me to get started in life. I admit that, but I paid for it in the end. Everywhere I looked there were rules for me to follow, and I followed them all. I even married the woman my father thought best." He fell silent for a moment, gazing into the depths of his tankard. "I saw my life laid out for me all the way to the end, and the pattern was old and familiar. I knew exactly what I would be doing at every age. It was as if my life belonged to someone else. I couldn't breathe." He paused. "Maybe you won't understand this, but I felt as if I didn't fit in my own life."

Sam, leaned back in his chair and crossed his arms over his chest. Watching Paul through the smoke that curled up from his pipe, he chuckled.

"What?" Paul asked.

"I spent the best part of my life feelin' boxed in by rules that didn't do much for me 'cept keep me in my place. I never thought a man from the quarterdeck could feel the same as a foremast hand."

"Not much difference then, is there?"

"No," Sam agreed, "not how you talk on it, leastways. Sittin' here in this tavern, it's easy to see why I'd want your life. But why d'you want mine?"

"I don't."

Sam ran his fingers through his long, dark hair, and rubbed his eyes. He belched loudly. "Too much," he muttered, pushing the tankard away. He wiped his mouth on his sleeve and belched again. "Then what do you want?"

"Look," Paul said, leaning across the table, "if I had wanted to go to sea, my father would have purchased a commission for me in the Royal Navy. But why? It's only another set of rules. For you, the merchant service was the same thing. You spent half your life at sea, and where are you? You're skilled at your work, yes, but what are you doing? You're still rigging ships! You haven't gotten anywhere, have you?"

"That's why I left home—to set my course for a new horizon. Make a new voyage."

"And that's why I left home, and walked away from it all."

"But—"

"You thought the rules were different here, didn't you? Well, they're not. Listen, my friend. The only real difference between *New* England and *old* England is the age of the buildings and the space between them. Everything else is the same—and you'll go on working for someone, never having enough money and never improving your life, until they carry you off in a wooden box. No one moves up, Sam, only sideways, and very often, down."

"Then why're you here? Why this place?"

"This is a place where I can easily step outside the line other people use to hold me back. I'm willing to do that." He looked Sam square in the face. "Are you?"

Paul's challenge was loud and clear against the din of the noisy tavern. Sam studied him with interest. "What course're you steerin', then?"

"Come with me." With a quick glance at Israel, who barely nodded his head, Paul introduced Sam to the real business of Great Island Tavern.

Food, drink, and a bed for the night were not the only commodities available for sale. Wool, from the many flocks of sheep, and whale oil were among the goods traded and wrangled over, and business was brisk. But the tavern's cellar held the truth about Israel's success. Smuggling and mooncussing were the old Cape Cod traditions that he used, with the help of Paul, Will and others, to successfully build an illicit market. The goods stored there moved in and out under cover of honest buying and selling, and when London raised trade tariffs, the dealings increased causing money to flow like wine.

"You'd be surprised at how easy it is," Paul said. They were in the cellar, both stooped beneath the low ceiling. "With import taxes so high and regulations so stiff, everyone wants to bargain. Plenty of people look the other way when there's money to be made. Israel's built up a sweet business here, and he's offering you a part in it. Now maybe you can get a piece of your own."

Sam studied the crates, barrels, and sacks of goods in the dim light of the lantern. "Aye, then, I'll sign on."

Paul shook Sam's hand. "Good, I'm glad. You won't be sorry."

2

Sam wasn't sorry. For the next few months, the money he earned from Israel's boatyard and smuggling business multiplied in his pockets. During his years at sea, the laws made in London by the few for the few—as Sam reasoned it—seemed to follow him wherever he sailed, no matter how far from home. In this remote, rural place, London felt farther away than ever. It was easy to turn a blind eye to those laws and throw the representatives of the Crown off the scent with a lie or a bribe.

Sam enjoyed his new life, but he was a sailor at heart and missed being at sea. One day, news came of Spanish ships sunk in a storm off the southern coast of Florida, and of their vast treasures of silver and gold lying on the ocean floor. He thought about this while he worked at the boatyard, eventually coming up with a way to go to sea and keep a good part of the profit for himself. After supper at the tavern he spoke with Paul. "I been thinkin' 'bout this, an' we can do it! We'll need a ship, supplies, an' a good crew. The sooner we get started the better."

"Just how sure are you about this?"

"How sure can I be? We got as good a chance as anyone. Knowin' how the Spanish are about gold, there's plenty—just for the takin'."

Paul thought for a while. "You know," he said, "this may be just the thing. If you can get Israel to put up half the money, I'll put up the rest."

Sam, whose working relationship with Israel had grown into a friendly tolerance of sorts, knew that the most direct way to his cousin's cash box was through his greed. He talked of gold every time he saw Israel, making liberal promises of success based on his skills as a seaman and his knowledge of Spanish shipping.

Israel, though, had doubts. "Oh, you'll find some gold, I suppose, you're clever enough. But what guarantee do I have you'll bring it back?"

"Why wouldn't I?"

"Why the hell would you?" Israel snorted a short laugh. "And what's to keep you from stayin' down there once you find all that gold?"

"When I give my word, I sticks by it. I ain't alone in this venture. I'll be back—an' with gold. Mark me on this."

They stood on a dock at the boatyard, Israel's shrewd eyes searching Sam's face for hidden meanings in his words.

"Are you putting up money for this trip?" Paul's blunt question to Israel broke into the silence between the two as he joined them. "Well, are you?"

"What's it to you if I am?"

"I'll match any ready money you have," Paul said. "I'm headed to Rhode Island to make arrangements, then I'll be going south with Sam."

"Hard to say if that makes me feel better or not," Israel remarked dryly. He stroked his chin, his eyes shifting warily from one man to the other. "All right," he said finally, "all right." He pointed a bony finger at Sam. "Just see that you keep it cheap."

Sam and Paul soon found that one of Israel's conditions was that they take John Julian along as a diver. Sam had worked with John since first coming to the boatyard, but several weeks had passed before he learned that John was a slave, and Israel owned him.

"Glad to be comin' with you, Sam," John said, soon after being told of the voyage. "It's the closest I been to home since I was born."

"Where're you from, then?"

"Granada. Mosquito tribe. Been feelin' a pull for a long time—to go home. Get's too cold here." He shivered in the June sun, but smiled at Sam, his unusually good teeth flashing bright white in contrast to his deep, coppery skin.

"Plenty warm where we're headed," Sam observed with a knowing grin.

"Aye."

"Wouldn't surprise me none if it was hard for you to come back north."

John's smile widened.

✠ ✠ ✠

The seamen of Cape Cod had heard all the stories of getting quick gold, one way or another, many times before. Making a living from he sea was a daily gamble under the best of circumstances, and they knew of easy death when brutal storms brought chaos to the Atlantic waters. This plan of Sam's, they decided, was beyond all common sense.

Far from being put off by their suspicious caution, Sam plunged into selling his plan with enthusiasm. His tongue was golden, and he told rich tales to nearly everyone he met. He was in Old Bill's chandlery one day when Josiah and Samson came to visit.

Samson had long ago recovered from his injuries. Though the joint in his foot would no longer bend and his gait was very odd, he frisked over to Sam, wagging his tail. Sam went down on one knee, petting and stroking the big dog's ears and head.

"Josiah! You hear 'bout Sam's big treasure hunt?" Old Bill asked, emerging from beneath his counter. "Well, I'm goin'."

"What the hell for?"

"Too bloody cold here. My joints ache more an' more each winter."

"If that ain't the most damn fool thing I heard in a long time. How you goin' t' work a ship? You're too old!"

"Sam's takin' me on as bosun. I know what I'm about—done it for donkey's years. I just got t' tell someone else what t' do, an' how t' do it, is all."

Josiah turned his glance to Sam, but he'd gone outside and was tossing a stick to Samson in the bright sunshine.

"He's cracked an' you're too old. Nothin' good's goin' t' come o' this. What about the shop?"

"Sold it. Don't ever plan on comin' back."

Josiah stared at his friend. "Thought you liked it here."

"I do—everythin' but the miserable winters. Why don't you come along? Sam'll take the dog. Start all over in the hot sun. You don't want t' sit around that jail forever, do you?"

"No, I don't. But I don't plan t' throw it all away on some muddleheaded treasure hunt, neither."

Outside the open door, Sam listened to their debate and Samson fetched the stick. After a while, he reached down to pat the dog, then walked to the boatyard whistling a little tune.

✠ ✠ ✠

At the tavern, whalers and seamen of every kind, locals and strangers, tradesmen and farmers all crowded in and talked about gold. Most had their doubts as they listened to Sam—but they did listen.

Sam put his own money on the table, and bought tankards of ale all 'round, played at cards, backgammon, and draughts, smoked clay pipes, and talked long into the night, every night.

"You're good for business, Sam," Susannah, Will Brown's plump, pretty wife, remarked. She put two tankards down on the table where he sat with a young fisherman.

"I say it's your lamb stew," he said, winking at her.

"Aw, don't listen to him, Nate," she said to the fisherman as she piled up the supper plates. "He's as daft as they come. Spanish gold, indeed!"

"Daft, am I?" Sam reached up with one arm and pulled her into his lap."Daft enough to take you along as ship's cook!" he said, laughing.

"Cook? For you? Huh! I'd rather roast in my own oven!" she said, getting up and smoothing her food-stained apron with mock dignity. "Some cook I'd be, spendin' all my time up-chuckin' over the side. No more nonsense from you, fresh boy! Go along with you now!" She cuffed Sam lightly on the ear and, gathering up the supper things, went behind the bar where she and Will broke into hearty laughter.

Nate Pound smiled at the playful exchange. He had listened to all that Sam said and liked how it sounded. For a while, he'd been worried that even the bountiful Atlantic couldn't fill his nets as fast as his wife could fill the family cradle, and he had to admit Sam certainly made it sound easy. Easier than it really was, no doubt, but still—a chance like this was surely worth the risk.

"Sign me up, Sam," Nate said. "May be that I can win over one or two others."

"Good!" They shook hands. "Give me word soon. Time ain't goin' to wait for us, none."

Nodding in agreement, Nate finished his drink and went to talk with a group of friends.

Through the crowded, smoky tavern, Sam caught Israel's eye. He raised his tankard in salute.

3

In the two weeks Paul had been gone Sam set his eye on a sloop and ordered supplies at Old Bill's chandlery. Although the ship had seen better days it was not beyond repair, so he went to Israel's house to work out the details for having it refitted at the boatyard. Conducting business with his cousin was never easy, and the headache he had was not helped by the Jamaican rum Israel poured so liberally into his glass. By the time he crawled into bed, Sam couldn't remember if a deal had been struck.

Israel's household was up and at work when he ventured out of doors. The early morning sun shone brightly and the May air smelled fresh and sweet. He gave up trying to remember what had been decided the night before and concentrated on walking off the effect of Israel's good rum.

Mariah was up early, too, and was walking home after delivering newly dyed yarn to a neighbor. There were shorter ways to go, but the path she chose passed a place where lilacs grew wild. They were nearly at their peak and their heady scent perfumed the air.

As Sam walked through the woods, the words of a song his sister used to sing when he was very small began to emerge from the fuzzy depths of his mind. He stopped and closed his eyes to listen more carefully, his heart swelling with the sound of Lizzie's voice. But in a moment he knew the singing was real and, curious, he followed the sound.

Sam caught his breath. Mariah stood by the lilacs breaking off small branches and filling her empty basket with blossoms as she sang the song he remembered. Her soft, light-brown hair was tied back with a length of rust-colored yarn and her bodice and skirt—an unusual blue, almost the color of a violet dawn—set off the pink, healthy glow of her face.

The shawl she wore against the chill held his eyes, its lustrous surface catching the light as she moved in the sun. For a few captivating moments he took in all the details of this pretty girl on this pretty spring morning. Then, rubbing his face to banish the feeling of bleary woolliness, he cleared his throat and, wishing his shirt was not so dirty, stepped into the clearing.

"G'mornin'."

Startled, Mariah stopped singing and turned quickly, dropping the flowers she held in her hands.

"I'm sorry," Sam said, picking up the branches and placing them in the basket. "Didn't mean to— Heard you singin', you know, a song my sister used to sing when I was a lad." He coughed and bowed his head, hoping the unexpected blush covering his face appeared to be the natural high color of exercise in the crisp weather. He coughed again and said gravely, "Samuel Bellamy, ma'am."

"Oh, I've heard of you!" Mariah smiled at him and her eyes twinkled. "You're Mr. Cole's cousin. My friend, Thankful, says she heard her father say he heard from a friend who said you're a rich merchant from London, you've been all the way around the world three times, an' you're plannin' to buy the tavern on Great Island. Is that true?" She paused for breath. "I'm Mariah."

"G'mornin', Mariah," he said with another little bow. Then he chuckled. "That's quite a yarn you been hearin'. I ain't no merchant, not by a long ways. I'm but a foremast hand, a bosun, in truth, who's seen a good bit of the world from the deck of a fine ship or two. I come to the colonies to find a new way for myself, so I live in Israel's tavern an' work at the boatyard. I'm from Plymouth—Devon by birth—not London; though I been there once." He paused. "I hope you ain't too much disappointed."

"Oh, my goodness, no. I don't care very much about money, do you? Tell me, please, about all the places you've seen. I've never been anywhere. You're very lucky."

Sam told her a little of his life in Plymouth and his years in the used to weave her fabrics, and the results were the same—rich and lustrous with patterns fanciful and unusual. She was interested in what he had to say, and he liked the way she listened.

"You've had an exciting life. It's very quiet, here." She turned back to the lilac bush and started to break off a branch.

"Please! Let me." Sam took out his sea knife and began cutting branches. They stood close together and when he accidentally brushed her hair with his hand, he felt a rush of warmth.

As she moved beneath her shawl, arranging the blossoms in her basket, he studied the pattern. It was very intricate, something he couldn't quite fathom—but the colors! He spotted blue threads, not unlike those in the fabric of her clothing; and russet-orange yarns, the same as the ones binding her hair. There were so many colors, he wasn't sure he could name them all. Some colors were dark and some were light; some yarns were dull and others shiny. Just for a moment, he remembered being in the parish school when he was very young, hearing the Bible story about Joseph's coat-of-many-colors. Had his coat been as glorious as this? Spellbound, he touched the edge of the fabric, very lightly, with the tips of his rough fingers. "When I first saw you, this seemed to shine in the sun."

"It's linsey-woolsey. I wove linen threads in with the wool because I like the smooth linen an' the fuzzy wool together. It's very warm."

"I like it."

"Thank you," Mariah said, smiling. "I'm glad."

He liked everything about her. They worked in silence for a few minutes.

"You're going away soon, aren't you? To look for pirate treasure. I heard that, too."

"Well, no, Spanish gold. From ships sunk in a storm. Gold all over the ocean floor. We'll have to dive for it. In the Caribbean." He continued cutting branches.

"That's one of those places where it never gets cold or snows, isn't it? I'd like to go to a place like that some day. It gets so cold here."

Sam's mind began to race as he listened to her.

"You're very smart," she went on, "an' clever, too, I think. Some day, you'll come back with bags of gold an' tell me all about your adventures."

Mariah looked up into his smiling face. Sam was not so remarkable in his appearance that he might turns heads, with his dark hair and eyes and ruddy complexion, although he was taller than average. He was lanky and well-muscled, with the tanned, leathery skin and rough callused hands of a man who'd worked out-of-doors all his life, much like any other man in any other sea-going community. But something in him held her gaze, and she could not turn away.

She pulled the shawl close about her and knew the heat she felt came from Sam. A little smile teased the corner of her mouth as a warm, liquid feeling flooded through her mind and body. At sixteen, Mariah had never given any real thought to love or its desires and pleasures until this very moment, and she blushed fiercely, dropping to her knees to gather the lilacs that had fallen to the ground.

Sam picked up the basket. Handing it to her, he knew his pleasure in her company was not solely lustful. There had been other women, exotic women from exotic ports-of-call, who had offered him a passionate hour or two, or a few nights of comfort. He'd never turned them down, but he'd never offered them his heart. One or two young women had tempted him enough to consider staying ashore to see what would happen, but his heart had never been engaged with them either and he'd eventually sailed away.

Now, suddenly, here was Mariah, healthy and sturdy, a pretty village maiden strong in her own way, with hands already coarse from working despite her sixteen years. She was not in the least exotic, and comfortably fit the plain, straightforward world in which she lived. Sam felt a contentment he'd not know for years, and he wondered if, in the fullness of time, he might not have with Mariah what he longed for the most: a home. His plans for recovering Spanish gold teetered on the brink of being cast aside as he considered staying with her, but in a moment he caught himself and resolved to conquer both his dreams: finding a place to call home with Mariah and the gold to make it possible.

Later that afternoon, Sam went back to the boatyard, and then to the tavern. At home, Mariah went about her chores in a distracted way. She saw his face clearly as she relived every word of their conversation while preparing for market the next day, but by nightfall his features had slipped from her memory no matter how hard she tried to hang on to them. The twelve hour market day dragged on three times longer than usual, the impatient Mariah was sure; and sleep, when night finally came, was nearly impossible. Early the next morning, after milking, she went to Israel's boatyard.

"I didn't think I'd be seein' you again. Leastways, not so soon," Sam remarked, smiling at her. "Been thinkin' 'bout you."

"I've been here before," she said, gazing out at Sam's sloop being towed in for repair. "I like to watch the work bein' done on the ships an' boats. Sometimes Old Bill's here, an' Josiah an' Samson, too."

"Your parents don't mind?"

"Not too much. I do my chores an' weave for market, so it

doesn't seem to matter to them where I go, or when," Mariah said. "I don't fit in my family somehow, at least I reckon it that way, so I come an' go as it pleases me, most times." Neither of them spoke for a few moments, then she smiled. "They don't know about you."

Sam met her eyes. "I'm glad you're here." The breeze blew her hair across her face, and he brushed it away. "I don't fit no better in my family. Pa says I was born to walk a different road."

They stood side by side, looking out over the water toward Great Island. Gulls flew around them, wheeling and shrieking in the sky, and one perched on the masthead of the sloop under tow.

"You think you might see your way to comin' to the tavern one day?" Sam asked, suddenly. "There's some fine people I been tellin' 'bout you. Will an' Susannah, the landlord an' his wife'll be watchin' an' takin' good care you get what you need. If I ain't here, someone'll take you over. Only got to ask."

"I've never been there, before." Mariah shielded her eyes, peering at Sam in the sun. "I think visitin' would be fine."

He took both her hands in his, and brushing them lightly with his lips, said softly, "I'll be lookin' forward to it. Thank you."

Paul had returned from Rhode Island and was in the tavern when Mariah visited for the first time. His manner to her was respectful and polite, and she felt at ease as they talked. She was pleased to find that she liked him. He was older than Sam, shorter and heavier built, but for all their physical differences, she saw how similar the two men were. Israel was also at the tavern, and although she had known him all her life, she always felt shy around him. It was Will and Susannah Brown who made her feel right at home.

"Well," Susannah said to Mariah as Sam introduced them, "so you're his pretty girl. Talked about you quite a bit, last two days. Look, Will, here's Sam's Mariah!"

Will came out from the back room, wiping his meaty hands on a bar towel. He touched his forelock. "Most welcome," he said with a shy smile. Then, looking awkwardly from his wife to Mariah, he nodded his head and vanished behind the bar.

"Now, don't mind him, love. He's big as a bear an' gentle as a kitten. Our two girls are newly married an' gone from home, an' he misses them mightily. He'll be glad to have a young thing like you around the place now an' then. Sam!" she called, laughing. "Don't stand there like a great lump! Draw some cider for our lass!"

The business of the day was in full swing, and the tavern was crowded. Mariah, used to her quiet life at home and many solitary hours, was overwhelmed by the activity. She took the cup Sam brought her and sipped the sweet liquid. Looking up, she spotted Josiah and Samson in a corner and went to sit with them.

"You all right?" he asked. When she nodded, he studied her closely from beneath his bushy eyebrows. "You sure you know what you're 'bout?"

"What d'you mean?"

Josiah looked to where Sam sat in earnest conversation with Israel, Paul, Will, and two others. Mariah followed his gaze. As she watched, Sam turned and smiled at her, and she wondered how she could ever have forgotten how he looked. He was not unlike the other men in the taproom. Farmers and seamen were much the same: weathered from a lifetime of working out-of-doors, strong and hard, some lean, some not, some taller than most, all calloused and rough. She'd noticed his work-scarred hands as he'd touched the lilacs and had known he could be gentle. As she studied Sam's profile at the table she recognized their kinship as the one trait she'd never forget. They understood each other, and in their understanding was acceptance.

"You don't know the first thing 'bout him," Josiah said, breaking into her thoughts. "An' don't be sayin' how you know everthin' you need to. Many's the lass who found out a thing or two when 'twas too late t' turn back." He pointed at her with his spoon to emphasize his words. "You just listen t' me, little missy. You're but sixteen year! It's your first time out o' the harbor, an' he's put his ship in many a port afore he dropped anchor here, an' that ain't no lie."

Mariah had been staring at her glass of cider as she listened, and looked up to see Josiah blush fiery red. "Well," he said, flustered, "I said my piece. Just be damned sure you know what you're 'bout. That's all."

Sam had turned back to the discussion at his table, and Mariah watched him for a few seconds longer. "Yes," she said, "I know exactly what I'm about."

✠ ✠ ✠

"I like her," Paul said. They were on the deck of the sloop, working to refit her for the long voyage south. Mariah had come to lend a hand as best she could. Paul watched her check a list with Old Bill as supplies from the chandlery were taken aboard. "She's pretty and all, but there's something more. She comes to the tavern and comes here any time she can. She's stepping across that line we talked of. No one's holding her back."

Sam was hauling on a halyard and he made it fast to a belaying pin. "Aye," he said, looking up at the mast. "Aye. She's a spirited lass, an' she suits me fine. We're—" he searched for the right words, "like-minded."

"Well, good fortunes for you both. I'm not like-minded with this hammer, though," Paul said with a frown. He looked at the work going on around him. "I never had to turn my hand to this sort of thing before."

"No worries, mate," Sam said, squinting at him in the sun, "you'll learn. Your real place is in the business of it all. It's been much easier dealin' with Israel now you come back an' put good money on the table. Just as useful as swingin' a hammer."

A dog barked, and they turned to see Samson trotting up the gangway. Josiah, close behind, still refused to join the crew, but worked on the sloop when he had the time. The old man came and stood beside Sam. "She's weatherly an' stiff," he said, looking out over the deck and avoiding Sam's eyes. "Got good lines. But mind how you handle her. You chart your course true an' she'll answer sharp. You run afoul o' her, an' it comes my way t' know, I'll see you dance with the devil an' no mistake 'bout it."

"Well, it ain't nobody who plans to run afoul," Sam said, shading his eyes from the sun and giving Josiah a quizzical look. "Don't think you got call to take it so hard. She's a old hulk, to be sure, but she'll serve well enough."

"Not the boat, you damned fool." Josiah spat over the side. As he walked away he said, "I mean Mariah."

✠ ✠ ✠

Sam and Mariah didn't have a formal courtship. Their friends at the boatyard and tavern gave them the support of a happy family, and they were relaxed and comfortable witheach other.

As mutual trust and faith grew, their friendship and love deepened. They met by the lilacs, walked over the dunes and sat on the beach. They shared their histories and their dreams. Eventually, in one of the bed chambers at the tavern, they shared their love.

4

Summer was a busy time on the Hallett farm, and Mariah was home more often than she would have liked. Not being with Sam was hard to bear; she never spoke about him. The first few times she went to the tavern she was sure Israel, or Ned Winslow, or some other neighbor, would speak to her parents about her new friend. She'd worried, until she realized it would not have mattered to her even if someone had.

She never worried that her day-long trips away from home to the boatyard or tavern would cause her parents to question her ramblings;

they were prepared to accept her ways as long as she got her work done. She always returned with her basket filled with plants and herbs. All summer long she dyed pounds of wool and flax to help prepare for market, and the long winter ahead.

One humid day in early August, Matthew stood in his barn staring at Sam in disbelief. On one of his trips to the tavern to trade fleece for goods, he had met the young seaman and heard his wild stories about Spanish gold. As he listened to Sam talk of his plans, he'd wondered what sort of man preferred such a rootless life. And now, suddenly, here he was hat in hand, asking to marry Mariah.

"How long has this been goin' on?" Matthew asked, his concern tinged with anger. "Look, Bellamy, I don't know how you met my daughter, or where an' when, or how you courted her, but you did it without my consent. Judgin' by what I heard of your plans an' the company you keep, you ain't the match I think best for her. Mariah needs a solid life with a husband willin' to give her just that. Accordin' to what I know of you, you ain't got nothin' to offer my girl, an' what you do got, you're puttin' aside to go on a fool's errand. An' one you might not come home from, neither. So I ask you, Bellamy, why you want to make a offer for my girl, if you ain't goin' to be here with her?"

"I'm makin' that voyage," Sam said, seeing at once that talking to Matthew was the fool's errand, "to give Mariah what she needs the best way I know how. Somethin' good'll come of it, an' when I come back, I can get some land an' build her a house." The plan sounded weak, even to himself.

Matthew raised a skeptical eyebrow. "An' take to raisin' sheep?" He gave a short laugh. "No, Bellamy. The answer's no. An' I'll say to you what I'd say to any man who comes askin' with a empty purse an' a load o' big ideas: Only when you can prove to me you got means to support a wife an' family, an' a place to house them in comfort, can you ask to marry my daughter. Not before. Good day, sir."

Sam's glib tongue failed him, and with a mumbled "Good day", he turned and walked away.

Matthew stood watching until Sam was out of sight. "Bloody hell!" he shouted, and kicked hard at a bucket, scattering the contents. Chickens, squawking loudly, flocked about relishing the sudden treat. Mary came out of the house.

"What's the matter? Who's that man?"

"Is there ever goin' to be a time when Mariah will do anythin' in the ordinary way?" He shouted angrily. "Where is she?"

"With Thankful. What's wrong?

He told her what had happened.

"Did you say no?"

"Of course I did! Oh, there's plenty in these parts who makes a honest livin' from the sea, but by all accounts he's a adventurer, a soldier of fortune. An' judgin' by his big talk, more'n likely a liar, too. Then there's that half-brained plan of his to find gold. Some're puttin' up good money to pay for it, an' some're goin' along, puttin' their lives on the line. For what? Nothin's goin' to come of it. Nothin'. How can I marry her to someone like that?"

"I'd hoped Lydia's weddin' would be the makin' of another," his wife said of their older daughter's recent marriage. "But no one ever shows much interest in Mariah."

"No, an' you wonder why? Oh, she's comely enough, but she's different, as everyone in these parts knows full well. Bellamy can't see it. Or, could be he don't care."

"What's his name?"

"Samuel Bellamy. Some cousin of Israel Cole's, which don't say much for him, neither."

"When did they meet?" Mary asked. "How did it get this far so fast? She never said a word to me. She must meet with him when she's away from home."

They looked at each other in alarm as the full meaning of the words hit them at the same time.

Matthew swore. "God's teeth. You think she's in the family way?"

"No. Oh, no. Not Mariah. She wouldn't do such a thing."

But standing together, among the clucking chickens, they feared the worst.

✠ ✠ ✠

A short time later, Sam came to the clearing by the lilacs. Mariah, sitting with Thankful, watched Sam walk up to them, his mouth set in a grim line.

"I'll go now," Thankful said, standing up. She smiled shyly at Sam. He nodded, but didn't return the smile. "I'm sorry for you both," she said, softly. Then kissing Mariah lightly on the cheek, she turned and hurried away.

For a long moment they were quiet, then Mariah rushed into Sam's arms. As he pulled her close, his embrace so completely surrounding her, she felt she had dissolved and become part of him.

"I love you so much." Sam's mouth was close to her ear and she could feel the warmth of his breath.

"I don't ever want to lose you. Not ever," she whispered.

"You never will."

"Then take me with you."

She felt his hold on her loosen a little as he pulled back and looked into her eyes. "I thought about that, but it's too dangerous—no place for a woman."

"But I'm strong! I can help!"

He smiled and stroked her hair. "I know you are, my love, I know. You'll be needin' all of that strength while you're waitin' for me to come back—an' I will."

Lilacs, for all their beautiful color and wonderful scent, have a very short life. They bloom for about two weeks or so, then wither to a rusty brown. Sam plucked a dead blossom from the bush.

"Wait for me, please wait. I got nothin' to give you but my love an' my heart, an' my promise to marry you. Please, please believe me.

I'll return before these bloom again." He twisted the flower in his fingers.

"I don't care what flower blooms, or when," she said, taking it from him and kissing his hand. "Just come back an' love me forever."

"Please have patience, Mariah. Don't ever give up on me." And when she kissed him, he knew she wouldn't.

✠ ✠ ✠

From the deck of the sloop, Sam looked again at the dock, slowly receding into the distance, and saw that Mariah had waded knee-deep into the water, her skirts bunched up in one arm as she waved with the other. And now, unbelievably, in that impossible place between advancing and retreating, he knew with more certainty than he'd ever known anything in his whole life: If he lost her, nothing else would ever matter to him again.

She was waving with both arms now, her skirts spreading out on the surface of the water so she looked as if she were floating. When she'd asked him to take her along, he'd said no because of the danger and now he regretted it. Every major choice he'd made that had propelled him forward in life, he'd made without regret—until now. If she really was the whole world to him, why wasn't he with her planning a life he was sure he wanted? Why had this treasure hunt become so important he'd leave the woman he loved?

Sam's brain whirled and his heart pounded. How easy it would be to come about, to go back and take her aboard. She'd come with him, too, without a second thought. He opened his mouth to give the order, but a catch in his throat squeezed hard. A lump grew and he couldn't swallow. They were moving steadily now, and she would soon be lost to view. He lifted both his arms and waved.

✠ ✠ ✠

Mariah walked miserably along the empty beach in her damp petticoat, her wet linen skirt in one hand and her soggy stockings and hoes in the other. She'd seen him at the stern, watching her, and for a brief moment wondered if he'd come about. She'd go with him, of course, without a second thought. Then she'd seen him wave. He'd promised to come back to her, and she believed with her whole heart that he'd try, but there were no guarantees with a sea voyage. The burying acre and the widows in their community were proof of that.

The August sun was hot, and she spread her clothes on the sand to dry. She sat, drawing her bent legs close, and rested her chin on her knees to look after the sloop as it disappeared from sight. She'd had the power to stop him all along. He would have cancelled the trip, had he known. He would have stayed. Or he'd have insisted on taking her with him. Either way, it would be better than the wrenching pain she felt now. Sam would always be with her.

She was filled with him. And she'd never been more alone.

The Second Part

First Dog Watch: 1715-1717

Pirates

GOLD RUSH FEVER WAS INFECTIOUS AND JUMPED FROM ONE PERSON TO another like fleas. By the time Sam and his crew walked along the Nassau waterfront, they were itching with excitement. Stories and rumors were everywhere, and the disappointment of those who had failed to find gold did little to discourage the treasure hunters who had yet to try.

It was mid-September, 1715, and it was hot. They had sailed from the cooler summer temperatures on Cape Cod into the southern heat during hurricane season, but the weather had been fine all the way. When Sam put into New Providence Island to take on supplies and make needed repairs, he found the harbor as crowded as the town.

New Providence Island and Nassau, its capital, were important safe havens for pirates. Sam and Old Bill had been in rough towns like Nassau before, so the crowded waterfront felt familiar to them. To Paul, John, Nate, and the Cape fishermen, however, it was a new experience. The tavern on Great Island, which could hold its own on rowdy nights, was no match for the lawlessness in the streets and taverns of this wild, notorious Caribbean town.

"Can't never say," Old Bill shouted in answer to Nate's question.

They were sitting with the others in a noisy waterfront tavern, where the barmaid had just laid food and drink before them. Bill's words were drowned out by a sudden explosion of laughter as she waited on the next table.

"Can't never say," he repeated. "They's a damn sight more gentlemen o' fortune than ordinary seamen in these parts. But with this lot crowdin' in, lookin' for gold an' all, maybe not."

"Is there any way to tell?" Nate asked. He'd moved in closer to hear Old Bill speak, casting an anxious glance at the crowd. It was almost as hard to see as it was to hear, and the sooty oil lamps, giving off a feeble glow, made little difference in the dim, dingy room. He'd objected to stopping at Nassau, but had given in to the practical insistence of Sam and Old Bill that it was as good a place as any for provisions, as well as a good a source for news of Spanish gold. Like most everyone on Cape Cod, he knew about the scourge of piracy in the Caribbean and up and down the North American coast, and like all seamen, he was determined to stay out of the way.

Old Bill shook his head in answer to Nate's question. "No. Sometimes, maybe a pirate got fancy clothes—ornamental like—what he takes as plunder off a fine ship. Now, in a place like this, maybe he got his share. It's lots more coin in his pocket for spendin' than what a ordinary seaman'll get in his lifetime an' beyond. Then, too, maybe he's better at drinkin' an' at fightin'. But, like I says, mostly you can't tell who is, an' who ain't, just by lookin'."

Paul, trying to listen to Old Bill, looked up when he thought he heard Sam speak to him. He cupped his hands behind his ears, but the words were lost to the noise in the room and he let them pass. As the racket died down, a man pushed through the crowd, and, standing behind Sam, put a hand on his shoulder.

"Sam!" the man called out, giving him a shake. "Sam Bellamy!" Sam turned and looked into the deeply tanned, craggy face. "Do you know me, Sam? Davy Turner, helmsman. We shipped together on the *Bonnie Celeste* in 1709."

"God's breath! It's Davy Turner! Aye, I know you! What're you doin' here?"

"Might ask you the same!"

"Well, come an' sit down!" Sam said, indicating a place on the opposite bench. "Lads, give my old messmate a place to drop anchor!"

Davy squeezed into the space between Old Bill and John Julian. Looking across the table at Sam, he flashed a nearly toothless grin.

"Ain't seen you since Lisbon."

"Worst floggin' I ever saw before—or since—an' I seen some bad ones," Sam commented after describing the event on the *Bonnie Celeste.* "Never set easy with me, tyin' a man up helpless-like, an' countin' out strokes." He shook his head.

"Had to do that many times myself," Old Bill put in. "Bloody rotters, some masters."

"I never thought you'd survive, Davy. Practically dead, you were, when we untied you. What'd you do, after we put you ashore?"

"Only thing I could do. Took my chances under the black flag."

Bill gave a grunt of agreement, but Nate, filled with suspicion and curiosity, lowered his voice and spoke to the newcomer. "You're a pirate, then."

"Aye, I'm a pirate; a gentleman o' fortune," Davy said with a laugh and mock bow. "But they's worse things, lad. Worse things in a world what looks t' other way when a man needs a hand up or a slice o' justice."

"Amen t' them true words," Old Bill said, lifting his tankard in salute.

Paul glanced around the tavern. "Is that why you're here? With your ship?"

"Aye, that's how I'm here. Point bein', Sammy, why're you here?" Before Sam could answer, Davy slapped his hand on the table and laughed. "No! You ain't after that gold, are you? Month or two late is what I been hearin'!"

As questions and comments came from the men around the table, Paul said, "Let's go outside. I can't hear anymore."

A short time later, they were aboard the sloop.

"It's like this," Davy said. "Them Spanish is goin' after their own gold, an' they got a system. They got ships scattered 'twixt Florida an' Cuba, an' they got good divers from Panama an' the like. Storin' most o' the gold in Havana, is what I been told."

"Then it's all been recovered and we wasted our time," Paul said, irritated.

"No, not hardly," Davy replied. "Twere the easiest to find that's been got first. But you know what they's like with gold, Sam, them Spanish. Where they got one coin, they got a ship full. An' like I says, they got their systems. Best part is," he continued, chuckling, "they was storin' some o' the treasure on a little island—Barra de Ayes, I think it's called. Anyways, Henry Jennings, he strikes his Jolly Roger, hoists the English colors, sails in as bold as you please, an' takes the whole lot right out from under their noses. Now, I heard it was upwards of 300,000 pieces-of-eight, an' them Spanish, they was hoppin' mad. Ain't no love lost 'twixt them an' the English anyways, an' this didn't help none. An' Jennings, well Jennings is smart t' lay low an' not go pokin' at them for a while."

"Who's this Jennings, then?" one of the Cape men asked.

Davy chuckled. "Oh, him an' Ben Hornigold is two pirate cap'ns worth reckonin', I'd say, as would most. Jennings hates them Spanish much as they hates him, Hornigold hates takin' English ships, an' mostly they hates each other. They ain't goin' t' give no quarter t' the seadog what crosses 'em, so it's best not bein' 'twixt 'em when they commence t' chasin' down the same prize."

In the silence that followed, the only sound was the sloop bobbing and creaking at her mooring as the tide rolled in under her.

"What're we t' be doin' now, Sam?" John asked after a while.

Sam had been standing apart from the others, leaning against the gunwale listening to Davy. "We up anchor an' make for the gold," he said, moving into the group. "We're here, an' we best be gettin' on with it while we still got a chance. I ain't goin' back beaten—not without tryin', leastways. I say we sail on the next tide."

"What about them two, as Davy was talkin' of?" John asked. "Jennings an' t' other?"

"Spanish gold's our aim," Sam replied, "an' keepin' well down wind of them two."

"Davy, do you know the best place to start looking?" Paul asked.

"We just head her sou'west an' stop anywheres them Spanish got a ship or two. They mark the spot. Pick a patch of ocean an' hope for the best."

"'We?' You signin' on, Davy?"

"Sure, Sam, why not? Spanish gold or anyone else's. I don't much care how I gets it, long as I does."

"What about your ship?" Nate asked.

"What about it? They'll think I took the sharp end o' a cutlass in a row somewheres an' sail without me. I got myself a new ship, now."

✠ ✠ ✠

Davy had been right about the Spanish Navy and their big war ships. They were well in control of each salvage site and went about the retrieval of their lost gold with unyielding efficiency. Sam's sloop, among other smaller vessels, pestered them like flies buzzing around an ox: darting in and out of the operation, looking for a choice spot to claim as their own. Like the ox, the Spanish reached out and flicked them away. And like persistent annoying flies everywhere, back they came.

For a couple of weeks, Sam and his crew hopefully dragged the bottom with grapnel irons and John did some diving, but the shallower waters had been picked clean. They teamed with treasure hunters on another ship, and with a rope hanging between them, swept it along the ocean floor. In the end, they had little to show for their efforts but the small handful of coins John had brought to the surface.

Bruised, battered, waterlogged, and hungry, they made their way back to the Bahamas, and it was there that the Cape men spoke up.

"We're through, Sam," said Nate. "We all signed on ships headin' north to be home before winter sets in."

"You can't go back now!" Paul protested. "We've got to try again! Try something else!"

"No, we're done. We took the risk an' it didn't pay. Some of us got wives an' children to go back to, an' the others got family, too. We don't belong down here—our lives're up north, so we're goin' home. James, Dan'l, Tom, an' me, we're sailin' on tomorrow's tide. Seth, Hal, George, an' them others got berths, too. It's over for us."

"What about you?" Paul asked Old Bill.

"Nothin' takes me back north no more," Bill said. "I stays right here where it's hot. Always said I would."

They looked at John.

"Israel's property," Old Bill observed. He nodded at Sam. "You an' Paul give your word you'd bring the youngster back, an' Israel's bound t' put a price on his head if you don't. That ol' skin-flint ain't goin' t' miss a chance t' get back what's his by rights."

"As I see it," Sam said, "there ain't no thought to give to the matter. Just tell Israel that John got hisself caught in a line whilst divin', an' when we fished him aboard, he was dead."

"Aye. Makes no matter t' us what he does," Nate said. He glanced at John. "Ain't the law goin' t' catch up with him someplace or t' other?"

"Nobody pays no mind, not in these parts," Davy said. "Too many like him about."

John closed his eyes. He'd been holding his breath, and exhaled a gusty sigh. "Thanks, t'one an' all."

"What about you two?" Nate asked Sam and Paul as he picked up his sea bag.

"We'll be back with gold in our hands, one way or another," Paul answered.

"Good luck t' you, then." He put the canvas bag over the side into the jolly boat and offered Sam his hand. "I'll be sure t' give Mariah your token."

"Aye," Sam said as they shook hands. "An' Godspeed."

Just as they cast off, Nate looked up at Sam once more. "What're you goin' t' do now?"

"I don't know. Somethin'll turn up. It always does."

✠ ✠ ✠

A canvas awning had been spread across the after deck, and Sam and his men sat under it, out of the hot Caribbean sun. They passed around a bottle of rum as they considered their futures.

"I put up a lot of money for this trip," Paul said, "and I want to recoup my loss."

"What about Israel?" Bill's muffled voice came from beneath the broad-brimmed hat that covered his face as he lay on the deck. A stiff wind had blown the hat down a street in Nassau and he'd snatched it up as it wheeled by. He'd worn it ever since, held on by two ribbons tied under his chin.

"That's a female's hat," Davy observed.

"Don't care. The sun's that strong on my pate," Old Bill replied. "Shades my face."

"Why's it they calls you 'Old?'"

"Look at him!" John said to Davy, laughing. "He's older'n dirt, I'll wager!"

Old Bill propped himself up on his elbows and cast a dark look at John. "Listen here, whippersnapper! My hair was snow-white afore I turned twenty year! Been called 'old' e'er since. Ain't never took no sauce about it then, an' I ain't goin' t' start now!" Against the soft laughter, he spoke to Paul. "Israel's took a loss, what with John, here, an' all. He's goin' t' be mad as the devil when t' others get home."

"That's his worry," Paul replied. "I took the same risk he did, and I'm going to do something about it. If there's money to be made, he'll get his share. He just has to wait."

"I ain't goin' home empty-handed," Sam said with conviction, "an' I ain't goin' back to the merchant service." Not many paths were open to him, now his great treasure-hunting scheme had failed. It would take too long to earn the money he'd need to offer Mariah a secure future if he went back to work for Israel or to fish along with Nate. Too much time had already been wasted. There was a solution to this problem, and it had continually pressed on his mind since running into Davy. It was dangerous and illegal—a capital crime that meant death, if caught. But to a clever, quick, and resourceful man, it might just yield enough to make the effort and risk worth while. They could quit when they'd had enough and head back home any time they were ready. He was willing to gamble. Were the others?

The conversation had died down, and just as Sam began to speak, Paul said, "Suppose we go on the account."

"Eh? What's that?" asked Old Bill, sitting up. "Turn t' piratin'?"

"You got a view to inside my head, Paul," Sam said, taking a drink from the bottle.

Davy got up and took the bottle from Sam. "I was wonderin' how long afore you two bright lads was goin' t' figure that one out." He drank deeply and wiped his mouth on his sleeve. "Who you goin' t' sign on with?"

"We ain't signin' on with no one," Sam answered. "We're goin' out on our own."

"Who's goin' t' sign up with us, then?" John asked, taking one of the ship's biscuits. "We ain't no pirates!" Breaking off a corner with his knife, he knocked out the weevils and crunched on the hard, dry cracker.

"How can you eat them things?" Old Bill asked.

"Got t' have teeth."

"Don't matter none what we are or ain't," Sam said. "You seen all that's goin' on around us. We ain't the only ones who got nothin' to show for all this work. Plenty's stranded here, an' plenty'll be ready to sign on with a new crew."

"Aye, Sam's right," Davy put in. "Most ain't got no life t' go back t', or leastways a life they don't want no more. Sailin' under the black flag gets 'em a piece o' the world they ain't goin' t' get no other way. All we got t' do is spread the word."

"You with us, John?" Sam asked.

"Aye. I ain't bein' no slave t' no one, no more."

"Ah, now you're talkin'," Davy said.

"I'm with you, Sam," Old Bill spoke up.

"I thought you just wanted to lie in the sun," Paul remarked.

"'Tis so. I just can't think o' no good reason for not bein' rich while I'm doin' it."

"Then, lads," Sam said, raising the rum bottle, "we drink to the black flag."

✠ ✠ ✠

The business of Nassau was piracy, and hundreds of these brethren of the coast roamed the town at any given time, while their ships lay at anchor in the busy harbor. Taverns, inns, and ordinaries bustled with activity, and it was to these establishments that Sam, Paul, Old Bill, Davy, and John went early the next morning to muster their crew.

"We'll be lookin' for sea-farin' men afore all else," Sam had told them before they set out. "There'll be plenty amongst the crowd who ain't, what with those who come for Spanish gold an' lost. But don't be countin' them out, neither, for maybe they'll have a skill we'll be needin'. Nor turn your backs on a fightin' man, cut loose from the war an' soldierin', who can hold his own with a weapon or two. Them lubbers'll learn their way about a deck soon enough. We want a crew that knows what it's doin' when it gets a order, an' takes that order with a good spirit."

In two days they'd signed on twenty-three men. Davy had come across two old shipmates who needed little persuasion to join the new crew, bringing the lot to twenty-five. With Sam, Paul, Old Bill, Davy, and John, they were thirty in all. Sam, satisfied at last, held a council aboard the sloop.

John Julian sat on the capstan watching Sam discuss the articles as he walked among the crew, speaking to everyone. Sometimes the talk was serious, other times laughter broke out. Paul came on deck with a book under one arm, and carrying an inkpot and quill pen. He laid the book open on one crate, sat on another, and began to write.

"You need to be part o' this, lad," Old Bill said, coming up to John. "You got t' say your mind."

"What's these 'articles' then?"

"It's the code, lad! It's the rules we lives by! Most pirate crews got 'em, so we're makin' up our own. We talks it all over, then Paul writes it in the ship's log. We votes on it an' swears a oath, so it's all official-like. Legal, as you might say. Then we're all equal, one t' other."

"My people ain't never been equal t' no one—'ceptin' t' other slaves, an' sometimes not even then," John said. "How's these articles goin' t' help me, eh?"

"The articles, lad, they make it so that what you got t' say is equal t' anyone else aboard ship, even the cap'n. An' as good as any other crew we meet up with, too. Nobody does nothin' without there bein' a council an' a vote. 'Ceptin' if we got a battle on our hands, or foul weather, or such like, then the cap'n's words stick, an' we heave to an' follow orders."

"Also," Sam said, coming up behind Old Bill, "you get your fair share of any prize we take." He saw John's doubtful look. "Well, I got to say that you bein' bought an' owned by another man makes you one that ain't got no freedoms at all. But even for the rest of us, there's plenty o' laws made to keep us in our place.

"Now, him," he continued, nodding at Paul, "he's born into a gentlemen's world, an' to my mind, the rules holdin' me down never touched a man like him. But I was wrong. You ever wonder why he's here? Why he worked with Israel? Because no matter how high you are, there's always someone bigger an' stronger with somethin' to say about what you do an' how you do it. An' some, like Paul, can't live with that no more'n you can."

"Paul an' me, we ain't the same, Sam," John said. "You know that."

"Aye, but I never said you was. Feelin' boxed in an' trapped is the same for all, high or low. It's the traps that're different. You left Israel knowin' you was never goin' back, an' if Paul an' me tried to force you, you'd've run off, eh?"

John took a quick glance at Sam, and turned away again. "Aye," he mumbled. "But if you can't go nowhere without it bein' all laws an' rules an' such, why're you makin' 'em up now? How's it different? It's still rules."

"Aye, it's rules, an' we got to have them. But the difference is we're makin' these rules for ourselves! They don't come from some far off king or parliament. Piratin's the only way o' life I ever heard of, on land or sea, what gives a man such freedom to make his own choices. Now, go on then! Speak your mind!" With a serious look on his face, John hopped down from the capstan, joining his shipmates in their discussion.

Paul took his seat as the lively talk settled down. Then, as each article was agreed on, he recorded it in the log, and when they finished he read them aloud.

"One: Every man will obey civil command.

"Two: Every man will have an equal vote on all matters of importance to the ship and ship's company. If a man does not sign these articles, he has no vote.

"Three: The captain and officers are chosen by the majority before a voyage or any other time the crew sees fit."

Paul continued until he'd read the entire list of fourteen articles, then Sam called for a vote. "Every man who swears this oath agrees to uphold these art icles. All who say 'aye,' sign your name or make your mark in the book." When the entire company had taken the oath, Sam wrote his name beneath the articles, followed by Paul, and watched as each man, in his turn, took up the pen.

"We elect officers now," Sam said after the last man made his mark.

Davy spoke up. "Been under the black flag for a time, an' them, too," he said of the four others standing near him. "We say t' the ship's company, that you'll get no better'n Sam Bellamy as cap'n, an' that's true."

"Aye," added Old Bill. "Give the business of it t' Paul. Make him quartermaster."

When the voting was over and the results entered into the log, Davy came to Sam. "Well, now, Cap'n Bellamy, sir, what's your first order?"

"The first order," said Sam, "is to get a new ship."

✠ ✠ ✠

Their salvage sloop was an awkward old hulk, barely seaworthy and not as quick to the helm as Sam would have liked. He wanted something fast, reliable, and easier to handle. The crew spread out, scouring the waterfront looking for a likely replacement. Davy spotted the two periaguas.

"Tied up abreast each other, Sam, out t' the end o' Long Wharf. Oars, mast, an' sail shipshape an' ready t' hand; neat as you like. Just the thing."

Sam and Paul walked casually past them for a good look. The vessels were canoe-like in their general shape, but rather flat, giving the appearance of small barges. The longer of the two was about forty feet or more, Paul guessed, and ten or so feet in the beam. Each craft had a raised stern, and a long tiller to operate the rudder.

Paul scratched his head. "Tell me how these—what are they called?—are better."

"Periaguas, so I hear it. The Spanish calls them 'piraguas'; Frenchies calls them 'pirogues', or such-like—don't reckon the French tongue too much. But, it don't matter none 'cause they're right for us," said Sam. He pointed to the oars, mast, and sail lying in an orderly fashion, fore and aft, on the plank seats. "Made to be rowed an' sailed. Ten or so oarsmen in each boat'll make them fast. Not a lot of work; easy to use. They'll hold the crew, with plenty of room for cargo an' loot." He glanced at Paul's doubtful frown. "Mark me, now. We'll be seein' a fair breeze afore long."

"Do we scuttle the sloop?"

"No!" Sam laughed and put his hand on Paul's shoulder. "Let's go. I have a plan."

In the dead of night, under a black sky, Sam and a skeleton crew silently crept aboard the two periaguas. They muffled the oars withrags and rowed out to the far side of the sloop, where the rest ofthe men waited to transfer supplies and tools to the boats. Finally, with everyone aboard, they pushed off, rowing out to sea against the tide. They left the sloop at her mooring, with her jolly boat, at the end of the painter, floating in the pool of light from the stern lantern.

"A good plan, that," Paul said, nodding toward the sloop. "It looks to all the world like we're aboard and asleep. Wrapped up and tidy."

"You know," said Sam, at the tiller of the longer periauga, "sometimes steppin' outside that line you spoke of—the one other people use to hold you back—ain't enough. Sometimes you got to convince people the line ain't there at all."

Paul smiled. "I do believe you're right, Sammy."

They were safely away from the harbor when they stepped the masts and trimmed the sails. Withevery man at an oar, they turned in a southwesterly direction. While under way, they mounted a swivel gun in the bow of each periagua. Davy had certainly played his part in finding them. Sam never knew where they came from, not that it mattered. They were symbols of his new life, and he felt power for the first time. Then, checking the compass, he corrected their bearings and they headed for the coast of Central America, making a small island off the coast of Honduras their first home port.

Sam planned carefully, learning from mistakes and gaining confidence withevery success. They plundered local shipping along the coast, taking loot and crewmen. The new pirates offered the crew of each ship they stopped a chance to sign on with them, and while most preferred to stay with their captain, many did not.

A year had gone by since Sam had come to Cape Cod. Now, in late March, 1716, as the small fleet sailed south toward Panama, plunder filled their boats and the crew had grown in number to more than forty. Captain Bellamy felt scrappy and tough, and was ready to take on the world.

2

In a quiet cove along the southern-most coast of Panama, Henry Jennings' fleet lay at anchor. He walked out of the great cabin on his flagship to find the early morning sun had dried the dew from the night before and the deck was already hot under his feet. Yawning widely, he looked at the hour glass which was nearly ready to turn. The high tide was at the turn, too, and his plan for taking his fleet out to sea was right on schedule. Eager to get on with the day, he flicked the top of the glass with his finger, but the sand streamed down at its steady pace ignoring his hint. Everything in its own time, he thought. Spotting his quartermaster and two other officers standing in the bow talking and pointing to something athwart his ship, he went forward to join them.

"God's teeth! Why the hell are they across my bow?" Jennings demanded.

"They just dropped anchor," the quartermaster said. "Not far off o' three bells." He stopped as the flagship's bell rang four times. Six o'clock.

"Did you hail them? What do they want?"

"Aye, we raised 'em, but they'll only talk to you, cap'n."

Jennings stepped over coiled rope and stood alongside the starboard deck rail. Two periaguas floated at anchor just beyond them, with their swivel guns, he noted, pointed away and toward the water. There were, he judged, twenty or so men in each boat, all of them looking intently in his direction. As he shielded his eyes from the sun, a tall, slender man stepped onto the raised stern of the longer periagua, near the tiller, and bowing deeply to Jennings, waved, while a great cheer came up from his men.

Jennings leaned forward and squinted at the scene before him. Then he turned to his quartermaster. "Who the hell is that?"

A Prediction of Success

HENRY JENNINGS COMMANDED SEVEN SHIPS AND 450 MEN, NOW THAT Sam's forty pirates and two periaguas had joined his fleet, and he felt unbeatable. He stood on the quarterdeck of his flagship with a glass to his eye, and studied the garrison for the hundredth time that day. It was perched on the edge of a cliff high above the wide harbor of Baya Honda, a town on Cuba's north coast, and inside was a cache of gold. Rumors of hidden Spanish gold traveled on the Caribbean air like tantalizing aromas, and over the years he had followed his nose to many a golden prize. He liked the game he played with the Spanish. They hid gold; he found it. They raised the price on his head; he grew bolder and the more insatiable his appetite for their gold became. He'd heard with pride that the latest reward for his capture was nearly equal to the amount he had stolen from them at Barra de Ayes, and he found the irony amusing.

Jennings was nothing if not particular; therefore nothing had been left to chance. He liked details. The planning and timing were perfect. One by one, his fleet of ships had sailed into the harbor and dropped anchor in well-thought-out locations. The ships flew flags of different countries at masthead or stern and appeared to be engaged in honest trade witheach other, and businesses ashore. Skeleton crews worked the ships and bogus cargo, while below decks pirates waited, keeping well out of sight. Every gun was primed and every man was on the alert. The strategy for his fleet was naval in its precision, and the campaign for the landing party was worthy of any general. Jennings liked the odds. He looked at the garrison again, and swept the glass over the harbor. All was well.

Sam had studied the garrison through his glass often enough to know he wanted no part of this maneuver regardless of the prize. He didn't like to attack towns—he preferred to do his plundering at sea. A chase through the open ocean was his thrill: out-thinking, outsmarting, and out-sailing his prey was his triumph. He'd grown skeptical of Jennings' plans—there were too many phases to the operation, too many things to go wrong, and too many ways to lose everything.

Sam, his crew, and his periaguas were crucial to the success of Jennings' plans. The size and canoe-like shape of their boats meant they could anchor in shallow water within easy distance of the beach at any tide. Tonight, on Jennings' signal, they were to wade ashore through the surf and lead the attack on land. A former sergeant of the Royal Marines, who had a certain amount of skill at land warfare, was to command the invasion. Men from other ships in the pirate fleet, veterans of the European war, were to join them. Muskets, pistols, cutlasses, pikes, and axes had been crammed into the periaguas. There were heavy knapsacks filled with grenades, fire pots, powder and shot. And all of it, Sam thought grimly, was at risk. He felt the surf passage would slow down the landing, and keeping weapons and ammunition dry would be nearly impossible. A retreat down the beach to wade back to the periaguas, especially at high tide, would make them easy targets for a counter attack.

The afternoon dragged on and Sam was tired of waiting. He put the glass to his eye, searching the flagship for some sign of activity. Then he looked again at the unknown ship.

The brig had sailed into the harbor flying a Spanish flag and had dropped anchor between two of the sloops in Jennings' fleet. Would she delay the attack? What purpose did she have at Baya Honda? Sam's mind drifted away from these questions while he admired the fine lines of her long hull. He considered her two masts and the canvas she could carry, and for a few moments he imagined himself in command as she cut through the water at great, unmatched speeds. Oh, she's bonny, he thought. With a sigh, he put his mind to the task at hand. Paul had taken a small crew to the flagship to find out what he could about the brigantine, and had been gone longer than expected. Sam grumbled and cursed while he waited for the news.

"She's a French merchantman, the *Ste. Marie*, selling smuggled goods to the locals," Paul reported, when he returned. "Captain's name is L'Escoubett. It seems the Spanish are as tough with their trade regulations as the English, and business is good."

"What's her cargo?"

"French linen, mostly. Wine and some other goods."

"All easy to sell," Sam said, and once again studied the ship through the glass.

"Sammy, that's not all. She's carrying silver—pieces-of-eight. From what I hear, she's rich."

"Aye. Then we'll seize her, too."

"Jennings won't touch her."

"Why not?" Sam asked. "By my reckonin' that ship an' her cargo can be taken in half no time. If she's rich, so much the better. Add to our shares, an' to the fleet. She's a bonny boat."

"You're not the only captain who wants that ship. Damier and Hastings are on board the flagship right now, voicing objections to sacking the town and letting the *Ste. Marie* go untouched. Young's there, too, but of course he won't think without Jennings' consent."

The crew was listening to their conversation, and Davy spoke up. "It's his way, Sam. He's like the bloody navy when he raids a town, Jennings is. Plans it all out, not wastin' no time on other things. His mind takin' one path, as you might say."

"There's no reason not to take both," Paul said. "We certainly have enough men and fire power."

Sam shook his head. "It ain't to my likin', besiegin' a town. Jennings' got his ways, as Davy says, but he snarled his lines this time." He watched two small boats row out to the *Ste. Marie.* "She'll be easy to take. An' a smuggler, too. By God, she's legal plunder for any to seize. We won't even be breakin' the bloody law."

"That's called 'irony', Sam," Paul said.

"Oh. Aye. Now, I want to know how many amongst us favors takin' both the town an' the ship. Put it to a vote, then we lay a course to that council. I mean to put in my words before the day gets much older."

After the vote was tallied, Sam and Paul, with four others of their crew, rowed to Jennings' flagship.

2

The great cabin was crowded, and men stood or sat wherever they found room. The only furniture was the heavy, ornate table behind which Henry Jennings sat on the equally ornate chair. They had been part of the plunder he'd taken from a rich Spanish ship during the War of Succession that had, luckily for him, been in the right place at the right time. The furniture had belonged to a bishop and Jennings prized it above all else—except for the priest's ring, which he wore on his left hand, and his chasuble, which he used as a light cover on cool nights. He had a particular fondness for stealing from Spanish priests and looked forward to the spoils from the church in Baya Honda, which was reported to be so lush with gold fixtures from Spain that the altar was covered with cloth-of-gold.

Liam Young was Jennings' right-hand man. He'd sailed with Jennings for many years, working his way into the captain's confidence and enjoying his role as trusted favorite. Despite opportunities to go out on his own, he was comfortable in the captain's shadow, jealously guarding his position, ready to eliminate any suspected competition. As the meeting began, he was in his usual place behind Jennings' chair. On the alert, he closely watched Sam and Paul.

Jennings liked Sam. He liked the bold, unusual way Sam had first approached him, anchoring athwart his bow and waving from the stern of the periagua, and was impressed with what the fledgling crew had achieved under Sam's leadership. As the men settled down, Liam, hovering and fussing in the background, poured wine into Jennings' heavy, gem-encrusted, silver chalice.

"It's our vote to seize the French ship," Sam said of his men. "There's enough here to spare a crew from assaultin' the town to take her."

"Aye, Bellamy's right," one of the captains said. "My crew voted likewise."

"An' mine," added another. "We're all rowin' in the same boat 'bout this, Jennings."

"The vote of the crew," Jennings said, "was to sack the town. Now it seems you've voted amongst yourselves and against me." He paused. "I don't like that."

"We ain't against you, Jennings," Captain Hastings said. "We're with you on sacking the town. We just don't want to pass up any ship what's carryin' silver, is all."

"It's only a rumor that's she's rich," Jennings said. "Any plunder we take from Baya Honda is worth ten times the loot aboard the *Ste. Marie*—if there is any. Why risk losing the greater gain on such a slim chance?"

"It's easier," Sam said. "Takin' a chance is what you're doin', layin' siege to the town. It's like a bloody war an' it's goin' to take time, which is one thing we ain't got. We know we can take the *Ste. Marie*, so I say take her—an' I mean the ship, too, for she's bonny—an' make for sea."

"I took you for sterner stuff, Bellamy."

"It's the wastin' of men, ships, ammunition, an' time that don't sit right with me, cap'n."

"He's a bloody coward," Liam Young said, his pent-up jealousy barely kept beneath the surface of his resentment. He stepped out from behind Jennings' chair. "A bloody, sodding coward who's not up to soldiering and taking that town. He's the weak link in your chain, captain. Only saving his own skin—"

Sam was face to face with Liam in a flash, his strong hands gripping the lapels of Liam's coat. Liam's hand went to the hilt of his sea knife.

"That's enough!" bellowed Jennings, slamming his desk with both hands as Paul and several others pulled the two angry men apart. "I say stand down! This isn't the time, nor is it the place, by God!" He signaled to Liam who, regaining his composure, smoothed his coat and refilled Jennings' goblet with wine.

Sam stood with Paul, crossed his arms and glared at Jennings. The other men, sensing a possible shift in the wind, watched Sam.

"The captain is right, as always," Liam said, his anger turning quickly to sickening flattery, his words soft and oily. "Perhaps not everyone here," he spoke directly to Sam and Paul, "recognizes the captain's superior skill in choosing the best course of action. The captain's successes are well known and respected. We all benefit from the captain's clear thinking—and faultless planning." He bowed toward Jennings with an empty smile.

Paul listened to this fawning speech and felt his skin crawl. How Jennings could tolerate Liam was beyond him. He stole a quick glance at Sam's expressionless face and knew his mind was busy.

"Well, Bellamy?" Jennings leaned back in his chair and folded his hands across his belly.

"Put off your attack on the town for one night more, an' tonight I'll take that ship without firin' a shot. By mornin' no one'll be the wiser that we got her, an' if she's rich, we all put to sea an' leave the town. If she ain't, I'll take her to sea, an' you take the town. I'll drop anchor anywheres you say an' we'll wait 'til you join us."

There was dead silence. Then the great cabin came alive with talk and laughter.

Paul, catching Sam's eye, raised a questioning eyebrow.

"Captain Bellamy," Jennings said, still chuckling, "that's quite a claim. But, I must say I'm intrigued. What if I give you this chance?"

"These men are the ones to give a chance, cap'n, speakin' as they do through election."

Jennings closed his eyes. He was usually able to count on Liam to help carry his point, but this time he listened as the only vote against taking the *Ste. Marie*, beside Liam's, was his own.

After a long moment he spoke to Sam. "You've had a lot to say. Now, what can you do? You want that ship—well, this is your chance to prove your worth. Impress us with your plan."

Sam stepped forward.

✠ ✠ ✠

Back aboard the periaguas with the rest of the crew, Sam and Paul held a council of their own. Paul had just finished an account of the meeting when Old Bill spoke up.

"Where're you headin' with this palaver, cap'n? Town's mighty rich—or so I hear."

"Aye, them's big words, Sam," Davy agreed. "You reckon we might vote you down?"

"If it be so, then so be it. But let the vote come from you lot—not them," Sam said, nodding toward the flagship. "It's your right, an' I don't say it ain't. But I'm askin' you to give a ear to what I got to say. There ain't much time, for the sun's well past its high point. Come nightfall, one way or the other, we ain't turnin' back."

"Supposin' the vote's against you, Sam? What'll happen?" John asked.

"Then with good sense we'll be puttin' to sea while it's dark, before Jennings gives the signal. There ain't much he can do to stop us without givin' himself away. We can drop anchor along the coast an' wait till his fleet passes us by."

"Don't like the idea o' hidin'," Old Bill muttered. "An' what 'bout them soldiers an' the sergeant an' such like we got aboard."

The sergeant spoke up. "Me? I'm stickin' with Bellamy." He shook his head. "Been soldierin' too damn long, an' got too much hard campaignin' under my belt as it is. If takin' yon ship's your plan, I'm stickin'. What the others do is up to them." The dozen or so men whose military experience was to have added power to Sam's assault on Baya Honda, agreed to stay.

"Aye. That's good, then," Old Bill said. "What's your course, Sam?"

Within an hour, it had been settled.

✠ ✠ ✠

"Was Liam Young aboard?" Davy asked later, as they prepared for the night's work.

"Do you know him?" Paul asked.

"Heard o' him. Not many as likes the cut of his jib."

"He's not happy with us being such a big part of this," Paul said. "Foppish prig."

"Don't let him fool you none," Davy said. "How he acts an' what he does is two different things. Some say he's Jennings' lap dog, the way he bows an' scrapes an' all, but he's da ngerous an' quick with a blade. He'd've cut you, Sam, sure as not. Stab a man in the back with his words or his knife afore he gives ground, an' he don't care which. Likes where he is—close t' Jennings—an' Jennings knows how t' use him."

"Very interestin'," Sam said. "Well, lads, I think it's time that snivelin' lap dog was pried loose."

3

Shrouded by the night's shadows, Sam and his crew muffled their oars with rags and rowed the flagship's jolly boat to the *St. Marie.* When they were close enough, they drifted toward her starboard bow and made fast to her anchor cable. They didn't speak. They moved as little, and as silently, as possible. Even through the thickness of her hull the French crew might hear the slightest unusual sound. The smells of her oakum-caulked timbers and the dank, salty low tide were strong on the warm night air. They sat in absolute silence for a few moments, listening as a ship's bell rang five times. It was ten-thirty.

They were armed. Sea knives, pistols and ammunition pouches were secured to leather straps and belts. Each had a length of coiled line and a length of canvas about four inches wide. A long pole, one end thickly padded with layers of canvas, lay along the bottom boards of the boat, ready to use to push away from the ship should they move together in the tidal currents.

Eleven men sat in the jolly boat; nine would board the *Ste. Marie.* Sam stood and gripped the taut hawser. He kicked up, swinging his legs around the thick rope and shinnied to the top. He managed a foothold on the bend of the hawser as it lay in the hawsehole in the side of the bow, and he peered over the deck rail. There was no one in sight. He signaled to the men waiting below in the boat, and he climbed aboard. One by one they followed him. One by one they melted into the deep shadows of the bow.

They crept through the darkness, keeping low, every sense on the alert. Their bare feet made no sound on the deck. Three men of the *Ste. Marie's* crew, standing watch on deck, stood together at the larboard side talking softly and watching the few lights still burning in Baya Honda.

With the calm efficiency of silent, patient cats, the pirates set upon each of the watch, grabbing them from behind. One pirate slipped the canvas gag around a man's mouth. Another brought the man down by tackling him at the knees. A third pirate pulled the victim's arms to his back and helped tie wrists to ankles with the length of line. Hogtied, all three sailors lay squirming on the deck.

With knives in their hands, seven pirates disappeared below decks, where the off-duty crew slept.

Sam and Paul slipped through the open doors of the great cabin. A man lay asleep in a make-shift bunk beneath the stern windows.

"Must be the captain," Sam whispered, as they looked around.

"*Monsieur le corsaire*, you are smarter than I took you for," said a voice from the bunk. Captain L'Escoubett was on his feet in an instant, sword in hand. "You were quiet, *mon ami*, but not quiet enough." At that moment, moonlight shone throuh the great cabin window behind him, cloaking Paul in darkness and falling full on Sam. L'Escoubett spluttered a short laugh. "*Pourquoi?* Why? *La!* But this is a parade!" For Sam, like every other pirate aboard the *Ste. Marie* that night, was completely naked.

L'Escoubett drew his arm back to thrust his sword at Sam—as Paul stepped out of the shadow.

He came up behind L'Escoubett and threw one arm around his neck, pressing his sea knife against the man's chest. "Drop it," he ordered in French. "Drop it or I'll slice you open and your gut will spill on the deck."

But L'Escoubett raised his sword and, brandishing it wildly, took a swing at Sam. Sam ducked, deflecting the attack with a counter blow that caused L'Escoubett to drop his weapon. Sam cocked his pistol, holding it to the captain's head. Paul released his chokehold and grabbing a hand-full of L'Escoubett's long hair, yanked hard and held on tight.

The Frenchman spat in Sam's face. Sam punched him hard in the gut. Gasping for breath, L'Escoubett bent forward, his arms around his middle. Paul's grip on his hair held him upright.

"You ugly, naked pig! You will never take my ship!" L'Escoubett spat again.

Sam wiped the spittle from his face, then wiped his hand on the man's shirt. "You're too late," he hissed. "I already got it." Then he swung his arm up and rammed his pistol hard in L'Escoubett's groin.

The captain screamed out in French, doubling over in pain. Paul spoke in his ear, then shoved him down on the bunk.

Sam raised a quizzical eyebrow at Paul. "So, you speak French. What'd you say this time?"

Paul shrugged. "I told him the next time you'd castrate him." He looked at L'Escoubett who had pulled his knees up to his chest and was rocking back and forth, groaning and sweating. "Chances are good he'll tell us what we want to know."

Davy poked his head through the great cabin's open doors. "We got 'em, Sam, an' they's all trussed up like Christmas plum puddin's. They was eight in all, sleepin' like innocent babes, each one. A real shame to wake 'em up. The rest is ashore like you said. How'd you know? John signaled t' McNabb in the jolly boat, an' he signaled t' Hastings an' Young. Boardin' parties're on the way. Who you got, the cap'n? Jennings is goin' t' like this." He disappeared.

✠ ✠ ✠

In the great cabin, L'Escoubett sat tied to a chair.

"It is not here," the French captain insisted, worn out from the crushing interrogation. "I tell you again and again, it is not here!"

"Then I ask you again an' again—where's the silver?" Sam demanded.

"It is ashore, in a place you will never find!"

"Ashore?" Paul walked around behind the prisoner, and grabbing him by the chin, jerked his head back sharply. "Now why would you keep French silver in a Spanish town? Does that sound like a reasonable thing to do?" He held his knife to L'Escoubett's throat. "I think *monsieur le capitaine* needs a shave, don't you, Sam?"

"Aye, he's got quite a beard, so make it a nice, close shave." Sam caught L'Escoubett's eye. "If he still refuses to tell us what we want to know, then cut from ear to ear—an' cut deep." He smiled at the captain. "Unless, of course, *monsieur* would like to tell us just where, aboard this ship, he's hidden all that silver."

4

Jennings abandoned his plans to raid the town. Taking his fleet and the *Ste. Marie,* with a prize crew and captives aboard, away from Baya Honda, they dropped anchor off a small island north of Cuba. The next morning, as Sam walked comfortably around the great cabin of the flagship, he knew a small wedge had been driven between Jennings and Liam. He'd heard their raised voices as he rowed to the ship, and now he looked into Jennings' smiling face and Liam's sullen one.

Jennings was suitably impressed. "Quite a coup, Captain Bellamy," he said, slapping his hand on the table. "Quickly and quietly done, and not a shot fired! Rather a brash touch, that business of stripping down. Really took them by surprise. Chests filled with pieces-of-eight and doubloons enough for a healthy share-out. This young buck has a thing or two to teach us, wouldn't you agree, Liam?"

Liam glowered at Sam. "Aye, captain, as you say." He forced his mouth into a smile and made a little bow toward Jennings. "Of course I agree." He stood by the windows in the great cabin, the look on his face as dark as the shadow he cast on the deck. "Half that French crew was ashore. Lucky for you, Bellamy."

"Luck?" Sam laughed. "No, Cap'n Young, opportunity. Luck comes in as bein' useful, but success comes from knowin' the enemy, an' knowin' when the time is right."

Liam's eyes flashed in jealous anger. He pulled his knife from its sheath, the blade catching the sun.

"Belay that!" Jennings' brusque order stopped Liam. "This isn't your time, it's mine. There's another smuggler down the coast at

Porto Mariel, and I want her!" He stormed out of the cabin.

"Damn you for a pox-riddled villain, Bellamy! There will be another time, you may count on it," Liam snarled. As he followed Jennings on deck, he pushed past Sam and gave him a shove.

Sam caught his arm. "Would you match yourself against me, cap'n?" he challenged. "My blade is ready at your pleasure."

They glared at each other, equally matched in their powerstruggle.

"Liam!" Jennings called.

A slow smile crossed Sam's face. "Your cap'n wants you on deck, Liam, ol' son. You better hop along now." He released his grip on Liam's arm.

Liam never moved his eyes from Sam's face. "Sod off, Bellamy. Weigh anchor and go to the devil. Do it soon, or next time I'll gut you for the scabrous dog you are." He turned and joined Jennings of deck.

✠ ✠ ✠

From his quarterdeck, Jennings scanned the horizon, watching for his ships to return. One of the sloops and a periagua had set sail hours ago in pursuit of the smuggler. Much too short a time had passed when they came back with bad news.

"She's a smuggler all right—the *Marianne,* she's called, and she's taken by Hornigold." Paul, who had been in command of the periagua, made the report. A thoughtful silence fell among his listeners, for Benjamin Hornigold's name always commanded respect. Like Jennings, he was a crafty, tough outlaw with a reputation for being brazen enough to take on any odds. Competition between the two pirate captains was often heated.

Jennings swore. "No! I will not lose to him! Liam! You and Bellamy take care of things here!" He strapped on his sword. "Get us out of here!" he shouted to his officers. "I'm going to seize that ship!"

As Jennings set his fleet in pursuit of Hornigold, Sam and his crew secured their periaguas to the starboard side of the *Ste. Marie* and boarded her. Young's sloop lay off the larboard.

"You know, there's 30,000 pieces-of-eight an' a small casket of doubloons aboard this ship," Sam said to Paul as they stood in the bow.

"Aye, Sammy, so there are." They looked at each other, sharing the same thought.

"Turn all hands up. Tell them to look lively—but mind the noise."

While Liam and his quartermaster went about the usual business of counting and listing the *Ste. Marie's* seized cargo, Sam and his men quietly transferred the entire treasure of coins from the *Ste. Marie* to one of their own boats. With chests of money and the whole crew stuffed into one periagua, they were about to cast off when Sam was hailed from the deck.

"*Capitaine* Bellamy!" Sam looked up into the face of a French sailor. "I will join you!" He tossed his sea bag into the periagua, caught a rope, and lowered himself down. Standing almost a head shorter than Sam, he crossed his arms and stuck out his chin. "I like you, *monsieur!* You are smart, clever—and fair. I have been in the French Navy and with this foolish *Capitaine* Young for too long. I am Jean Taffier, a gunner, and at your service."

The sail was set and the crew leaned into their oars, pulling away from the *Ste. Marie* just as Liam came running up on deck. "Bellamy! You bastard!" he roared, watching the loot sail away. He ran to a swivel gun and fired it at the periagua, but the shot went wild. He shouted, swearing at them as they sailed out of the harbor. Sam grinned and waved.

"See?" the Frenchman smiled. "With you I predict success!"

"Welcome aboard," said Sam. He looked at the new crewman. He'd noticed Taffier before, set apart from his shipmates by the large white feather tied to his head scarf.

"Ah, you wonder about the feather, *monsieur le capitaine*. Many years ago, while on the Barbary Coast, I plucked it from the wing of an angel." With a quick wink, he turned and picked up an oar.

Well, Sam thought, looking at Taffier, now that's something: an angel on the Barbary Coast. No matter what else happens, we're sure to have a good time.

When Jennings got back to the *Ste. Marie* after a fruitless search for Hornigold, he found the treasure gone and an embarrassed pirate captain who had been unable to stop Sam and his crew. He flew into a rage at Liam, at Sam, and at himself for his foolish lack of judgment, then scuttled Sam's periagua and Liam's sloop. Still in a seething temper, he turned his back on the Cuban coast and took the *Ste. Marie* and what was left of his fleet out to sea.

A Death's Head with Bones Across

EDWARD TEACH STOOD BY THE FLAGSHIP'S LARBOARD SHROUDS watching the *Marianne* as the work to refit her commenced. Benjamin Hornigold's crew had taken the French sloop not a week before, outrunning Henry Jennings who arrived on the scene too late and had pointlessly given chase. The image of the defeated Jennings returning to his own prizeship, the *Ste. Marie*, only to discover Bellamy had sailed away with the treasure, appealed to Teach. He gave a small grunt of satisfaction.

As he raised the glass again to search the *Marianne's* deck for Sam, his long black beard stirred in the mild breeze. Teach disliked the new pirate captain, despite having a secret, grudging admiration for the cheeky bit of skullduggery it took to out-fox Jennings. What had really raised his hackles was Hornigold's reaction to Bellamy's story. The old man had rewarded Sam for betraying Jennings by giving him the *Marianne*—a command Teach fully expected to be his own.

Unlike Liam Young, Jennings' toady, who would have seethed with envy and resentment and pulled his knife on the spot, Teach was on his guard and held his hand. It was not an unusual reward, to be elected captain of a prize-ship, nor for the voting to be influenced by a commander like Hornigold. But Sam was different—an outsider, and dangerous. He'd taken Teach by surprise, and Teach did not like surprises.

He kept his thoughts to himself, waiting to see which way the wind might blow. You never knew with Hornigold. It often took fancy footwork to stay on his right side, and he, Teach, wasn't ready to step down yet. He had plans of his own, and they didn't include Sam Bellamy.

Hornigold joined Teach at the deck rail and watched in silence for a while. Then he asked: "What d'you think o' Bellamy?"

Teach shrugged. He reached up and gripped a ratline. "You raise up any man, cap'n, what takes Jennings down a peg."

"I like what he done an' how he done it. Jennings ain't no fool, but when Bellamy comes out o' nowhere, cuts Jennings' cables an' runs for sea, well, I got t' admire that. Got a loyal crew, too, an' that speaks well o' him."

Teach nodded. Without taking his eyes off Sam he added, "He's smart, an' he got ideas. Always thinkin'. Spills the wind out o' one man's sails, he'll do it t' another."

Hornigold stared thoughtfully at the *Marianne,* considering what Teach had said. "We'll just have t' wait an' see what happens."

✠ ✠ ✠

The *Marianne* was his to command. Sam walked across her deck and liked the feel of her under his feet. She was sea-worthy and trim and he knew she'd answer sharp. Her shallow draft would serve them well in the chase, and allow them ease in running from the enemy.

"Aye, cap'n," Old Bill said, hands on hips and looking at the work going on around them. "She's a bonny ship. Sound, an' dry below, too. She'll take us along nice for a while. Hornigold's prize is Jennings' loss an' our gain."

"Hornigold's got hisself a mighty big name for many years,

Sammy," Davy added, "an' they's many a man now sailin' 'neath the black flag what learned his trade off him. One o' 'em's Teach."

"What'd you know 'bout him?" Sam asked.

"Teach? Not a lot, 'cept I wouldn't want t' make him mad. Sticks by his cap'n, but got hisself a followin' amongst the crew. Got no loyalty t' the king."

"It shook him when the old man gave us the *Marianne*," Paul said. "He'll be watching us closely, now. Davy's right—I wouldn't want to cross him."

"No, nor me," Sam mused. He stood at the gunwale looking across to the flagship at the spot from which Teach had kept watch. "But it don't matter none, lads," he said, turning back to his crew, "'cause we got this ship, an' he don't. So we trim our sails an' shift our ballast for a smooth voyage." He stopped to make his point. "But we keep a sharp lookout for a hidden reef. If a good wind blows our way, well, we make sure we don't miss our tack."

Jean Taffier had been chosen master gunner in the same election that had returned Sam and Paul to their positions as captain and quartermaster. After the articles had been reviewed, and revised where needed, they boarded their new ship and he looked over his guns.

The *Marianne* already had eight cannon and now had six swivel guns, after the two from the periagua had been added to her battery. Taffier put his crew to work and cleaned, oiled, and primed the fourteen guns, making them ready for use at a moment's notice.

"It is like this, *capitaine*," Taffier had said when they first boarded the *Marianne*. "In the navy, everything is precise. We will be no different. There will be target practice, and we will drill and drill until there is no mistake and we are perfection itself." He kissed the tips of his fingers.

"The success of the whole, *Monsieur* Taffier," Sam said, turning a swivel gun so that it pointed out to sea, "depends on the success of the parts." There was no gun deck on the *Marianne*, and he squinted at the water reflecting the bright sunshine. "With you," he continued, repeating the words Taffier had once said to him, "I predict success."

The next few months were good ones for the captain and crew of the *Marianne.* Sailing with Hornigold paid off as Sam gained experience as well as loot. He had plenty of chances to put his quick thinking andambitious nature to the test, and was soon a master of the sweet trade.

2

From the maintop, high above the deck, John Julian saw the English merchantman tack into the wind and pass far to larboard of their flotilla. The *Marianne* was too far behind Hornigold's flagship for him to see most details with the naked eye, but he was sure that had they hoisted the black flag, he'd have seen it. He shielded his eyes and squinted. No—the signal to pursue and attack did not appear; Hornigold had let another prize sail away. Looking down, he heard Jeremy Burke, the bosun, shouting loudly to the men aloft, echoing Sam's order. "Stand down! All hands stand down!" John climbed down the shrouds and dropped to the deck, joining Old Bill.

The angry, protesting crew had gathered amidships, weapons still in their hands. Sam hoisted himself up on one of Taffier's guns and sat waiting while the men had their say.

"Cap'n! This ain't square!" John called out. "We're free-booters, an' it's our right t' plunder our fill!"

"Aye! Look what we're passing up by not takin' them English ships!" cried another.

"Every time we raise one, the old man don't give chase!"

"They's as good a prize as any, them English ships!" Old Bill fumed. "You see how the water were nearly t' her gunwales? She was heavy an' ripe with plunder!"

"Aye," Sam agreed, "no one could say different. But—" The crew interrupted, protesting again, and he raised his voice to be heard. "Belay that! Belay that, now! Hear this, one an' all! Hornigold was above board with his ways when every man here put his name to the articles, or made his mark. We know this from when we took the oath to follow him as cap'n of this fleet."

Jack Lambert, the sailing master who'd signed on soon after Sam and his crew had left Jennings, spoke up. "That vote don't make no sense. Not no more. Hornigold's ways ain't right."

"Crew's counseled amongst ourselves many times afore on this very point," Old Bill put in. "This ain't how we want t' go about things, Sam, it just ain't."

"Then seein' as how so many of us are on the same tack," Sam announced, "we take a vote an' record it in the log. When next we drop anchor, we chart a new course."

Shortly after the voting was finished, Paul spoke to Sam. "There's a sizeable number among Hornigold's own crew who disagree with him and will follow you—if you play this hand smart."

"You mean walk away—or walk away with it all."

Paul glanced slyly at Sam. "Oppose or depose. It's your deal."

Sam returned Paul's smile.

✠ ✠ ✠

It was in a safe harbor on one of the Windward Islands that Hornigold and Sam set their men to careening the fleet. The backbreaking work of scraping barnacles and other marine growth off the ship's hulls, then caulking the seams, could take more than two weeks to accomplish. During that time they would also attend to much-needed repairs. Fresh food and water would be taken aboard before leaving, and until then, the island's bounty was there to be enjoyed by all.

The discussion started on the starboard side of the *Marianne*. Supported by tall timbers on her larboard side, she had been beached for careening, and now a half dozen of her crew were standing side by side on a raft in the shallow water scraping her exposed hull clean.

"Ol' Hornigold's running afoul o' his crew," John commented, "not takin' them English ships."

"Aye," Davy replied. "It's a sore point that. What about Teach, then, eh? He don't fancy the old man's ways none, either. Why don't he do somethin'?"

"Why don't Sam do somethin' is what I want t' know," John demanded.

"The ol' man ain't goin' t' take kindly t' bein' crossed," Davy said. "Got hisself too big a name t' give way t' Teach, or t' Sam." He shook his head. "How many in Hornigold's crew would fancy sailin' with us, do you reckon?"

"I don't know," John said, scraping at the barnacles with deliberate attention. "But I'm goin' t' find out."

✠ ✠ ✠

Sam sat on the beach splicing rope and taking pleasure in images of Mariah. Even when his mind was active and filled up with immediate concerns, she was always there, ready to spring from his memory and occupy all his thoughts the moment his mind was clear.

He smiled at her prettiness, and in his dreams he saw her with him, wherever he was. What had Josiah said of her? She was mettlesome. He liked that word, but preferred daring—same thing, really—only because it helped him picture her at sea, sharing the quarterdeck with him and maybe taking her turn at the wheel.

He touched the patch she had specially woven to repair his ripped shirt and remembered watching her nimble fingers as she took tiny, neat stitches all around the edges. Even his roughly calloused hands could feel the soft, raised words she had embroidered on the patch with fine linen threads of the same color. "SB Keep My Heart MH." It was something of hers to hold and feel—a token to cherish, until he could once again have her.

Sam let the marlinespike drop to the sand, and he sat, arms resting on his knees, rope still in his hands. He stared out to sea, his mind closing down to the sights and sounds around him.

"Sam. Sam!"

A voice broke into his daydream. He closed his eyes, then looked up as Old Bill sat on the sand beside him.

"No sleepin' on watch, cap'n," Old Bill said laughing. "Though, can't say's I blame you none. Mighty peaceful. Could sit right here 'til the end of my days." He picked up a length of rope and started working. Off in the distance they heard Tinker, a foremast hand, playing a tune on his penny whistle. "Now why ain't he workin'?" Old Bill started to get up. "Too much t' be done for him—"

"Leave him be." Sam forced the iron spike into the twisted strands of rope and wondered if it had come from the ropewalk in Plymouth. "Let him play."

They had been working in companionable silence for a while when shouting erupted down the beach. John and Davy had taken their questions and grievances to Hornigold's crew, and the heated discussion had come to blows. Sam got to his feet and ran toward the angry men.

As he hurried along, Teach, standing head and shoulders above most of the crowd, pushed two of the battling pirates apart. "Avast!" he shouted. "We ain't settlin' it this way!"

"Cap'n!" John called out as Sam joined the group. "Cap'n! This ain't right! There ain't no good reason for us not takin' them English ships, I say!"

"You say!" yelled one of Hornigold's men. "What'd you got t' say on it? Cap'n's got reasons enough for what he does, an' they's nothin' you need t' know of!"

"Whatever his reasons is, they ain't enough if half his crew wants t' ship with Sam Bellamy!" John reached for his sea knife and Teach's big hand came down hard on his shoulder just as Sam stepped into the brawl.

"Leave it now!" Sam's order was brusque. "Leave it! Back to work while there's still good light. It'll be clear tonight."

✠ ✠ ✠

The entire company gathered on the beach for a share-out that night, and a council followed.

"The crew's been holdin' fo'c'sle councils of late, Ben," Sam said, slowly walking around inside the circle of attentive pirates, "an' they're takin' a mighty exception to this turn of events, as you could say. There's too many who question why you don't raid English ships, an' too many who wants a simple answer."

"I ain't never kept that a secret. I'm a Englishman an' loyal t' king an' country."

Voices broke out from the crowd. "We don't serve no king!" "Nor do we got a country, neither!" "There ain't no flag but the black flag!" "Aye! The Jolly Roger's our flag, an' none other!"

Old Bill's voice stood out. "Pipe down, you scurvy lubbers! The cap'ns is got t' set the true course."

"Aye, Bill," said Sam, "but each man's word is equal to mine— an' Ben's. Let them speak out." The debate continued against the background of comments from pirates taking both sides. "If you don't hold English ships to be as good a prize as any," Sam asked Ben, "then why ain't you offerin' your services to the king? Or take to sea as a privateer?"

"I ain't goin' t' share my plunder nor answer t' no one else, no more'n you, Bellamy. Not even the crown."

"Answerin' to the king's law ain't my way, neither. But I come to be cap'n by a honest election, same as you, so I got to answer to this crew as laid out in the articles, which we all signed—even you."

Hornigold matched his stride to Sam's as they slowly paced inside the circle. The campfire cracked and snapped between them, sending sparks flying up into the night sky. "Aye," he said. "Aye. But it's by them same articles that this crew voted t' let King George's ships pass free—even you, Bellamy. An' on this point my word is law."

The low, hoarse murmuring of voices that came from the restless pirates got louder. Sam heard them moving, and without taking his eyes from Hornigold's face, let the tension grow before speaking.

"Ah, now, Ben, you know the rules! An' if you don't, I do—as do these gentlemen of fortune who sit around us here. Givin' chase, or in battle, or in foul weather, no man'd deny your claim. But it ain't the question, now, is it?"

Among the gabble of raised voices, one was clear and insistent. "Speak t' the question, cap'n! What about them English ships?"

Hornigold looked sharply to his right. It was Teach who had spoken. Scowling darkly, he turned back to Sam. "I ain't goin' t' plunder no ship belongin' t' my countrymen, an' I hold by that." He paused, one hand closing around the hilt of the cutlass at his side and the other resting on his pistol. "I hold by that," he repeated. "An' my crew'll hold by me in any election."

"Will they?" Sam's fingers curled lightly around the handle of the sea knife in his belt. "By any reckonin' these lads believe in free plunder on the open seas. They know it to be their right to take what they want from any ship. Now, it seems like we hit rough water an' there's some who wants to chart a different course. A vote ain't goin' to go your way, Ben."

The two men, facing each other across the fire, were bathed in the deep golden-red of the flickering light. As he stepped down wind of the smoke, Hornigold drew his cutlass and raised it above his head.

"Belay that, cap'n!" Sam's sea knife seemed to leap in his hand. "Even from this distance I'll find my mark first. My blade'll split your ribs before you get close enough to strike." The fire light danced on the surface of his knife as Sam dropped to a crouch and moved forward a few steps.

Hornigold stood firm, feet spread apart. He cursed and spat. "You need t' be mindful as t' who's cap'n o' this fleet!"

"Aye, 'tis Ben Hornigold who's cap'n of this fleet, sure enough, but he's losin' favor of his crew! You called for blood—then come at me steel to steel!"

In the stillness, the only sounds were the waves breaking on the beach and the crackle of the driftwood in the flames. Absorbed by the fire-lit scene before them, the men were tense, ready to spring to action. Barely breathing, their eyes shifted from one captain to the other.

Hornigold brandished his cutlass. With a throaty growl, he advanced on Sam. "I'll spill your blood afore I let you take my command!"

"I ain't takin' nothin' from you, cap'n. It's your men who want to sail with me!"

"Damn your eyes, Bellamy! You're a clever bastard. You wanted it all—right from the beginnin'!" He charged forward, his stored-up anger erupting in fury. "I'll rip the tongue from your head!"

Sam sprang at him, knife ready. Horniold's cutlass swept down in a whistling arc close to his ear, slashing his cheek. Blood ran down Sam's neck as he ducked away, using his left arm to block the attack, but the flat of the deflected blade struck a glancing blow to his shoulder. Gripping Hornigold's forearm, he forced it back, twisting it remorselessly until, with an oath, Hornigold went off balance, letting the cutlass fall from his grasp. The momentum carried Sam forward and the two men locked in a deadly embrace. They struggled pushing, kicking, gouging, with every muscle strained. Pressed in hard against each other, Sam heard Hornigold's raspy, heavy breathing and smelled his rotting teeth. He felt the other man's strength and weight as he drew his right arm back. His knifepoint pricked Hornigold between the ribs.

"That's my blade you feel," Sam hissed. "All I have to do is force it home. I'm half your age—an' I'll win. Stand down an' live."

Hornigold's body tensed as he continued to stand his ground, then suddenly he pushed hard at Sam and backed away. "Be damned for the devil you are!" he growled, picking up his cutlass. He pointed it at Sam. "If you don't swing sun-dryin' at Execution Dock, somethin' else'll stop you, an' when it does, not even God hisself 'll keep you from the blazin' pit o' hell!"

"Wind's shifted, Ben, an' we're takin' another tack." Sam sheathed his knife and turned to face the men. Blood and sweat on his face glistened in the fire light. He took a moment to catch his breath and wipe his forehead with his arm. "Time to put this to a vote. Who'll be cap'n of this fleet?"

The tension broke, and the pirates exploded with loud opinions.

"Did you never see the like?" John asked. "What'd Hornigold want t' fight him for? How'd he ever expect t' win? We could've split up, you know—them as wants t' follow Sam an' them as wants t' stay with the old man."

"Still goin' t' happen, youngster," said Old Bill. "The vote'll say what's what accordin' t' the articles. Just wait."

"Hornigold knew he was losin' his command, but he had t' stand his ground," Davy put in. "Could've been t' the death—but Sam ain't like that, nor's Hornigold neither, as it turns out."

Before he joined Teach to conduct the voting, Paul came to Sam With a wet cloth. "Seawater," he said. Then eyeing Sam's bloody shirt he added, "You all right?"

Sam nodded, putting the cloth to his wound. The slash from Hornigold's cutlass ran across his left cheek from close to his ear to his chin. The salt stung, but the water was cool on his hot face. Paul peered at him in the half-light. "It's not deep, but you're going to have a scar."

✠ ✠ ✠

"I knew you'd cross him, given time." The election was over, and Teach spoke abruptly to Sam before joining the defeated Hornigold on what was once the flagship.

Sam raised an eyebrow in surprise. "It was comin' on, wasn't it?

He left a big hole in his command, by not takin' them English ships, an' me an' my crew sailed on through—takin' most of his men." He paused. "But not you. Why? You spoke out some against Hornigold in council."

Teach studied Sam through narrowed eyes. "I don't got t' say nothin' t' no one—least o' all you. I sticks with the cap'n, for the time bein', for reasons o' my own. He ain't over yet, an' I ain't got no taste t' ship with you." A heavy canvas bag sat near him on the sand and he lifted it, shouldering it with ease. "You're a smart one, Bellamy, but only time'll tell as t' how long you last." He turned away. Sam watched him walk along the shore.

"I hadn't expected that," Paul remarked, as Teach headed toward the ship to join his captain.

"No," Sam said, "nor me. But it makes me wonder how long afore one of them runs afoul of the other."

✠ ✠ ✠

Sam now commanded ninety men. Two days had passed since parting with Hornigold, and they celebrated their new strength by stopping the first English ship they raised and stripping her clean. High above the deck of the *Marianne*, the new black flag caught the wind.

A white death's head with two bones across had been Sam's choice, and from now on he and his crew would be known by this design and the warning it held. The Jolly Roger spoke the truth—that those who sailed under it, living outside the law, were "dead" in the eyes of authority. When the black flag was at the masthead, another captain knew his time was running out and he was expected to surrender without argument or suffer the consequences. Sam knew the world had opened up to him and this means to an end—this sweet trade of piracy—offered him limitless power. He felt invincible.

3

Paul squinted forward through the smoke and flying timber to see Sam shout in his direction, but the deafening roar of cannon fire swallowed his words. He hated the acrid stink of gun powder and the dirty, burning air. It stung his eyes. His throat was raw from shouting.

Thunderous sounds of the explosive discharge from their cannons pounded remorselessly inside his skull until he wanted to scream in sheer agony. The *Marianne* shook with the firing, and the recoil and tremors of her big guns traveled through his body. Long after the smell and taste of battle disappeared, he would hear it and feel it. There was no escape.

For more than an hour the crew of the forty-gun French warship tried to gain the advantage and deliver a critical broadside to the pirate's sloop, but Sam out-maneuvered them each time. The *Marianne*, smaller and easier to handle, slipped in and out of range of the warship's two stern guns. She tacked and came about, bringing first her larboard, then her starboard four-gun battery of cannon to bear on their target. Taffier and his crew paced the cannon fire so the big guns went off in succession, raking the French ship's vulnerable stern as they ran by. Their round shot shattered the glass windows of the great cabin and splintered the weak wooden structure that surrounded it as they once again passed out of reach of the French guns.

Paul couldn't hear what Sam had said, but he saw what Sam had done—and he did the same. Dropping to the deck, he scuttled to the shelter of the starboard bulwark. The heat from the cannon was like hell's own fire but he ducked down, covering his head with his hands. Men crowded in near him. Bar shot and chain shot, musket balls, and scraps of metal from the man-of-war's two stern guns, rained down on them. As the pirates moved from under cover, a third, louder, report broke the air. A powerful hail of debris and small shot tore through rigging and canvas, bringing down part of the topsail yard, crushing and shredding flesh and bone when it landed on deck.

"Lay off her! Lay off her!" Sam shouted to Jack Lambert. "The mainsail's tore but holdin'! Burke!" he called out to the bosun, "get a crew aloft to her gaff!" As he hurried by the helm he yelled, "Take us out of range!" But Davy, reacting to the situation almost before reacting to Sam, had spun the wheel and steered the *Marianne* out of the wind.

"What damage?" Sam asked as Paul came to him.

"We're tight and dry below. Thirteen wounded—one burned by cartridge misfire, some from the raking, others from battle damage."

"What's bein' done?"

"Furguson's tending to them," Paul replied, speaking of the *Marianne's* surgeon. "Sam, it's time to turn away from this. We can't take much more."

"Burke! Are we sound? Can we make another pass at them?" Sam asked, ignoring Paul.

"Aye, cap'n, for time bein'," the bosun said. "But if we're hit again, I ain't answerin' for it."

"Sam!" Paul cried. "No more!"

"They're comin' about!" Jack Lambert pointed to the warship.

"She's takin' on wind!"

"Davy! Stay in her wake," Sam ordered. "Taffier!" He called to the master gunner. "We're runnin' by her one more time. Load your larboard battery witheverythin' you got. Aim for her rudder. Davy, bring us in close as you can."

"Sam!" Paul said, grabbing his arm. "Sam—it's enough!"

"No! No, it ain't! You want to do somethin'? Then pray the wind don't drop 'cause if it does, an' they rake us again, we'll lose our canvas an' we're done!"

✠ ✠ ✠

The French ship fired once more at the retreating *Marianne*, narrowly missing her stern as her sails filled with wind and she moved swiftly away.

Sam and Jeremy Burke assessed the damage. The topsail was shredded, the yard snapped in two, the line hanging loose and tangled. There was considerable damage to the starboard deck rail—it would all take time to repair. "There's work ahead of us, Jeremy. We'll put in somewhere safe for a while, an' take our time." He turned to Davy. "Now, put some miles between them an' us."

"They ain't givin' chase, Sam!" Davy said, looking back.

"Nor will they," Sam said with a grin. "We'll be long gone afore they repair their rudder!"

"Sam!" Old Bill made his way through the debris. "Sam, Tinker's dead. Got it full in the face."

"Where is he?"

"Foredeck."

"Any more?"

"No, just him. The wounded's bein' took care o'. A couple o' broken bones and burns an' all, but ain't none too bad, considerin'."

Tinker lay sprawled on the deck. What was left of his skull, neck and upper chest was imbedded with shards of metal debris, musket balls, and iron nails. His skin was shredded and burned. Sam squatted by his body and watched the pool of blood run toward the scuppers. He touched Tinker's arm—and then he saw the penny whistle.

Tinker had fashioned a lanyard of thin leather cords so the whistle could hang around his neck. He'd kept it tucked into his shirt, ready for the moment his hands would be free to play a tune. Sam cut the lanyard with his sea knife, and scooping seawater from a bucket, washed blood off the whistle. He put it to his lips and blew a small note.

Riding high on his successes, Sam had had little trouble building his men up to the level of enthusiasm needed to engage the forty gun ship. The *Marianne* had come up on her stern with guns blazing and had held her position for nearly an hour and a half. Even as they turned and ran, he felt justified. He had flexed his muscles by disabling a ship that outclassed them, and he saw himself as a growing force to be reckoned with, by any man's navy.

Death at sea was routine and Sam had long ago become hardened to its inevitability. What he hadn't bargained for was the dull, hollow feeling that wrapped around him now. "His whistle," he said, holding it out. Paul joined him, and they stood watching some of the crew wash Tinker's blood off the deck and prepare him for burial.

"She had forty guns, Sam!" Paul exploded. "What the hell were you thinking? Did you really expect to take her? To board her?"

"Crew voted for it."

"You knew they would! This crew will follow any course you want, knowing that course to be dead on. There's always logic in your plans and in the way you act on them. That's your strength. It's where your success comes from, and it's why any crew will choose you as captain. But this time there was no logic. This time your plan was for yourself. It was your pride that brought us up against a ship with five times our fire power—and at what price?"

Sam said nothing and stared aft as the French ship disappeared on the horizon. He twisted the flute in his hands.

"Look," Paul continued, "I can see how it is. Tinker was favored by the crew. Now you've got his tin whistle and you're feeling some remorse. Any one of us might have died today, in this needless skirmish, at your command. I've known you to take up weapons and use them when you had to, but not like this. Not just for the sake of doing it. This isn't your way."

"Would it've made a difference to you if we took that ship?" Sam asked. "Come away with plunder?"

"I don't know. Maybe. But that's not the point, because that's not what happened, is it? We might've lost it all! All of it! The crew, the ship, and the loot, as well!" He looked into Sam's eyes. "And what the hell for?"

Sam watched Paul walk away. He rubbed his face with his hands, exhaling deeply. Well, he thought, that's just the trouble with people like Paul. Sometimes they're right.

4

Three days later, Sam woke up on the beach feeling stiff and clammy. They'd put into the harbor of a small island for repairs and long overdue relaxation for the crew, and he'd been in the tavern playing at dice with some of his men for longer than he could remember. Brushing sand from his face and hair, he ran his tongue over his dry, salty lips, sniffed the fresh air, and peered cautiously into the early morning sun. The *Marianne* floated quietly at her mooring. He swore, anxiously patting his shirt for the small leather purse that held his winnings from the night before—yes, it was still there. Then he swore again—he was to have taken the Middle Watch. He barely recalled staggering from the tavern and heading to the dock to look for their jolly boat. He'd dropped to the sand and had fallen asleep on the spot.

Now as he scanned the harbor, he saw it—the blue sloop. Rubbing his eyes, he looked again. Yes, he'd been right. She had come in on the night tide and that meant only one thing.

La Buze was on the island.

The Thrill of the Chase

SAM ROUSED HIMSELF, AND WITH A GROWING SENSE OF URGENCY crossed the beach to the tavern where he had last seen some of his crew. Walking through the door, he waited until his eyes became accustomed to the darkness of the dingy, sour-smelling room. He blinked a few times, then spotted Old Bill and Davy asleep where he'd left them hours ago, dice and wine bottles still on the table.

"Wake up!" he said, giving each of them a shove. "Come on, move! Where's Paul?"

He picked his way through the debris on the floor and found John lying under a bench near a pool of dried vomit. He prodded the still body with the toe of his boot. John stirred and moaned.

The landlord had been making his way through the remaining crowd, tossing out the straggling customers and jabbing at the sleeping ones with a broom handle in an effort to clear the place out. He poked hard at John. "This'un dead?"

"No."

"Well, get him out, then, an' be right quick about it, or by God's wounds he'll suffer for stayin'." He took a stab at Bill and Davy. "Them's your'n too? Move 'em, or they be carrion for yon gulls. Got t' clean." He banged the broom handle on one of the tables. "All right!" he shouted. "Every bleedin' one o' you mangy scupper-louts out o' here! Let's go! Move! Go on, get out! Aye, you too, y' shallow pated sprat." He pushed a sulky customer toward the door.

Old Bill got up, and mumbling something, staggered away. Davy looked up at Sam and groaned. "What you want? Uh! My head." He picked up a wine bottle and turned it upside down. "Empty."

"Help me get him out of here," Sam said, moving the bench off John. "Grab his feet." They carried John out of the tavern to the beach and dumped him on the hot sand. "Where's Paul?" Sam asked, wiping his hands on his breeches.

Davy belched loudly. "Don't know." Then, swaying gently, he collapsed, asleep before he hit the sand.

The wide stretch of beach curved around the bay, and thick stands of palm trees spread close to the high-tide mark. The rough buildings that seemed to grow in a clearing sat on the sand facing the water and were the only things that violated the natural shoreline. Sam and his crew had come to this island to repair the *Marianne* after their skirmish with the French warship and had stayed on to enjoy the many pleasures of this active port town.

A week-and-a-half later, the pink-white sand served as a berth for dozens of sleeping men. Sam wondered how many members of his crew were among them. "We been here too bloody long," he grumbled.

The ships moored in the harbor had swung wide on their anchor cables in the changing tidal currents, and Sam now faced them bows on. He glanced at the *Marianne*, and studying the blue sloop, thought about Oliver "*La Buze*" Levasseur. Then, for the second time that day, he headed across the beach to the tavern.

✠ ✠ ✠

"Paul!"

"Morning, Sam!" Paul came walking down the sandy road, his arm around a soft, curvy barmaid. "What's the matter? You look like hell! Remember Meg?" Meg untangled herself from Paul's embrace to grab Sam's arm and smile flirtatiously at him. Paul grinned. "Friendly, isn't she?"

"Levasseur is here," Sam said, ignoring Meg.

"What? You've seen him?"

"No. He dropped anchor durin' the night. Not too far from us."

"We need to meet him."

Sam nodded. "An' it's best to be gettin' back to sea whilst we still got a crew."

"Run along now," Paul said, removing Meg from Sam's arm. "It's business."

But Meg's saucy eye had already turned to another. "Oh, aye, now here's a rare one! Look at them laces an' ribbons an' frills an' such-like he done hisself up in, an' all t' make a lady swoon." She touched the deep neckline of her bodice. "Mighty fine t' be havin' the touch o' them fancies near my skin. Mighty fine t' be havin' him there, too."

The man who had caught her admiring gaze walked along the wharf-side in the company of three others, making a stately parade that attracted the attention of more than just the women of the town. He advanced to Sam. With a perfumed flourish he removed his broadbrimmed, feathered hat with a neatly gloved hand, and bowed deeply.

"*Capitaine* Samuel Bellamy, is it not? It is my greatest pleasure to meet you at last! I," he bowed again, "am Oliver Levasseur!"

"Cap'n! Cap'n, sir!" The landlord of the tavern came scurrying out into the bright sunshine, broom in one hand, and bowed nervously to Levasseur. Flinging his free arm toward the building, he gasped, "Cap'n, they was so many—stayed so late! We was— You— It were so— I—" He stopped. With ingratiating politeness he bowed again, flashing a smile of broken brown teeth. "We ain't quite ready for your kind visit, cap'n, sir."

"It is of no matter. We are here now." Levasseur nodded at two of his men, who silently entered the tavern, each carrying a crate.

With a cry of dismay, the anxious proprietor dashed after them. Stopping short at his door, he turned and bowed to Levasseur, to Sam and Paul, and to the small crowd that had gathered to enjoy the scene. Flushing, he looked up at his tittering neighbors and bolted inside.

Meg had been slowly circling Levasseur, taking in every detail of his fine clothes and inhaling the spicy sweetness of his cologne. As she touched his lacy jabot, the landlord burst through the door again and rushed to her, grabbing her roughly by the wrist.

"Here, now! That's enough, you stupid piece o' baggage!" he snapped, and headed back to the tavern, tugging her behind him. At the door, when she turned to wave at Levasseur, the landlord pulled her inside.

Levasseur turned to Sam and Paul. "You will join me, *s'il vous plaît?*" Without waiting for their answer, he entered the tavern.

"Well, split my sides," Sam remarked. "A sport an' a entertainment all for one price."

Paul looked straight ahead. "It's best not to laugh."

They stepped into the cool darkness of the tavern. The landlord, still fussing about with his broom, cleared up the last remnants from the night before. Meg fetched bread and cheese.

The table and bench where Levasseur sat were covered with sailcloth. Knife in hand, he cut thick slices of the dark, brown bread. On a nearby table, also covered with canvas, he had neatly placed his hat, coat and gloves. One of his men unwrapped soft cloth from around four goblets, and the other placed two bottles of wine on the table.

Levasseur looked up. "Ah! Welcome! Come, come, my friends! Please—!" He indicated the opposite bench. "I am on this little island three or four times a year, and the landlord, he obliges, *n'est ce pas?* You will now taste this wine from the Bordeaux region of my country. I think you will like it!" As he poured the wine, his quartermaster joined them. "You will meet Henri Eugene Benét. He is most interesting. Once, he collects gold—the taxes—for the king. And then—*voila tout*! He steals the gold for himself! It is a better life, *non?*"

As Paul, Levasseur, and Henri talked, Sam considered all he'd heard about the pirate who sat across the table from him. Sometime during the twenty-odd years of his career, Levasseur had gotten the nickname *La Buze*—the vulture—and he'd earned it. Could it be that this vain, fashionable—and very clean—man was really as wild and merciless as the stories told? Time, Sam decided, would tell.

"And now, *mon ami*," Levasseur said, turning to Sam and startling him out of his musings, "what are these reports I hear of you, eh? One hears about Samuel Bellamy everywhere! First Jennings, then Hornigold, and then—ah! *Mon Dieu!* A ship of his gracious majesty, *le roi de France!*" He crossed himself. "It is monumental! You must tell me all!"

He snapped his fingers, and as two more bottles of wine were placed on the table, Sam and Paul told their story.

"So!" he laughed when they had finished, "the little fish gobble bigger and bigger fish until they are the biggest fish of all! Congratulations, *mes amis. C'est bon.*" He turned to Sam. "I, too, once sailed with Hornigold. I did not like his ways, either, but then, I did not want his command. Tell me, the big man, he is with Hornigold still?"

"You mean Teach?" Paul asked. "He stayed with Hornigold after we split up."

"Of this, I am surprised. He has no limits, that black-bearded one. He will always do just as he pleases. Very untidy." With the repellent vision of Edward Teach's dirty, black beard in his mind's eye, he adjusted his lace jabot and thoughtfully stroked his own well-groomed beard.

"Come to my hearin'," Sam said, taking a long look at Levasseur, "that you was once a priest."

A look of delight brightened the Frenchman's face. "Ah, but this is superb! I am overcome with honor that you have heard my little story." He bowed modestly.

"I haven't," said Paul. "If *monsieur* will pardon the observation, it seems hard to believe, given what one hears about *Capitaine La Buze*."

"*Oui*, it does, does it not? Ah, but we were all someone else, once, *non?*" Levasseur sighed dramatically, and bowed his head. "Alas, I am but the second son. What does one do in such a lowly place? My *maman*, she lay dying, and sitting with her is her uncle, a bishop—a most unsavory man. But, to her, and to him, I make the promise to enter the priesthood, so at the end, she is happy." He leaned forward. "Then, one week before my final vows—it is finished. This, I cannot do. I ask *le bon Dieu* to explain to *maman* that I tried, but I hear no such call from on high. She will not understand, but she is in paradise and will not be angry." He reflected sadly for a moment, then flashed a wide smile. "And so, *mes ami*, I am here! This life," he picked up his leather gloves, "he fits me like *les gants de cuir*, *non?* But now, we will sail together, *eh?*"

Draining his glass, he put on his hat and coat. "Come, my friends. Aboard *le Postillion*, I have a wonderful wine from the Champagne region of my country I think you will enjoy. We will drink to our success!" He raised an eyebrow and glanced at Meg, who was smiling coyly from behind the bar. "Then perhaps I will return and see what else this tavern has to offer." He pulled on his gloves. "She is friendly, is she not?"

As they headed to the dock where the jolly boats were tied up, Levasseur walked ahead, the feathers in his hat stirring in the ocean breeze.

"I'm told," Paul said quietly to Sam, "he dresses like that all the time."

"Tales of him rippin' an' cuttin' don't jibe with his manner of dress, none," Sam replied. "Mistress Meg ain't the only one who'll be findin' truth 'neath them frills an' fancies."

Sam and Levasseur, eager to sail in consort, rushed through the usual business of reviewing the articles and put to sea within two days of their first meeting. They raised a Dutch merchantman not long after that, and approached with black flags flying. Despite the double warning, their quarry had chosen to run.

Davy stood at the wheel reading the weather, the merchantman, and the sea, all at once. Like any good helmsmen, he hardly needed to follow Sam's commands, but instead reacted to the immediacy of the chase. His skill was vital support for Taffier's skill as master gunner, and they worked together to make the best use of wind, powder, and shot. The *Marianne* gained the weather gage. As she pulled past the Dutchman's larboard side, Taffier fired one of his starboard cannon, scattering bar shot across her bow, snarling her forward lines and tearing her fore course. The Dutch fired their two larboard eight pounders in return, narrowly missing the *Marianne's* stern as she slipped by.

"She ain't struck her colors!" Old Bill yelled as the Dutch fired their larboard guns once more and the heavy balls fell into the sea. "They're goin' to stand an' fight! What the hell's the matter with him?"

"She's comin' into the wind! They're goin' to heave to!" Sam shouted, running toward the quarterdeck. "Bring us about! Bring us about!"

The *Marianne* lay off the Dutchman's larboard bow. Sam grabbed the glass, watching the *Postillion* take the weather gage and close in on the merchantman. Levasseur worked her well, bringing his ship alongside their quarry. The pirate cannons fired bar shot and metal scraps across the merchantman's deck. Levasseur's men threw grenades and firepots to scatter and disorganize the Dutch crew, and fired musket shot into the masts and spars to bring down the armed men. Under cover of thick smoke the pirates threw grapnel irons over the side, and lashing the two ships together, swarmed aboard with pistols, axes, pikes, and cutlasses, ready for battle.

From the deck of the Dutch ship, the sounds of fierce hand-to-hand combat drifted across the water to the *Marianne* and her tense crew. Taffier, his white feather stirring gently in the breeze, paced anxiously behind his starboard guns, patting the breech of each one as he passed. Every so often he looked up at Sam, waiting for the order to resume firing.

The men shoved and elbowed their way to the starboard deck rail, keeping a tight eye on the battle. Sam, up in the shrouds, watched the activity through his glass with intense interest. The Dutch had certainly fired first, foolishly choosing to stand and fight, but they were poorly armed, and the cargo ship, with its small crew, was no match for Levasseur and his men. The attack was savage, and it seemed to Sam an excessive amount of force to subdue so small a target.

"I don't see him!" Paul shouted.

Sam scanned the deck of the Dutch ship through his glass, looking for the *Postillion's* captain. Where was Levasseur, if not in the thick of battle? The smoke was dense and the acrid air filled with falling debris. He looked for something that would make the Frenchman stand out in the confusion—his red coat, perhaps—but there was nothing.

A shout came from one of the crew. "He's taken her!"

Sam watched Levasseur's men lower the Dutch flag from the masthead. "Mr. Lambert!" he yelled to the sailing master. "Bring us alongside!"

✠ ✠ ✠

"What's the cargo?" Sam was aboard the Dutch ship.

Paul brought him the news. "Cocoa, coffee, and tobacco. Not too much coin. We're going to reckon it up now. Still haven't seem him, Sam." He nodded at Henri, as the French quartermaster came up on deck with the ship's log under one arm.

Henri came to Sam. "*Monsieur, Capitaine* Levasseur wishes you to join him aboard *le Postillion,* when you are ready."

"Where is he now?" Sam asked, glancing around the battered ship.

"That I do not know, *capitaine.*"

Sam took his time looking over their prize. The stench of blood, gunpowder and smoke filled the air. Masts and yards were shot with holes, sails shredded, rigging badly damaged. Spilled powder had ignited, burning part of her fore deck, and the charred timbers still smoldered, though wet with seawater. He had seen Levasseur avoid inflicting the damage that would make repairing the Dutchman at sea nearly impossible, but here was senseless destruction. Sam knew it for what it was: *La Buze*—the vulture's—deliberate show of his absolute power.

Woven through the splintered and shattered wood were splintered and shattered men. Blood ran freely from their bodies, forming pools and mixing with soot and ash to make an ugly red-black mud. Sam stepped cautiously among the wounded and the dead. Flesh and bone crushed by falling spars and tackle, slashed by flying metal, pierced by shot, or burned—the injuries were many and gruesome. He looked up to see John Ferguson, the *Marianne's* surgeon, with the *Postillion's* doctor—Sam never knew his name—lay out their tools on a hatch cover and set to work helping whom they could.

He crossed the deck toward the *Postillion* and spotted the Dutch captain sitting on an upended bucket, cradling his broken arm. The man stood and spoke first in his own language, then in rapid-fire French, his face showing a mixture of hatred and pain.

Sam's few words of rough French were useless, so they stood amid the rubble and faced each other in silence. Finally, pointing to the injured arm and the dead and wounded sprawled on the deck, he said, "Next time, don't run. Strike your colors."

The Dutch captain glared darkly at him, then turned away and sat again. Sam turned and boarded the *Postillion* in search of Levasseur.

✠ ✠ ✠

In the great cabin, Sam once again wondered about *La Buze*. The fancy clothes were neatly stowed, he knew, in various storage places around the cabin, and the collection of hats and wigs hung from pegs near the top of the bulkhead. He took down a dark-red hat, decorated with a wide leather band and a yellow feather, and was examining it closely when a crewman came into the cabin and tossed a brace of pistols and a cutlass on the deck.

"*C'est la guerre*," the man said, and turned to look at Sam. "*Eh?*"

Sam pointed to the weapons. "Where—Levasseur?"

The seaman pulled off his headscarf, and wiping his sweaty face with it, tossed it into the pile. He ran his hands through his short, matted hair, and grinned at Sam.

"But of course, I am here! Just as you see!" He opened his arms wide. "*Mon Dieu!* What did you think?"

Sam chuckled. "Now I know why I didn't see you on deck."

Without the wig, hat, and the extra height created by the high heels of his fine boots, Levasseur looked very different. He was dressed in the clothes of an ordinary seaman and was dirtier than Sam could ever have believed possible. Instead of the sweet fragrance that usually accompanied him, *La Buze* smelled of battle—gunpowder, sweat, and smoke.

"From the blade," he said, looking at the bloodstained tears in his shirt. "I wipe her clean many times." He threw his belt and ammunition pouch to the deck, and dropping heavily into his chair, tugged at his sea boots.

"Ah, it is what I like. You do not see me, but I am there—always." He glanced at Sam, who was still holding the hat. "So! You are thinking: what hat does he wear? What wig goes into battle? Never! For the fight, I am thus! In battle, the foe—he looks for *le capitaine* and then—" he drew his finger across his throat. "But me," he said with a shrug, "I am just a sailor. I do not know where he is, *le capitaine*.

Clever, *non?*"

Sam hung the hat back on its peg.

Levasseur peered up at Sam. "Ah. You are not happy, *mon ami. Pourquoi?* Why? We have the miserable little vessel, and her miserable little cargo we will sell for gold to add to our—bah, *mon Dieu*, how do you say—coffers, *non?* The cocoa—I will keep," he said more to himself than to Sam, "for it makes a nice drink." He paused. "My friend, your face is too long—he goes down to the deck!" He gestured, pulling at his own beard. "What troubles you?"

"You nearly destroyed her. Why?"

"But she is not destroyed. The hull, she is sound. The rudder, he will steer the ship. The rigging and sails, bah, they can be fixed. So?"

"There's too many dead, Levasseur. They had no chance against you, but you engaged them, givin' them no quarter. Why? The prize was easy enough to take without this slaughter."

"Why? Because he runs, this demented captain. *Mon Dieu*, Sam! *Le Postillion! La Marianne!* We fly the black flags. We give the warning. But does he stop? *Non!*" Levasseur shrugged. "So, I am there, I board, and *voila!* It is over." He looked at Sam. "It is nothing, *mon ami*, nothing. These little Dutchmen—now they feed the fishes."

"Your crew—"

"*Eh!* Some are here, some are dead. Of this, I do not worry. Everybody wants to sail with *La Buze!* They appear, they sign up. *Toujours, mon ami, toujours.* Or the Dutch, they will oblige me and some will join us, *n'cest pas?* All will be well again. You will see."

Sam leaned back against the bulkhead, his arms crossed. "This ain't my way."

"Ah, no." Levasseur got up, fetched a bottle of wine and uncorked it. "You will like this," he said, pouring some into two tankards. "It is from the Burgundy region of my country." He sat down again putting grimy, bare feet on the table. "*Non.* We are not alike, we two. You are *le renard*—the fox. You think, you plan, you wait— *Alors!* The little chicken, he thinks he is safe, but—" Levasseur snapped his fingers. "Alas! He is trapped, and gives everything he has to you, including the other chickens. Me? I am *le taureau*—the bull. I do not wait; I charge!"

Unsheathing his sea knife, he threw it at the bulkhead where it held tight, vibrating from the force of the blow. "*Voila.* So."

Sam yanked the knife out of the wood. Gripping it tightly, he raised it above his head and brought it down, stabbing it deeply into the table near Levasseur's feet with such force the blade snapped off at the tip. "So."

Levasseur picked up his knife and examined the broken blade ruefully. "Huh. *La bonne dague*—once she was good." He tossed it over his shoulder and it clattered on the deck with the pistols and cutlass. Arching an eyebrow, he looked at Sam. "So?"

"A fox an' a bull is both after the same thing. Each one ruttin' an' strong—wantin' to take the prize. But they follows a different nature. So. What say you?"

"Bellamy, *le renard.* I like you, a*bsolument.* We sail in consort as agreed."

"'Til a shift in the wind," Sam said.

"Until the wind, he shifts and blows us each our own way."

"One thing more you can tell me, Levasseur."

"*Oui, mon ami?*"

"Do all regions of your country have the best wine, then?" He looked skeptically at his partner, took a tankard, and drank the dark red liquid.

Levasseur threw back his head and laughed. "But it is absurd, this question. Of course! All French wine—*c'est magnifique!*" He kissed his fingertips. "You can do no better! Drink, *mon ami!*" He held out his tankard. "We did well today, eh?"

Sam touched it with his own. "Aye, that we did."

3

Paul Williams stood on the beach and looked across the water at the *Marianne,* riding at anchor in the small, peaceful cove. I'm the master, he thought to himself, still finding it hard to believe. She's my ship—mine to command.

He had not put his name forward in the last election. Jack Lambert, the sailing master, wanted the *Marianne* and had lobbied hard, but when Sam had suggested that Paul might do the job, the voting turned out to be just a formality.

"Here's luck to you, cap'n," Old Bill said, coming up to Paul. "You know her, she's a trim vessel. You'll do all right."

"Aye. I was just remembering when we started out in Nassau, in the periaguas. Sam said things would improve, and he was right. They have."

"Got the gift, Sammy does, an' now he got the *Sultana.*"

They had seized the *Sultana,* a two masted galley, off Guadalupe toward the end of December, 1716, after spending the fall and early winter plundering throughout the Caribbean. They sailed in and out of ports of call where Paul and Henri bargained, traded, and sold their prize cargoes to merchants willing to do business with pirates. Cash stored in common chests awaited the next share-out.

It was early January, 1717, when the *Marianne* and the *Postillion* dropped anchor off Blanquilla, an island just north of the Venezuelan coast, and work to refit the *Sultana* was under way. She had yielded more than expected, for in a sheltered pen on the deck was a prize bull being shipped to its new owner. The *Marianne's* cook, Hendrick Quintor, pleased and excited when this great treasure was discovered, got to work and planned a feast.

The beach on Blanquilla was crowded with more than 200 pirates, newly rich from their share-out, and the air was filled with the delicious scent of roasting beef. Quintor and the *Postillion's* cook butchered the animal, and the best parts were slowly turning on a spit, the fat snapping and crackling as it dripped into the fire.

Levasseur was lying on the beach, breathing in the heavenly aroma as it wafted by his nose on the breeze. "Ah! The 'fatted calf'—not long now, eh, Sam?"

But Sam was thinking about his new ship. Levasseur had been right about the *Sultana*. She was bigger than the *Marianne*, and having even a little more room was a prize all in itself. Like the two sloops, the *Sultana* had a shallow draft, but unlike them she carried twice the canvas, which made her faster, and Sam liked that.

"Why didn't you want her?" he asked Levasseur.

"Eh?" Levasseur took his mind off eating and turned his attention to Sam.

"They elected me cap'n of the *Sultana,* but you never stepped forward. Why didn't you want her?"

Levasseur propped himself up on one elbow and looked out into the harbor at the three ships. "You knew I was on that island before we met, yes? You saw *le Postillion*, the blue sloop, before you saw me. Well, that is why, *mon ami.* A small ship with a lot of blue paint is easier to remember than a large ship with a little blue paint." He took off his hat and wig and placed them on the sand. "Bah. Sometimes it is all too much trouble, this *la mode*."

Hendrick Quintor banged a heavy pot with a large metal spoon, and as Sam and Levasseur got up to join the eager crowd, Davy, John and Old Bill hurried by, sea knives unsheathed and pewter plates in their hands.

"Oh, what a day!" Davy said. He jangled his canvas purse and fingered the coins inside. "All this here loot, the new galley, an' this meat. Now, ain't this a fine life!"

"What'd'you say we put it t' Sam that we go back t' Nassau?" John asked. "Or Tortuga?"

"You finally come 'round t' spendin' like a pirate, John," laughed Old Bill. "Last time we was in Nassau, you sat on your hands—an' your coin. We got another share-out an' smoke's a-curlin' out that purse o' yours!"

John looked down at the canvas sack hanging from his belt. "It' s one o' your better feelin's, havin' coin t' spend. Don't ever plan on goin' back t' having nothin'." He looked at the *Sultana.* "Now we got her, cap'n'll take us far, you watch. Sam's always hatchin' some idea or other."

"What do you think o' Taffier?" Davy asked, spotting their master gunner among the French pirates. "You think he'll stick with Sam or go with *La Buze* when we split up?"

"Can't say," Old Bill replied. "Spends his shore time with 'em, true enough, but takes his watch on the *Marianne,* just the same."

"I say he sticks," John said. As they moved closer to the beef, he licked his lips. "Remember how he come aboard when we left Jennings? Impressed with Sam then, an' still is."

"He goes amongst 'em for the lingo," Old Bill observed. "Dicey, that French tongue. Never could fathom how they talk it so fast." He craned his neck and looked up ahead. "Wonder if they got a nice gravy up there."

John turned to his friends. "You goin' t' stick with Sam, or sail with Paul?"

"Well, if that ain't the most fool-like thing a body ever said!" Old Bill chided.

"Why?" John asked. "We're all goin' t' the same place at the same time, ain't we?"

"We sticks with Sam, an' that's enough about it." Davy said, firmly. "With him you got a future more'n just your coins, an' don't be forgettin' that. Now, turn into the wind an' get your ration."

They reached the head of the line and held out their plates.

"Aye, just pile it on," Bill said, smacking his lips. He looked at the two cooks. "You got a nice gravy?"

✠ ✠ ✠

Levasseur picked up the wine bottle and put it to his lips for a long drink. "Ah, what a feast!" He belched happily and sighed.

Sam's bottle was nearly empty. After taking another swallow, he held it out toward Levasseur and said, his words slurred, "We did good, eh? Mighty good. One good success"—he hiccoughed—"after another." He held up his bottle and studied the dark-red liquid inside. "Is good. You're good. I'm good." He belched. "Is all very good." They clinked their bottles together and drank. "Where you"— he hiccoughed again—"headed for, then?"

"I think—we stay in these waters, I think. Follow the wind.You?"

Sam leaned back on his elbows and watched a gull float on the breeze. "Don't know. North. Hispaniola, maybe. Or not. Or the Leewards. Or not."

Levasseur gathered up his hat and wig, put them on, and got to his feet with a groan. "*Mon Dieu*, that was good. If I can get the crew to the ship, then we leave on the next tide. Or the one after that," he said doubtfully, looking over the crowded beach. He bent down and grabbed his wine bottle. "Always red wine with beef, *mon ami*, you will remember that, eh? Red like blood."

Sam got up, and they walked along the beach to the *Postillion's* jolly boat.

"So, now Sam Bellamy has two ships," Levasseur said. "You will do well! Come! I will make you a present. You will choose a hat, yes?"

"No. Thanks, but no."

Levasseur laughed as he climbed into the boat with some of his crew. "As you wish! *Bon voyage, mon ami!*"

Sam stood in the shallow water, watching as they rowed away. Paul waded out to join him. "What did he say?"

"He offered me a hat."

"Did you take it?"

4

Walter Hamilton, governor of Antigua, had had his fill of Samuel Bellamy, pirate captain. Sam's lightning raids in local waters had become more than frustrating to him. With the latest news of another lost cargo still ringing in his ears, he firmly decided to meet fire with fire.

"And the next time I hear this devil's name," he thundered, "it's because you have arrested him, or hanged him, or both!" Red-faced and hoarse, he pounded the desk with his fist, and fell into his chair.

Captain Francis Hume, commander of the flagship *HMS Scarborough,* took quick advantage of the lull to speak with what he hoped was positive assurance.

"Bellamy is clever, but not clever enough, Your Excellency. We are well-equipped to handle this rogue." He produced a map, which he unrolled to lay flat on the governor's desk. "Now, if Your Excellency will follow along—"

Governor Hamilton watched Hume's finger trace imaginary lines on the map. He hated maps and he hated Sam. As Hume droned on, he sighed and looked over the captain's shoulder through the open window at the calm, turquoise sea.

Focusing again on the things at hand, he stopped Hume. "Look, I don't care what you do or how you do it, captain, just stop him. I want that devil out of my waters. Kill him if you must, but I'd rather see him hang. And Williams, too. Both of them." He narrowed his eyes and set his mouth in a grim, satisfied smile. "Both of them, hanging together, swinging in a nice sea breeze. Very fitting. Now, go out there and get this done!"

Captain Hume rolled up his map, and bowing, turned to leave.

"Captain!" Hamilton called out to him. "Bring me those two ships! The—" he checked his notes, "the *Sultana* and the *Marianne.* I want everything that's aboard them. Every single thing!"

✠ ✠ ✠

Francis Hume set his fleet in search of Sam and Paul. Always one step behind them, he dashed from port to port coming up short every time. But a few gold coins spent in exchange for information brought the Royal Navy to the island of St. Croix, where the Irish pirate, Michael Kennedy, sailed into their well-laid trap.

"Where's Bellamy?" Governor Hamilton roared when his secretary brought him the news. "And who the hell is Kennedy?"

"But, Your Excellency! This news is good! Captain Hume took on all five pirate ships, captured two, sank two, letting one escape with Kennedy himself, unfortunately, but he is bringing back the two ships laden with booty! We'll have more than 100 pirates to stand trial!"

Hamilton stood up, and placing both hands on his desk, leaned forward, shaking his head. "Good news, perhaps," he said, glowering at his secretary, "but not Bellamy."

"Ah, no, Your Excellency. Not Bellamy."

Governor Hamilton swore.

5

"Aye, about five days ago, near's we can figure. An' it were only then we finds out the bloody navy was after you!" Fifteen of Kennedy's men sat aboard the *Sultana,* glad, once again, to be among their own kind. They had taken refuge on St. Croix after the British sunk their ships and had remained hidden until rescued by Sam's crew.

"They lie waitin' for you," the pirate continued, his frustrated glance taking in both Sam and Paul, "an' we comes along, caught unawares, as you might say. Three of them sets upon us, shootin' their guns—one of them was carryin' a hundred guns, at least. An' all of them thinkin' we was you. We never had a chance."

Sam glanced at Paul. They had been heading for St. Croix and would have arrived there around the same time as Kennedy, but were delayed when they stopped to take on fresh water and make repairs.

"Well," Paul said, "we certainly had a stroke of luck there. That was a lot of fire power."

"We been livin' on luck," Sam replied. "Seems a bit unusual for a ship of the line to be patrollin' like that. They must've wanted us real bad to send more'n a hundred guns. Makes you wonder who's so glad to see us go to Davy Jones—or the hangman's noose."

"Whoever's behind it knew where we were headed. Although," Paul said with a laugh, "look how they helped us in the end. We've got fifteen more men. So, where to now?"

"We'll head to Cuba." Sam looked up to the masthead of the *Sultana*. "Something ain't right here."

"Here? In St. Croix? What's wrong? The navy's satisfied. They're not coming back—at least not for a while."

"No—that ain't it," Sam said vaguely. "I ain't—" He hesitated, searching for the word. "Settled. I need—" His voice trailed off.

"Well," Paul said, "I'm going back to the *Marianne*. What do you say we put to sea?"

Not long after leaving St. Croix, they were headed north through the Windward Passage between Hispaniola and Cuba, when the lookout shouted from aloft. "Sails! To the larboard bow!"

Sam grabbed the glass and hurried forward. Studying the ship through the lens, he whistled softly.

"What is she?" Taffier came to stand beside Sam. He took the glass and looked ahead. "Ah, *c'est magnifique!* A galley. 300 tons, maybe. We go after her, *non?*"

"Aye. We go after her."

The unknown galley cut through water like a porpoise through a calm sea. Sam kept a sharp eye on her through the glass, his blood racing as the desire for this ship grew witheach passing hour. They put out extra canvas and the *Sultana* soon left the *Marianne* behind—but it didn't matter; he knew Paul would catch up. It was late February, 1717, and a year-and-a-half had passed since leaving Mariah and Cape Cod. The ship they were chasing was a bonny boat—a prize unlike any other Sam had seen since coming to this part of the world. And he wanted her.

The Free Prince and the Whydah

ABOARD THE *WHYDAH*, CAPTAIN LAWRENCE PRINCE WATCHED the *Sultana* closely. She was flying English colors, and he hoped, like his own ship, was following the same course back to Europe with her hold full of cargo. On the morning of the third day she was still at his stern, but he was surprised at how quickly she'd closed the distance during the night. Whoever commanded her was certainly a master mariner to have caught up so fast. He studied her through the glass and then handed it to his mate. "What do you think?" he asked.

The first mate put the glass to his eye. "She looks— Captain! She's clappin' on stuns'ls!"

Prince grabbed the glass again. For the last two days he had ignored the knot growing in his stomach as he tried to convince himself this unknown ship was simply a merchantman. "She's struck her colors!" He watched in dread and the knot grew tighter. "God's wounds! It's the black flag!" Bile rose in his throat and he swallowed the hot, acidic liquid. "Mr. Hale! Put out extra canvas and get us away from them!"

"Aye, captain." And Martin Hale, the cat-o-nine tails hanging from his belt, turned to give the crew their orders.

From the *Sultana*, Sam watched the other ship crowd on sail and willed his own ship to pick up speed. The wind was with them, and when they came up on her weather side, Taffier's starboard gun crew was ready for action.

Bar shot and chunks of metal whizzed across the *Whydah's* bowsprit, ripping her inner jib and snagging and cutting the forward lines. Lawrence Prince felt the concussion from the hit in his churning stomach. "God damn these bloody pirates right to hell! Not this! Not now!"

"Return fire, captain!" Hale shouted. "We can outrun them!"

"No. Turn into the wind and heave to. Take in sail." Hale didn't move. "I told you what to do, Mr. Hale, now do it! And strike our colors!"

Prince stood at the poop deck rail as his ship came to a stop and the *Sultana* maneuvered alongside. He'd given orders to his crew. "Don't resist. Let them take what they want. Maybe we'll come out of this alive—and with this ship."

The pirates threw grapnel irons over the *Whydah's* deck rail, drawing the two ships together until they lay deck to deck. Their fierce battle cry filled the air and they swarmed aboard the prize, weapons drawn and ready for battle. Two elegantly carved companionways, curving gracefully down from the poop to the main deck, flanked Prince's crew on both sides as they stood with their backs to the great cabin bulkhead. The rowdy boarding party, finding no opposition, came to a ragged halt, their hot energy checked. They faced their captives in the edgy, unexpected silence. Above them, at the poop rail, Prince watched the tall figure standing amidships on the larboard gunwale.

Sam had boarded the Whydah with his cutlass in one hand and his pistol in the other, but when the battle failed to take place, he'd remained on the gunwale taking in the scene before him. He knew Prince was watching, but instead of acknowledging this, he jumped to the deck and turned his attention to his new ship. He looked up at her three masts silhouetted against the deep blue sky, remembering how she'd cut through the water with full sails as he gave chase. It had been more luck than anything that he'd caught her. She was new, and expensive, too, judging by the quality of her fittings. On her bronze bell, gleaming in the bright sun, were the words "THE ✠ WHYDAH ✠ GALLY ✠ 1716". The *Whydah,* he thought to himself, is a bonny boat.

The lookout aloft on the *Sultana's* maintop raised an alarm. "Sail on the larboard quarter!" Prince went to the *Whydah's* taff rail and raised his glass. His heart lifted for a moment. Was this help? Then the lookout shouted again. "It's the *Marianne!*"

The cramp in Prince's gut kicked hard. "Sodding, bloody pirates," he said under his breath. The bad situation was about to become worse, and he was resigned to his fate. He made his way to the main deck to receive the pirate captain.

Sam approached Prince. "Cap'n Samuel Bellamy, master of the *Sultana*, an' now the *Whydah*. She's a fine ship; I'm glad to have her. Your name, sir?"

"Prince. Lawrence Prince."

"Cap'n Prince. Aye, cap'n, it seems you played your hand right smart. Spoilin' her in battle would've been a loss too hard to bear. I wasn't happy about riskin' it, but you made it easy, an' I like that." He gave Prince a little poke in the chin with his pistol. "Now, join your officers."

From the poop deck, Prince's eyes followed Sam and his men as they ransacked the ship. He felt a small movement and glanced behind him. Hale had loosed the cat-o'-nine tails, and was slapping the whip softly against his leg. "Are you mad, Hale?" Prince whispered. "Keep that thing out of sight!"

"I know him," the first mate said, never taking his eyes off Sam. His tanned face flushed with anger. "Bellamy's his name, and I owe him a taste of justice."

"For God's sake, man, use your head. It's not our advantage. I don't want to lose any chance to save this ship."

"Aye, captain. Sir." Hale said between clenched teeth. "By all means we must save the ship."

Prince closed his eyes and sighed. He hadn't known about Hale's reputation when he'd taken him on as first mate, the last time he was in Africa. He knew now that he'd rather deal with pirates than have Hale aboard his ship for one more day.

Dick Noland, Sam's quartermaster, came from the great cabin with the ship's log. "She's a slaver, captain," he said, handing the book to Sam, "and by the look of her papers, a mighty successful one. On her way back to England." He moved in closer, excitement in his hushed voice. "She's rich, Sam, very rich. Only took a quick glance to know there's a fortune in saleable goods and lots more besides."

"Well, keep at it, then." Sam glanced at the sails in the distance. "Paul'll be here soon."

Taking the log, he climbed to the foredeck and sat leafing through the book, studying the entries.

The *Whydah* had twice transported human cargo on a journey through the infamous "middle passage" from Africa to the New World, where the prisoners were sold as slaves in the Caribbean and north along the American coast. She had been on the last leg of this second voyage, heading back to England, when Sam'd stopped her. As he read Prince's words, the activity on the ship slipped into the background.

> "Africa. 14 April, 1716. Port Whydah. Sky clear. Prevailing winds from East. Very hot. Forenoon Watch. 2 bells
> 52 days in port and have finally taken aboard and stowed 562 males and females, prime and healthy, all. The goods we had to trade: cloth, tools and utensils, liquor, arms and gunpowder were all well received. One local king has provided very fine specimens, his

raids on other tribes yielding enough cargo to nearly fill the hold. He tells me his men go deep into the interior regions, and assures me the long trek back has not damaged the captives. By the look of them, he is right. Quite a number on this voyage are prisoners taken after a recent war between rival tribes the winner being in a position to profit not only from said war, but from selling their prisoners to us. This same king said he is glad to be rid of the prisoners; after keeping some as slaves for himself, he is happy to sell the others as a profitable alternative to feeding them. Have sent Martin Hale below to deal with the constant howling and wailing coming from these soulless creatures. I do not entirely approve of his methods, but anything to keep them quiet. I will be glad when we make port in Jamaica and are finally rid of them."

Sam closed the log and looked across the deck to where Prince sat captive with his crew. Was this the same Martin Hale he'd known aboard the *Bonnie Celeste*? He'd given up looking for Hale years ago. Was he aboard the *Whydah*?

Sam thought about the miserable human cargo once chained below and the riches taken in payment for them, now stowed in their place. He thought about Martin Hale and the "justice" he handed out with the cat-o'-nine tails. The buying and selling of human beings was a major enterprise with a life of its own, and impossible to stop, but he could stop Hale; Hale was only one man. With no clear idea in mind, he gave the log back to Noland and went below.

Up on deck in the fresh breeze of the beautiful, sunny day, Sam had been unprepared for the stench in the cargo hold. He tried to imagine the shackled prisoners jammed in together, suffering inhuman conditions and Hale's ghastly discipline for the endless weeks of the long voyage between Africa and Jamaica. The air was hot and fetid, and he gagged on the acidy vomit creeping up his throat. He swallowed and sniffed, noticing another smell, and he looked around in the dim light, trying to identify it.

John stood alone in the shadows. "Vinegar," he said as Sam joined him. "They use it t' wash down the deck t' get rid o' the stink.. Don't work." He paused. "I knew she was a slaver. I could smell her afore we come alongside. Got their own stink, they do."

Sam studied him. "We were upwind of her. How could you—"

"Don't know." John shrugged. "How does a body know his own kind? My mam used to tell us young'uns stories 'bout her pap. Come over chained in a ship just like this. Grabbed while huntin', he was, by another tribe, an' sold on the coast. I used t' get nightmares from her stories, Mam's an' others." He paused and looked around. "Never thought I'd set foot on a slaver."

Sam had heard stories, too. Nearly one third of all pirates sailing in the Caribbean and the North Atlantic were African or of African descent, and the composition of his crew was no different. Seizing the *Whydah* would not stop the slave trade, he knew, but putting her out of commission would stop Prince and the owners—at least for a while.

"Then we'll take this ship for your gran'pap. Go topside an' breathe some clean air."

"No. I want t' stay right here an' see how much them owners got for their slaves."

"Cap'n!" A voice shouted into the hold from above. "The *Marianne's* come along side."

"I will purge her of this poison!" Sam swore as he climbed the companionway and into the sunshine. He glanced around the crowded main deck and spotted the sailing master. "Mr. Lambert!"

"Aye, cap'n."

"Open every hatch an' gun port. Open everything that can open, even rat holes, an' let the fresh air move through this ship. Have Mr.

Burke take some men an' holystone her slave deck as best they can. Toss anything that can't be cleaned over the side. Get rid of that stink!"

"'Tis the stink o' death that's hangin' over this ship, cap'n." Lambert's grim words matched his dark, somber face. "Fresh air an' muscle ain' goin' t' clean her o' her bad luck. She was unlucky for them as was chained below an' died there, she's unlucky for yon cap'n," he added, nodding at Prince, "an' she'll be unlucky for us."

Sam's attention had been momentarily caught by the sight of the *Marianne's* crew boarding the *Whydah,* and he turned back to the sailing master. "There ain't nothin' unlucky about this ship. She's new, she's fast, an' no superstition's goin' to stop us from takin' her an' all her cargo. You know what she's carryin', Jack? Her treasure'll make you richer'n you ever dreamed!"

"Aye, an' that treasure's keepin' you from seein' what she really is, Sam. She's rigged up like a tart, with her fine fittin's an' all, temptin' you with her cargo like a wanton, godless woman shows herself down t' the docks. No good's goin' t' come o' this. Afore long we'll be callin' on Davy Jones ourselves, the way o' them poor, wretched souls what died below."

"Believe what you want, Jack, but keep that way of talkin' to yourself," Sam said, lowering his voice. "Don't be spreadin' your tales of doom amongst the crew. There ain't no such a thing as bad luck or curses, an' I ain't havin' talk of it aboard my ship."

"Your ship?" Jack asked with a scornful laugh. "You ain't got this ship, she got you! You're captive aboard her just like them as was chained deep in her hold." Turning his back on Sam, he called out to the bosun. "Mr. Burke! It's cap'n's orders for you!"

"He's a Cassandra, isn't he?" Paul had come to join Sam on the *Whydah's* deck but stood apart, listening to the exchange.

Sam snorted. "If that means he's a bloody doomsayer, then aye, you're right. Does a fair job of work, but he's comin' on to be more of a trouble than he's worth. Damn, bloody fool. This ship's no different from all the others we been takin', an' he's first amongst the boardin' parties an' ready for his portion in a share-out every time. So why's he spoutin' off like this now for?" He gave a grunt of disgust. "Hell, all we need is for the crew to make him out to be a Jonah."

"He's got a strange religious zeal mixed up with a deep belief in superstition," Paul observed. "Best keep a sharp watch that he doesn't encourage more of a following than he's already got. Many's the crew that's been turned from sensible ways by a loose tongue like his." He suddenly grinned. "But Sammy! What plunder! Fletcher and Noland are below having a grand time going over it all. The list keeps getting longer and longer."

"Aye, it'll take two quartermasters to go through that manifest," Sam replied with an absentminded laugh. "A lot of totalin', I expect." Jack's words had cut deeper than he liked to admit. Seamen were a superstitious lot, as a rule, and while Sam considered these old wives' tales to be harmless, he was very much aware of the speed with which bad ideas could spread through a ship. Jack Lambert's superstitions were not the danger—it was his power to persuade that worried Sam.

Paul's happy voice pulled him back to awareness. "Our Captain Prince is quite a reader. Look at all the books he's got!" They were in the great cabin sorting through Prince's belongings, and Paul was on his knees rummaging in an open trunk. Sam had just lifted the lid of a smaller trunk when Davy rushed in with news.

"Sam, Martin Hale's aboard. Got a beard now, but I seen him, an' I knows for sure. What're you goin' t' do?"

"Nothin'—for now. The right time'll come along, it always does."

"You ain't too surprised t' hear this," Davy said.

"His name's in the ship's log. I just didn't spot him, is all."

"Got t' think o' somethin', Sam. Hale ain't square."

"Aye, I know that," Sam replied, thinking of the *Whydah's* log. "Just lay soft. Let it rest for a while."

"Why?" Davy asked. "Look what he done to me!" He pointed to the ragged scars on his bottom lip. "Why ain't the time right for this?

Or this?" He turned and pulled up his shirt. Raised and rigid, the red scars ran over his back, some straight and some crossed, like the crooked furrows in a field plowed by a farmer who had lost his sense of direction. Sam had seen these scars many times before and remembered the raw, bleeding, pulpy mess that had been Davy's back as he lay half dead on the deck of the *Bonnie Celeste.*

Davy spun around. "Sam! You can't say this ain't the time!"

"Aye, I can, an' I do. There's more at stake here'n a score to settle!"

Frustrated, Davy looked from one man to the other, then went back on deck.

"What are you going to do?" Paul asked.

Sam shook his head. "I don't know."

✠ ✠ ✠

They followed Davy on deck. The sun was directly overhead and everything was hot to the touch, including the air. Sam shielded his eyes and looked at the prisoners on the poop deck. He locked eyes with Prince, who scowled back at him, his arms crossed tightly against his chest. Sam sought out the man he now knew to be Martin Hale, and Hale glared back with fire in his eyes.

Sam spoke quietly to two pirates who were standing close by. "Bring me the master an' his mate." Prince and Hale, their hands bound behind their backs, were headed down the companionway to the main deck.

"Cap'n! Sam! Look what this one's kept for hisself!" One of the pirates held Hale's cat high above his head, swinging the nine tails in the air.

"Well, cap'n," Sam said with a brief nod at Prince, but facing Hale square on, "what about this mate of yours, eh?" He took the cat and wrapping the tails around his hand, gripped the handle and held it up straight. "Martin Hale, it's the second time I took a cat-o'-nine-tails from you. First time it went over the side, but not so today."

"You bilge-sucking bastard!" Hale's eyes burned with hatred. He struggled in his bonds. "You think you've won, Bellamy. I knew I'd face you again. Nobody gets the better of me and lives to tell." Saliva bubbled from between his lips and dribbled into his beard. His face glowed deep crimson as a torrent of curses came from between his clenched teeth. "You'll swing at Execution Dock, you mutinous, puling maggot—if I don't get you first!"

Sam took the cat and rammed the butt of the handle hard beneath Hale's chin, cutting off his words. Hale's tongue was caught between his teeth, and a trickle of blood ran from the corner of his mouth.

"Now, now, Mr. Hale! Still quick to anger, I see. Years ago, I told you not to forget the day you made a enemy of me, an' it seems you ain't. Your mistake was not killin' me with the cat when you had the chance." He gave Hale a sharp poke under his chin with the cat, then hopped up on the hatch cover to address the entire crew.

"Lads!" Sam said in a loud voice. "There's many a mother's son amongst us who's heard the story of how Davy Turner got his scars."

Murmurs of "aye" came from the crowd as Davy stood beside Sam and pulled off his shirt, obliging the ship's company with a good view of his mutilated back.

Sam glanced up at the poop deck and noted pirates and prisoners standing shoulder to shoulder, watching intently. "An' there's many amongst us who knows of Caleb Jones an' Martin Hale."

"Aye."

"It seems we got Martin Hale as first mate on this fine ship an' those of you as knows him, also knows his cat." He held it high as the grumbling chorus rose again. "It was on Jones' orders that Hale brought the cat down on Davy, diggin' its nine sharp claws deep into his flesh an' givin' him his stripes. Him an' so many others afore an' since, all flogged by Hale's own hand." Sam paused. "An' there's some amongst the *Whydah's* crew, I'll wager, who's still feelin' the sting of lashes from this cat."

Sam looked around at the tense faces, then swung the whip high above his head for all to see. Catching the tails as they circled in the air, he pulled them taut. "Lads! Now, who owns this cat?"

"Hale does!" "Aye! He's the bastard!" "Hale owns her!" "Nay, 'tis the devil hisself!"

"An' what does Hale do with his little cat? Why he pets her an' strokes her 'til she purrs an' does his biddin'. He uses her to beat a honest man again an' again, takin' his pleasure withevery stroke. Eh, Mr. Hale? Takin' more pleasure from a whip than from a woman? Or so I been told."

"You bloody bastard!" Hale cursed and struggled in the hands of his captors. "Damn your eyes!" He spat, and a mouthful of foul, bloody saliva landed on the deck.

The men had been worked up by these words and Sam stepped back letting the angry shouting build. After a few moments he spoke again.

"Now, we all know how Jones happened to wash overboard, sudden like in that squall years ago. An' we all know how he's down in the dark place navigatin' the foul weather o' hell, never to know a calm sea again!"

"Where he should be!" someone shouted. Angry voices from Prince's own crew joined in with the pirates.

Sam raised his hand for quiet, holding the *Whydah's* log high for all to see. "As written in this log, Cap'n Prince, here, gave Hale free hand in keepin' order below decks, amongst the captives. An' it's written here that twenty-eight—that's twenty-eight!—African natives were murdered aboard this ship because of Hale's discipline!"

Sam waited again for the angry crowd to quiet down. "Hale had his reputation long afore Davy an' I shipped with him in '09, an' nobody's stopped him 'til now. I say to the ship's company, this is bigger than the score between two men that needs to be settled here!" While a loud chorus of "ayes" came from the crowd, Sam stepped down from the hatch cover and Dick Noland and John Fletcher, the two quartermasters, stepped up to face the crew.

Fletcher spoke first. "Article Fifteen is written in our log, thus: 'If a man is to strike any of the ship's company, he will suffer punishment as the majority sees fit.' Is this article seen to be useful here?"

"Aye!" the pirates agreed.

"Then what punishment—"

"Moses' Law!" someone shouted.

"Moses' Law is put before the ship's company. If you agree to this, vote 'aye' by raising your hand!"

"The vote is a majority," Noland announced to the crew. "And it's recorded in the ship's log. Moses' Law, forty stripes less one, is to be delivered on Martin Hale's naked back in the sight of the ship's company."

"Thirty-nine lashes," Fletcher continued, "are to be given by three men, thirteen lashes from each man. After Davy, here, decide which two amongst you is to give the rest of the strokes, whilst Hale is made fast to the grating."

As the pirates lifted the hatch cover to lean it against the mainmast, Hale's red face became dark purple. His gasping breath stopped, and as he gagged and choked, his eyes turned up, the whites showing brightly in his deeply tanned face.

"He's swallowin' his tongue!" Old Bill shouted, watching Hale become rigid and fall to the deck. Tremors shot through his body as he raised up, his back arched. For a terrifying few moments he seemed to balance on his head and feet, then falling again to the deck, he lay still.

There was absolute quiet. Then Prince spoke. "Is he dead?"

Sam squatted by the body. "Aye."

"Now ain't that a shame," Davy said, giving Hale a sharp poke with the cat.

"Were it a demon in him?" John asked in a frightened whisper.

"No, lad, though some might say it were so," Old Bill remarked.

"Seen this once afore. 'Tis a sickness they calls the convulsives."

"You seen everythin'," John commented.

Old Bill grunted. "When you're my age, you'll've seen everythin', too."

"That's one prize we didn't take, the A'mighty steppin' in like he did," Sam said, standing. He looked down at Hale. "Wind him in some scraps o' canvas. Round shot'll weigh him down."

They laid Hale on the canvas, cannonballs at his side.

"Hold fast!" Old Bill said. "We can't send him to Davy Jones' Locker dressed like that."

"What's wrong with how he's dressed?" John asked, sitting back on his heels.

"He don't got t' be dressed at all, not where he's goin'. Take my point?"

John took the point right away. "Then I get his shoes."

They stripped him naked, dividing up his clothes and possessions.

"You know," said Old Bill, putting on Hale's belt, "this is like the part in the Bible where they takes the Lord's clothes afore they nails him to the cross. Only they was playin' bones, an' this one," he nodded at Hale, "ain't no god. Leastways, it's almost the same."

"'Tain't the same at all, an' you knows it well, Old Bill Lee," Jack Lambert said, breaking through the crowd. "Bad enough we're takin' this ship, fouled as she is with the stink o' death. An' bad enough you three layin' more curses on us by the takin' an' wearin' o' a dead man's clothes. But now you're bringin' down holy wrath by speakin' the Lord's name in with the likes o' his. Sure an' true, if God A'mighty don't strike us down in his anger, Satan'll snare us for his pleasure."

"Oh, belay it," Old Bill remarked, standing to face Jack. "I knows that ol' superstition, an' no bad luck ever come of it. 'Cept t' them as talks 'bout it all the bloody time. If what we got here—" he indicated the *Whydah* with a broad sweep of his arm—"ain't *good* luck, well, then, I don't know what it is. An' how we come by it ain't no mystery, neither. 'Twas brung by Cap'n Samuel Bellamy hisself, an' none other.

I been t' sea longer years'n you been drawin' breath, Jack Lambert, an' I ain't never seen a lad smarter'n our cap'n."

A cheer came from the men who heard this speech, and Jack, squinting in the afternoon sun, said softly, to no one in particular, "Mark my words—this ain't over yet," and he made his way below decks.

John, holding Hale's shoes and wool stockings, which were stuffed down into the toes, turned to Old Bill and Davy. "I want these shoes an' stockin's," he remarked simply. "I got need of 'em an' he ain't—not no more. But if havin' 'em puts a curse o' bad luck on the ship's company, I'll put 'em over the side."

His companions looked at each other for a few moments, then Davy spoke. "'Tis just as Old Bill said, youngster. A superstition—a made-up way o' thinkin'. You just wear them things an' don't pay no mind to Jack's yarns." He rolled up Hale's shirt and trousers, and tucked them under his arm. After a few moment's thought, he added, "Let's give him this t' take t' Davy Jones, so he got somethin' t' do." He put the cat-o'-nine-tails into the canvas burial cloth, then finished winding the cloth around Hale's head, securing it with a length of cord.

Martin Hale's body was carried to the seaward side of the *Whydah* and rested on the gunwale.

"Anythin' t' say, cap'n?" Old Bill asked.

Sam looked at the shrouded body. "No. Just tip him in."

"Amen t' that," said Davy. And Hale sank beneath the waves.

✠ ✠ ✠

Dick Noland was reading a list to an attentive group of pirates. "Ivory elephant tusks, indigo dye, quinine bark, sugar and molasses, gold and silver coin, native African jewelry made of solid gold, and a casket of gemstones with what Paul says is a ruby—the size of the top of my thumb!"

"And so it is, lads!" Paul added. "So it is!"

Noland held up his thumb and looked around at his spellbound audience. "It's all listed in the *Whydah's* log," he continued, lifting the book high above his head. The men jostled for a better view and compared the first joints of their thumbs.

"What's the shares t' be?" one of the pirates called out. "How much in coin?"

"Hard to say, now," Fletcher said. "We still have to reckon it all up. Also, there's a lot to sell and convert to coin. But it's safe to say we'll be rich men."

Lawrence Prince stayed in the shadows of the fo'c'sle and leaned heavily against the larboard deck rail. Someone started to play a fiddle, and he listened as cheers and singing erupted from the pirates. He wasn't surprised when several of his own crew danced by in a lively jig, arm in arm with their captors.

Nor was he surprised by the three huzzahs shouted by the pirates after Sam climbed up on the capstan. He spoke in a soft voice that everyone seemed to hear, "Lads, we've gotten enough. It's time to go home. But there's one thing still to do—one more prize to take." Looking directly at Prince, he jumped down, and amid the cheering men, made his way across the crowded deck to the *Whydah's* master.

"Cap'n," he said when they stood face to face, "I will have this ship."

Prince swore silently. "Captain Bellamy, I have not opposed you and have forfeited a considerable treasure without resistance. I respectfully request to be allowed to make my way home in my own ship."

"Oh? Do you own this fine ship, then, Cap'n Prince?"

"No. I do not."

"Ah. The crew—they got a stake in her?"

"They work this ship for a day's pay like any honest seaman."

"An' aboard the *Whydah* your word is law?"

"Aye. My word is law."

"Your word is law. Caleb Jones' word was law. Martin Hale's cat was law. An' where are they now? Takin' orders from Davy Jones hisself—whose word is always law."

"You're no different from this Caleb Jones, or Hale, or from me, for that matter," Prince observed recklessly, feeling he may as well hang for a sheep as for a lamb. "A vote for Hale's fate is still murder. The crew calls you 'captain', and votes you the power that comes with being ship's master, but it's still dishonor among cutthroats."

"Cap'n Prince knows the ways of a sea rover!" Sam observed with a laugh. "Aye, it's these gentlemen of fortune whose votin' makes it so, an' in that way do we make our own laws. I come to the quarterdeck by their will, an' I remain by their favor. Our ships an' everythin' on them is kept an' shared equal, or be done with as majority sees fit. An' it's honor an' fairness amongst equals, cap'n."

"A pretty speech, Captain Bellamy, but empty. Since you live outside the laws that govern our society, the rules you design carry no weight. You're a thief and a villain. Piracy is a crime well deserving of its capital punishments."

"A thief, am I? An' a villain, too, by God. Well, lads, we're all cut of the same cloth, an' no doubt some of us'll swing with chains a jinglin' at Execution Dock at the pleasure of King George, hisself. Thieves we well may be, but we steal things, Cap'n Prince—objects, goods, an' money. You steal people. You see profit from the transport an' sale of human souls."

"As distasteful as my cargo may be to you, I ply my trade within the same laws you break."

Sam laughed. "Laws made by rich men to protect their own lives, possessions, an' comfort don't carry no weight with us. We ain't obeyin' laws we had no voice in makin'."

Prince wondered why he was still alive. Why was this pirate captain allowing him to argue these points? He was thinking that with a knife at his throat he would at least know where he stood, when Sam advanced with his cutlass drawn and pressed the cool flat of the blade against his hot, flushed cheek. He closed his eyes and his pulse raced.

"I speak," said Sam, "for all them as sails under the black flag, which stands here for the power of our laws—the ones we make. I'm a free prince with as much authority to make war on the whole world as a king with a hundred ships at sea. There's only this difference: Those you serve rob the poor under the cover of the law. We plunder the rich under the protection of our own courage an' strength." He paused, and holding his cutlass at arm's length, pointed to his crew. "Look around you, Cap'n Prince, at these men."

Prince had been keeping a sharp eye on Sam and had forgotten about the pirate crew. He caught his breath when he noticed that they had closed in, their weapons at the ready.

"Of the 183 men who sail with me, fifty-two's come to the West as slaves—survivors, if you will, of the laws you serve. Many of them was ripped from their homelands and suffered the journey to this side of the world in the bellies of ships very much like this one. I'll take this ship, Cap'n Prince, for myself 'cause she's fast an' new. I'll also take her for my partners, here an' about you, so they'll sail her as free men an' owners, instead of chained like beasts in her hold."

Sam walked around Prince, and facing him, held the point of the cutlass to his chest. "An' before you protest again, cap'n, think yourself lucky that you ain't spendin' the rest of this voyage shackled in the hold of our ship."

✠ ✠ ✠

They put into the deep harbor of a small island in the central Bahamas, where the pirates began work transferring booty, stores and weapons from the *Sultana* to the *Whydah*. Jean Taffier mounted four more swivel guns and added ten cannon to the *Whydah's* battery of eighteen, directing the ship's carpenters to cut new gun ports in her sides. Nearly a dozen heavy guns were stored in her hold.

Bit by bit, the *Sultana* was stripped of all but the barest essentials. When a barrel of fresh water and enough food for a day had been taken aboard, Prince and those of his crew who had chosen to remain with him, were allowed to sail her to the nearest port.

In his nearly thirty years at sea, Prince had run up against pirates more times than he cared to remember. Each encounter had been different, and each time the pirates had taken what they wanted. This time he'd lost it all: his fine new ship, the precious cargo, and ten of his crew. Surely the owners would understand the circumstances and be lenient. Still, he'd come away with his life, for what it might be worth when he got home.

"'Free prince,'" he grumbled as he gave the order to set sails and weigh anchor. Taking the helm himself, he guided the *Sultana* out of the cove on the evening tide. "A bloody common criminal is the truth." As he turned his back on his finest command, he angrily mulled over the past few days and his unusual conversation with the pirate captain. What had all that talk been about, anyway?

Captain Lawrence Prince never understood.

2

The *Whydah,* the "paradise bird" of the West African coast, was now a heavily armed ship of prey. Ten members of Prince's crew had become pirates: seven volunteers had signed on after Hale died, and three others, having much-needed skills, had been forced into service. As the *Sultana* sailed away, one of the impressed seamen passed closely behind Sam and said, "Slaves still aboard the slave ship."

Sam, givng no sign he heard the man, felt something he'd not known for a long time: a twinge of conscience. As he looked around at the work still going on aboard the *Whydah*, a dark cloud passed over the brightness of his success and dampened his spirits. Jack Lambert's foreboding words refused to go away, and he stood in deep thought.

"Cap'n. Cap'n!" He was suddenly aware of Old Bill shaking him by the shoulder. "Sam! We're castin' off."

Sam looked up at the white sails filling with air, and let the stiff breeze blow away his gloomy mood. As the *Whydah* plowed through the waves, south toward Hispaniola, her bell rang out the watch change and he listened with pleasure to the clear tones. He was at the top of his career, and the only thing missing from this perfect scene was Mariah. She was his ultimate prize; the only gold in his life that really mattered. Closing his eyes, he saw her sweet, pretty smile, and vowed to turn north as soon as possible to claim her as his own.

✠ ✠ ✠

In the days that followed separating from the *Sultana,* the *Whydah's* treasure was revealed to the astonished pirate crew. They talked of little else, and many spent their off-duty hours watching bags, trunks, and crates opened for inspection and counting. They planned and dreamed, joked and quarreled, and more than once Sam, or Burke, or Noland or Fletcher, or even Jack Lambert had to step in between two or more men squabbling over shares they had yet to receive.

"There's so much they got t' weigh it out on them scales an' put each share in a sack," Davy said. He'd been keeping a close eye on Noland and Fletcher as they tallied and divided up the *Whydah's* treasure, and he brought regular reports to Old Bill and John. "They's sellin' them goods an' breakin' up that solid gold jewelry from Africa. Each share's weighin' up t' maybe fifty pounds!"

"How much is that in money?" John asked.

"You ever tote a fifty pound sack o' corn meal or flour?" Davy asked. "Well, that's how much. They doin' it that ways 'cause it's too much t' count."

John whistled. "Fifty pound dead weight. That's a mighty sum. Be near as old as my gran'pap when I get done spendin' it all. An' he went at ninety year."

"You ain't goin' t' last ninety days if Israel catches up with you, youngster," observed Old Bill.

"Ain't no chance o' that ever happenin'. We ain't goin' back north."

"Don't be too sure."

"What d'you know 'bout anythin'?"

Davy, who had been calculating on his fingers while they talked, spoke up. "We been sailin' in an' out o' these little islands, addin' t' our loot, more'n a week since the *Sultana* cast off. Why's Sam been lookin' so somber of late, then, eh? You'd think he'd be happy. I am."

"Wants t' go back north, I expect," Old Bill said with a side-long glance at John. "Got a sweetheart on Cape Cod. Pretty lass, name o' Mariah."

"Sam's goin' back for her?" John looked at Old Bill with surprise. "What for? We got everythin' we need right here on this ship, an' more. An' what we ain't got, we can get somewheres else. If he needs a wench, there's plenty around."

"You knows Mariah, John, an' she ain't no wench. I think Sam's a-fixin' t' head north t' do some swaggerin' on Great Island, too. Isarel's goin' t' be bloody surprised by what we got stowed aboard this ship. Sam'll bring Mariah along, an' we'll go somewheres t' lie low for a pace." He paused. "Comin' t' think on it, I'd be mighty happy showin' off t' Josiah all he missed by not shippin' with Sam."

Thought you was goin' t' stay in these southern climes," Davy said, "'cause o' your bones."

"Well I was, but now I ain't. I'm stickin' with Sam every where he goes. Question is, what's John goin' t' do if we goes north? Israel's put a price on his head already, I'll be bound."

"Thought you was goin' t' find your people," Davy said. "Down t' Nicaragua."

"Ain't got nobody t' call kith an' kin nowheres that I knows of. 'Ceptin' who's aboard this very ship, which is what Sam calls brothers o' the coast. So, I'm stickin', too. If we go back t' Cape Cod one day, I ain't never got t' see Israel. Just put me ashore in Provincetown an' take me aboard on the way out o' the Bay."

Old Bill raised an eyebrow in surprise. "The lad's tellin' a new yarn," he said to Davy.

"It's his purse a jinglin'," Davy said. "Coin'll make any man change course."

"Aye," Old Bill said. "Changed mine."

"Julian!" Jeremy Burke, the bosun, interrupted and spoke to John. "Lay aloft an' see t' the main t'gallant." John looked up at the sail, its corner whipping loose in the wind, and scrambled up the shrouds.

"I seen many a topman with the gift," said Bill, watching him as he coiled a line. "Had it myself, once upon a time, but ain't never seen anyone the likes o' him. He can climb anythin' an' balance in a gale once he's there. Wasted, workin' on land." He frowned at Davy, who had been following him as he went about his tasks. "You're off duty. Ain't you never goin' t' sleep? You ain't goin' t' miss nothin'. Someone'll wake you when we got a share-out." He coiled another rope and looked aft toward Sam. "I think we'll be headin' north real soon. Just you watch."

3

About two-and-a-half weeks later, in late-March, 1717, the *Whydah* turned northward from the Caribbean and moved into the Gulf Stream toward home. As they made their way along the American coast, they raided and plundered inward-bound shipping taking advantage of smuggling businesses that had sprung up in defiance of heavy taxes and trade laws. Some colonial governors were apt to look the other way when money was to be made, and smugglers, privateers, and pirates were all welcome in their ports. By mid-April, Sam's fleet included the *Anne*, a two-masted galley-built "snow" from Scotland they seized off Virginia. Sam liked her; she was trim and fast. Dick Noland had been put aboard to command the prize crew, and the *Whydah*, the *Marianne*, and the *Anne* now lay at anchor off the

Delaware coast.

Paul came aboard the *Whydah*, after their most recent share-out, and sat with Sam in the great cabin. "I want to go home."

"We're goin' home," Sam replied, surprised.

"No, I mean to Rhode Island. I need to see my family, my mother and sisters."

Sam understood how Paul felt. "I ain't seen mine in almost two an'- a-half years. I'm—" He hesitated. "I ain't the same man they knew," he said, thinking of his father and his brothers and sisters—and especially Lizzie. "I ain't sure they'd understand what I done."

"Most people wouldn't," Paul observed. "My wife wouldn't. I'm not proud of what I did, leaving her and my children so I could work with Israel and go off to Florida. But I'm better for leaving, and she's happier now I'm gone. My mother, well, she's cut from a different cloth. Sharp, smart, and sly, the old lady is." He chuckled. "I'd like to have seen her go head to head with Jennings. She'd have ground him up like minced meat in no time. My sisters, too. Just like our mother. What pirates they would've made."

"Not my family. Content, happy, an' satisfied, all of them. I just never fit in, not even as a lad. Always out of step, I was. No, ain't them I worry about." He stopped.

"Mariah? I don't think she'll have much trouble understanding all this. There's more to her than meets the eye. I think my mother would like her." Paul stood up, stretched and groaned. "I've got ten years on you, Sam. I'm feeling my age." He looked at his friend. "We've done all right since leaving Cape Cod. Remember when Nate Pound and the others left us to go back home? I remember telling him we wouldn't be back until we had gold in our hands. In our hands! Oh, Sammy! Wait until Israel sees this ship and what we've got stowed in her. He'll split a gut. Now, keep in mind when you pay him back, just give him what he laid out—he didn't ask for interest."

Sam laughed. "We'll sell some of our loot through his tavern. That'll make him happy."

On deck, Sam leaned against the starboard deck rail and watched Paul row back to the *Marianne*. April was almost over, and they'd planned to meet again in two month's time on Green Island in Maine. As he wondered about those months, he thought of Mariah. How long would it take to get to her—five days? A week or more? Spring weather was tricky in the North Atlantic, and you could never tell.

He'd carried the memory of her nearly every day of the year-and-a half or so they'd been apart, and he'd tried not to forget a detail. But his conversation with Paul had awakened fears he had, for the most part, managed to suppress. How would Mariah react to what he'd become? Would his outlaw's life frighten and repel her? And what about his treasure? She'd claimed not to care about money. Would she spurn him because of his great wealth—or worse—find it hard to resist? Gold did things to people, as he knew full well. Paul's assurance had helped, but too much had changed. He'd changed. His hand went to his left cheek and the long red scar that had formed after his knife fight with Ben Hornigold. Nothing was the same anymore.

Sam looked up into the rigging and masts as the crew prepared to go to sea. Every spar had a name; every rope, every sail, every tool, every plank of wood, piece of metal, task, command, position, and direction had a name. Even the way a rope and its fibers were twisted had a name. Everything on a ship was orderly; it had to be when your life depended on it. There was security in knowing everything was exactly where it should be at a moment's notice and in proper working order. He spotted John Julian and his crew on the main topgallant yard as they let go the sail. And everyone, he thought, exactly where they should be, when they should be, too. Sam was a man who liked to be sure, as much as possible, when facing the unknown. While he could never predict an outcome, he was willing to take any risk when the things and people he counted on were in place. And that, thought Sam ruefully, is just the problem. Would Mariah be the same after a year and a half? He wasn't.

He thought about her simple, quiet life, her weaving, and her animals. What had happened to her during the months that followed his departure? He'd never considered the impact his leaving might have had on her. She'd promised to wait for him, but had she? His hand automatically went to the patch on his shirt where she'd embroidered their initials. It was stained with blood—his own blood—that had run freely down his arm after his cheek had been slashed by Hornigold. And suddenly he knew. He knew that home was not his family and Plymouth. Home was where he wanted to be. Home was Mariah.

Homeward bound was the sailor's love song from ages past that had different words in every version, but the same sentiment every seaman felt in his heart. The ship creaked and groaned her song as her sails unfurled, cutting off his view of the horizon. The men at the capstan sang, pushing and straining as the huge anchor rose slowly through the water. There were unknowns ahead, but one thing he knew for certain: Whatever he needed to do to be with Mariah, to make her happy, he wanted to do right now. With a sharp turn of the wheel the sails filled with wind and the *Whydah* followed a course toward Cape Cod.

Second Dog Watch: 1715 – 1717

The Tavern

MARIAH SAT HUDDLED ON THE BEACH AND STARED BLANKLY AT THE empty horizon. Although the late August sun was hot, she shivered in the ocean breeze. She had come to see Sam one last time before he left on his treasure hunt, then waded into the sea waving goodbye as his ship moved slowly away from the wharf. She had wanted to plunge in and swim after him; to be hauled aboard, and held, dripping wet, in his arms as they headed into Cape Cod Bay. But she hadn't moved. By the time his sloop disappeared from view and she walked up the beach, her skirts hung heavy with sea-water.

Now she spread her wet clothes on the hot sand to dry and sat in her petticoat with her legs drawn up tight, her chin resting on her knees. A few weeks ago, at the tavern, Sam had drawn a rough map showing the shoreline of the American colonies and the Caribbean so she could see how far his trip would take him, and why he'd be gone so long. Mariah kept the scrap of paper carefully hidden in the small chest by her bed, and she thought of it now: the scrawling lines representing places with alien names; places she'd never see; places far away. No letters would go back and forth, no news would come. Sam would fill each of his days with his unfolding adventure and she would wait as women have always waited for their men to return from the sea. But Mariah would lie and pretend his absence meant nothing to her, and she'd keep lying until the day came when she could no longer pretend.

A small flock of sea-gulls landed on the beach in front of her, squabbling and fussing over some bit of food. Mariah watched them for a while, her dispirited thoughts miles away. She tossed an empty seashell into their midst, and one of them turned to her with a reproachful gleam in its eye.

"Don't look at me like that. I know I should've said somethin'. I should've—an' now it's too late." The catch in her throat grew and squeezed her words into whispers. Tears stung her eyes. She gripped her bent legs tightly and rocked back and forth remembering how close she'd come to telling him. So often had the words been on her lips, she'd been sure Sam would taste the truth when they kissed. But he hadn't, and all the opportunities to stop this trip and keep him home were gone forever.

The ebb tide that took Sam from her would soon reach the low-water mark. It would turn immediately, inching its wide apron of foam farther and farther up the beach to where Mariah dug her bare toes in the sand. It would not bring him back.

✠ ✠ ✠

As the long summer days shortened and took on the crispness of fall, Mariah resigned herself to Sam's absence and kept her secret well hidden. She seldom left the farm now, except to go to church and market, or to see Thankful. On her rare visits with Josiah, she hardly ever spoke of Sam. Josiah cocked an eyebrow at her silence, but never asked questions. Once, when she asked his opinion about the length of the trip and a time of expected homecoming, he answered as best he could. "Afore winter sets in, t' be sure." There was no way of knowing, of course, but his guess made her happy, and she went about her work with high spirits, sure his prediction would come true.

On a late-September day, newly spun wool rolled and boiled in the large kettle of dye over an open fire behind the house. Mariah stirred the bubbling mixture and tended the fire, singing happily at her work.

"She's fittin' in nice," Mary observed to her husband. "She does well at market with her yarns an' fabrics, an' four people came by last week for her potions. It's a wonder how she's changed."

Matthew watched his daughter thoughtfully. Although there had been four peaceful years since the trouble with Samson, he had to admit that ever since the unsuitable Bellamy had finally sailed away, life had become smooth and productive. "If this change in her lasts through to spring," he muttered with resolve, "I'll speak to Ned Winslow 'bout his oldest boy. Ready to take a wife, I should think. Been talkin' about startin' his own flock." He narrowed his eyes against the smoke that blew into his face.

"Thank God for whatever makes her like this," Mary said, her thoughts drifting to a summer wedding.

The queasy stomach that plagued Mariah early on had finally stopped, and she was grateful for never having been sick. That would have been hard to hide from her mother. She joined her parents for every meal, pink-cheeked and glowing, and ate with a healthy appetite. By early November, the hard New England winter began to make itself known, and on the day first snow fell, news came that the Cape fishermen who had gone south on the treasure hunt for Spanish gold were finally all home. Everyone had come back except Paul, Old Bill, John—and Sam.

✠ ✠ ✠

"Israel? Israel!" In the Great Island Tavern, Susannah Brown gave him a gentle poke, but he sat still, his jaw clamped shut, anger clouding his face. Adding up both the loss of a valuable slave and his start-up money was too much for the tight-fisted man, and he sat consumed with rage at Sam, Paul, John, the Spanish, and everyone else.

"Ain't never seen him like that," Josiah said. "Not a happy man. I wonder what's become o' them others."

"All Nate said is they stayed behind to try again," Will Brown put in. "By rights, they should've brung somethin' to prove John bein' dead. Maybe best Sam an' Paul didn't come back empty-handed, considerin' him." He nodded at Israel.

Samson hobbled over and sniffed at Israel's hand, then went to sit near Josiah. Susannah sighed. "Well, I'd rather he was stompin' 'round an' yellin' like he usually does. This ain't natural."

"No, ain't never seen him like this," Josiah said again. Then he paused for a moment. "News ain't goin' t' sit well with Mariah, none, either."

✠ ✠ ✠

Sam hadn't come home.

Mariah heard the news in a matter-of-fact way from her father who'd been to the tavern to do some trading and had come home at the end of the day with goods and gossip. She sat quietly at her loom as he repeated the story he'd heard from one of the men who'd gone on the trip and called himself lucky to be back with his life and his senses.

"It's best you're rid of him, Mariah," Matthew said.

"Yes, Papa."

"He'd've brought you nothin' but trouble. Probably dead by now, anyways."

"Yes, Papa."

Later, alone in the barn, Mariah finished the evening milking. Wrapped in her shawl and a blanket against the chill November air, she sat on the low stool watching the barn cats investigate the three filled buckets that waited to be carried to the house. Never had anyone inflicted more pain than her father had that night. His words and her tangled thoughts crowded into her aching head and banged around like stones inside an iron kettle. Sam had not come home. The others had returned to their wives and sweethearts—women Mariah knew and chatted with on market day or at church; women who would openly commiserate with each other over the rash foolishness that had taken their men so far away; women from whom she might seek sympathy and consolation as the one in their group whose man had not come back.

She was in over her head because she'd trusted a man she barely knew, and now, caught in the undertow, she was being dragged out to sea. There was no one to throw her a lifeline. Fear and pain washed over her like breaking waves on the beach and she struggled for her mental footing.

"No. No. This'll be all right. Sam loves me. I know he does. There's a good reason he's not here. Paul an' Old Bill didn't come home, or John, either. They're tryin' again, is all. Or maybe they're on their way back right now. Maybe they'll sail up to Israel's place tomorrow. Or next week." She nodded. "It'll be all right."

Five cats had risen on their hind legs to lean over the rim of the buckets and lap the steaming milk. One of them stopped to lick its face, then jumped into her lap and started kneading the blanket. Mariah gathered it close and nuzzled its fur. "He isn't dead. He isn't. I know it." The cat felt the vibrations from her voice and started to purr. "Then why isn't he here? Why?" But there was just one reason Mariah could think of beside death or injury that would keep Sam away, and she would not speak the words aloud. But they were there just the same, and she could not get away from them: He'd forgotten about her.

The words stayed with her as days dragged on and no news came.

Sam did not return.

2

November was bleak and dreary. It snowed, then rained, then froze, then snowed again, making a dismal weather pattern that kept everyone indoors. Mary prepared hot tallow to dip candles and watched Mariah at the loom. She had matured since summer, and the differences were quite obvious. Not only was there a new concentration about her work, but she'd grown softer and more compliant. Even her slight figure had begun filling out nicely rounder and womanly, less like a boy.

The fire filled the great room with warmth and light, and Mariah, fetching a ball of yarn to rewind the shuttles, looked up when she heard her mother cry out.

"Mama! Are you hurt? Are you burned? Mama?"

They stared at each other for a long moment, then Mary gripped her daughter's hands tightly. "How long?"

Mariah caught her breath. She whispered, "Four months."

"Is this Sam's child?"

"Yes."

"Why did he leave you alone? Why isn't he here with you?"

"He doesn't know."

"Why didn't you tell him?"

"He needed money so papa would let us marry. If he knew about the baby, he wouldn't've gone away to try to get the gold."

"Don't you think you'd be married now, if he'd stayed with you?"

"But papa—"

"Papa would've insisted—an' we'd've managed."

Mariah recognized the truth of her mother's words and her throat closed. "What've I done? Oh, Mama—what've I done? I thought this was the only way. I didn't tell him. I didn't tell him! Oh, God, what'll I do? I thought he'd be back! He said he'd be back!"

"But he didn't come back, did he? We may never know what's happened to him. He may be dead."

"No! Don't say that! God can't be that cruel. I know he's coming back, I know it! I know it!"

When the tears came, Mary sighed, and holding her daughter, stroked her hair. "Dearest girl," she said softly, "don't cry so. We'll work this out somehow." She dried Mariah's red, puffy eyes with the corner of her apron. "Papa will be in soon for his dinner. There's just enough time to splash cool water on your face an' lay down for a spell."

The evening meal was not a happy event. Matthew, speechless as a thousand thoughts filled his head at once, found his voice as he paced about the room.

"You broke commandments an' sinned against God! Your loose wickedness'll bring shame on you—an' on our family! We'll all be tainted by this. Even Lydia an' her girl will feel the shadow of your sin!"

Mariah sat silent before him, her head bowed.

"You're ruined. Ruined an' soiled. What decent man will take you to wife now? You're no better than a whore."

Mariah recoiled as if struck by his words. "That's not true. It's a terrible thing to say. Sam loves me an' he'll be back!" she insisted hotly. "You don't know everythin'. He promised to marry me, an' I believe him."

"He will not!" her father bellowed. "An' don't you take that tone with me, my girl! That man is a fast-talkin' liar an' cheat—an' you, stupid girl, believed him! He took what he wanted from you an' left. An' for what? Spanish gold! I heard that story, too. Lies—all lies. How are we to face everyone now that you're...you're...like this?" Mariah looked at her hands clasped tightly in her lap, an angry scowl on her face. "I'll bring you to my Aunt Abigail. She'll take you in an' when this"—he motioned at her with his arms—"is over an' done with, you'll stay in her house as companion an' housekeeper."

"Papa, no!"

"It is enough an' it is done! I will hear no more of this!" His stern glance took in both his daughter and wife.

Alone in her room, Mariah closed the lid of the small trunk she had packed and lay on her bed, curled in a ball, a lump tightening her throat. The delicious smell of the shepherd's pie her mother had prepared wafted through the house, but she had not eaten a bite. Now, in the dark, she pulled the covers up and dissolved into choking sobs.

Mary pushed uneaten food around on her plate and listened to her daughter cry. She thought of Aunt Abigail, a severe, grim old lady, and knew Mariah would have a difficult time in her house. Fighting back her own tears, she thought: This is wrong. Mariah should be home. She looked across the table at her husband as he wolfed down his food. The self-assured conviction that he was absolutely right seemed to have sparked his appetite. She watched him eat, washing his meal down with cider. I'll speak to him tonight, she decided. There must be another way.

Mariah lay huddled under her quilt, exhausted from the physical effort of crying. Her head throbbed, her eyes burned, and her nose was so stuffed she took shallow breaths though her mouth. Papa's sending me away so Sam can't find me, she thought miserably. He'll come back and I'll be gone. They'll never tell him about Aunt Abigail. I should've gone with him. That's what I should've done.

She could not fully visualize life at sea or in foreign ports, but she lay in the darkened room snuffling quietly, remembering Sam's stories and the images he'd conjured up. She jumped when she heard her father's raised voice.

"No! Don't speak to me of this again. All her life she's defied my authority, an' all her life I've been called to account for what she done. I ain't goin' do it no more."

"She's our child, Matthew. She'll need me when her time comes. Please, let her stay. When Sam comes back—"

"Sam? Bah!" he interrupted, and snorted scornfully. "He ain't comin' back. If he ain't dead, he forgot about her is all. No honorable man leaves a woman in that condition."

"He doesn't know. Mariah didn't tell him about the baby."

"Bein' stupid don't fix nothin'. The sin is there just the same. We ain't goin' to be tarnished by bringin' her shame into this house. She'll go to Aunt Abigail as a servant an' that ends it." He shook his finger in her face. "You will obey me, Mary, an' say nothin' of this to no one. No one." He picked up his fork. "We leave at sun-up."

✠ ✠ ✠

The house was still when Mariah got up and dressed. She put her best bodice, her shawl, and a few other things in her basket and went quietly down to the great room. As she stood by the front door putting on her heavy wool cloak, a soft whisper came out of the darkness.

"Mariah."

"Mama?"

"Are you goin' to the tavern?"

"What? How do you know?"

"It doesn't matter. Will you be all right there?"

"Yes— But Mama, how— Does papa know?"

"No, he doesn't. Don't ask questions, child, just go. An' take these." She put some objects into Mariah's hands. There was a coin, but what were the others? "My grandmother's combs. Her name was Mariah, too. Wear them when you marry Sam."

"Oh, Mama— We love each other so much! An' papa's wrong. Sam didn't forget about me, he didn't."

"Yes, yes, I know. Now, go quickly, an' God be with you. Write soon an' tell me you're safe." She kissed her daughter's cheeks and slipped back into the darkness.

Low voices came from her parents' bedroom, and she froze, her cloak in her hands. She barely breathed. In a moment it was quiet once more, but she waited—just to be sure—then silently left the house.

In the cold hours before dawn, Mariah arrived at Israel's boatyard and let herself into the shed where rope, sails, and tools were kept. She wrapped her cloak tightly about her, and yawning widely, stretched out on the work bench. The shawl made a soft pillow. Closing her eyes, she wondered about her great-grandmother until sleep finally came.

3

"Wouldn't you be better off home, with your mama?" Susannah Brown asked.

Mariah had come to Great Island, huddled on the deck of a small boat, shivering in the thin sunshine of the cold, November dawn. Now, in the warmth of the tavern's blazing fire, she ate a hearty breakfast with Will and Susannah.

"I miss mama," she said, "but I can't stay at home. Papa will take me to Aunt Abigail, an' mama—she'll do exactly as papa says. If I go away, Sam won't know where to find me"—she smiled shyly, "find us—when he gets back. Please let me stay."

"Oh, love!" Susannah said, getting up to hug Mariah. "Of course you can stay! Can't she, Will?"

Will swallowed his bit of cheese and looked up cheerfully. "Aye. Always welcome, you know that."

Mariah's grateful words were muffled as she snuggled deeply into Susannah's warm embrace.

"We'll keep you an' your baby safe until Sam comes for you, won't we, Will?" But she caught her husband's eye over the top of Mariah's head. *If* he comes back was their shared thought.

"Now then!" Susannah said, giving her a reassuring squeeze. "Let's finish up here an' get you settled!"

Mariah felt at home right away and insisted on working for her room and board. She served customers at tables and at the bar, helped in the kitchen when there was a crowd at meal times, carded and spun yarn, and knitted during the long evenings. She saw Josiah more often than she had all autumn, and they'd sit together listening to Nate Pound tell stories of his trip south with Sam, of the pirates they'd seen on New Providence Island, and of the Spanish and their sunken gold.

It was during her early days at the tavern when Nate gave her the shell. "Never seen one like it afore," he said. "They ain't a bit like the ones we got up here, in these north waters. Don't know what it's called. Sam says they're usual in the south. 'Course, most everything's different down there. Bright. Lot of colors." He smiled shyly, and turned back to his friends at the bar.

Mariah took the shell. It was about half the size of a hen's egg, and had a soft beige color that turned golden pink on the inside where the little sea-animal had once lived. This was something from Sam—a token to keep—and her heart leaped for joy. He hadn't forgotten! He'd been thinking of her when he'd picked it up off the beach, when he'd given it to Nate, and every time he imagined her holding it in her hand—just as she was doing now. That night she sewed a pouch from a bit of calico to put the shell in and attached it to a cord to hang around her neck. When she was working, she tucked it inside her bodice where it was safe and near her heart, like their baby.

4

"Sorry now you didn't go along after all?" Susannah asked Josiah one bright, sunny December afternoon.

"Can't say, now, can I?" His eyes twinkled. "Listenin' to Nate, here, got t'say no. Ain't sorry one bit. Have to wait 'til the others get back afore I knows how t' answer proper, then, eh? Got to see what they bring, now, don't I?"

The comforting routine of the tavern suited Mariah very well. Susannah and Will had come to think of her as family and looked forward to the birth of her baby as if it was their own grandchild. Acquaintances of her parents often came to the tavern, but if they told her father they'd seen her, she never knew. And after a while she didn't care.

By the end of January, 1716, Mariah was well into her sixth month, her belly swelling with the growing child. On one cold, snowy night, she lay on the settle with her head on Susannah's lap, drifting in and out of sleep. Three tavern guests sat with them, and one, a whaler from Nantucket, drew deeply on his pipe and closed his eyes in the silence. The old story he'd been telling, Homer's *Odyssey,* was new to his small audience. They were spellbound by his words, and each gazed into the fire seeing the fantastic monsters, witches, maidens, and heroes come to life in the flames.

"Now, here you are, Tom!" Will came back into the room with a tankard of ale. "Wet your whistle an' finish your yarn!"

"Thanks kindly, landlord. Here's a health to you an' to your good lady. An' ma'am," he nodded at the sleepy Mariah, "my best regards to you." He took a long drink. "Ah!" he said with a happy smile. Wiping the foam from his mouth with his sleeve, he sat back in his chair and took a long pull on his pipe. He looked up at the ceiling and blew smoke into the air.

Susannah shifted on the settle. "There, love," she murmured softly, stroking Mariah's hair, "now we can listen proper."

Tom took another drink and leaned forward, elbows on his knees. "It seems that all the while this here cove, Odysseus, was tryin' his best to get home an' his son was out there lookin' for him, his lady wife was runnin' through storms of her own. Penelope was her name, an' her father, well, he was no one but the king of Sparta hisself. She was besieged by a gang of suitors, every one of them sniffin' 'round an' claimin' her husband wasn't never comin' home, an' she should marry one of them. Like hungry sharks they was, all circlin' for the kill.

"Now, Penelope hatched herself a scheme to put them sharks off. She was mighty tired of that lot anyways, cruisin' by, day in, day out, hopin' to splice their line to hers. So she told them she wasn't goin' to take no new husband until she finishes up makin' a shroud for her husband's old father in case he should die one day soon. Well, the sharks, they say it's all fine with them, so they drops anchor an' waits.

"But Penelope, she don't ever give up thinkin' her husband'll sail up one day, so—"

"Like me!" Mariah sat up, wide awake and interested. "That's like me. Sam'll be back—I know it. He will. What did she do?"

"Well, she took to her loom—"

"Her loom?"

"Aye. She took to her loom an' began to weave the most wonderful cloth a body could ever've seen."

"An' when she finished?" Mariah asked.

Tom smiled slyly through the smoke and took another drink. "Oh, she was a clever one, that lass. She took to workin' at the loom all the day long. Then, every night, all secret-like, she unravels the cloth, thread by thread, 'til there weren't nothin' left. Then each morn she strings up the loom again an' starts afresh."

"They never knew?"

"Well, they was rich, them suitors, but nobody could say they was sharp."

Mariah got up and wrapped the shawl tightly about her. "Did he come back? Did he?"

"Well, now, lass, that would be tellin'. There's lots more of this here tale to come afore a body gets to know that."

"Please! I have to know. Sam! Will he come back?"

"Mariah, love!" Susannah's voice rose in concern.

"Suppose I tell you in secret, lass, so as not to spoil the story for them others."

He spoke quietly to Mariah, and in the ruddy glow of the fire, her face beamed with a bright smile.

"Thank you. Oh, thank you!" Without another word, she climbed the stairs to bed where she dreamed of angry sea gods, six-headed dogs, witches who turned men into pigs—but mostly of Sam.

5

On a beautiful, mild day in April, Mariah walked down the path to the beach to collect some plants and stood at the water's edge thinking about Sam. She had not walked very far, but the effort made her unusually breathless, and the baby kicked hard. Rubbing her belly, she murmured happily, "Don't worry so, little one. Your papa will be home soon."

She picked up her basket, but as she walked to the tavern, her legs and back ached with every step. Her belly felt heavier and heavier, and a dull pain started as the baby began to press down hard at the base of her spine. "I can't—do this," she gasped, her breath coming hard. "I have to—Oh, my God!" A tightening surge of pain shot through her as the pressure increased, and rivulets of sweat ran down her face, stinging her eyes. She stood in the sand and looked ahead to the tavern door, but the short distance seemed impossible to cross without help. The spasm passed and she took a few cautious steps. When she could breathe easily, she walked slowly home.

She was nearly there when pain gripped her again, suddenly, horribly. It doubled her over, squeezing, crushing, sharp, and hot. She cried out, and gripping her belly, dropped to a squat, her knees far apart.

Susannah came running. "Oh, my God! Will! Will! Come quick! Now!" She knelt down, her strong competent hands holding Mariah until the waves of pain slowed to a stop. "Can you stand? The pain, did it happen before?"

Mariah nodded, and wiping sweat and tears from her face, she stood, leaning on Susannah. She took a small step, and stopped as a sudden gush of warm liquid ran down her legs. "I'm wet! I'm bleedin'!"

"No, it's your waters breakin'," Susannah said, looking at the puddle. She brushed Mariah's damp hair back from her face. "You're all right, love. Baby's nice an' low an' ready to come, is all. It's your time! Let's get you inside. Will!" she called, holding Mariah tightly. "Come along right smart an' give us a hand here!"

The baby came, wailing and strong, late that afternoon. After Mariah nursed him and fell asleep, Susannah swaddled the tiny child and brought him down to the taproom.

"Come an' see," she said softly to the men who had been waiting. She pulled aside a bit of blanket, and they gathered around to look at the small, pink face. "He's got his papa's dark hair an' eyes." She gently touched his cheek with her finger. "Got his name, too. She calls him Samuel."

✠ ✠ ✠

"Ain't you been happy here?" asked Josiah. "Thought you was."

He sat with Mariah outside the tavern door in the afternoon sun. Samuel, now more than a week old, was tucked into the crook of his mother's arm, fast asleep. Josiah refused to hold the baby, saying the only newborn things he had ever touched were puppies—and that had been enough.

"I am happy," Mariah said wistfully. "But the closer I came to birthin' him, the more I missed my mama. Now he's born, I—I want to go home."

"Ain't goin' t' sit well with your papa."

She stuck out her bottom lip defiantly. "Samuel's here. Papa won't like it, but he'll change his mind once we're home. I know it."

Josiah shook his head. "You ain't thinkin' this through proper, girl. You talk t' Will an' Susannah 'bout this?"

"Will arranged for a boat."

"You're goin', then."

They sat together silently for a while.

"Josiah, Sam'll come here first, to the tavern, you know, because of Israel. Will an' Susannah say they'll tell him where I am. You have to promise, too, what ever happens."

Josiah leaned forward, elbows on his knees, and studied the ground. "'Course I will," he said gruffly. "This just ain't a good idea."

✠ ✠ ✠

"If this don't work out," Susannah said, kissing Mariah on the cheek, "remember to come back to Will an' me—any time." They had walked to the end of the dock, and when Mariah was settled in the boat, Susannah handed her the baby.

"I'll never forget, but I'm sure we won't have to, because everything will be just fine. I know it will."

Susannah waited as they cast off, the sail filling with wind. She raised her hand to wave and heard Mariah call out, "Thanks again! I love you!"

As the boat moved into the bay, she sighed deeply, shaking her head. "Oh, my girl, you sayin' everythin'll be fine sure ain't goin' to make it so."

The Barn

IN THE TIME IT HAD TAKEN TO WAVE GOODBYE TO SUSANNAH AND cross Billingsgate Bay to Israel's boatyard in Eastham, Mariah began to regret her decision and almost changed her mind about going on. The boatman who'd taken her across had offered to take her back to Great Island, but once on land she rallied and grimly shook her head. After all, nothing had really gone wrong—she'd simply forgotten her heavy wool cloak. And if being chilly was the only problem she encountered on the way home, it would be easily fixed once she got there.

The two-mile trek to her father's farm lay along a rugged path through the wilderness that covered the outer Cape between both shores—Cape Cod Bay and the Atlantic Ocean. She'd walked it many times from the boatyard when only plants and herbs filled her basket. This same basket now held her few belongings. Juggling it and Samuel made this part of her journey much more difficult than she'd imagined. She tripped and stumbled along the uneven ground, unsure of her footing, and stopped often to rest and sooth her fussing, squirming son.

"Ah, hush, now, hush, sweet baby," she said as she sat leaning against a tree. "Frettin' won't make goin' home any easier. If you're scoldin' me for leavin' the tavern, well, I reckon I deserve it. I should've gone with your papa—that's what I should've done, an' you'd've been born at sea. Sleepin' on a ship must be like sleepin' in a giant's cradle." She groaned as she struggled to her feet. "Well, we best get movin'. Sun's slippin' down faster'n I can walk."

Samuel, his tummy full, found his comfort and slept while Mariah negotiated the path in the gathering dusk and contemplated what lay ahead. Could she slip into her familiar life at home with her baby, or would she find that world as filled with stumbling blocks as this walk through the woods? In her happiness with Samuel she'd imagined the joy his presence would bring to her parents—just as Lydia's daughter had—but the memory of her father's anger squeezed at her heart. Everything was different, everybody was different; and her sleeping child was no basket of herbs. Neither of her parents had come to her, sought her out, or asked about her baby. Not even a word from her mother, who'd given her money and her great-grandmother's combs in that dream-like moment before she left the house. They had abandoned her to her fate.

"I shouldn't be here," Mariah said ruefully. She wiped tears from her eyes and stepped gingerly through a wide patch of tree roots that crossed the trail on a downhill slope. "This is wrong. When I get home, everything'll be just as it was the night I left. Nothin' will have changed. They don't even care about me. Why didn't I go with Sam? Why didn't I stay with Susannah? Why didn't I listen? I shouldn't be here."

The darkened woods were alive with the rustlings of night creatures by the time Mariah stopped to catch her breath and look around. She was half-way home, and too cold and tired to go on. The Knowles' farm was nearby, and a tempting haven despite the unwelcome possibility of meeting the man himself. But the thought of passing a warm, sheltered night in his barn was worth the risk.

✠ ✠ ✠

From the shadowy edge of the woods, Mariah looked out across the newly plowed fields to the barn. The activity of the day was over. Smoke curled from the chimney of the house, and the cool, fresh breeze blew delicious aromas of the family's supper her way, teasing her nose. She glanced impatiently at the setting sun. It stubbornly refused to budge from its comfortable spot above the treetops, and its deep golden rays cast long shadows across the open land. The baby was nestled against her chest in a snug cocoon-like pouch she made by wrapping her shawl tightly around them both. She cupped her hand behind his head and kissed his downy hair. He woke up, stirring softly.

"Samuel, we're almost there," she whispered as she fed him. "We just have to wait until it's dark. You can wait, my sweet little lamb, can't you?"

Shifting from foot to foot, Mariah shivered in the chilly air of the late April evening. The buildings were blackened silhouettes against the sun's vivid light, but the windows of the house, lit with a rich amber glow that spilled out onto the ground, made her long for the warm comforts of home. As she paced back and forth, grumbling and yawning, the sun finally disappeared behind the stand of trees. She waited a little while longer, then walked through the night and entered the barn.

In the near pitch black, she stood very still, listening to the sounds that swelled around her. Animals snorted and snuffled as they moved in their stalls. A horse whinnied softly. The earthy smells of hay and manure were reassuringly familiar. When her eyes grew accustomed to the dark, she inched along carefully, groping for the ladder to the hayloft. It was free-standing, but stationary and nearly vertical. She passed her hands over the slats of wood that served as rungs, then up and down the sides, giving the ladder a good shake. It felt secure, and she prayed the top of the ladder would allow easy access to the hayloft floor. She hitched up her skirt and petticoat, tucking the hems into her waist-band.

"Here we go, Samuel. Now, hold on."

The hayloft was about ten feet above the barn floor and climbing up was awkward, even in daylight. Mariah's center of balance was thrown off by the baby, still strapped tightly to her chest, so she couldn't lean into the ladder and hug it to prevent a fall. Her arms were almost fully extended and her body bent to keep Samuel safe from knocking into the wood. At each step she stopped to readjust readjust her grip and catch her breath.

The two long boards that formed the ladder's sides mercifully continued beyond the top of the ladder giving her the leverage she needed to haul herself up the last bit and onto the hayloft floor. She inched forward on her hands and knees then dropped on her side.

Samuel let out a shriek and bawled loudly at the abrupt change of position. The horses whinnied nervously at the unexpected sound, their heavy hoofs clomping in the straw bedding. Barn swallows and doves, roosting on the beams, took off in a startled cloud of feathers, and from somewhere in the barn frightened sheep bleated.

"God's teeth," she muttered. "We're raisin' a mighty alarm." She cooed, cuddled, and calmed her son while she made a nest in the hay and lined it with her shawl. Sitting with the hungry baby, comfortable in her arms, she fed him, then ate the last of the bread and cheese Susannah had given her.

Stillness settled over the barn creatures, and lying so close to the sleeping Samuel, Mariah could just hear his gentle breathing. "For someone so little, you had a big day," she whispered, pulling a bit of shawl over him. Then she took Sam's sea shell out of the little pouch she'd sewn at the tavern. She couldn't see it, but she could feel its conical shape, the spiral that came to a point at one end, and the wide opening for the creature that had once lived inside.

"When your papa chose this shell for me, he didn't know about you, little one. It belongs to me just like your papa—an' just like you." She returned the shell to its pouch, and yawned.

A mouse rustled in the straw, and an owl hooted in the distance.

The night closed over her, and in a moment she slept.

2

Thankful Knowles entered the barn early the following morning thinking about Mariah. It was nearly five months to the day since they'd last seen each other at church and word started to get around that Mariah had gone to live with her father's maiden aunt. The November disappearance of her friend seemed too sudden for Thankful, too rushed. She initially felt hurt when Mariah didn't come to say goodbye, but she soon began to doubt what she was told, and grew determined to learn the truth.

"It's best she's gone from the neighborhood," had been her mother's vague reply not long after Mariah vanished. "It's what your father wants, and he always knows what's best." She would not meet Thankful's eyes, and Thankful knew better than to argue or press her point. Her mother was completely under her father's thumb, and would no more speak her own mind than she would sit on the roof and howl at the moon.

Then, on an unusually mild Sunday in February, when the little church overflowed with neighbors eager to escape the confinement of their homes after the long, hard, isolating winter, Thankful spoke with Mary Hallett.

Mary had cast a furtive glance at her husband, who came and hovered close behind her while she spoke with Thankful. "She's doin' quite well there, enjoyin' her work an' all." She would say no more, and looked away. Thankful noticed that both Mariah's parents looked drawn and ill, and had aged in the three months since their daughter left home. Matthew's anger showed in the hard set of his mouth, and the frown lines etched deeply into his weather-beaten skin. Mary's face was more difficult to read, but Thankful was sure she saw worry and fear in those troubled, reddened eyes.

It had been frustrating for Thankful, and it still was. Even Mr.

Treat believed Mariah had gone to Aunt Abigail. The person she hoped to see was Josiah, for she was convinced he'd know the truth. He didn't often attend church, and now that spring had come and people were again out-of-doors, she'd hoped to see him around and about, but this idea failed, too. The rumor was that he spent more time than ever at the Great Island Tavern, but she couldn't go there, nor could she look for him at his usual Eastham haunts.

Thankful was blocked at every path she tried to follow to the truth about Mariah, and in due course unwillingly accepted her friend's absence as part of life. And while she didn't give up wondering, the unanswered questions had, for the most part, drifted to the back of her mind where they stayed until this April morning.

It had been a year since Mariah, bright-eyed, happy—and a little shy—told Thankful about meeting Sam Bellamy. Thankful thought of this as she worked in the barn, and she remembered her friend's happiness with the tall, rugged sailor. There was only one explanation for the mystery that made sense to her: Mariah had run away to find Sam. But even this theory was flawed. Surely Mariah would have shared this secret with her. Surely Mariah's parents would be reacting differently to such an event. Surely there'd be talk, rumors—

"Ssssst! Thankful!" A bit of straw floated down from the hay loft and Thankful looked up. "Ssssst!"

"Mariah!"

"Ssh! Come up!"

Thankful peered over her shoulder at the wide barn door standing open to the farm yard, then climbed the ladder. She went straight to her friend's open arms.

"What's happened? Where've you been? Nobody will tell me anything and I've been so worried. My mother said you went to an elderly aunt to be her housekeeper. Even your mother said you were happy in your work. But I didn't believe—" She turned and saw Samuel.

"He was born at the tavern ten days ago," Mariah said softly.

Thankful took a small step backward. With a sharp intake of breath she looked at her friend. "You mean—you and Sam— Mariah, how could you?" She stared down at the baby. "That means he's a—"

"He's a child of God," Mariah said. "He come into the world same as everyone because his papa loves me. Susannah said words over him, an' he's free of sin, just like all the little ones blessed in church. If there's fault, it's mine an' Sam's, not his. You know this." She was quiet a moment. "Thankful—?"

Tears prickled Thankful's eyes as she struggled with what she had been taught to believe and what she felt at that moment. She knelt and put her finger in the tiny fist. "He's so beautiful. Do you call him Samuel?" Then she sat in the hay and picked him up, cradling him between her knees in the hammock-like sling of her skirt. "So he's why you disappeared. I never guessed. Why didn't you tell me?"

"I thought about tellin' you. Every day I wanted to write," Mariah said, "but I was afraid your father'd find my letter. You'd be lyin' to your parents as much as I was lyin' to mine, if you knew the truth, an' I didn't want to do that to you." Sitting next to her friend, she told the whole story. "So much has happened an' so much is wrong," she said with a sigh. "I thought I wanted to go home, but now I know they were right, Susannah an' Josiah, an' I should've stayed at the tavern. But I also want to see my mama. Maybe I should've gone with Sam. I don't know what I want, an' I'm tired. An' cold."

"If you had gone with Sam, then I'd really never see you again."

"Can I stay here for awhile 'til I decide what to do? Please?"

Thankful frowned and bit her bottom lip. It was her duty, she knew, to tell her father everything, and she hesitated—but only for a moment. "They're plowing and lambing now, and everyone's mostly out in the fields, so I suppose it'll be all right for a while. But you must leave as soon as you can. I'll bring some food later. Now, I've got to do my chores!" She lingered for a minute, studying the baby's dark hair and eyes, then took hold of his feet. He straightened his legs and pushed hard against her palms. "He's a strong one," she laughed, "just like his papa."

She kissed Mariah lightly on the cheek. "I'll be back when I can."

But as she went about her daily tasks, Thankful worried about Mariah and her baby, and thought of the handsome sailor whose dark features were so pleasing in his son. He had captured her friend's heart and she wondered, not for the first time, if Sam Bellamy would ever come back to claim his love—and now his family.

Thankful came as promised, after supper, and brought bread and two cold roasted potatoes. "That's all I could get," she said as Mariah gobbled them down. "Here's some water, too, and this old quilt. Now, I've got to go. I'll come early tomorrow." She kissed Samuel and disappeared down the ladder.

The next morning, Mariah quietly left the barn before sun-up and returned a few minutes later to find a lantern burning inside the open door. She crept close, and hearing no sound, cautiously went inside. When she'd climbed the ladder far enough to be eye level with the hayloft floor, she searched anxiously for the place where she'd left Samuel only moments before, swaddled in her shawl. But her view was blocked by a pair of heavy, brown boots. The thick soles were encrusted with mud, and she caught a whiff of fresh muck from the animals. She knew before she looked up at the owner that they belonged to John Knowles.

Mariah clung tightly to the ladder with both hands, and leaned back to look up into his face. It struck her that she'd never seen Thankful's father look sad, and she wondered why—until the bright color of her shawl caught her eye. It was oddly out of place in his rough, dirty hands and she stared at it, bewildered. Something was wrapped loosely in the shawl, and he held it, protectively, close to his chest. Among the folds of the draping fabric she saw Samuel's legs small and very still. His soft baby skin already had a waxy, gray cast, and as his blood, obeying gravity's pull, collected in his little feet and tiny toes, turning them deep scarlet.

"This is *your* sin and crime, Mariah Hallett. May God almighty have mercy on you."

Her wail of anguish cut into the silence and filled every space in the barn. She let go of the ladder to reach out for her dead child, and fell to the barn floor, striking her head on the top edge of a horse stall. In the moment or two of groggy confusion, heavy foot steps came to her and an angry voice floated down from somewhere above. "She is the child's mother, and has done this wicked deed. Take her outside."

Knowles' hired men hauled Mariah to her feet. Her knees gave way and she sagged, the barn floor tilting wildly as she struggled for her footing, but they held on to her and walked her outside. They heaved her into the back of the farm cart where she lay in dirty straw and muck.

"Mariah! Mama, it's Mariah!" Thankful ran from the house. Her mother watched from the kitchen door, silent and frightened. "Papa! No! What are you doing? Where are you taking her?" She stopped short when she saw Mariah's dead baby in his arms. "Samuel!"

"What do you know of this?"

She shrank back from him, almost unable to speak. "Nothing, Papa."

He glared at her, and his eyes were cold and fierce. "For your sake, and for your salvation, let it be so." He climbed in the cart and it rumbled away.

3

John Knowles stood before the magistrate's large oak desk an hour later, triumphant and self-righteous. He had taken the frightened Mariah directly to the court and pressed for a swift judgment. "Her sin against God is a sin against our community," he said. "To delay prosecution is to open a door for the devil to come among us. Once again we stand in peril—"

The magistrate banged his gavel for silence. "I will consider this when I know, with exact words and true, what has happened."

Justice Joseph Doane sat in judgment on the wrongdoers of Eastham, and the surrounding area, twice a week. Today he was facing a docket filled with the usual crimes and complaints playing out in front of the usual group of listless spectators, who never seemed to have anything else to do on the days court was in session, and he was feeling the usual tedium. John Knowles, interrupting the proceedings with Mariah Hallett—of all people—in tow, presented a problem he was glad to tackle. The spectators perked up and strained to see.

Knowles stepped forward, placing Samuel's body, still wrapped in Mariah's shawl, on the corner of the desk. "I came to my barn before sun-up to tend my beasts and put them out to pasture," he said. "In the stillness, I heard a small sound I thought to be one of the cats taking a mouse. But as I listened, I knew the sound to be coughing or choking, and it came from above—from my hayloft. I went to look and found a newly born child, dead. I picked him up and turned to see Mariah Hallett coming up the ladder."

Mariah stood still, as if the weight of her heavy iron shackles anchored her to the spot. She glanced at neither man, but stared blankly at the floor.

"I know of this witch-girl and was not surprised," Knowles continued. "For her heart belonged to the devil when she was a child, and it still does. You see she does not speak, neither does she weep. She has killed this child, surely, as if she had sucked the very breath from him while he slept."

There was a sudden movement, and John Knowles lifted Mariah's shawl to reveal her son. She stared, unblinking, at Samuel. There was no mistaking death for sleep, his stillness was like stone. His eyes were open. She wanted to touch him, but turned away.

"You see she does not care!" John Knowles cried. "She does not mourn, as all who are here bear witness! She must be brought to trial for conceiving and bringing forth this child outside the law, and for his murder. She must also answer the charge of witchcraft, as seen in her unnatural ways with animals. God's moral laws are just and must be enforced or we will suffer the judgment of Sodom and Gomorrah for giving shelter to a disciple of the devil!"

Justice Doane knew of John Knowles' strong principles and religious beliefs. He also knew that with Knowles' extreme devotion came an irrational need to go to any lengths to prove his point. He remembered the unpleasantness that had centered around Mariah, when she was only twelve years old, and had mysteriously cured the dog, Samson. Now here she was four years later at the center of another potential storm—and here was her dead baby. Struggling for rational thought, he turned his stern face to the prisoner.

"Mariah Hallett, you stand accused of terrible crimes and sins against God and man. How speak you to these accusations?" He waited for her to answer, but she said nothing. "Look upon this dead child. Did you conceive and bear him outside God's law, then willfully murder him? Have you consorted with the devil and been his instrument in this community? Will you not answer these charges, Mariah? Will you not confess?"

The magistrate frowned darkly at her and banged his gavel on the desk. "You would be wise to speak, else your silence be taken as admission of guilt." He waited again. "Mariah Hallett, you will be placed in Eastham jail until such time that a decision shall be made and sentencing pronounced, for your silence has condemned you. Constable, take her away." The gavel banged again.

✠ ✠ ✠

Mariah sat on the small three-legged stool in her cell and stared into the dark. A thick mist, like a heavy black veil, seemed to swirl in front of her eyes and ooze into the deepest corners of her mind. Occasional words pierced the misty veil and darted into her head. She groped for them in the darkness, but they leaked out before she could grasp them and understand. There was nothing now—nothing but endless emptiness.

Josiah had been shocked when the county constable brought her to the jail that afternoon with instructions to lock her away. He'd argued and shouted, but orders are orders, he'd been told. She hadn't said a word to anyone and wouldn't speak to him, either, no matter what he said or how he tried. After night-fall he went into her cell with a lantern and found her asleep in the straw bedding. "Best for you," he said, covering her with an old quilt. He picked up the dish of uneaten porridge and waited while Samson licked her face. Then he locked the door and went to his bed, feeling older than his seventy years.

4

"What's wrong with them people?" Susannah asked the bread dough early the next morning. She kneaded it, then picked it up and slammed it down hard on the floured board with more force than necessary. "Just the sweetest girl who got herself in big trouble, is all."

"Who's that?" Will asked, coming into the kitchen with a bucket of milk.

"Well, now, you just listen to this piece of news come over from Eastham!" Susannah's eyes flashed angrily as she put dough-covered hands on her ample hips and told her husband about Mariah. "You'd think she's the first one ever to put makin' a baby before the weddin'. An' murder? Why anyone who knows her or seen her with that babe knows it ain't true." She punched down the dough and kneaded it again. "An' witchcraft? I ask you. John Knowles is behind this. You know that as well as I do. Preachin' an' carryin' on like he does, got everybody all fired up by sayin' she's evil an' all. She's—" Tears ran down her face and she wiped them away with her floury hand. "The poor, wee babe—"

Will stepped in closer and held his sobbing wife in his big, bear like embrace.

5

Mary Hallett heard occasional news of her daughter from Josiah and knew of Samuel's birth. She said nothing about it to her husband, just as she kept silent about her involvement the night Mariah ran away. Matthew's anger at finding his daughter gone wasn't explosive—he withdrew into himself and refused to talk about her. He silently dismantled her loom and stored it in a shed.

When he heard, sometime during the winter, that Mariah was living at the tavern, he, too, kept the news to himself. The deep gulf he created between his heart and his daughter—and his wife for that matter—became unbridgeable. Saying Mariah's name meant he accepted what she had done, and that was one thing he could not do.

He said nothing when he heard the news of Mariah's arrest, but walked to the shed and stared at the parts of her loom piled against a wall. He thought about the animals she had nursed there—the fox, the pheasant, the rabbit, and all the others. He thought about Samson, and his dead grandson.

"My girl—oh, my poor child," he began, but choked, unaccustomed to the tears welling in his eyes. Then he sat on the loom and cried.

The Jail

MARIAH'S SLEEP WAS DEEP AND DREAMLESS. IT HAD RAINED OFF and on the last three days, since leaving the tavern, but when she awoke on the morning after her arrest, the sun was shining through the small face-sized window in the heavy oak door of her cell. She lay in the straw watching hay and dust particles float in the shaft of light. There was something familiar about the door, and she puzzled over it, her mind slipping sideways as she tried to grip onto her reality.

The jolt of recognition hit her hard, and she was overcome by a surge of fear. Her empty stomach churned, sending a hot, sour flood up to her throat. She crawled into a corner, retching until she was weak and drenched in sweat. She rinsed her mouth with cool water from a bucket and wiped her face on her skirt. She sat miserably in the straw with her head in her hands for some time.

It was all there, and it was all clear. Memories, like midges, flew at her, and she tried to fight them off. Images of little Samuel flashed before her eyes. "I won't look!" she insisted, willing her mind to cooperate. "I won't look. It's not true. It's not!" She paced in her small cell, hearing his birth cry and soft murmurings of contentment. Desperate to shut out the sounds, she pressed her hands over her ears. "I won't listen! I won't! I won't! It didn't happen!" She looked around wildly, realizing even in her panic that she couldn't hide from these truths. Her aching breasts, swollen with milk, leaked and stained her bodice, betraying her into facing what she most wanted to deny.

✠ ✠ ✠

Earlier that morning, Josiah had awakened at dawn after a troubled night's sleep and fussed about with cornbread and milk. He ate some, then carried a filled dish and a bucket of fresh water into Mariah's cell. He flung an empty sack over his shoulder, and taking his gun, whistled for Samson. They walked together into the woods.

✠ ✠ ✠

The Reverend Mr. Samuel Treat awoke that same morning thinking about breakfast. The delicious smells wafting in from the kitchen, accompanied by mysterious clangs and thumps, told him his wife was preparing his favorite dishes. He heard the light laughter of his daughters as they helped.

He rolled over in bed and looked through the window at the beautiful spring day. Then the memory of Mariah jarred his mind. His heart raced, and he felt a flush of heat rise to his face. He threw back the covers. There was a lot to do today.

✠ ✠ ✠

John Knowles was also up before dawn. He took care of his early morning chores, then went to his bookshelf. Taking down a small red volume, he smiled to himself. "This will do."

For the third morning in a row, he saddled his horse and rode off without saying a word.

Thankful, rubbing her eyes, stood beside her mother at the

opened door. They watched him ride away. "What's he going to do, Mama? What's going to happen?"

"I don't know," Mrs. Knowles whispered. "I don't know."

✠ ✠ ✠

At the same time, Justice Joseph Doane sat at the head of his breakfast table with his wife and seven of their eleven children. His bound girl brought in a tray loaded with steaming porringers, and his wife tended to the fretting baby, but he noticed none of this. Earlier that morning, a courier had ridden to his house from Israel's boatyard carrying a leather pouch filled with legal papers from the General Court in Boston, and a newspaper that had also arrived on the pre-dawn ship. He read a certain article again and again, with scant hope the news had not circulated throughout the community. Daily pressure from John Knowles made the situation bad enough, but this—

He took a drink of his tepid tea. The best thing to do, he thought grimly, is to conclude this matter as quickly as possible—today, in fact. Gathering up the papers, he left the room without a word.

"Joseph, what's happened?" asked his wife as he walked out, hastily adding a sharp "Sit!" to the seven-year-old who was about to follow him.

✠ ✠ ✠

At the tavern on Great Island, another copy of the newspaper from Boston had come on a trading vessel that put in and unloaded at the dock very early that same morning.

"Weren't he around a bit, year or so back?" the ship's captain asked as he sat in the taproom shoveling in hot lamb stew and warm bread. "Remember him. Big talker."

Will read the paper, then thrust it at Susannah when she came in with a tankard of ale. "Read this!" he said. "I'm goin' to wake Israel."

While Mariah paced in her cell that morning, Will, Susannah, and the others involved in the smuggling business, counted their eggs before they were laid. Israel, a man of little humor, actually smiled.

2

The jail held the cool dampness of the night's rain well into the day. Josiah spread fresh straw in a prisoner's cell every morning, but he couldn't remove the unhealthy stench of human waste and misery that had soaked into the wood and stone building over the years. Mariah's misery added yet another layer. Her skirt and bodice had been soaked from the mucky straw she'd lain in on her trip to court in John Knowles' farm cart. In the dank cell, nothing would dry and the stink would last. There was no way to get away from it, no place to hide, no fresh air to breathe.

Mariah went to the cell-door window and looked outside. When she put her hands on the iron bars, the door moved. She pushed it again, and again, and it swung open on well-oiled hinges. She stood in the doorway for only a few seconds, then walked outside and into the beautiful, mild spring day.

Josiah was nowhere to be seen, but Mariah didn't care. She sat on an old weathered bench and lifted her face to the warmth of the sun. The fresh air, tinged with the sweet smells of pine and the salty sea, chased away the closeness and stink of the cell. She inhaled it deeply.

"Mariah." A voice came out of the shadow that had crossed her face, and someone sat next to her. "Mariah, it's Samuel Treat." He took her tightly clenched hands in his, but she turned away. "Will you speak with me?"

Samuel. She'd heard him say his name—Samuel. Samuel. Sam. Her mind drifted into blackness and snapped back when she heard him speak again.

"Almighty God, our heavenly Father, who of His great and tender mercy hath promised forgiveness of sins to all them that with hearty repentance—"

"No." Her scratchy voice was barely a whisper.

"I want to pray for you."

"Don't."

"I can help you find peace."

"Can you bring back my baby?"

"You know I can't do that."

"Then go away."

"A person can know God and know that he can bring peace amid the storm, Mariah, no matter what has happened. He watches over his children."

"Why is my baby dead?"

"I don't know. We are not always able to understand what God chooses to do."

"They say I am a witch an' a murderer."

Mr. Treat hesitated. "I don't believe that, but painful, terrible things have caused you great suffering. I once told you that to be in torment was to have pain and misery in your heart and mind. Do you remember? Let me help you to relieve that torment now. Please."

Mariah got up and walked back to her cell. "Go away. I got no use for you or your God." She pulled the heavy door shut, closing herself in the dark.

✠ ✠ ✠

A few hours later, John Knowles reined in his horse and dismounted in front of the Eastham jail. His spurs jingled as he crossed the yard, walking toward the two cell doors. He liked their sound. He had never worn them before, but he thought they gave an earthly authority to his heavenly mission—as if being God's instrument in the face of the devil wasn't enough. The sun was bright, and he let his eyes grow accustomed to the dim, gloomy cell as he peered through the small window.

"Mariah Hallett!" he shouted. "Come and stand before me!" He banged his fist on the door. "Mariah Hallett!" He went to the second door and shouted again. "Mariah Hallett! You cannot hide from God's judgment! Come to this window at once!" He stepped back from the door. "Jailer! Jailer!"

Samson ran around the side of the building followed by Josiah. "What's the trouble, then, eh?"

"I have come to read to your prisoner," he said, holding out his small red book, "but she does not answer my call. Unlock the door and bring her before me."

"Why? Read at her through the window."

John Knowles narrowed his eyes, his anger rising. "Would you stand between this devil worshipper and her salvation?"

"She ain't no such a thing! I'd never take to standin' twixt Mariah an' anythin' that'd be good for her, but I'd stand 'tween her an' you if ever I gets the chance!"

"I do not see her. Open this door at once and show me that she is there." The two men stood face to face, glaring furiously at each other, then Josiah went to Mariah's cell door and pulled it open. "It is unlocked? You leave the witch's door unlocked?" Knowles went into the cell and came back, his face red. "She's gone, jailer! You fool. You have allowed her to escape!"

Josiah looked into the cell and stood with his arms crossed against his chest, deep in thought.

"You have done this, Barrett!" Knowles continued. "You have allowed Satan's daughter to once again move among the people of this community. She has bewitched you!"

"Now, how stupid can one man be. Walked to the ocean, is more'n likely." Joisah whistled for Samson who came trotting out of Mariah's cell. As they headed for the cliffs overlooking the sea, he could hear John Knowles raising the alarm.

3

Justice Joseph Doane's house was the biggest in the area. Not only did it accommodate his large family and two indentured servants, but the great room, to the right of the front door, served twice a week as

A small, noisy crowd had gathered outside. As he watched from his window, he marveled at how quickly news traveled in the spread-out community. Perhaps it was borne on the cross-breezes, the way the smells of the sea were. In any case, judging by the activity, word had gotten around.

He turned back to his desk, where there was a pile of books he'd gathered to help him sort through the muddle of facts and emotions surrounding Mariah's case. He'd read and reread them many times. The Bible, two books on English law, and two by Cotton Mather—one, *Wonders of the Invisible World,* he'd purchased after the terrible trials in Salem Village nearly twenty-five years before. The writers were so sure, so positive in their convictions, although their insightful points did little to clear the way for him. On the desk was the newspaper he'd received earlier that morning. He picked it up and turned back to the window.

"Good day, Joseph," Mr. Treat said, coming into the room. "I knocked—"

"No, no, it's fine, Samuel. I didn't hear you. Please." He gestured toward a chair. After another worried look at the crowd, he sat behind his desk. "How may I be of ser— You've come about Mariah Hallett, haven't you?"

"Yes. I went to see her this morning. But before we discuss that, what has, or is about to, happen?" He nodded at the growing number of people outside the house.

"She escaped from prison this morning," Justice Doane said, "and a search party has been out for these past two hours at least. When John Knowles raised the alarm, he said she had bewitched Josiah Barrett into leaving her cell door unlocked." He looked at the gathering again. "That lot has come out of fear and concern."

"That lot is hungry for the sensation Knowles is feeding them," Mr. Treat said. "When I saw Mariah this morning she was sitting in the sun. Josiah told me he'd left the cell door open so she might breathe the fresh air. An act of kindness, not witchcraft. And where could she have gone? To the ocean? Israel's boatyard?"

"The point is she's escaped. I've written the indictment and when she's apprehended she will answer these charges today. Josiah Barrett, too, for giving aid to a murderer."

"How can you hold Josiah guilty if you believe Mariah cast a spell over him?"

"I don't believe— Well, it's all the more reason to get this sorted out as quickly as possible."

"I agree. Mariah isn't a witch, Joseph, and neither did she murder her child. There's no evidence to support John's vengeful accusations. You know how he thinks."

"Yes, I know—all too well. But it seems to me," Doane said, looking with narrowed eyes at his friend, arms crossed against his chest, "that there was a time when you were not as sure about Mariah as you are today. I remember the doubts you had at her baptism"—he held up his hand as the minister started to interrupt—"and the time you took to speak to Matthew about your concerns. I also remember how troubled you were when she cured Josiah's dog. Those were heavy burdens for you, Samuel, and today they are not."

Mr. Treat's face was serious, and he leaned forward. "Yes, those were burdens, and I did not take them lightly. Facing evil, possibly the devil, is a critical undertaking with far-reaching consequences. Mariah isn't evil; she's very unusual, and perhaps gifted by God." He looked into Doane's stubborn face. "My friend, John Knowles will have people believe what he says because of his own needs and fears. There is no proof of the devil in Eastham, nor in Mariah."

Justice Doane picked up a pile of papers and waved them in front of the minister's face. "Oh, yes there is! In the three days since her arrest, many have come forward to testify that shortly after accepting Mariah's cures—potions and such—their animals have fallen ill and died. One woman swears that after an argument with Mary Hallett, which Mariah witnessed, her daughter fell violently ill. Many will also testify that her 'shape' has appeared before them in the night."

"In other words, a convenient memory for squabbles and misadventures has now become useful to Knowles' purpose, to say nothing of admitting dreams and fancies as evidence!"

"It's here! All here!" Doane threw the papers back on his desk and turned away, frustration in every line of his body.

"No one cried 'witch' at the time, did they?" Treat asked. "Now, though, everyone speaks of witchcraft. Wild stories and opinions are running unchecked through the village." The minister paused and looked at his friend. "For heaven's sake, man! Many folks come to Mariah for her cures. How has Knowles prompted the good people of Eastham into remembering these events his way?"

"They are prompted by their own values of right and wrong. Of good and evil."

Mr. Treat got up and, walking to the window, looked out at the villagers arguing and waiting. "Can't you see what's happening here? John relishes the memories of the witch trials as if he'd been there. This crusade of his has less to do with God and the devil than it does with his own glory and importance. Mariah is his victim."

"His victim? The only victim here is that dead child, and his death must be explained and the person responsible brought to justice."

"Joseph, many children die in their first year. Hardly a family exists that has not suffered this loss. Childbirth is a most dangerous time for the babe and its mother. You know this is true!"

"Then you believe Mariah to be innocent of these crimes?"

"Of witchcraft and murder, yes, I do. She has borne a child out of wedlock, but surely this charge can be dropped since the child is dead."

"Murdered!"

"No!"

"Mr. Treat! I ask why you cannot accept the possibility of her guilt?"

"Mr. Doane, I ask you! Why do you believe her guilty? What possible motive could Mariah have to kill her own baby?"

"Oh, motives a-plenty, I assure you."

"But—"

"Revenge!"

"Revenge?" A small chuckle teased the corner of Reverend Treat's mouth at the absurdity of this idea. "Why that's pure lunacy! Against whom?"

"Apparently," Justice Doane said stiffly, "you are the only man in Eastham who does not know of this." He handed Mr. Treat the newspaper he'd gotten that morning, and the minister sat back in his chair to read.

> "*The Newsletter* – Boston, April 14, 1716. It has recently come to the attention of this writer that Captain Samuel Bellamy, originating in Plymouth, England, and late of Eastham, Cape Cod, has been known to be sailing in consort with the infamous buccaneer, Captain Benjamin Hornigold.
>
> "Mr. Hiram Turnbolt, of this town, who brought us this terrible news, is one of the unhappy persons upon whom a villainous act of piracy has been committed. Formerly a member of an innocent and defenseless crew aboard a merchant vessel that had been brutally ravaged by criminals of the most odious and detestable kind, Mr. Turnbolt, a joiner of some skill, was forced by Captain Bellamy to sail with his crew. It was only after serving seven weeks in this terror-filled capacity that Mr. Turnbolt did effect his escape and return to tell his story.

"'Black Bellamy', as this pirate captain is called, owing to his dark and vile deeds, commands a ship with more than eighty in the crew. Serving as his second in command is Mr. Palgrave Williams, a gentleman, to judge by his speech, Mr. Turnbolt says, from Newport, Rhode Island, and late of Eastham. There are others, among this wicked crew, who also come from Cape Cod.

"Mr. Turnbolt recounts the following events in the hope that such a recitation will be most beneficial and useful to the public; that any person or persons so inclined to turn to a life of wickedness by raising a sword against the weak may learn they do so without concealment from our vengeful all-seeing, all-knowing God; and that upon capture shall pay the ultimate price as expressed by the laws of our sovereign, King George I."

Samuel Treat stopped reading and looked up at Justice Doane's triumphant smile. "This is…most regrettable and unfortunate, to say the least, but aside from Bellamy fathering Mariah's child, I fail to see—"

"Is it not obvious?" Doane asked, jabbing the article with his finger as he took back the newspaper. "He is a pirate! A criminal of the worst kind, he leaves her with child, penniless and disgraced. He refuses to give her gold to compensate for her unfortunate condition, and she extracts the only justice she can. She kills his child."

"Ridiculous! Who would believe that?"

"It's what everyone believes. Look!" The magistrate gestured at the window.

"Bellamy may have been many things while he lived among us," Treat said, "an adventurer, a dreamer, possibly a liar, and most certainly involved in the smuggling on Great Island— Oh, don't say it.

They're all involved out there. I'm even willing to believe he truly loved Mariah. But he was no pirate, and no one can say that he was, including you." Treat held up his hands to stop Doane's protest. "Be reasonable, Joseph. Bellamy's crimes have nothing to do with Mariah's case. You cannot twist these facts because you need a conviction. You begin to sound like Knowles."

They were quiet for a moment, the only sounds coming from the agitated people outside.

Then Doane slammed both hands on his desk and looked intensely at Treat. "This must be dealt with! She's broken our laws and faces two charges; either of which, if proved, carry death sentences. What am I to do, Samuel? She says nothing—nothing in her own defense. There are no witnesses, other than Knowles, who got there after the child was already dead. Did she speak to you? Has she said anything at all?"

"No, no, she hasn't. But I'm convinced she did not murder that baby."

"Yet the public's need for justice must be satisfied. I must find a way to pronounce a verdict that is not extreme." He paused.

"Will you charge her with witchcraft?" Treat asked softly.

Doane exhaled slowly and closed his eyes. "No." He looked at his friend. "No. If I do, Knowles will see to it that Salem's horror becomes ours. He must be stopped before this gets further out of hand. Mariah Hallett is no witch."

"Praise be to God! 'Blessed are the merciful,'" quoted Treat, "'for they shall obtain mercy.' It should be written on the walls of every court in the kingdom."

Shouting from the crowd outside suddenly interrupted them. The two men went to the window, and when Doane opened it, they heard a woman speaking loudly.

"T'ain't no other reason for that cow t' go dry like she did, her bein' as good a milker as any! T'was a curse sure as not! I say for all t' hear: The Hallett girl's a witch!"

"Take more'n one dry cow for me t' believe that," a man replied, looking around at the few who nodded agreement.

"Oh, there's lots more if you think on it," the woman said, trying to continue, but some shouted her down. "Don't tell me t' be quiet!" she yelled back. "You listen t' me! You'll see! Nearly everythin' she done since that business o' the dog four years back could well be looked at two ways!"

"Well, then," someone objected, "look at it so she's innocent."

Several voices shouted at once. "Innocent!" "How can she be innocent? She's a pirate's whore!" "Pirate's whore, an' worse!" "Who's to say that dead baby ain't the devil's spawn?"

Someone screamed, and what had started as a shouting match turned into a brawl. Mr. Treat ran into the mob to join the few trying to stop the fight. "You must end this!" he yelled as he helped pull two formerly friendly neighbors apart. "Fighting solves nothing!"

As he moved among them, his parishioners grew suddenly quiet. Then a voice called out, "Murderer! Murderer!"

The crowd parted, and Treat looked down the road. John Knowles appeared, riding his slowly walking horse, sitting tall and straight like a victorious general returning from battle. In one gloved hand he held the end of a rope. At the other end was Mariah, stumbling along, the rope tied to her iron shackles.

"Oh, dear God!" Treat whispered. Then he shouted, "No! No!" and ran to her. Knowles continued to the front door of the Doane house and dismounted. He pulled the rope, hand over hand, bringing Mariah closer to him. Mr. Treat had his arms around her, shielding her from the shouts and taunts.

"Murderer!" "Whore!" "Where's his gold, witch?"

"This is madness!" Treat said, when he and Knowles were face to face. "Look at what you've done, man! You've divided our village and destroyed this child with your fanatical ideas! How can you say this is God's work?"

With a self-satisfied look on his face, John Knowles took off his gloves. "Take her inside," he said to the constable. Turning to the minister, he sighed, revealing more condescension than patience with his exaggerated tone. "Many times have I tried to explain this to you, but you've refused to see the truth. I am chosen by God to seek out Satan and cleanse our community of his evil imprint. My life's work is at last bearing fruit. Mariah Hallet is the devil's handmaiden, and when she—"

"You're the one what knows the devil!" Josiah shouted, leaping on Knowles from behind. "You leave her be! She ain't done nothin' t' you, mad-brained rotter! You—"

"Josiah! Josiah! No!" As Samuel Treat yelled, Will Brown, who had come from the tavern to see Mariah, pushed his way through the watching crowd and pulled his friend off the angry Knowles. "Stop! Stop, I say! This will not do!" Treat yelled again as Josiah struggled in Will's big hands.

Knowles picked up his hat and brushed it off. "You see the truth," he said, straightening his coat. "The witch-girl does the devil's bidding and casts her spells even in the face of God's holy work. You have not heard the last of this." With a steely glance at Josiah, he turned and went into the courtroom.

The people who had watched in breathless silence outside rushed in after him, jostling and pushing for the best place to stand. Justice Doane gave three sharp bangs of the gavel, insisting on quiet, and the hearing began.

Still outside, Mr. Treat raked his hand through his sweaty hair and glared angrily at Josiah. "What in God's name were you thinking? We all want to help Mariah, but that isn't the way!"

"Parson's right," Will said. "Best to keep a cool head."

"What happened at the jail, Josiah, when Knowles came by?" Mr. Treat asked. "Everything was quiet while I was there."

"And so it were, all mornin'. Me an' Samson, we went out after a rabbit or two, an' when we come back, he"—Josiah jerked his head toward the courtroom—"were shoutin' an' hollerin' that he'd come to read out o' this little red book he were wavin' about, an' she'd escaped—by puttin' a spell on me. Stupidest damned thing I heard in a long time, an' I told him so! So we headed out t' the cliffs, Samson an' me, 'cause I know she's like t' sit there an' watch for Sam. Then, Knowles comes back here. Doane swears him in, an' they gets up a search party that goes off in all directions. When I gets back with Mariah, the constable puts the irons on her, an'—" He coughed, covering up a sob. "You seen her, Parson. She's wastin'. She ain't had nothin' but water for three days."

"Why was she tied up like that? Was it Knowles' doing?"

The old man nodded, tears in his eyes. "Aye, he done it, all right. He done it t' make sure she don't escape again. He done it t' be sure everybody knows he's bringin' in Satan's daughter an' that she's right at the end o' a rope where she ought t' be. Only next time, he says, it's another kind o' rope an' she'll be danglin', not walkin'. I tried t' stop him. I tried! But they was too many…too many. He's out o' his head, Parson!"

The gavel sounded again. "We'd better go inside. Thank you, Josiah, you're a good friend to Mariah. You'll help her most by not shouting and not taking on Knowles any more. Do you understand?" Josiah nodded stubbornly and shook off Will's hand. Together, they went into the house.

The magistrate was reading the charges against Maria as Reverend Treat elbowed his way to the front of the room. "Whereby it is ordained that Mariah Hallett, to the high displeasure of Almighty God and in open contempt and defiance of His Majesty's good and wholesome laws, did conceive and bring forth a male child outside the bonds of holy matrimony, and did on the eleventh day of this child's life willfully and wickedly cause his death, shall stand before this court and be found guilty of fornication and murder by her own confession, or by her refusal to plead, or by the oath of witnesses taken on this day of our Lord, 28 April 1716." He looked directly at Mariah. "How speak you to these charges?"

Silently, the spectators craned their necks for a better look. Mariah's heavy chains bound her thin wrists, and her hair and clothes carried the stench of her cell. She said nothing. Frightened, she stared hollow-eyed at the magistrate.

"You must speak, Mariah," Mr. Treat said, gently taking her arm.

"She ain't done nothin'!" Josiah yelled, shoving and pushing through the crowd. "She ain't no murderer an' she ain't no witch! It's all Knowles' lies! He's the one t' lock up!"

Loud noise and talk erupted from the spectators, who stood wedged tightly together in the courtroom. Mr. Doane banged his gavel hard. "Bailiff! Take him out of here. If anyone else disrupts this hearing, all spectators will be removed!"

The room grew quiet as John Knowles approached the magistrate's desk. "If I may speak, I will ask the court to consider that the charge of witchcraft has not yet been brought against Mariah Hallett. I have known this girl to use her powers to command animals to follow her ways, not God's. She does as she pleases outside her parent's control, for they have been bewitched into believing her wanderings to be innocent. She has consorted with a criminal and claims Satan as her master. She has denied God and is deaf to all prayers. Her hardened heart cannot receive holy blessing!"

The spectators, who had been straining to hear every word, now talked excitedly among themselves again.

"Order! Order! I will have order in this court!" Doane insisted. The crack of the gavel sounded above the noise of the crowd.

"These words are false!" Mr. Treat said firmly, after the commotion had died down. "These accusations are the inventions of John Knowles' imagination. They have never been true. This young woman," he said, still holding on to Mariah, "has unexplainable gifts, to be sure, but I believe her to be a child of God. And perhaps, as Josiah said four years ago, her gifts are heaven-sent. Many of us here in this room have benefited from her ability to bring a cure." A few people murmured in agreement.

Mr. Doane turned to the red-faced John Knowles and pointed at him with the gavel. "Be aware that should you bear false witness in this court and before God, you will face the penalties demanded by all laws!"

"God has provided the proof, and I have brought it to this court," Knowles insisted, and taking the papers from Doane's desk, shook them in Treat's face. "You have long refused to see the righteousness of this holy quest, but I have it here in the written testimony of witnesses and victims—good, God-fearing people—who have come today to deny Satan and present their evidence in court."

"These statements are fantasies, John, and you know it," Treat replied.

"This is evidence!" Knowles shouted. "We must put on the whole armor of God that we may be able to resist the wiles of the devil, which work through his daughter, standing here before us." He held the papers above his head for all to see. "Here is the truth!"

"As you know it!" an angry voice shouted from the back of the room. The spectators, fired up by Knowles' words, took both sides in the argument and heated discussions broke out.

Justice Doane had small hope that this would be the last disturbance of the day. He surveyed the spectators and sighed, allowing the noise to go on for a while.

John Knowles took a seat by the window. Mopping the sweat from his forehead, he coughed loudly while he studied his book.

Josiah returned to the courtroom to talk angrily with Will.

Reverent Treat, who had been holding Mariah's arm throughout the proceedings, guided her to a seat opposite Knowles. She looked up at him, and he saw the sick fear in her eyes.

"Will they hang me?"

She asked the question in a whisper so soft he had to lean in close to hear. He took her hands in his, and squatting beside her, made his promise. "No, they won't. I don't know what will happen, but you will not die," he assured her. "Mariah, you must deny these charges. Please speak. Your silence does not help you, that is most certain." But as he waited for her response, her eyes closed and she retreated again inside her own world.

The magistrate brought down his gavel, and Samuel Treat spoke up. "May I continue?" he asked. When Doane nodded, the minister addressed Knowles. "John, you must stop this witch-hunt. You see evil because you look for it. In your zeal to find devil worship and witches in our midst, you have forgotten how to look upon other human beings with understanding and compassion. We are all imperfect—with flaws, agonies, and pain. You must look into your heart to find the same mercy for others that God has for you."

"She is a witch!" Knowles shouted. He crossed the small room to face Mariah. "The Lord God Almighty says, 'Thou shalt not suffer a witch to live.' With these holy words, I battle the devil and the powers of darkness, for our souls are at stake. Woman! You must confess and repent to save your life and soul—now!"

His words struck Mariah like deadly blows, and she cowered from their sting. Doane banged the gavel on his desk with great force. Treat stood before her and faced her attacker.

"You sound, John, as though you hope the madness of Salem might repeat itself here—today."

"It will! It did! Four years ago! Here in our village, it began in this sinful woman!" He held up his book. He coughed and his voice broke. "I have here the words of the great theologian Dr. Cotton Mather. In his book, *Wonders of the Invisible World,* he documents those glorious trials in Salem. He knew witches! He was among them! 'Witchcraft,' he said, 'is a curse upon the conscience of New England.' It is through sinners like Mariah Hallett that the devil enters in. I know this! I know it! Look upon her! See the mark—the mark of Satan! See—"

The book fell to the floor with a small thud, and gasping for air, he clutched desperately at his throat. His eyes bulged and the veins in his temples pulsed. Sweating heavily, he staggered to a chair and dropped into it, pushing away all attempts to offer help.

No one said a word. Mr. Doane lifted his gavel to strike it, but instead put it down on his desk. The only sound was John Knowles' rapid, scratchy breathing.

Facing the magistrate, Mr. Treat said, "God's mercy takes many forms. Let it come to Mariah Hallett through our human laws."

Justice Doane looked around his courtroom, then rested his eyes on Mariah as she stood with Reverend Treat. He remembered the sunny, chattering little girl she had once been, and now he thoughtfully studied the frightened, distressed woman she had become. He made his decision.

"An offense against God is an offense against his people. Mariah Hallett, your immoral principles have dishonored God and have threatened the faithful. The effect of your sins has been destructive to the welfare of our community, driving us one from the other. Therefore, in the face of your refusal to defend yourself or to repent and confess to the charges brought against you, and for the sake of the citizens of Eastham, it is my judgment to banish you to Lucifer Land for the rest of your days, never again to be amongst God's children or to hear his Holy word."

Turning to the spectators, he said, "I instruct the people of Eastham thus: You must drive her from your hearts and minds, and it must be to you as if she had never been born. Dispense your charity to her parents, good people who have suffered doing God's work, and to her sister and her child, for they are innocents in this sinful brew. From this moment on, Mariah Hallett does not exist. She is an abomination in the presence of God's divine majesty, and we must leave her to Lucifer Land where she belongs."

✠ ✠ ✠

Mariah was released from Eastham jail that afternoon. Curious villagers watched as she went by, and there were shouts of "Witch!"

and "Pirate's whore!" from among the small crowd. Someone threw a rock that hit her in the back, and though she stumbled, she walked on. The constable who kept her under guard left her when they got to the edge of Lucifer Land—he would go no farther. She looked ahead at the hard, wind-beaten land and walked alone to the sea.

Lucifer Land

THE EAST WIND BLEW OVER THE SEA, UP THE BEACH TO THE SANDY cliffs on the backside of the Cape, and across Lucifer Land. No one could say this land was entirely barren, for weeds, sea-grasses, stunted trees, and shrubs were everywhere. It was said that the devil had once farmed there and his poisonous crops had ruined the soil so nothing useful would ever grow and flourish. Many years later a man built a cabin and tried to cultivate the land, but failed. Then one day he was gone, never to be seen again, leaving everything behind and smoke still rising from his chimney. Knowing the land to be cursed, locals took other routes to the beach to avoid crossing the area. Those who did enter Lucifer Land never did so without saying a prayer to save their immortal souls.

Mariah stood by the cabin near the edge of the cliff, watching seagulls wheeling against the silvery-grey clouds. Every once in a while the ocean breeze came up under them and they rode the wind, hanging still like blackened silhouettes. The salt air blew through her hair and clothes, and she inhaled it deeply.

The desolate little cabin was hardly more than a hovel. There wasn't much left from the days of the poor farmer, for the locals, saving their best prayers for entering Lucifer Land when it suited their needs, had taken what they wanted from the cabin long ago. A musty, ragged quilt still covered the old straw on the rough wooden bed, and overcome by physical and mental exhaustion, Mariah lay on it staring vacantly at the opposite wall. The constant sea breeze whistled as it blew through the chinks in the walls, but she didn't hear or feel it. Grief and fear had made her body numb, and her head throbbed so fiercely she could not think or rest. She closed her eyes and bit by bit her body relaxed until she felt weightless and drifted on the currents of sleep as the seagulls drifted on the currents of air.

When she awoke, sunlight streamed onto the bed through the half-open door and she blinked in the brightness. Propping herself up on an elbow, she looked around at the cabin's crude, dirty interior and its meager furnishings. The enormous task that lay ahead of her—simple day-to-day living—never entered her head, and instead she focused on the door. This door meant freedom.

The broad sweep of the moor that was Lucifer Land, the wide beach, and the sparkling ocean stretching to the blue horizon held her fascinated gaze as she turned slowly around, taking it all in. She walked the few dozen yards to the edge of the cliff and looked down at the beach. Here she could watch and wait for Sam. He would pass this spot on his way north to round the "hook" of Cape Cod. She sat in the sand and squinted at the shimmering sea. The tide was out, and in the distance she could see white water breaking on the shoals. Below, on the beach, a few seagulls ran in and out of the surf as it spread wide and sank into the wet sand. Apart from them, she was alone.

She had no idea what day it was, or how long ago anything had happened, and except for her vigil on the cliff, she had no interest in daily life. But her instinct for survival did force her to look for food and drink. She explored Lucifer Land and the woodland that grew farther back from the shore. Along the way, her practiced eye noticed the edible plants that grew wild and she nibbled some, sparking the first hunger pangs she'd known for some time. A small stream of fresh water trickled through the woods on its way to or from one of the many kettle ponds that dotted the area, and she knelt to drink thirstily from her cupped hands. She splashed the refreshing water on her face, and sitting back on her heels, looked around. It was an easy distance for a daily walk with the wooden bucket she'd noticed in a corner of the cabin. I'll need to make a basket, too, she thought. And vaguely surprised at having practical notions about daily life, she walked back to the cliff where she sat watching the sea.

Mariah didn't think of her family. The people she had known all her life and the traumatic events of the past days had melted together in a muddled blur and ceased to exist. But her memories of little Samuel were sharp, so she kept them buried deep in her heart and refused to bring them to light. She thought mostly of Sam. He was a pirate now, they'd told her. Well, good for him, she decided. I'm glad. It'd serve them right if he robs everyone in the village when he comes back for me.

The few mild days that had teased everyone with promises of warmer temperatures disappeared as quickly as they'd come. The weather turned cool and rainy—typical of the long Cape Cod spring that waits to explode into summer all of a sudden one day in late June. Mariah had neither her shawl nor her cloak to keep her warm, and she shivered on the moldy quilt at night with only her petticoat as a cover.

On one colorless day, she wrapped herself in the petticoat and walked to the cliff. The sun, hidden by a dove-gray sky, cast no shadows. The ocean was dark and looked very cold. While she watched the sea, the wind whipped the surface of the water into a herd of white horses, racing to the beach and breaking on the sand in an apron of frothy bubbles that crept toward the base of the cliff.

Mariah let her dark memories flood over her. Horrible scenes unfolded, and she studied them intently, remembering every detail: John Knowles' boots; her dead baby in his hands; Samuel, still and lifeless, lying uncovered on Justice Doane's desk; jeers and taunts of "witch", "murderer", and "pirate's whore"; and the dreadful specter of the gallows hovering over the courtroom. The black mist that had protected her for so many days and nights dissolved, leaving emotional wounds that were open, raw, and bleeding. She saw the brutal truth. John Knowles had been right. Mr. Treat had reassured her in his soothing pastor's voice that Samuel had died choking on bits of hay and hay dust. But he'd been wrong. She knew now it had been her fault.

"I killed him," she said softly. "I killed him, Sam. I killed your son." She stood on the cliff, looking out at the seagulls and the shoals. "Sam!" she yelled into the wind. "I killed our son! I killed him! It wasme! Me! I'm a murderer!" Pacing back and forth, her screaming became frenzied. She balled her hands into fists and punched at the air as she let out all the hurt and anger that had tied her in knots for so long. "I did it! I killed him! I killed him!" Her throat was sore by the time she collapsed on the ground and gave way to bitter crying, her strained body heaving with wrenching sobs.

✠ ✠ ✠

Mariah awoke later that afternoon lying on her side near the edge of the cliff. The salty east wind blew off the ocean and she felt clammy and sticky, but she stayed there, unwilling to move. She scooped up handfuls of sand, and funneled them through her fist like the sand in an hourglass. She had no time; she had endless time. Time was running out; time was piling up. There was no past; there would be no future. There was only now.

She rolled onto her front and buried her face in her folded arms. The sun had come out while she'd slept, but the honey-colored glow that washed over the ground couldn't warm it, and the damp chill penetrated through her clothes, leaving her stiff and achy. With an effort she got to her knees and struggled to stand. She wiped sand from her face and hands with the petticoat and turned away from the cliff, stumbling through the shrubs and weeds toward her new home.

A man stood near the cabin backlit by the setting sun, his figure dark and featureless. She stopped. Her heart pounded as she saw him raise his arm, and she backed away, crying out in fear. But he waved and called her name. A dog bounded around the corner of the small building and put its paws on her skirt, wagging its tail. She knelt down to hold Samson, and buried her face in his black fur.

"Come t' see you," Josiah said. Mariah, still kneeling with her arms around Samson, looked up at him. "Brung this." He opened his sack and handed her a loaf of dark brown bread that was still warm. "Other things, too. Put 'em inside." He disappeared into the cabin, followed by Samson.

She pressed the bread to her cheek, inhaling the delicious aroma of the simple gift. Its warmth, whether it came from an oven or an act of friendship, flowed through her, and she felt alive again.

"From Susannah," he said when she joined him inside. "Went t' the tavern with Will after you left the jail. She says anythin' you need, just ask. Will honed the knife afore I left. Good edge."

Mariah picked up the hunting knife. A cooking fork, a pewter plate and cup, and a spoon lay on a freshly cleaned quilt. Tears brimmed in her eyes as she looked at his weather-beaten face. "Josiah, I— Tell Susannah—"

"Don't say nothin', girl! You ain't et for more days'n I know o', so eat now." She tore off a chunk of bread, her stomach growling as she chewed slowly. "Good firebox an' chimney," he said, looking around. "Good kettle. Wonder why nobody took it."

She drank some of the milk he'd brought and wiped her mouth with her hand. "How long have I been here? Is it still April?"

"May. You left the tavern on a Tuesday, an' Knowles found you Thursday. I know it, for 'twas Doane's day t' do his judgin' an' he brung you straight t' court, Knowles did. You was in the jail 'til Monday, which is Doane's other day for judgin'. Then Knowles brung you t' court second time, an' after that fool hearin', you come out here. A week's come an' gone since then, an' it's Monday again."

"Three weeks since my baby—" She stopped. Josiah, uneasy with tears, peered warily at her out of the corner of his eye, but she asked him a question instead. "You don't mind comin' to Lucifer Land, then?"

Josiah chuckled. "Just superstition 'bout this land, ain't it? Remember my pa tellin' me 'bout the fool who come out here t' farm. Nothin' ever grows this close t' the sea, now, does it? If you believed everybody who sees Ol' Nick behind every corner, you'd never leave your house." He paused for a moment. "Not all in the village is hard as Knowles," he said kindly. "There's talk amongst the good folk."

Mariah would not meet his eyes, and looked down at the bread.

He cleared his throat. "Well, sun's droppin' down, best be movin' on." Then picking up his sack, he left the cabin, whistling for Samson, who came trotting from the edge of the cliff. Mariah followed Josiah outdoors and put her hand gently on his arm. "Thank you."

The old man looked down at Samson with sudden interest and coughed. "Aye." He coughed again. "Be back when I can," he said, and walked off into the late-afternoon sun with Samson hobbling along at his side.

2

Thankful had come as far as the western boundary of Lucifer Land and could go no farther. She was determined to go to Mariah's cabin, but her courage failed her and she walked slowly along the little stream, a worried frown on her face, trying to work through the problem of delivering the gifts she had brought for her friend. She put down the basket and looked anxiously across the hardscrabble land to the sea.

"Thankful."

She looked up at the sound of her name and saw Mariah standing a small distance away. They stared at each other for awhile, a strange awkwardness between them. Thankful took a step forward, but

Mariah didn't move. "I've been so scared," she said, "and worried. Father—he's ill and stays in bed. And mama—she prays all day long. People are yelling and fighting all the time. It's been so awful." She blushed with shame, conscious of the words tumbling out of her mouth. "My father, he—oh, Mariah!" She dropped to her knees, gasping sharply as she put folded hands to her mouth, tears running down her cheeks. "I'm so very sorry for what my father did! Please, please forgive me." Covering her face with her hands, she bent forward, her body shaking as she sobbed.

Mariah watched her for a moment, then put the bucket down and knelt before her friend. "Don't cry," she whispered, taking Thankful in her arms. "You didn't do anythin'. Don't cry."

Thankful, aware of Mariah's thin, bony frame and the stench of her filthy clothes and matted hair, murmured softly, "I'm sorry for Sam not coming back—and for little Samuel, too."

"I know you are. Thank you," Mariah answered. As she sat on the ground, she noticed what Thankful had carried with her. "That's my basket."

Thankful sniffled and wiped her eyes with her fingers, then sat with Mariah. "Yes, it was"—she hesitated—"in the hayloft. I've brought some things for you," she said, unpacking the basket. "Here are a few coals, in case you haven't been able to start a fire." She put a little tin box on the sandy ground, and Mariah held her hands near the friendly heat. "Here's a clean petticoat. It's old, but useable. Carrots, a few potatoes, a bit of bread, and some cornmeal—" She hesitated, then put several balls of yarn in Mariah's lap. "I wondered if you'd dye these for me. Your colors are always so beautiful, and I—well—"

Mariah picked up the yarn. Was it only two weeks ago she'd been sitting in the tavern knitting? "I don't see how—" she began doubtfully, then remembered the kettle Josiah had discovered amid the debris in the cabin. "I think I can. Yes, I can. Thank you for bringin' everything, an' especially for the—"

Thankful was holding her shawl. "After they took you to"—she paused, embarrassed—"away, I went up into the hayloft and collected your things. I found these, too." She held out the two tortoise shell combs.

Mariah took the shawl and ran her hands over the lustrous fabric. She'd worn it when she first met Sam, and when he'd first held her in his arms. It was the one in which she'd wrapped little Samuel when she cuddled him close. It had come back to her, making the circle complete.

"Josiah came the day before yesterday," she said, smiling as tears welled up in her eyes, "an' brought bread an' milk. Today you brought my great-grandmother's combs an' my shawl. I'm blessed to have you an' Josiah as friends. Thanks for rememberin' me."

3

Mariah gathered the materials to make rough tools, and started the project the next day. She stood by the fire outside her door watching Thankful's yarn roll and swirl in the boiling dye. While she worked, she considered her surroundings. The emotional release on the cliff, as well as the visits from Josiah and Thankful, helped awaken her from the terrifying, confusing nightmare that had held her captive for so long. Now, she faced the difficult task of living in the dilapidated cabin on this bleak and inhospitable land. She poked the fire. "It's too bad I'm not a witch after all. Magic would come in handy just about now."

Pulling the yarn out of the kettle with the broom handle, she studied the color. Then, when it was ready to dry, she hung the yarn on a clothes line she'd made by tying the ends of sea grass together and stretching it from a corner of the cabin to a nearby tree. It wouldn't support her own clothing, or stand up to a stiff breeze, but until she could get some rope, it would do. While the kettle boiled again, to make soup, she shook out the old quilt, laying it over nearby bushes to air. Then she replaced the old straw bedding with fresh pine boughs. She'd made the broom from a stout stick with sea grass and pine branches lashed to one end, and it did a credible job. She swept the cabin clean, and the small fire burning in the fireplace got rid of the damp, musty smell. The plants, roots, and wild herbs she collected for dyes and medicines hung from the rafters to dry. The ones she'd chosen for her soup rolled and swam in the simmering broth.

"Witch!" A fist-sized rock flew through the air and landed with a thud by her feet. Two young men walked toward her, laughing and passing a bottle between them. "They say the witch-girl's a whore. She look that way t' you?" They came closer. "Look at her!" the first man continued, "stirring her witch's brew! An' she's all alone!"

The second man drank from the bottle. Liquid ran down his chin and he wiped his mouth with the back of his hand. "Aye, Bellamy's wench! Ain't so pretty now, is she? Where's his gold, then, eh? We come all the way out here t' see you, witch, so you got t' give us what we come for! First we come for Bellamy's gold! Then we come for a piece o' you, whore—"

As Mariah backed away, a small current of air blew the smoke between her and the men, hiding them from view. In the few seconds that she heard them cough, rage and fear burst out of her. "Get away from me! Get away! Don't touch me!" she yelled, holding the broom like a weapon. The wind shifted again. "There's no gold here!" They came toward her, their drunken taunts more cruel and abusive. She touched the end of the broom to the fire, catching the sea grass and pine in the flames. It sputtered and crackled then blazed hot and bright. Sparks and smoke trailed behind as she swung it through the air. "You call me a witch! The devil will take you before you lay a hand on me!"

Sooty and disheveled, she wildly shrieked out her curses. "Get away from me, or I'll burn you with the fires of hell an' damnation!" Crouching low, jabbing and thrusting the smoldering broom, she moved forward. "Get off my land! It's my land—mine an' Lucifer's! Get away!"

Suddenly sober, the frightened men ran toward the woods, dropping their bottle as they went. Mariah picked it up and spilled the last of the alcohol on the fire under the kettle. The men paused to look back at the witch-girl from the safety of the edge of the woods, and watched in horror as the flames burst high and wild around her cauldron. She saw them, and touching her broom to the fire once more, took a few steps in their direction. They ran off, and this time, didn't bother to look back.

"No! No! No!" she screamed. "Stay away!" She took the broom and swung it, beating it, over and over, against the corner of the cabin. With each crack of the broom handle she shouted louder and louder. "Stay away! Leave me alone!" She flung the broom away from her, and it sailed high in the air and into the brush. Her throat was sore and her eyes stung from the smoke. Then, dizzy from the force of the blows, she staggered slowly toward the cliff.

The mild spring day had turned noticeably cooler, and gathering clouds darkened the sky. She sat in the sand looking down at the ocean, her anger spent. The Atlantic had been calm earlier that morning, almost like a pond, and now the east wind churned up swells and breakers, sending a fine, salty mist over the land. Shivering, she drew her knees up close, wrapping her arms around her legs.

Mariah had been numb during the days following Samuel's death and since coming to the cabin she'd barely noticed as one seemingly endless day melted into the next. The dream-like black veil that once shielded her from pain had finally been destroyed by hard, grim truths—and now it was gone for good.

Icy cold emptiness grew from the core of her soul as the reality of her banishment crushed her beneath the weight of the deepest sorrow. She could never go back. She'd been condemned to spend her life unloved, untouched, and unwanted; drifting alone in this desolate, evil place without laughter and warmth, from that horrible day forward, as if she'd never been born. She'd been sent to Lucifer Land to die.

4

Mariah's exile from Eastham made her more of a presence than she ever had been, even while living there. That night in the pub, the two young men who had tormented her told a hushed audience the story of their narrow escape from the witch-girl's fiery broomstick and flaming cauldron. People were still divided on the question of whether Mariah was a witch doing the devil's work. Some saw the story as confirmation of John Knowles' dire predictions and were glad to say they had known the truth all along. Others, equally sure it proved less than nothing, knew that had Mariah taken the burning broom to the men and set fire to their breeches, it would have been just what they deserved. Josiah didn't hear their story, having gone to Great Island for his usual visit, and the two young men, who were fisherman, were advised to be at sea before he got back.

Immediately following Mariah's release from jail, both her champion and accuser fell gravely ill. Samuel Treat heard the news of Josiah's visit to Lucifer Land from his sickbed, where he lay recovering from a strange paralysis that affected his speech and movement. It had come upon him once before in a milder form and passed quickly, returning him to good health. This time he lay stricken, and as the weeks of Mariah's banishment passed slowly by, full recovery seemed doubtful. The story of the attack had stung him, but he staunchly planned a visit of his own when he regained his strength.

John Knowles had also taken to his sick-bed, following Mariah's hearing, fighting fever and delirium. But he recovered in time to issue directives regarding the burial of her child and the hiring of an interim minister.

That both men had fallen ill so soon, and at the same time, gave rise to the speculation that Mariah had placed curses upon them. Stubborn contrariness, coupled with nonsensical points-of-view, fanned the flames of gossip leaving nothing unexamined and no opinion unspoken. It was all very unsettling, and even her most staunch supporters were chilled by the notion that no one was safe.

5

Mariah, however, grew to welcome her solitude. The wild stories about witchcraft and the curse of Lucifer Land kept the curious away, which was exactly what she wanted. She had no use for the people of Eastham. Making no distinction between those who had harmed her and those who had not, she turned her back on them all. Josiah and Thankful were her only friends and they continued to visit, generous with their help and love. She was glad for their company, but the only person she really wanted was Sam.

At night she walked to nearby farms in search of food. Root vegetables, flour, and some fruits preserved for the winter were often stored in outbuildings, where she helped herself, filling her basket. The luscious bloom of early summer was everywhere, and soon kitchen gardens and fields would provide her with fresh vegetables and grains. Occasionally, she took eggs, and if she was able to get to a grazing cow before the farmer arrived with his bucket and stool for first milking, she brought home fresh, creamy milk.

It was hard to think about winter during the bright days of summer, but she knew everything she put her hand to now would be needed to increase her chances of living through the cold months ahead. Neither the nighttime trips scavenging for food nor the plants she harvested from the land about her would yield enough for basic long-term survival. She needed a plan.

Late one night in mid-June, someone knocked on her door. She froze, holding her breath, unable to move. The familiar, friendly sound did not belong here. She stared at the door, and the knock came again. Inching forward, she strained to hear some reassuring sound.

"Mariah Hallett! Seen your light." She looked at the small stub of a candle she'd stolen from a farm. "I know you're in there. It's Sylvanus Harding. Mariah?" He knocked again.

"Why're you here? Who's with you?"

"No one. I'm alone. I need your help. It's about Emma. Please."

Mariah stood very still, her heart beating wildly. She cautiously opened the door.

Her parent's neighbor stood before her, bathed in the soft glow from his lantern. "She got the colic," he said, "real bad. Got my own mixture I been givin' her, but it don't work. My boy's with her walking her so she don't go down an' roll. Came along here 'cause you know what else to do. Please, Mariah."

Confusion and disbelief swirled in her mind. She thought: Why should I help any of these people? But looking into the farmer's worried face, she pictured Emma. The big, sweet-natured draft horse, an innocent and in pain, was life's blood to this man.

"I'll pay you," he pleaded.

"I don't need money."

"You must be wantin' for somethin', out here, with nothin'—"

"A hatchet."

Mr. Harding swallowed. "I—all right. A hatchet. Help me, please. I can't lose that horse—she's all I got."

Mariah stepped back, nodding at him, and he followed her inside. "This will work," she said, handing him some tree bark. "White willow."

"No. Tried it an' it don't work."

She collected some dried plants and a piece of root. "Take this. Cut the root in small pieces an' boil it 'til the water turns brown, an' add it to the white willow. When it's cool, she'll drink it."

"Thank you," he said. "I'll bring the hatchet tomorrow night." He stepped outside, then turned back. "You still weave? My wife wants to know."

Hope suddenly flooded through her. "No. Not now."

"I'll tell her. Thanks again." He tipped his hat and walked away into the darkness.

Mariah hadn't expected this. Sylvanus Harding needed help, and his fear of losing Emma had been stronger than his superstitions. It had been a test of his faith to venture into Lucifer Land alone at night and knock on the witch-girl's door. Would others come? Perhaps Josiah was right about the locals after all.

She collected her basket and headed out into the night. Walking through the moon-lit woods, her mind was busy with questions and plans. How could she get her loom? Would she be able to weave enough to barter for her needs? Sylvanus Harding—would he come back with the hatchet? She'd been about to go to his farm to steal eggs when the man himself knocked on her door. Considerin' this turn of events, she thought, I'll go somewhere else tonight.

6

How to get her loom was the problem that ran through her head for the next few days, and when she met Thankful at the brook she heard the bad news.

"After you, uh, left, your father took all of your things out of the house. Your loom, too."

"My loom?" Mariah's heart sank. "But mama weaves, why isn't she usin' it?"

"I don't know." Thankful looked sadly at her friend. "My mother says your parents never speak your name, and my father—my father sees this as just. I'm so sorry."

"It doesn't matter. Just tell me what happened to my loom."

"It's in an outbuilding. I think he plans to sell it."

Determined to have it, Mariah arranged to meet Josiah at her parent's farm very late one night, not long after her conversation with Thankful. Together they carried the heavy, cumbersome sections of the loom to where he had left a borrowed pony and cart.

"Does anyone know you're helpin' me?" Mariah asked. She took the pony by his bridle.

Josiah steadied the loom. "Not a one. What'll your papa say when he finds it gone, then, eh?"

"I don't care." She clicked to the pony. "Walk on."

Josiah came back the next day and helped put the loom together. They'd found all the pieces—all but the bench—and he promised to go back for that as soon as he could. It took up most of the floor space in the cabin, but it didn't matter. She would have to crawl under it or squeeze around it to get to the hearth, but it was a small price to pay for peace of mind. She took pleasure in weaving—sending the shuttles flying back and forth, sliding the yarns in place, and watching the colors and patterns of the fabric emerge. Was it possible that this could be her salvation, as well?

Josiah made sure this news got around. He told Mr. Treat, who was recovering, though not as quickly as anyone would have liked, and he stopped by the Harding place to make sure Sylvanus' wife knew Mariah was ready to work. When he returned from Great Island, he had a large sack filled with the yarn Mariah had spun during the winter she waited for Samuel to be born. Susannah had asked her to make whatever she could for trade at the tavern, or for market, sending along with the yarn two loaves of bread, some cheese, and all her love.

Sylvanus came by one night, delivering the hatchet as promised and reporting on Emma's recovery. He also brought her yarn with a request for six pairs of stockings and six pairs of mittens for his six children, in exchange for whatever was needed. She asked for a spade, knowing it to be a useful tool, and the next morning went out in search of some birch branches to make into knitting needles. She peeled off the bark, sharpened the ends to points, and got to work.

It wasn't long after she'd taken her loom that Josiah brought the bench.

"Was it hard to find?"

"No, your papa brought it t' the jail. Wondered about his comin' t' see you."

She stared at him open mouthed. "I got no use for my parents."

"That's a might hard."

"Hard?" She glared at him. "How can you say that to me? To me! After all that's happened! They never once come to see me when I was in—durin' that time! They never once saw Samuel! Thankful says they don't mention my name—as if I was never there! Why should I see them? Why?"

"'Cause it's healin', girl! 'Cause he's offerin' his hand t' you, an' you oughta take it. That's why." He looked at her angry face. "You're feelin' bad, an' you got a right." He started to leave and paused in the door. "Best t' think on it, I say."

"I don't need to think on it!" she shouted as he walked away. "I don't need anythin' from anyone! Why do you say this to me? I thought you were my friend! Go away, an' tell them to leave me alone!"

She'd never raised her voice to him before. Ashamed, she ran after him, taking his arm. "Wait! Josiah, don't go! I'm sorry—please, don't be hurt! I promise I'll think about it, I promise!" She looked up into his face, and, flinging her arms around his neck, kissed him lightly on the cheek. "You are my dearest friend. I would have died without you. I owe you so much."

He flushed deeply as heat pulsed through him. He longed to put his arms around her and gather her to him, to comfort her and stroke her hair, but instead he turned away. "Be back another time," he mumbled, and walked off toward home. She watched him until he was out of sight.

7

Mary Hallett stood in the outbuilding and stared at the place where the loom had been stored. She was sure Mariah had come one night—probably with Josiah—and taken it. The thought made her glad, but she worried as she looked toward the field where her husband worked. She nervously bit her lip, caught up in her own tangled thoughts.

She and Matthew rarely spoke now. They ran the farm together, but kept apart, each hiding behind private thoughts. The place in their lives that Mariah had once occupied was now filled with an icy cold that spread like a malignancy, freezing and killing everything that had once been alive. Lydia, their elder daughter, lived too far away to visit daily, and used that excuse not to come at all. Friends and neighbors were polite and sympathetic, but kept their distance. Mary needed to comfort, and be comforted by, her husband. They shared the land, the house, and the bed, but could not share their grief.

They ate another supper in almost total silence. He told her of the broken fence, and she said the turnips were doing well in the sandy soil on the south side of the house. She studied his face while he chewed slowly, as if each mouthful needed deliberate concentration. He had aged so in the last year. The lines etched in his face from a lifetime of working out-of-doors were deeper, and the corners of his mouth were pulled down with the weight of his worries. He never looked directly at her anymore, but she knew that the anger she'd once seen in his eyes had been replaced by pain.

"Matthew—" Supper was finished, and Mary looked up from her knitting. "Matthew, we've got to talk about Mariah." He was repairing a harness, and she saw him stiffen, but he kept at his work. "She's taken the loom. You must know that we have to talk about this. She's our daughter."

"Lydia is my only—"

"No!" She threw down her knitting and stood up, confronting him. "No! No she isn't your—our—only daughter. You always say that, an' I won't listen. No more." He put down his work, the old anger in his eyes returning. "Don't look at me like that, Matthew Hallett. I—I won't live like this any longer!" She drew a deep breath, sobs choking her words. "She's in trouble. We're in trouble. Everythin'"—she looked around desperately—"everythin' between us is broken an' cold. For God's sake! For Mariah! For us! Talk with me, please!"

He walked away from her without a word. Alone in the bed, in the dark, he listened to his wife's snuffles as she moved through the house closing up for the night. He'd gone to see Reverend Treat a few days before to ask about his recovery and had gotten an earful about forgiveness for his trouble. He liked the pastor, so he listened politely, shifting from foot to foot, but the message had been too difficult to hear. "You must find it in your heart to forgive, Matthew," the minister had said from his sick bed. "Even the Lord, as he hung dying on the cross, found the strength to forgive his tormentors. So must you find this strength in yourself, for without forgiveness, you will never be free."

Free? Free to do what? he wondered, remembering their talk. There was nothing to do, no place to go—the future was bleak and barren. Who was he supposed to forgive? Mariah, Sam, John Knowles, Joseph Doane, the people of Eastham, the devil, God—it was too much to sort out.

He closed his eyes and listened to his wildly beating heart. As he lay there, the answer rushed in, and he knew the truth. I did it. I threw her out. I threw her to the wolves, let her go through all that—that horror, alone. I never fought for her, never stood by her—my own dear child, my own girl. He heard Mr. Treat's words again and understood at last that the person he needed to forgive was himself.

Shame brought tears to his eyes. No, I can't—it's too hard. I'm guilty. I did this to her.

His wife came into the room, and he smelled the melting tallow of her candle as she passed by. She settled in bed, and they lay back to back as they had been doing for so long.

"Mary—"

A few moments later, she answered. "Yes?"

"Help me." They turned toward each other, and she held him as he cried softly in her arms.

8

All summer Mariah traded and swapped her skills for food, clothing, or some useful tool, always keeping in mind that a long, cold winter was only months ahead. She filled the chinks in the walls and roof with a mixture of mud, grasses, and roots, and carried baskets of seaweed from the beach to pack against the base of the outer walls to help eliminate drafts. She made a woodpile on the lee side of the cabin and added to her supply of plants and grains. Although her stockpile of provisions grew every day, she worried that whatever she did, it wouldn't be enough.

The warm, sultry days of August finally passed. The clear skies, cooler nights, and low humidity of September were a welcome sign of the glorious Cape Cod autumn yet to come. Lucifer Land glowed with a beauty of its own, and the sea sparkled like diamonds floating on the deep blue of the reflected sky.

Mariah kept her daily vigil on the cliff, watching and waiting for Sam. He'd been gone just over a year now, and she longed for his warm smile, his love, and his voice—especially his voice. When she closed her eyes, she could see his face and feel his touch, but she couldn't hear him say her name, and she wanted that most of all because it was the hardest to remember.

She ran her fingers over Sam's sea shell, and wondered where he was. The only news of him was the newspaper article Mr. Treat had told her about—and there'd been nothing since then. It was so hard, not knowing. Josiah had told her stories of pirates, and what happened to them when they were caught. It was horribly possible that Sam had been— No. Somehow, some way, Sam would be back. He'd asked her to wait, and she would, no matter how long it took. And after he came back for her, she would leave with him and go wherever his ship took them, far away from the cursed land and the people who put her there.

On a warm day in early October, Thankful brought Mariah an

injured barn cat. "I don't know what happened— I think she's been in a fight. Father would have drowned her, had he found her first. Can you help her? She's a sweet puss."

Mariah stroked the ginger cat's head and examined the wound. "It's a bite of some kind, an' it's festerin' real bad. Yes, I can help her, poor little thing."

"I saw your mama at market last Friday. Susannah Brown had some of the things you made for sale, and I saw her touching them. She's so sad. Can't you—"

"No." Mariah gently placed the cat in her basket. "I promised Josiah I'd think on it," she added, seeing Thankful's disappointed face. "I promise you, too."

"Mr. Treat is quite poorly. His new assistant is taking more and more of the services. He's so thin, and he can hardly walk. I saw him once at church, and he whispered that he's wanted to see you for a long time, but he's not able to get around. Do you— Would you say something I can tell him?"

Mariah held the basket against her chest. "Tell him I said thank you." She paused. "Thank you, too." She nodded at the cat. "I'll take care of her."

The little cat grew stronger as the days passed and was soon eating and moving slowly around the cabin. Mariah stroked and cuddled her new friend, grateful to share her life with such a good companion.

Then, early one morning, she discovered a sick nanny goat outside her door. There was no message, nothing to say who'd left her, but she took the animal in, and in time both patients were strong and healthy. The two creatures formed a special bond during their recovery, and she noticed that where one went, the other always followed. They snuggled together for sleep, and when she put down a bit of fish for the cat, the goat would stand alongside, nibbling at a nearby bush. "For whither thou goeth, I shall go; and where thou lodgest, I shall lodge," she quoted, smiling at them. She called the cat Ruth and the goat Naomi.

While the weather was still mild, Mariah kept the outdoor fire going and her kettle bubbling day after day. The villagers, who were determined to keep an eye on her, watched from the safety of the woods as she stirred her witch's brew, and noted the company of her familiars—a cat and a goat. The words of those who knew the kettle held a meal, a potion, or dye, and that the animals were merely pets, did nothing to stop those who wanted to believe Mariah was a witch who hoarded secret gold. After all, they argued, how else could she be managing if she weren't casting spells?

But Mariah didn't care what anyone thought. She walked along the cliff every day and watched for Sam. The truth about his piracy never once caused her to doubt their love. She knew he would be back. All she had to do was wait.

Winter

THE FIRST FROST CAME EARLY. IT WAS STILL OCTOBER WHEN THE AIR turned suddenly cold, and at night freezing mist settled all around leaving ice crystals in the morning. Several mild days followed, but Mariah, having grown up knowing a comfortable winter depended on a successful summer, took the icy warning seriously.

Wandering through Lucifer Land and the woods, hatchet in hand, Mariah looked for anything that might burn. She scoured the beach, hoping to find debris washed up at high tide. Tidal pools yielded seaweed and some shellfish, and on one trek she found a dead seagull, which she took home and roasted. There were fish drying on the rack she'd built on the west side of the cabin where they could get the most sun, and dried fish were stored in a rough wooden box with a lid to keep out animals.

More than once she considered going back to the tavern. Susannah and Will, caring nothing at all for the court-ordered banishment, had often sent word with Josiah that she must "Pack up an' come home. Cat an' goat, too." There was good sense in going to Great Island, where she'd be welcomed and cared for, and Mariah knew it. But despite the warmth, security, and happiness she'd known last year waiting to birth Samuel, spending another winter in the tavern would bring back the ache of missing her baby. She would stay where she was.

It was on one of those mild autumn days that Mariah came out of the woods with her water-filled bucket, and stopped at the edge of the moor to look at the scene before her. Lucifer Land was alive with the blazing reds, rich oranges, and golden yellows of fall that dazzled against the blue backdrop of sky and sea. The effect was so intense she blinked and shielded her eyes. The air seemed to vibrate with the shimmering hues, and she inhaled great gulps of it as if there was nourishment in every breath.

Mariah took her time walking along the well-worn path to her cabin. "How *can* this place be Lucifer's land?" she asked, admiring the wide range of vivid colors in the shrubbery and bushes as she passed by. "If ever God showed his hand, it's here."

The happy thought kept her occupied until she got to the cabin. Just beside the door was a large basket covered with neatly folded dark wool. Ruth, curled in a tight furry ball, had made a bed of the fabric and was asleep in the sun.

Someone had come while Mariah was at the brook. She'd seen no one on her walk, and she saw no one now. At the edge of the cliff she looked out to sea and along the great, wide beach below her. It's emptiness stretched far in both directions. Returning to the cabin she pulled the basket indoors, grateful for whatever was packed inside.

The basket was the one in which she'd kept yarn when she lived in her father's house, and the dark wool that hid the contents was the cloak that had been left behind at the tavern. Beneath the cloak were two pairs of wool stockings, candles, mittens, potatoes, turnips, apples, a small jug of cider, and several hanks of yarn. At the bottom was the quilt from her bed at home. Puzzled, she sat on the bench and looked thoughtfully at the collection of things laid out on her bed. Someone had done this good deed, but who could it have been? Josiah, never secretive about his visits, always came in to sit for awhile. Thankful, who was afraid to enter Lucifer Land, would never come to the cabin. Remembering what Josiah had said, she thought of her father. Had he done this? Or had Will come all the way from Great Island? Her benefactor had left neither clue nor note.

2

The winter of 1717 was the worst in memory, and its arrival took everyone by surprise. The temperature dropped rapidly. Snow started falling in late November from dull, overcast skies the color of pewter. When the clouds parted, the sun did not shine strong enough to dry the sand, warm the earth and air, or melt the snow. The long stretches of arctic cold and the great snowstorms that tormented the mainland colony did not usually come to the outer Cape. But when snow came that year, it fell steadily across the narrow land, blowing, drifting, and banking against anything that got in its way. It blew into deep, dunelike drifts on farmlands, marshes, meadows, and in woodlands, as well. Roads and tracks became impassable, and for weeks no one went anywhere.

Winter wind blew off the ocean, banging hard against Mariah's little cabin. She felt the walls and chimney vibrate, and the frigid air crept in through chinks gone unplugged. The same sharp wind that blasted sand against the north and east walls also blew some of the light, powdery snow from Lucifer Land, exposing shrubs and grasses.

She lived closer to the land than she ever had before, and without a community of family and neighbors to rely on in hard times, she was never more at its mercy. A heightened awareness of nature's changes caused her to sleep lightly. She heard the sudden silence when the wind dropped, or she would wake up when the fire died down enough to let icy cold fill the room. She sensed the rhythms, sounds, and smells of the sea and learned its currents, patterns, and colors. This purple-black, wintry ocean that rolled, swelled, and crashed on grayish sand that never dried was her only physical connection to Sam. She didn't know where he was, but she knew the ocean he saw was a different color. The sea was important to Sam, and she felt a unity with him as the sea became important to her, as well.

The short winter days seemed longer and passed slower than ever before. When it started to snow, she had been weaving a blanket for a local farmwife, and now that it was finished, the fabric folded neatly on the bench, snow and time were all she had left. She had little room to pace—the small cabin was crowded with the loom, her bed, Naomi, Ruth, the woodpile, and her provisions—but she did, back and forth in front of the fire. She grew restless and stared at the empty loom trying to fight off the tedium that gripped her as tightly as the winter's cold.

She had once welcomed her solitude. Those who had come to barter for her skills kept her busy, and she had not minded the isolation. But now, in this remote, freezing place, loneliness bore into her and reached to depths of neediness she had never known before.

Wrapped in her shawl and a quilt, she lay on the bed thinking of Susannah and the winter she'd lived at the tavern waiting for Samuel to be born. Staring at her empty loom and the folded blanket, she remembered the whaler from Nantucket and the story he'd told that cold January night.

"You didn't hear it," she said to Naomi and Ruth. "A story about the lady an' her loom." She sat up, a spark of energy lighting her eyes. "It's an adventure about— Oh, I forget his name, but I remember his wife, Penelope, because she weaves—like me. An' she waits an' waits for her husband to come home, like I'm waitin' for Sam. She wove a shroud durin' the day an' unraveled it every night to fool some men." Mariah picked up the blanket. "What do you think?" she asked the animals. "I could do that, too. Only this isn't a shroud." She wound the yarn into a ball and eyed the door as it rattled and shook. "Though, if the weather gets any worse, it could be mine."

Mariah began weaving, unraveling, and reweaving the same yarn over and over again. She tried different patterns and worked out new techniques, trying to keep her mind occupied while her stomach ached from emptiness.

After the New Year, there was a break in the weather. At Christmas, a nor'easter had roared across the area, blasting sand and sleet against the little cabin. High seas had crashed on the beach below the cliffs, sending icy spray high in the air. The storm had raged all through the day and night, but in the morning the sun came out. When the wind finally stopped the air was much milder, and Mariah ventured outside to survey the damage. On the second nice day, Josiah, on snowshoes, took the long three-mile hike out to her cabin.

"Josiah! You're here! You're here! It's so good to see you! Was it hard to get through? Come in, please come in!"

His large frame seemed to fill all the vacant space in the cabin, but he squeezed by the loom and sat on the bench near the fire. "Be lyin' if I said t'were easy. Barometer's up, so thought I'd come out here afore it snows again—an' it will." He bent down to his pack. "Brought you some things." Barks and bleats came from the corner as Samson drank from the water bucket and settled by the fire with Naomi and Ruth. Josiah warmed his hands on the mug of hot steeping herbs Mariah gave him. He watched her sort through the parcel to find bread, cheese, two frozen rabbits, and twenty-odd candle stumps.

"You always bring me so much. How do I thank you? I never know what to say."

"Somethin' I can share."

"But so many candles! How can you spare them all?"

"Some from the tavern, an' some from the jail. Got more'n I need 'cause now I got a oil lamp. Thought you'd be wantin' for them, so I brung 'em along. Good weather for keepin' things outdoors," he added, nodding at the rabbits. He blew on the steaming mug. "You havin' some?"

"I only got one cup."

He flushed pink. "Oh. Well. Thank you." They sat in silence for a while. "There's news."

"Yes—of the good, righteous folk of Eastham." Mariah picked up her knitting needles; part of the unraveled blanket was now becoming a sweater, and she was finishing a sleeve.

"Please tell me."

Josiah gave a low chuckle. "Well, the weather keeps most indoors, but them as thinks you a witch've been busy. They say you brung this hard winter, vengeful-like, playin' dice with Old Nick. Winnin' the game, too."

Mariah snickered. "An' do they say Old Nick is favorin' me in exchange for my soul?"

"They say you barter with him. Signed your name in blood, too." His eyes twinkled. "Then, there's Sam's gold."

"If I had Sam's gold, I'd have Sam himself, an' I wouldn't be here. Those pious judges haven't got one brain among them—or heart, neither."

"Jail's empty—too cold t' bother doin' mischief. Three dead in the village—one, the parson. Can't bury 'em; the ground's frozen solid. Have t' wait 'til spring thaw."

Mariah looked up from her knitting. "I'm sorry about Mr. Treat. He was very good to me." Then she gave a small scornful laugh. "They should have Mr. Knowles talk hellfire an' brimstone at the ground in the buryin' acre. All that heat would melt any ice, an' they could plant the parson an' the others right then an' there."

The old man glanced at her from under his bushy eyebrows and smiled. "A might peevish today, eh?"

"Peevish is the least of it. Why should I care about these people?" Resentful, she got up, and, standing by the fire, kicked at the stone hearth. "Where'd they bury my son?" When he hesitated, she turned to him. "Where?"

"Down by the buryin' acre," he said, "under the apple tree, outside the fence. I marked the place with some stones, so you'd know."

"Outside the fence? Why'd Mr. Treat do that? Susannah said the right words over him right after he was born."

"He didn't. Had no say. Took t' his bed right after you left the jail—couldn't move nor talk. 'Twere Knowles behind it, sermonizin' like he does, an' from his sickbed, too. Oh, there was a fierce row 'bout it, some folks sayin' as how Samuel ain't been baptized proper, an' can't be lyin' amongst the saved." He shook his head. "Moved right in an' had it done his way. When the parson begun t' come 'round, he was mighty angry, but the deed 'twere done."

Mariah stared into the fire. "John Knowles. John Knowles. I thought about him plenty, you can be sure. He's the one who should be lyin' dead, not Mr. Treat. He's the one who should be lyin' in an unblessed grave, not my baby."

Josiah stole a quick glance at her, uneasy that she might cry. But Mariah's eyes were dry—she had no more tears.

Josiah and Samson headed home just after noon. Looking up at the deep-blue sky, Mariah wondered if he was right about the weather. Probably is, she thought. She bundled up as best she could and set out for the burying acre, taking the spade along to dig through the snow that drifted across the mile-long trail.

It was mid-afternoon when she reached the spot between the cemetery fence and the apple tree. The snow wasn't very deep. She shoveled enough away until she could see the place where little Samuel lay alone in the dark, frozen earth. She knelt down and ran her mittened hand over the ground, remembering how he kicked and squirmed inside her and how he fought his way out into the world. She remembered his soft sweetness as he snuggled against her, wrapped in her shawl. "Ooh, oh, my baby," she crooned, "your papa's gone a-sailin'. When he comes back I'll bring him to see this place, an' I'll tell him all about you."

Stray snowflakes began to fall. The sunlight had become thin and watery, with gathering white clouds moving in, taking over the sky. She touched the ground again. "I'll tell your papa all about you," she repeated softly, "an' what these saintly people have done."

The snow was falling steadily. It would be dark and even colder before she got back to Lucifer Land. There was snow in her shoes, and her hands and feet were numb with cold. She turned away from Samuel's grave, the cold inside her more brutal than anything nature could unleash, and started the long, difficult walk home.

3

The winter's rage never let up. Small pockets of sunshine passed too quickly to make much difference in the temperature, and the gray sky was as oppressive as the mounting snow that constantly fell from it. A second nor'easter careened onto the Cape, blowing the powdery snow in all directions, washing layers of it away with freezing rain leaving an icy coating on everything in its wake.

Mariah was out-of-doors nearly every day, scrounging for food and firewood. She slipped and slid down the old path to the beach and trudged along the high-water mark gathering whatever she could find, willing to eat almost anything. Her frozen hands could not grip the heavy driftwood she found, so she hacked away at it with the hatchet. Then, dragging it in pieces, she slowly climbed back up the path and crossed the land to the cabin.

She rationed her food carefully, sharing the little there was with Naomi and Ruth. But her hunger pangs grew, and thoughts of eating made it impossible to think about anything else. On a dark morning in February, she walked to the woods and set out snares. As she trudged through the ankle-deep snow she spoke aloud and the words came from her mouth surrounded by a bluish vapor that disappeared in the frigid air taking the sounds with it. "I got to eat. I got to eat. I got to eat—"

An angry voice inside her head interrupted and began to argue. *You must stop this, Mariah.* "I got to eat." *You must stop this, Mariah.* "But I'm hungry!" *You must stop—* "No!" she shouted. "No! I'm not doin' wrong. I'm not guilty." *You're stealin' meat from our neighbor's stewpot.* "Whose stewpot?" she asked. "Not mine." *Stop this, Mariah. Who taught you how to do these things? Who? Tell me!* "I don't know! It just happens!" She crouched down to put bait in a snare. *The devil's daughter sets snares.* "No!" *The pirate's whore steals from stewpots.* "No! Go away! It's the other person who sets the snares—not me. Not me. I'm the hungry one. Not me."

The argumentative voice in her head was quiet, and as she finished setting the fourth snare, she stood to look over her work. The spade and hunting knife were in the snow, where she'd been kneeling, and she picked them up. "Not me," she said softly. "Not me."

✠ ✠ ✠

When Mariah got home, she put more wood on the fire and set her shoes and wool stockings on the hearth to dry. She spread her cloak over the loom, partly to dry it, but also because it formed a barrier that helped to keep the heat contained in a smaller part of the single-room cabin.

Naomi and Ruth crowded around and she parceled out a meal. Josiah had taught her how to make the dense, dry ship's biscuits, meant to last long months at sea, and when she'd made them during the summer, there had been plenty. Now, with nearly everything else gone, she ate only one each day, soaked in the thin seaweed broth.

Her rough, cracked, bleeding hands hurt too much to do the intricate work of weaving or knitting, and her tools were silent and still. She climbed into bed wearing all her clothes and burrowed under both quilts, with her shawl wrapped around her feet and her head on the rewoven blanket. To take her thoughts off her empty stomach, she tried to remember the verses she'd stitched in her first sampler. But it was too cold to think; the words would not come, and her mind stayed blank. She lay very still. In the silence she counted her heartbeats. There was an overwhelming sense of marking time—of waiting, counting, expecting, beat after beat, hour after hour, like a spring being coiled tighter and tighter—counting, anticipating, waiting.

On the third day she could bear it no longer, and went out to the woods to check the snares. Her feet and hands hurt as she walked through the snow, and the pain constricted her throat. A weasel had been caught in one of the snares, driven by its hunger to the bits of dried fish she'd left as bait. Desperate to get free, it had struggled and gnawed at the foot caught in the rope, spattering the pure white snow with its blood. It had died, freezing to death in the same weather that forced her to trap it.

"No! Oh, my God, no!" She knelt down by the little creature and ran her hands over its sleek wintry-white coat. "Oh, dear God, I'm sorry! I'm so sorry!" She picked it up, and holding it to her, rocked back and forth in the snow, tears freezing on her cheeks and eyelashes. "God forgive me. God, please forgive me."

As she struggled to her feet, snow began to fall. Her cloak slipped down around her shoulders and dragged behind her as she walked through the woods removing the snares she'd set. Slowly, she went home, stumbling, dazed, and cradling the dead weasel in her arms. Sleet mixed into the wet, sloppy snow of late winter, and the bitter east wind blew hard, leaving an icy crust on her clothes, face, and hair.

Ruth nosed and pawed at the weasel as it lay thawing on the hearth, and when the time was right, Mariah dressed it for cooking. "It goes into the stewpot, like papa said," she whispered as the room began to tilt and spin around her, "so the neighbors don't go hungry." When it was cooked, she gave the cat its share, while the goat, which had developed a liking for dried seaweed, munched quietly in the corner. Her plate went untouched.

The thought of food turned her stomach, and the pain that wracked her hands and feet spread through her body. Every muscle ached as she put the last bit of wood on the fire. The blaze lit up the room and threw out heat, drawing Ruth and Naomi in close, but she couldn't get warm. Her whole body shook with a chill that didn't come from the winter, but started deep inside and worked its way out to her skin. She wrapped herself in the heavy cloak and the quilts, and lay curled up in bed, her teeth chattering so hard she couldn't speak. Pulling two sections of the newly woven blanket up to her chin, she could smell the lanolin in the wool. It's my shroud after all, she thought, and closed her eyes.

4

"Mariah?" Josiah knocked on the cabin door and listened to the meowing and bleating. "Mariah! You in there?" He rattled the handle and knocked again. "I'm comin' in. Mariah?" He pushed the door open and Naomi and Ruth rushed out. Squeezing past the loom he looked around in the dim light. The fire had gone out, leaving the room in stale coldness. The bench lay across the hearth, one end in the ashes and slightly charred. He set it near the loom and noticed the hatchet embedded in the heavy frame. He pulled it out, running gnarled fingers over the gash. "Now, what's she been at?"

Embers glowed in the ash. He found some kindling and started a fire, adding the wood he'd found outside. There was a plate with some sort of congealed meat on it and a big pile of tumbled bedclothes on the bed, but no sign of Mariah.

As the flames grew and lit the room, he noticed her shoes. "Somethin' ain't right," he mumbled. He went outside again, calling her name. Samson barked and hobbled past, barking again from the side of the cabin. Josiah followed and found him nosing an animal carcass. "Weasel skin," he said, examining it. "Must be what's on that plate. Now where'd she get to?" he asked, ruffling the big dog's black fur. "Where'd she go? An' barefoot, too. Somethin' bad's happenin'."

The fire had taken some of the deadly chill out of the room when Josiah went back in, Samson trotting at his heels. He cleaned up the mess the animals had made in the corner, and when he came in again, Ruth had snuggled into the bedclothes and was licking her paw. Samson, his head burrowed under the covers, whined.

"That's just ol' Ruth, boy. You leave her be." Then, for the first time he looked closely at the bed, and his heart stopped. Without breathing, he pulled back the covers.

5

A large black dog with a goat's head barked and bleated. It jumped into a snow bank, followed by a long parade of weasels that jumped in, too. In single file, they snaked their way across the snow, coming down the chimney and into the room, the last weasel stopping to light the fire. The blaze burned, making the room brighter than mid-day and heating it until it felt like summer. It was crowded with people, and the dog-goat barked and bleated until it and the weasels were put outside. One weasel stayed behind and, purring like a cat, snuggled close. Mariah could feel the heat from its little body and touched its soft fur with her fingertips.

A woman bent close to her, speaking softly and stroking her hair. She had rough, hard-worn hands, but her touch was a mother's caress. One man, old, grayed, and grizzled, stood close by, his watchful, worried eyes never moving from her. Another man, standing in the shadow, had no face. He was someone she should have known, and she struggled with this until she heard the old man whistle and call out a name. "Samson!" He whistled again. "Samson!" The dog-goat barked. There was a loud, scrabbling noise and the "weasel" meowed and jumped off the bed.

Mariah turned bleary-eyed to the faceless man and called out to her lover. "Sam! Sam!" She struggled in the covers, trying to go to him. "Sam!"

"No, no." The woman soothed her, and with strong hands gently pushed her down. "No, sweet child, that's not Sam—it's your papa. Don't! You must lie still! It's papa."

Breathing heavily, Mariah lay back. The dream was over; the nightmare finished. The pieces were back where they belonged. She knew the faceless man, and turned to the woman. "Mama—"

"It's all right now. Sleep, an' don't worry. You're so much better. Just sleep."

Later, Mariah sat in bed, a bowl of warm milk and bread in her lap, and fought back a giggle. They were all lined up, silently watching her every movement, noting every spoonful she brought to her mouth: Mama, Papa, Josiah, Samson, Naomi, even Ruth, curled up in her mother's lap—all so serious and still.

She coughed to cover the laugh and took another spoonful. "What happened? I don't remember anythin' after snarin' the weasel."

"Come t' see you a few days back," Josiah said. "Found you lyin' there. Thought you was dead at first, but saw you was sick, real bad. Brain fever, more'n likely, by the way you was talkin' wild 'bout weasels an' goats an' such-like. Went right off t' your mama, an' your papa brung us out here in the farm wagon. Good thing, too, as I don't think you would've lasted much longer." He grinned at her slyly. "Looks like you took a swing at your loom with that hatchet. For the fire. Tried t' burn your bench, too."

"I don't remember any of that," she whispered, looking at the loom with wide eyes.

"We wanted to bring you home, but you were too sick to move," her mother said. "Perhaps now—"

"I am home."

"There's no reason to say out here," her father said gruffly. "John Knowles an' the others— None of them can tell me what happens to my family. I—"

"Matthew." Mary Hallett reached up and touched her husband's arm. He found her hand and squeezed it before letting it go. Mariah watched this little exchange with the spoon halfway to her lips. This was new. "Thank you, but I'll stay here just the same," she said quietly, avoiding their eyes.

Mary came every other day for a while, either with Matthew or Josiah, and each day Mariah got a little stronger. As she rested and ate her mother's food, she gradually got back some of her youthful softness, losing the hollow-eyed, death-like appearance she'd had while sick with fever. Her cracked and bleeding hands had healed, but her feet had not. She lost the small toe on her right foot to frostbite. When she was able to, she took her first steps with aid of a walking stick.

"It's time to come home, Mariah," her father said one day in early March. "Gettin' ready to plant an' I can use your help come lambin' time."

"No, Papa."

"This… banishment… " the word was hard for him to say. "Nobody'll care if you come home, not any more." They stood side by side on the cliff, but did not look at each other. "You can go back to your old life, the way it was before. Ned Winslow's boy is of age an' lookin' to take a wife, so you—"

"How can you say this to me?" she interrupted, hurt and angry. "Was it so good before that you or I would want that life again?"

"Don't raise your voice to me, my girl! I'm still—"

"My father? You forced me out of your house! My dead baby lies outside the buryin' acre, an' you never saw him. The people of Eastham put me in jail, sayin' I murdered Samuel an' you didn't stand up for me. They banished me from their village an' you never came to me. I don't have an 'old life'—I only have now. The life I want is with Sam an' I'm goin' to stay here 'til he comes back." Leaning heavily on the walking stick, she started back for the cabin.

The rebuke stung, but he accepted it, knowing it was deserved and hers to give. He watched her slow steps over the uneven ground and offered his hand to steady her if she faltered, but she looked ahead, brave and determined, and he knew he'd lost her. "If you don't want to be at home," he said, trying again, "then wait for Sam at the tavern. He'll drop anchor off Great Island—when he comes."

"I'll see him here first—see his ship, when he sails by."

"So many ships pass by here," he said doubtfully, looking back at the sea. "How'll you know—"

"I'll know."

"It don't matter to you that he's a pirate? What kind of life is that to offer you? Livin' amongst outlaws—"

"When he comes back I'm leavin' with him. I don't care how he lives or where. Why do you keep talkin' to me as if I don't know what I want, an' how I feel isn't important?"

"I—I only want to give you comfort." He paused. "I'm sorry, Mariah."

She stopped to rest. "Josiah said that takin' your hand would be healin'. I expect Mr. Treat would've said the same. Thank you for comin' when I was sick." She looked out over Lucifer Land. "Some who call me a witch say I'm well suited to this place. Maybe I am, but I don't care what they think. It was the righteous ones who sent me here to die. Well, I'm goin' to beat them at their own game. I'm goin' to stay right where I am. I'll win, an' I'll survive."

7

A week later, Mariah walked slowly to the brook, her bucket in one hand and the walking stick in the other. Winter's touch was still visible, but the days were longer, and the spring thaw was well under way. She stood by the brook, watching the sparkling water hurry along, and noticed the first green shoots growing in places where the snow had finally melted. The damp earth smelled rich and loamy, and full of promise.

"Mariah!"

"Who's there?"

"It's me! I saw you coming along and I—" Thankful went to her friend and kissed her thin face. "I saw your mama at church and she told me what happened. How are you? I should have known—I could have helped. Come out with your mother—"

"To Lucifer Land?" Mariah teased with a little smile. Thankful blushed. "It was a hard winter, an' that's the truth. You did help, you an' mama—papa, too, in his way. But Josiah—"

"He's done so much for you," Thankful said softly.

"I would have died without him. He told me we were alike—'akin' he called it—because we're both outcasts. Did you know he thought about goin' along on the trip to Florida? He says when Sam comes back for me, he's leavin' with us. He says it's fittin' for a jailer to turn pirate." She stooped to pick up the bucket, but Thankful grabbed it first.

"No, let me fill it. I'll carry it for you, and we can walk for a while. You look so tired." They walked in silence. Thankful, self-conscious of her healthy body, cried out shamefully, "I wish I'd done more! I wish none of this had happened, that it was all different—"

"But it's happened an' there's no goin' back. All I want is Sam." Mariah smiled at Thankful and squeezed her arm. "You couldn't do more than be my friend. Every time you come here, you defy your father. Maybe that's the greatest gift of all."

✠ ✠ ✠

Mariah stood under the tree by the cemetery, looking at the three new graves inside the fence. The ground shimmered in the white moonlight, as if it were still covered with ice and snow. Samuel had been barely two weeks old when he died, and now it had been a year since his birth. She imagined him laughing and babbling, taking his first steps, holding his father's hands.

"We're outsiders, Samuel—you, me, an' your papa. We can't live among them, an' when we die, we can't lie among them. Your papa's comin' back very soon, I know it, an' when he does, we'll go far, far away from here, an' from these people, too. But no matter where we go, my sweet little lamb, we'll always keep you in our hearts."

Thinking of Sam, she turned her face to the sea and walked home in the sweet April breeze

The Third Part

First Watch – April 26, 1717
The Storm at Sea

IT HAD RAINED CONSTANTLY FOR THE PAST WEEK, BUT HERE AT last was a bright day. Morning sunshine streamed through the stern windows, lighting the floor of the great cabin. Pirate captain Sam Bellamy, master of the *Whydah,* rolled out of his hammock, and with bleary eyes looked out at the North Atlantic. The sea and sky were a different color blue than in the Caribbean, and he wondered, not for the first time, what Mariah would think of the bright, vibrant colors of the south. He yawned widely, and stared out at the sea a few minutes longer. The *Anne,* the Scottish snow they'd taken off Virginia's coast a few weeks before, came into view with her sails all set, rolling along before the brisk, southerly breeze.

Raking his fingers through his long, dark hair, he tied it back with a leather cord then gave his face an invigorating rub. The ship's bell rang seven times. It was the morning of April 26, 1717, and the *Whydah* and the *Anne* were approaching Cape Cod. Sam went on deck in search of breakfast.

"Will you look at that sun," Old Bill said, coming up on deck with Davy and John. "May turn out t' be just a little bit warmer today."

Davy squinted into the sunshine. "Aye. But it takes more sun t' heat the air in these northern climes."

"Why's that, then?" John asked. One hand on a ratline, he looked up at the main course, filled with air. "You really know, or you just spoutin' off?" He brought his gaze down to Davy. "As per usual."

Old Bill hooted with laughter. "Oh, ho! Listen t' him!"

"Well I never!" Davy said with mock offense. "It just so happens that them southern parts is closer t' the sun." The *Whydah's* bell rang the watch change, and John took a last bite of bread. He threw a skeptical glance at Davy, climbed up on the gunwale and scrambled up the shrouds. "It's true! I learned it off a book!" Davy called after him. "Sounds like he don't believe me."

"You can't read!" John's voice floated down from aloft.

"An' you can't lead him 'round no more, neither," Old Bill said still chuckling. "Gettin' smart at last, our young John is. Mornin', Sam."

The captain was at the helm, one hand on the wheel and a chunk of dark bread in the other. "Beggin' pardon, cap'n," Davy mumbled. Stepping aside, Sam gave him the compass bearing and took a bite of bread.

"Quintor sure plays his part with all this bread he's been bakin'," he said to Old Bill, his mouth full. "Next time we take a ship—if there is a next time—we stop her only if there's food an' drink aboard."

"What's your meanin', Sammy? You ain't turnin' against the sweet trade?" Davy asked.

"I'm meanin' this ship's so full she's ridin' low in the water an' ain't answerin' sharp. We ain't goin' to be able to run if we got to, an' I don't like that. Those bloody cannon we got below don't give us much advantage, weighin' us down as they do. We come through that storm off the Carolinas a few weeks back, but ain't nothin' that says we'll have that luck again."

"You sound like Jack Lambert," Old Bill observed.

Sam snorted. "Mark my words. They'll come an albatross, if we don't put them over the side."

"We'll be needin' them up to Green Island, I'm thinkin'," Davy said.

"Maybe. We'll be plottin' a new course in Maine, with or without them big guns."

"When do you reckon to raise Great Island, cap'n?" Old Bill asked.

"Middle watch. Early hours tomorrow, if we don't run into dirty weather." Sam thought: Less than twenty-four hours 'til I see Mariah. Time ain't movin' fast enough.

"Well," Old Bill said, rubbing his hands together, "I'm goin' t' take my time enjoyin' the look on Josiah's face when we sails up an' drops anchor on his door step—in a manner o' speakin'. An' Israel, by God, he ain't goin' t' know where t' look first when he lays his eyes on this booty. Nor will any of t'others at the tavern. Worth the trip just for that fun."

"Sails off the larboard bow!" called the lookout.

Sam hurried forward. "What do we got?" Jack Lambert had the glass to his eye.

"She's a pink, by the looks of her—an' her hold's full, too. See how low she sits in the water." He handed the glass to Sam. "She's ripe for the pickin'."

Sam looked at the merchantman, with her round bow and three short masts, and knew the *Whydah* would easily catch up. He felt his high spirits sink as he thought of the time it would take to seize her, and he begrudged every minute of it. He wanted to get to Cape Cod, he wanted to see Mariah, and he wanted it now. No prize ships, no stopping, no waiting, no share-outs, no more—just go. But he had no choice. "Aye. If it's what the ships' company wants, then so be it. Turn the hands up for a council."

From the poop deck, where he stood at the wheel with Davy, Sam listened to Jack pitch his plan to the crew. They wanted the ship and they didn't need convincing. But this was the first time Sam wasn't in the thick of things, and for the first time he didn't care.

"Don't fathom his way o' thinkin', none, Sam," Davy said of Jack.

"One day he's callin' down fire an' brimstone, foretellin' a bad end for us all, an' the next he's workin' out plans for takin' a ship, an' gloatin' over her cargo. Don't make no sense. How can one man be sailin' afore the wind an' into it all at the same time?"

Sam arched an eyebrow and chuckled. "Ain't worked that out yet, eh? He wants to be cap'n—one way or the other."

Davy grunted with amusement. "Got as good a chance o' that as a one-legged man goin' aloft."

"Oh, I don't know, Davy lad. A bosun's chair'll get your man to the masthead."

"Eh? What's that? Sam?"

But Sam had gone amidships. "Hoist the black flag an' get on with it," he said when Jack told him what he already knew, and he recorded the vote in the log. Sam thought: I'm just like Jennings an' Hornigold. They had their reasons for not doin' things, an' now I got mine. But a crew is always ready with good reasons of their own for doin' what they want, an' there's always someone new to step into the breach to lead them into outvotin' the cap'n.

"Ain't you boardin' her, Sam?" John asked, putting a handful of musket shot in his ammunition pouch.

"No."

"You ailin'?"

"No."

John joined the rest of the crew, but looked over his shoulder in time to see Sam climb the main shrouds.

The crew of the pink offered no resistance when the *Whydah* easily took the weather gage and came alongside with her boarding party ready. Grapnel irons went over the side drawing the two ships together, and from his vantage point, Sam watched his men swarm aboard and take their prize. He noticed the officers and crew of the *Mary Anne* pull together in a tight group out of the way of the pirates who, following Jack's orders, tore through the ship looking for plunder. He'd lost count of the number of times he'd been in Jack's place amid the wild scramble for loot, and for an odd moment, it was like watching himself take the ship, intent on his goal, having little or no regard for the captives. Feeling vaguely disconnected from the scene playing out before him, Sam leaned back against the shrouds and frowned in thought. If Jack wants my command, he can bloody well have it.

Excited voices called out from the pink. "The cargo's wine! Barrels an' barrels o' wine!" Sam dropped to the deck and waited while the *Mary Anne's* officers and some of the crew were brought aboard the *Whydah*. He received the ship's log and papers from the resentful, but resigned captain, and was surprised to feel an apology forming inside his mouth. He clamped down on his tongue. What's happenin' to me? he wondered.

"It's a good seven thousand gallons o' Madeira wine, Sam! Seven thousand!" Old Bill appeared beside him with the news. "An' look at what we got from the cap'n's own stores!" Two wooden crates with a dozen bottles each of the fine Portuguese wine were carried to the *Whydah's* forward hatch cover.

Eager hands grabbed them. "Aye, that's right, drink it down." "Ah, ha! Plenty more where that come from." "Watch it, watch it! Don't spill it—too good t' run in them scuppers."

Old Bill gleefully snatched a bottle. Holding it high, he hurried to the poop deck, where, after taking a drink, he passed it to Davy. "Ever taste the like o' that afore?"

Davy put the bottle to his mouth letting the red, fruity liquid slide down his throat. "Can't say's I have—till now." He smacked his lips happily. "Oh, Billy-boy! Ain't this the life!"

Someone handed a bottle to Sam. He used his sea knife to scrape off the red wax and gouge out the cork, then he drank deeply, hoping to drown the uncomfortable thoughts flickering in his head. In an effort to grab on to the familiar, he spoke to Jack. "Get a prize crew aboard her. John Brown!" He called to a pirate who had jumped down from the deck rail, bottle in hand. "Brown, I'm givin' you a crew. Take the *Mary Anne.* You, Peter! Ahoy, Simon! Tom! Thomas Baker! Go with him!"

"I'll go, Cap'n Sam," said a soft, musical voice close by.

"Quintor!" Sam looked at the ship's cook in surprise. Hendrick Quintor's talents in the galley were considerable, and this big, gentle (but surprisingly vicious when he had to be) Dutch-African was one crewman Sam had determined would stay aboard the *Whydah*, come what may. Still, they'd put in to Great Island in a matter of hours and he could reassemble his crew then. He laughed. "Aye, you big galleyrat. Go on, then."

"Fog bank! Fog bank, ahead!" The look-out on the foretop called out the alarm.

Sam hurried to the bow. He didn't need the glass to see the band of dark clouds stretching along the eastern horizon as far as it could go in both directions. Even as he watched, it rolled swiftly toward them.

2

Scanning the fog with his glass, Sam looked for a spot of color, a shape in the gloom—some sign to alert him to unwanted company. He saw nothing but gray—no sky, no water, no horizon. Staring glumly up at the main top as the mast disappeared into the mist, he willed the wind to pick up. All sails were set, and even the slightest breeze would take the *Whydah* out into open ocean, away from the dangerous shoals. But the moist air was heavy and still. A fine layer of water had settled on every surface, and he wiped the wetness from his face. The soggy chill soaked through to his bones.

Impatiently cursing the delay, Sam drew his coat closely about him and walked aft, his eyes on every detail. Lookouts posted on the foredeck and bowsprit, and on either end of the foresail and mainsail yards, listened and watched. Crewmen lining the deck rails, their senses alert for any sound or movement, were tense and quiet. The big guns were primed and loaded, the gun crews ready for action. He caught the eye of master gunner Jean Taffier, who nodded assurance that all was well and patted the breech of one of his cannons. No one spoke. The only sound came from the ship's bronze bell, which slowly tolled out a warning.

On the poop deck, Sam stood by the helmsman and stared forward into the gloom. The light from the ship's lamps gave the swirling clouds a cheerful honey-colored glow that reminded him of the time, when he was a boy, he'd gotten lost coming home from talking with Billy White on a particularly dark, foggy night. He'd carried a lantern with a candle inside, and the small flame had cast a comforting, amber blush on the misty air. It'll be all right, he remembered thinking, as long as the candle stays lit. When the candle blew out, he'd wandered, alone and frightened, for what seemed like hours, until he'd heard the bell of the nearby church ring the watch hour. The bell had guided him to the open air of the churchyard, and then to the safety of home, just as the *Whydah's* bell gave them a measure of safety in the fog. The ship's lanterns, like the candles in the windows of his family's small house, gave out their tawny lights: one as a warning, the other as a welcome.

"God's teeth, Sam," Davy said, "if this ain't the worst fog I ever seen. So thick you could shovel it right off the deck." He stood at the wheel and his soft words jerked Sam out of his reverie. "You sleepin', cap'n?" he continued, chuckling softly and glancing at the compass. "Well, one thing, we're stickin' on course. Not that there's much o' anyplace else we could be goin' till the wind picks up."

"Can't do nothin' but wait," Sam said. He studied the English flag hanging wet and limp at the stern; its shape appeared flat in the grayness. "Lamps don't throw enough light for even a shadow," he muttered, peering into the mist.

It had been a long time since Sam'd wandered through that foggy night on the Plymouth waterfront, and years since he'd left the safety of his father's house to wander through the world. He'd been back to

Plymouth often enough, between voyages, and sometimes he'd stay in a foreign port for a month or two just for the feel of good, solid earth under his feet. He'd belonged nowhere for a long time, until he'd met Mariah, and now he knew he belonged with her. Shivering inside his coat, he turned up the collar and thought of her: This warm, golden girl was his light, his welcome home. She was his beacon, guiding him back to Cape Cod, and he was nearly there.

The Whydah creaked and groaned as a gentle swell rolled under her, and Sam turned his attention back to the present. "Bound to be someone else out here. This weather ain't goin' to stop local fishin' an' shippin'."

"We done all right so far, cap'n," Davy observed. "Fog don't last forever—only feels that way." After a few moments, he spoke again. "Hold fast, Sam. Sea lawyer Lambert comin' up on your starboard side, tackin' t' cross your bow. Got hisself a delegation, too."

Sam swore. Most crews had a man labeled "sea lawyer" among them, and Jack Lambert, the sailing master, had quickly gained this negative reputation within days of signing on by questioning or debating nearly every order, direction, or suggestion coming from the poop deck—or anyplace else. Although Sam couldn't fault him for not doing his job, for he was an able navigator, Jack's superstitions and bleak prophecies wore heavily on everyone.

Half a dozen men had followed Jack aft and joined him on the poop deck to face the captain. "Well now, Mr. Lambert," Sam said, "I see you lads've taken time for a fo'c'sle council durin' this unfortunate event, as you might call it."

Jack didn't hide his boldness and stood with his hands on his hips. "Aye, cap'n. There's more'n a fair number amongst us who's got cause t' challenge your orders an' wants t' break out the sweeps. Puttin' a crew t' the oars'll get us out o' this sea smoke in good time, for we been here long enough."

"Since my orders was for all hands to keep their eyes seaward in this dirty weather, who's been standin' your watch whilst you seven've been in council?" Sam asked. "And findin' your courage in wine an' rum, by the stink of you."

"Stick t' the point, Sam." He jerked his head back in the direction of his mates. "This is grievances we're bringin'. That English flag ain't goin' t' fool nobody. Why the hell don't you run up the Jolly Roger an' have done with it? We're sittin' here waitin' for trouble with that bloody bell ringin' over an' over."

"You been shiftin' your ballast, Jack," Sam observed with a wry smile. "You spoke out strong in open council against usin' the sweeps, especially in this passage, dangerous with shoals as it is. Every man includin' you—voted to stay this course an' sit out the fog, ringin' the bell an' hoistin' the king's colors like any honest merchantman."

Their exchange wasn't loud, but it had attracted the attention of the crew, and all eyes were on the poop deck.

Jack glared intently at Sam. "We been at dead stop for nigh on twelve hours by the glass. Twelve hours! How long afore you do somethin', cap'n? An' what about the gold, eh? Every hour we spend waitin' for somethin' t' happen, is a hour we could be at the oars! We got t' make for open ocean afore more bad luck takes us! "

Out of the corner of his eye, Sam saw a flash of yellow light. Old Bill had drawn his weapon and the blade caught the glint of a nearby lantern. "The treasure's stowed safe, an' bad luck ain't followin' us," Sam said. "Never was." Some of the larboard watch had joined Old Bill to support the captain and stood to the ready behind Jack's men. "Though, not to say that some who searches for bad luck, regular like, soon enough finds it."

Jack had known the folly of standing against such a popular captain, but so strong was his conviction that fear of reprisal fell to the side. "I'm speakin' out as is my right," he insisted, looking around him. "It ain't no call for arms t' be drawn amongst mates. This ain't no mutiny. 'Tis but my honest speak o' the curse that was laid upon us when we took this here unlucky ship, an' that which put us in this fog waitin' t' be found out. The curse that come when them three—an' I mean Old Bill, John Julian, an' Davy, here"—he scowled at the helmsman, "started wearin' a dead man's clothes bold as brass. That act bein' one which always brings powerful bad luck t' a ship."

"Hale's clothes ain't brought no bad luck," Davy retorted. "Look at all we been through since that day. Mighty good luck I call it, what with all that gold down below. Them, too, they say no different." He nodded at his crewmates and grunts of agreement came from the men. "An' sure as hell no bad luck ever brung this fog, nor any other weather."

Jack ignored Davy and turned back to Sam. "Look, cap'n, we say the faster we get out o' here, the better for us all lest we lose everything! An' we'll do what's needed t' make it so—even callin' for a vote that sets you aside!"

"You want to have it out with me? Fine! It's your rights, an' I'll take you on! You an' any of these mates of yours who wants to cross me. But when we're under clear skies again. 'Til then, I'm cap'n here."

"Aye, an' rightly so," Old Bill called out from behind Jack. "It'd take more'n you an' them others t' depose Sam Bellamy. This crew's tight as oakum about him, an' ain't goin' t' follow none other."

"An' what's his right t' speak up?" Jack said, his anger exploding. "We're in hell's own mess out here, 'cause o' him an' them others! Even if we was t' get out o' this an' head north along Cape Cod, bad luck'll keep us from ever goin' 'round the hook, whether you're cap'n or not! An' the gold! It's a fortune that's too big! Bad luck'll keep us from knowin' its pleasure! We'll lose it all! You'll see! You'll all see!"

Sam had had enough. "I'm givin' you fair warnin'! Belay that talk an' lay soft! Don't do nothin' more to throw the crew off balance. Fog watch ain't easy for a man, an' I want this ship run tight!"

"This ain't been resolved—"

"By God, I say it is!" Sam took a step closer to Jack. "I'm orderin' you an' them as follows you to stand down. Go forward an' take up your watch or I'll clap you in irons faster'n you can draw your next breath!" He went to the poop deck rail and spoke to the crew. "An' to all you lubberly wharf-rats, cut the cable on this matter an' let it drop like a loose anchor. Mark me: there'll be no more talk about it! All hands to your posts an' look sharp!"

The sailing master narrowed his eyes, glowering at Sam. "Then we're dead men, Bellamy, every mother's son of us, for there ain't no way out o' this curse. Be it on your head alone."

Jack and his men elbowed their way through the crowd to the foredeck. There was no easy give-and-take between Jack's six and the rest of Sam's men, and they snarled and shoved at each other as they returned to their posts. Sam crossed his arms, waiting at the poop deck rail until silence once again fell over the *Whydah*. Then he fetched the bottle of Madeira he'd kept for himself and walked to the starboard side, where, leaning on a swivel gun, he took a long drink and stared out into the fog.

The air smelled saltier than usual, and he tasted it on his lips mixed with the sweetness of the wine. For a while his mind raced, his thoughts falling over each other as he tried to unscramble all the talk about Jack's dire predictions, the weather, and the treasure. Weather was always unreliable. Jack—well, Jack was a fool. But the treasure—Sam swallowed more wine.

Everything they did was connected with the treasure. Where they went and what they risked depended on keeping it safe. They squabbled and fought, counted and planned. Lives were exchanged for gold; lost for gold; used for gold. Gold taunted and teased. It set you up and let you down. It drove you on and held you back. And although it sparkled and shone like a thousand suns with its promise of abundance and ease, it hung heavy as a millstone around a man's neck, weighing him down with the fear of its irretrievable loss.

The wine was nearly gone. Sam yawned and stretched. He had no idea how long he'd been awake, and he was bone tired. He held the bottle up to the light from one of the lamps and studied the flame through the glass. Dull. Lost brilliance. No beacon fit enough to guide you. No welcome. No belonging.

The Madeira took effect and he relaxed, his thoughts drifting aimlessly. He closed his eyes, swaying on his feet slightly as gentle swells rolled beneath his ship. He heard the soft flap of canvas as a sail caught a breeze. Yawning widely, he listened to the *Whydah's* bell, its measured stroke counting time as a church bell at a funeral counts the years of dead men. He thought: Will a bell toll for me? More'n likely I'll die at sea, an' maybe they'll bury a empty coffin. I seen it done.

The bell's single warning note floated into the menacing silence, an echo gave answer. A lighter sound, the echo was a counterpoint to the deeper voice of the *Whydah's* bell, and Sam listened to the music, his eyes half closed.

Suddenly, he was awake. He was alert; his muscles tensed. This was no echo. A second bell was ringing. He hurried down the companion way to the main deck just as a voice hailed them from the fog.

"Ahoy!"

Sam cupped his hands to his mouth and shouted, "Where away?"

"Off your larboard quarter," returned the voice as a small sloop came into view.

"Who are you?" Sam asked.

"The *Fisher,* Robert Ingols commandin'. Homeward bound for Boston. Who are you?"

"The *Whydah*, bound for Cape Cod. Samuel Bellamy, master. Do you know these waters, Cap'n Ingols?"

"We know 'em well. Can we help, Cap'n Bellamy?"

"Aye! Can you pilot us through these shoals?"

The *Fisher* had come broadside to the *Whydah*, and almost before Ingols could answer, the pirates had grapnel irons over the sloop's deck rail and were hauling on the lines to bring the ships side by side. Two men on the yardarm held the Jolly Roger between them, and it hung heavy and menacing. Ingols cursed the pirates under his breath. In all his long years at sea he'd never been stopped before, and now, because of an act of kindness, he'd come to this sad end.

Ingols and his mate, captives aboard the *Whydah* and resigned to their predicament, waited while the pirates put a prize crew aboard their ship. The pirate captain was speaking, but his attention had been caught by the activity on the deck of the *Fisher* and when he finally turned back to listen, he looked right into Sam's face.

"Cap'n, it'd do you well to attend to me, because I always plan to have the advantage," Sam said to the resentful Ingols. "But, today it's not to my advantage to do you harm. If you guide us safely through this fog to open ocean, I'll return your ship to you—an' maybe the cargo, as well. Mark my words, cap'n, an' have no fear. Hold to a true course, an' in time, all will be well."

Sam and Ingols stood at the helm with Davy. A southerly breeze blew up, and the four ships stayed close together as they moved slowly northward through the fog. The sky gradually brightened and the thinning mist took on a golden glow from the setting sun. The breeze stiffened to a brisk wind, blowing the fog inland.

Sam felt he could breathe for the first time since entering the fog bank. The air was clear and the sky in the southwest, tinged with red spilling out from a sunset hidden by the fog, turned the indigo sea purple at the horizon. The air over the ocean off Cape Cod remained quite cool well into June, but the unusually mild wind pushing in from the south made this late April day feel like summer. Sam took off his hat and coat, pulled off the leather cord binding his hair, and let the fresh, dry air blow away the dampness. He caught Ingols' eye. They stared at each other for a long minute, then Sam smiled. Ingols, in no mood to forgive, smiled in spite of himself and offered Sam his hand.

The *Whydah* and her consort ships, the *Anne*, the *Mary Anne*, and the *Fisher*, their sails set and trimmed to hold every bit of the steadily growing south wind, ran northward along the treacherous eastern shore of Cape Cod. Shadows lengthened to darkness as twilight dissolved into night. And the north wind, still touched by the imprint of a brutally cold winter, churned up the great Atlantic waters as it barreled south.

3

Aboard the *Mary Anne*, the prize crew, with no little effort, broke open a wine barrel and were drinking themselves to the bottom of it, one ladle-full at a time. They had kept close by the *Anne's* starboard side while fog-bound, and had replied to each signal in reasonable time. Even if they'd known Lambert had crossed Sam, and Sam had taken the *Fisher*, they were well past caring. When the south wind blew the fog inland and the other pirate crews had given a great cheer, the pirates aboard the *Mary Anne* who could still stand, tapped the second barrel and settled down to the business of celebrating.

Within an hour, the *Mary Anne* rolled and pitched as she took the growing swells, and the pirates, asleep on the cargo deck, slid into the larboard bulkhead in an ungainly heap. Sea water washed in through the open hatch, flooding the deck and rousing them from their groggy stupor.

"It's blowin' up a gale! It's blowin' up a bloody gale an' we're takin' on water! You soddin' bilge-rats, get up! Man the pumps! We can't work her alone!" One of the *Mary Anne's* own crew had come below for help and splashed through the shallow water prodding each man with his boot, and barely keeping his footing. When John Brown, the *Mary Anne's* new master stirred, the seaman kicked him hard in the ribs. "Get up man! We're takin' on water! She's goin' t' split a seam!"

Brown groaned, but got to his feet. Suddenly alert and desperate, he shouted to his men. "We're losin' her! Move! Now! You four—to the pumps! Tom! Tom South! Get a crew an' see t' the seams!" Sobered by the fear of losing the ship—and their lives—the pirates rushed to their stations, and Brown climbed the ladder to the deck.

The high winds hit him square on, and he gripped the life line. In the gathering darkness, he could just make out the glow of a ship's lantern, and although he didn't know which ship it was, or precisely where they were, they plowed ahead through the growing storm.

Aboard the *Anne*, Dick Noland lost sight of the *Whydah's* stern lantern as night closed in and the north wind bore down on them. No matter which way he looked it was impossible to navigate. With a rush of fear he felt the *Anne* rise up on the heavy surf and move toward the shore. I waited too long to come about! he thought in a panic. Too late to turn into the wind! He shouted his order. "Drop anchor! Drop anchor! Don't let her run aground!"

The heavy anchors splashed into the water and held fast to the ocean's floor. The *Anne* came to a sudden stop, straining at her cables, and throwing Noland and his crew roughly to the deck. He stood and looked over the side into the inky blackness as the surf pounded the hull. With luck, he thought, they might just pull through the storm with their ship intact. He went below with his crew to wait until morning.

The *Fisher*, severely damaged, followed the *Anne's* lanterns as she turned to the shore. She dropped her anchor and it held, but the small ship swung about sharply, pulling hard at her cable, and took the brunt of the storm bow on.

The crew of the *Mary Anne* abandoned the pumps as her bilge filled with water, and put all their effort into turning her into the wind, even as the ship moved toward the shore. But she ran aground broadside, grinding and scraping along the bottom of the sea, shuddering and screaming until she stopped short and was still. The only sound was the storm as it raced and sang through her rigging and tattered canvas. Like the *Fisher* and the *Anne*, she would be battered by high seas and brutal wind all through the long, seemingly endless night.

In the leaky hold of the *Mary Anne*, pirates and prisoners sat huddled together. A lantern threw off a dim glow, and in the dusky light a young prisoner read aloud from the Church of England's *Book of Common Prayer*. The pirates listened intently and soberly considered their bleak future.

"O most glorious and gracious Lord God, who dwellest in heaven, but beholdest all things below: Look down, we beseech thee, and hear us, calling out of the depth of misery, and out of the jaws of death, which is ready now to swallow us up: Save us, Lord, or else we perish… O send thy word of command to rebuke the raging winds, and the roaring sea…"

"Lord, have mercy upon us," one of the pirates cried. "Christ, have mercy upon us," another answered. And every voice spoke, "Amen."

No one knew what had become of Sam Bellamy and the *Whydah.*

4

With the night came the north wind.

Sam had seen the lanterns on the other ships in his fleet glowing in the gathering dusk. Through the glass he could make out the *Mary Anne* lagging behind, but it didn't matter. The prize captains had gotten their orders and in a few hours they'd be in Cape Cod Bay, dropping anchor off Great Island. The fleet was running before the strengthening south wind at a good clip, with the shoals well to their leeward. But Sam had kept his eye on the weather all the same. The North Atlantic was unpredictable in the spring. The swells, growing since the fog had blown inland, rolled under the *Whydah*, lifting her up and gently dropping her down—felt, but barely seen in the shadows and had not, in themselves, been worrying. It had also become noticeably cooler, although in this latitude it was not cause for alarm. But together—

The last of the purple twilight dissolved into an indigo night sky and there were stars a-plenty, but Sam, worried about the weather, had loose equipment secured, hatch covers battened down, and prepared for a squall. The *Whydah* began to roll and pitch as a strong wind blew from the north, and the swells became steeper. Davy, watching Sam work the ship, anticipated the order and prepared to turn her into the wind.

The mighty northeaster slammed into them with the power and roar of a hundred cannons, catching the fleet in the middle as the two winds collided. The ocean surface broke apart into gigantic swells and troughs deeper than hell. The blackness of the night was streaked with the white of breaking waves.

The sea swept across the *Whydah's* deck, burying her bow, loosening what had been secured and washing it overboard. Water streamed into her hold adding extra weight to the sixteen cannons stored below. They manned the pumps, working continually. Life lines had been run from the bow to the stern and the men clung to them as they made their way about, bare feet in wet boots slipping and sliding on the deck, blisters and sores ignored. When the rain came, it was driven sideways by the force of the wind, stinging like a thousand pinpricks, blowing into ears, eyes, and open mouths. The few men wearing coats shed them, for the weight of the heavy, wet wool made it impossible to do the work the *Whydah* required. Water was everywhere—inside, outside, above and below. No longer able to light the lanterns, they rode through the storm in total darkness. And alone.

The *Whydah* pitched violently as she plunged into the valleys and headed up the steep sides of the rolling mountains of black water. She staggered and shook as waves crested and broke under her, and she slewed off her course as she slid, broadside, into a trough.

"She's broachin'! Hard over! Hard over!" Sam yelled as Davy put his strength to the helm.

"I can't hold her!" Davy shouted. He grabbed the wheel and braced himself, using his weight to hold it in position. Sam and another man went to the helm and pushed hard. If they could swing her back into the wind and head her out to sea—

"Breakers dead ahead!" came shouts from the deck.

"Here, you! Put your back to it!" Two seamen took Sam's place to help hold the wheel steady. "I'm goin' to club-haul her!" Sam shouted to Davy. "We can't let her roll!" Davy nodded. Sam struggled forward.

The *Whydah*, broadside to the ferocious wind, heeled to the leeward. Men and loose debris slid toward the sea.

"Let go the starboard anchor! Let go the starboard anchor!"

The heavy anchor fell into the heaving water and held tight. The cable snapped taut, straining with the weight of the ship and the force of the storm. The *Whydah* turned into the wind.

"Cut the anchor cable!" Sam shouted. Jeremy Burke and his mate swung hatchets down on the thick hawser.

Suddenly freed from the heavy anchor, Sam felt the *Whydah* leap forward, but the wind had picked up again, whipping around from the east and became as hard to push through as stone. Snow mixed with rain, and the temperature dipped so fast the difference was felt in minutes. Slush ice covered everything that needed men's hands. Injured, stiff, and numb fingers had to stay nimble in the desperate cold. Soaked to the skin and frozen to the bone, the pirates of the *Whydah* had no place to go for warmth. Private tears froze on despairing faces as their ship—and the storm—demanded more and more from the weary men.

Above, the main topsail yard let go, swinging widely with the pitching of the ship. It ripped through her rigging, and halyards, sheets, and braces snaked wildly in the wind. John Julian and his crew went aloft to cut it loose, and they secured themselves to the main course yard to work in safety. The canvas sail, hard and as heavy as slate, was snatched from their hands and the mighty wind carried it out to sea, dragging the yard and the rigging behind it, like a giant kite with a dozen whipping tails.

Sam kept to his position by the helm. The only chance they had of staying on course was the rudder, and Davy and two others struggled with the wheel as the *Whydah* shook and pitched with every massive assault. The colossal swells came on them unseen in the dark of night, rolling under them, and lifting them out of the troughs, up and over the cresting waves and dropping them down on the other side. Sam faced forward, squinting into the darkness and the rain, barely able to see his ship or his men. He would not give up hope—as long as they could steer and stay afloat, there was a chance to ride out the storm and move away from the threatening shoals.

The storm bore down on them relentlessly screaming and shrieking like a chorus of wailing banshees. It didn't slow or break its pace, pounding faster and harder, demanding more and more of a crew that had less and less to give. The *Whydah's* jib and staysails blew in tattered ribbons, and the yards swung back and forth, straining at the rigging. She struggled out of a deep trough and up the side of an oncoming swell, her bowsprit piercing the water like an immense needle, and as she crested the wave, it broke, sending tons of water crashing across her deck. She heeled far to larboard and Sam gripped the pinrail at the mizzen, hanging on tightly, waist deep in freezing water. Two of Taffier's cannon broke loose, and set in motion by the pitching deck, crashed through the larboard deck rail taking men and deck debris with them. When the *Whydah* rolled back, Sam made his way to the damaged rail.

"Can we repair this?" he shouted to the bosun, Jeremy Burke. "Where's Tom Davis?"

"Workin' in the bow!" Burke shouted in return. "We'll rig up somethin'!" He disappeared in the darkness.

The sea found the wide opening in the deck rail and flooded the deck, bringing the body of one of the crew with it.

"Put him over the side!" Sam shouted. The *Whydah* rolled to the starboard, and water sluiced across the deck, taking the limp body with it to rest in the scuppers.

"Who is it?" someone shouted.

"Don't know! Face is half gone!"

"I said put him over the side!" Sam shouted again.

Two pirates put the dead man over the starboard rail. Sam gripped the lifeline and watched helplessly as the angry ocean washed him onto the deck twice more before finally keeping his body.

"It's a omen!" Someone yelled close to his ear. Lightening flashed and Sam looked into Jack Lambert's face, startled by what he saw. Jack squinted sideways in the blowing rain, his eyes darting back and forth. He was smiling broadly, showing his broken teeth. "I told you!" he shouted, pointing at Sam. "I told you the Lord's wrath'd fall on us, didn't I? That fog—it 'twas a warnin'. An' now we know. Now we know how we're t' face God's judgment! Where we're goin' is lower'n Davy Jones, 'cause the sea don't want us—it sends back our dead! It don't want us! The sea don't want us!" Jack stared at Sam for a moment, then started laughing. The *Whydah* pitched forward, her bow under water, then she rolled heavily to her larboard. Sam held tight to the lifeline with both hands, just as Jack let go. "It's a omen—"

"Take hold of the line! Jack! Take hold!"

A wave broke on the *Whydahs's* deck washing Jack Lambert into the sea. It did not send him back.

Sam turned away from the wave and was lifted up on its crest, but he held on tightly to the life line, finding his footing when the ship rolled again. He turned aft, and hauled himself along the deck and into the great cabin. The stern windows were miraculously intact, and although several inches of sea water sloshed on the deck and the contents of the cabin had tumbled freely, the air was dry. He put his coat on over his wet clothes and heard the *Whydah's* bronze bell ringing. The clapper swung freely, keeping time with the pitching of the ship and he wondered whether it had been ringing all along or had he only just heard it. Its rich sound once rhythmically marked the passing time, but tonight it was wild and frantic—like the storm and the men. He looked sadly around the great cabin and at the elegantly framed stern windows. The *Whydah*—a bonny ship. An' she knows how this will end, he thought. She knows.

"Breakers astern!"

Sam went back to the poop deck and grabbed the glass. He could hardly make out the breakers, but the white water was there, and much closer than it had been not long ago. All his effort had kept them afloat, but they had not gained any distance. The massive seas were bringing them closer to certain death, and this time there was no way out.

He returned to the helm, tasting the warm, salty sweat that was running down his face and into his mouth despite the rain and the cold. He leaned into the wheel, using all his strength to help Davy head the *Whydah* into the wind, and he felt her grow tired in his hands. Her battered rudder resisted his commands, wanting to give in, but he insisted, putting his strength into keeping her on the course he'd chosen.

The *Whydah* crested a wave and slid down into the trough bow first, her rudder well out of the water. She seemed to twist on her bow, and her stern hit the wall of an oncoming wave knocking Sam and Davy to the wet deck and jerking the wheel out of their hands. As Sam slid away from the helm, a breaking wave washed him hard against the bulwark. He hit his head and was momentarily dazed, but managed to stand. The *Whydah* pitched violently, and he fell, grabbing a line to keep from going over the side. He inched across the deck on his belly.

Davy had fallen into the wildly spinning wheel where he lay trapped, its spokes beating him about the head and neck. When the rudder snapped, Sam stopped the wheel as it slowed and pulled Davy free. His head had been battered and broken; the pulpy mess washing away in the rain and sea foam. He stared down into his friend's lifeless, bloody eyes, remembering the flogging he'd gotten at the hands of Martin Hale. Death had cheated Davy out of his revenge when Hale died aboard this very ship, and now Death had won again.

"I'm sorry, Davy, I'm sorry." Sam struggled to his feet and gripped the dead wheel, exhausted.

"Sam! Sam!" Old Bill came aft with the news. "Cap'n! She's opened a seam! The pumps—"

He saw Davy lying by the useless wheel and looked into Sam's desperate, rain-soaked face. They stared at one another for a long, wordless moment. Then he put one hand on his captain's shoulder.

"It happens," he yelled into the storm. "T'ain't nothin' nobody can do. Everythin' ends—for us all. It's over, an' it's time t' stop fightin'."

"No—no! I ain't never givin' up!" Sam wiped the rain from his eyes and looked at the old man. "Bill, if you see Mariah, tell her I love her."

The *Whydah* was doomed. Her only chance of riding out the storm had been lost with the headsails and the rudder. It was finished. Sam had lost—the ship, the treasure, Mariah. All lost, all gone. For these men, the fight was over. All their thoughts and reactions, the small victories that had come while working their ship in the face of disaster, the terrified panic that comes while there's still hope of survival if no one makes a mistake—all washed overboard and drowned. The only sliver of hope that remained for his crew—for himself—was to somehow make it to shore.

Sam looked up from the ruined deck to see Jean Taffier and noticed that the feather he always wore was gone. Had it been hidden safely below deck, or had it blown away? He was just beginning to wonder how Jean was going to swagger proudly without it when he heard what the Frenchman was saying. "*Pater noster…*" Our Father…

He stared at what Jean had already seen and stood frozen in place as each terrifying second ticked slowly by. The rudderless ship had broached and was taking an oncoming swell broadside. The wall of black water rose high on her starboard side, invisible in the night; they could not see its crest. Its height caused the wind to drop, and in the unnatural quiet Sam could hear the hissing of the water as it collected, building strength and size. The cold, briny smell was overwhelming. The *Whydah* rode the enormous swell higher and higher. Then it broke and crashed, violently drowning her; rolling her to larboard, her bare masts and spars dipping beneath the massive explosion of water. The ocean swirled all around and was swallowed by the opened hatches. Sam, gripping something—he didn't know what—held on for his life as he was plunged into the churning sea.

The icy Atlantic closed in above him. The water was shockingly cold and pain shot through his body, freezing him and making his head ache. He hung on tightly, his lungs bursting from the effort of holding his breath. His throat constricted. Pressure built up behind his eyes. He needed to breathe. His desperate lungs screamed for air. Suddenly he didn't care. His body felt loose, warmer, and serenity replaced panic. Take a deep breath. Now—

Sam landed on the deck with a heavy thud, his strained breathing coming in great gasps. The *Whydah* had miraculously righted herself, pulling him to the surface, and he lay there, stunned and disoriented. His lungs ached; his eyes burned from the salt. He'd swallowed seawater, and his stomach heaved. Struggling to his hands and knees, he vomited on the deck, tasting the hot acid and sweetness of the Madeira. Amid the ear-splitting roar of the storm, he heard the bell ringing. He and the *Whydah* were still alive.

Bone-tired and freezing, he sat back on his heels in the suffocating rain and wiped his mouth on his sleeve. Lightening flashed and he looked around. He had no idea who had survived—who was left, who was below. Some men moved on deck. Davy's body was gone.

White water tumbled angrily around the *Whydah* like a cauldron of witch's brew as she moved toward the shallows. The pounding surf broke on the shoals, and the sea lifted the helpless ship, grounding her on a sand bar. She groaned loudly, a low, rumbling, dreadful sound, as though in pain, as the sea heaved her off again.

In a streak of lightening, Sam saw Old Bill. He was half-crouched near one of the larboard deck cannons, gripping the gunwale, and watching the main mast arc like a bow. Rigging, strained by the bending mast, snapped and pulled free, snaking wildly through the air taking block and tackle with it. "Bill! Get down!" Sam shouted the warning, but the wind stole his words.

Helpless, he watched the deadeye at the end of a whipping line swing through the air and hit Old Bill, twisting his neck and snapping his head back so hard, and so far, Sam was sure he heard the old man's bones break despite the ear-splitting noise of the storm. The impact lifted him off the deck, and for a moment Old Bill hung in space before dropping into the swollen sea.

The main mast broke with the sound of cannon fire, and crashed across the deck, smashing the starboard bulwark, a mass of shattered wood, yards, canvas, and snarled line. The man aloft as watch, still lashed to the top of the mast came down with it and disappeared beneath the high seas. The screams of the men trapped beneath the heavy wood, the groaning of the ship, and the howl of the wind all seemed to join together in a single, desperate wail of agony.

On the poop deck, Sam clutched the mizzen pinrail, watching the carnage in the flashes of lightening. The *Whydah*, his bonny ship, was dashed to firewood by the sea. Her spars, felled like trees to a woodsman's ax, tossed and whirled together in the deluge that flooded the deck like so many straws in a pond. And her line hung useless and dead like a broken spider's web.

Dead men lay in crumpled heaps on the deck, washing from side to side, and some sliding overboard as the ship pitched and rolled. Others clung to life, as Sam did, waiting for the end—or for salvation. They were once pirate kings and masters of the sweet trade. Ships, men, and loot had fallen into their outstretched hands almost at will. They'd yielded to nothing—and to no one—rising to the top of their world, their futures secured in fifty-pound bags of golden plunder stored in the belly of the *Whydah* where slaves had once suffered the voyage of the damned. The pirates were damned now, their brittle human souls and bodies breaking apart like their ship, and tossed about like ragdolls in the jaws of the sea.

Throughout the long night of terror, the *Whydah's* bell had rung out in alarm, its clanging voice made more frantic by the ship's pitching and tossing in the turbulent sea. As she sat almost motionless on the crest of a swell, her bell spoke out again—slow and mournful, lamenting for the desperate men and their dying ship.

"No!" Sam roared at the bell. "No! Don't toll for me!" He clawed his way to the starboard gunwale, and grabbed hold with a grip of iron. "I will win! I will live!"

In an unearthly silence, lightening flashed and the swell broke. The *Whydah,* seized once more by the pitiless sea, capsized and crashed hard on the shoals. Heavy cannons and prize cargo stored in her hold burst through the decks to the ocean floor, crushing and burying the pirates caught beneath their weight. The bell, finally voiceless, broke loose and sank in the dark icy water. The violence of the wreck drove what was left of her masts through her hull, breaking her back and letting in the wild Atlantic.

The Storm on Land

MARIAH STEPPED FROM HER CABIN INTO WHAT PROMISED TO BE A perfect spring day and walked to the edge of the cliff. She stared down at the sea, thinking of Sam, as she had for the year she'd lived in Lucifer Land. The tide was coming in, but for all the forward motion of the surf as it edged its way up the beach, the water was very calm. The action of the waves always reminded her of kneading bread—pushing in, folding over, and pushing in again. How long would it be until she was kneading bread for Sam? She let the happy thought play in her mind as she watched seagulls run in the wet sand.

On this beautiful morning of April 26, 1717, Mariah turned her face to the sun, letting the warmth flood through her body. She'd recovered from her illness, and although she was still too thin, being out-of-doors in the mild spring weather had put some color back in her pale cheeks. Naomi wandered off to graze in a patch of fresh undergrowth, and Ruth pounced on something moving through the ground-cover only she could see. Mariah smiled at the peaceful scene, but knew she'd only be content with Sam.

She spent the early morning dyeing yarn a farmer's wife had brought to her, but kept her eye on the weather as the hours went by. The bright sunlight had become thin and watery, and the breeze shifted, now blowing from the south. She'd hoped to dry the yarn in the sun, but casting a doubtful glance at the soft gray clouds gathering on the southern horizon, went indoors. She draped the yarn over her loom, and buil6 up the small fire.

Dense fog covered Lucifer Land when Mariah got back to the cabin with a bucket of water. "An' just in time, too," she said to Naomi and Ruth. "If this sea-smoke got any thicker, I'd never've found my way home."

Working at her loom that afternoon, she felt unsettled. She sent the shuttles back and forth and made a few mistakes, but didn't have the concentration to put them right. After a while, she gave up, and wrapping herself in her shawl, went outside into the wet, gray world. The animals trotted out with her, nosing the damp ground, and sniffing the air which was heavy with the strong briny smell of the out-going tide.

Every view was masked by the thick, billowing fog. In the few feet of visibility, she followed the well-worn path to the cliff, carefully stopping short of the edge. There was nothing to see: no sky, no horizon, and no ocean. The sea had risen, and she heard the surf break on the beach and spread toward the base of the cliffs.

The northeasters of last winter had broken off a foot or two of the cliff in several places, making the edges unstable, and undermining the place where she walked and watched for Sam. Roots of trees and bushes poked out of the cliff 's sandy face as a reminder of the time when the shore extended farther into the ocean than it did now. Her cabin had stood fast for many years, too far back to be in any real danger, but she worried when clouds gathered, just the same.

The fog's drops of heavy moisture turned to a light rain. Mariah hurried back home bringing in wood from the pile on the cabin's lee side. She stepped back as Naomi and Ruth trotted indoors and shook off the wet before settling by the fire.

She pulled some dried herbs down from the rafters and brewed a cup of tea. Breathing in the scented steam, she wrapped the ends of the shawl around her hands to hold the hot cup close, and took a cautious sip. The tea and the cabin were warm, and she began to feel drowsy. The animals were asleep; she let her eyes close.

The south wind was blowing steadily when Mariah woke up a few hours later and went outside. The fog had blown inland, and the sky was a clear, deep blue, darkening in the twilight, with a blush of pink from the last of a hidden sunset. The water was choppy—whitecaps crested the swells of the incoming tide, but the air was refreshingly mild. She walked along the cliffs for a while, collected some plants, then headed home for a supper of the bread and cheese she'd gotten from her mother.

It grew steadily colder as the evening wore on, and Mariah put more wood on the fire. The wind shifted suddenly, blasting across the Atlantic from the northeast and crashing into the southern winds, catching Cape Cod in between. The two winds merged and screamed through the grasses and shrubs of Lucifer Land with a force that shook and rattled the frame of the old cabin.

She snuggled into her shawl, and peered through the little window seeing nothing but darkness and splatters of rain. "Do you think this'll be the storm that blows us away?" she asked the animals. Listening to the fearsome sounds of the shrieking wind, she pressed her hands against the walls of the cabin, reassuring herself of their sturdiness. "There's only got to be one big storm." She gathered Ruth into her lap and huddled close to the hearth.

An unexpected sound pulled her out of her worried thoughts. "Do you hear a bell? It can't be! Where—?" She looked around her as if the source of the sound was in the room. "There's no bell in these parts. How—?" She listened intently. "There it is again! I knew it! It *is* a bell!" She opened the door, and the pelting rain hit her face. The ringing was clear and loud—not the measured strokes of a church bell—but frenzied, wild and desperate, and coming from the sea.

"Sam! Oh, my God, it's Sam!" With all her thoughts on the man she loved, Mariah ran out into the storm.

Blinded by driving rain, she pressed into the wind and fought her way toward the cliff. Lightning flashed, casting hard shadows of the shrubs and grass on the sandy ground. In the uneven darkness, the edge of the cliff was barely distinguishable from the blackness where the land dropped to the ocean—like the end of the world and the void beyond it.

There was nothing to hold on to. She leaned against the wind, but was unable to move forward. It knocked her down. When she tried to stand, it knocked her down again, rolling her over. She wrapped her shawl tightly around her, tucking the ends into her skirt. Keeping low to the ground, she crawled and clawed her way along the path on her hands and knees. She clutched at the sea grass and scrub bushes that, whipped by the wind, reached out and tore at her clothes, scratched her arms and face, and cut her hands. Rain blew so hard she could barely open her eyes. Sand blasted and scraped her skin, getting into her mouth, nose, and ears.

Mariah wriggled to the edge of the cliff, and was soaked by the spume of a breaking wave. Spluttering and choking, she spit out a mouthful of sea water, and wiped the salt from her eyes. She struggled to stand, but fell back as the ground gave way beneath her, and a piece of the cliff tumbled to the beach below and into the raging surf. Digging her hands and feet in the sand, she dragged herself back from the edge. She grabbed hold of a bush and pulled herself to her knees. Blinking in the rain, Mariah shielded her eyes to squint at the fearsome ocean. The bell's wild ringing held her in its grip. She could not move.

Above the noise of the crashing surf a new sound came to her. She bent into the storm straining to hear. A low moaning swelled out of the darkness, not unlike the sound of the wind roaring through a stand of trees, bending branches and trunks. A trick of the mind, Mariah thought. But she listened to the sounds grow louder and louder, building layer upon layer; piteous groaning keeping time with the frantic clamoring of the ship's bell.

The heart-breaking sounds were human—tortured voices that

flew at her out of the dreadful blackness, surrounding her like a maelstrom. They wrapped around her, cocooning her in their terror and agony, clinging like her wet hair and clothes as if they had no place else to go. Overwhelmed by the wretched misery of the voices, Mariah gave herself up to them and she no longer heard the storm. There were words, but she made no sense of them. They ran together, their edges blurring, their meanings gone, but in a moment of clarity she knew she'd heard Sam.

"Sam! I'm here! I'm here!" She faced into the wind, calling to him, shouting his name. Huge waves broke on the cliffs, and the foam, driven high by the powerful wind, spread across the sand where she stood, swamping her feet in icy water. She moved and pushed toward the end of the land, desperate for some human response from him; something that told her he knew she was there. As the brazen alarm of the insistent bell rose again in Mariah's awareness, its frenetic pace stopped. A dreadful death-knell sounded in its place.

"Stop! Stop!" She placed her bloody hands over her ears. "Don't toll for him! He's not dead! He's not!" She folded her hands in prayer and looked toward the angry heavens, her pleas blending with those of the desperate men. "Lord! Please, help them! Look down on Sam an' these men, an' save them from this terrible death! Oh, God! Calm this storm with your endless power! Have mercy on them! Please have mercy!"

The voices died away, lost forever in the screaming of the storm. She waited, paralyzed in the eerie silence, barely able to breathe. Lightning lit the sky, and she saw a ship capsize and crash on the shoals. "No! Sam! Don't leave me! You can't die! Oh, God, no! No!" Gasping and choking on her words, she watched the ship in its death throes, the hull broken and beaten by the sea.

Mariah dropped to her knees, her hands clenched in tight, angry fists. Her voice was strangled and hoarse. "God! Why couldn't you spare him? Why? You took my son—wasn't that enough? Why did you let me suffer so long? Why did you bring me here just to watch this an' hear him die? Why? I don't understand! Sweet Jesus, I don't understand!"

She covered her face with her hands and knelt alone in the storm.

Middle Watch – April 27, 1717
The Wake of the Storm

THANKFUL KNOWLES LAY AWAKE THROUGH THE NIGHT listening to the frightening storm, falling at last into a fitful sleep shortly before dawn. The strong east wind was still blowing when she awoke, but the faint glimmer of daylight that brightened small patches of the heavy cloud cover held promise that the night's stormy turmoil was finally ending.

She pulled the covers up to her chin and listened to the quiet, steady breathing of her younger sisters. The storm had alarmed them, but they slept soundly through the worst of it. For Thankful, though, there was no more sleep. Turning in bed, she watched the clouds blow by and the light mist bead up on the small window. It was hard to remember a storm this bad, and she worried about Mariah, alone in the cabin by the edge of the sea.

I've got to go see her, or go to Josiah, or— She stopped, her thoughts interrupted by the sound of men's voices, hushed and anxious, coming from the great room. Her father's and some others'—what were they saying about the storm? She walked silently to the top of the stairs and listened as their words floated up to her.

"It's bad, John, real bad. Doane's sent word to Boston already, an' he an' Josiah's down to the beach now. News'll get 'round right fast an' the beach'll be crowded in half no time. You know how folks are, when there's a wreck."

"Has the ship been identified?" Knowles asked.

"No, no way to tell yet," another voice spoke up. "Been down there myself. You can still see her—bottom up on the shoals. What's left of her anyways." There was quiet for a moment. "The wreck ain't the only thing washin' up, neither."

"Aye," the first man said. "Never seen the like of this before, to be sure. Some say it's the worst ever in these parts. Doane'll be wanting help till the Crown gets here. You coming, then?"

"Yes," Knowles said, "yes, I'll come. You go ahead, and I'll be there as soon as I can."

The front door closed behind the men, and hearing her father walking toward the stairs, Thankful scurried back to her bedroom. A short time later he left the house, and when he was out of sight, she dressed quickly, put on her cloak, and slipped out into the cold, wet morning.

Many ships had wrecked on the backside of the Cape during her lifetime, and although she'd never gone to the beach to see the debris wash up, Thankful knew what happened after a storm, for she'd heard the stories. As she stumbled along in the dim light, she thought of Mariah. Was she safe in the cabin? Had she gone to the beach?

Lost in nervous thought, Thankful looked up to find herself on the edge of Lucifer Land. As she stood in the stiff wind, looking toward the sea, she wrestled with her fear. Her father would not have taken this path to the beach and would not pass Mariah's cabin, so she knew she wouldn't meet him along the way. But still she hesitated, remembering the curse on this land. "Standing here all day won't get anything done, you goose," she chided. "Mariah never said a word about evil spirits. Well, there's nothing for it but to just go." She took a deep breath and walked on.

"There's nothing to be afraid of, I'm doing a good deed. Mariah needs me." Thankful continued to reassure herself as she walked through the wet undergrowth, and while the last of the storm blew around her, she started to sing. Yet, as she glanced anxiously for signs of Satan and his minions, she was vaguely surprised that Lucifer Land looked just like every other rough moor near the ocean. "Whatever did I expect?" she mumbled, acknowledging her own common sense. "Scorched earth?" But she said a little prayer to save herself from the devil and all his works, just the same.

When she came to the cabin, the door was wide open. "Mariah? Mariah!" She got no answer, and stepped inside the tiny room for the first time. For a moment, Thankful forgot her purpose as she looked sorrowfully around the bleak place where her friend had lived for a year. Storm winds and rain had created a mess, and Naomi and Ruth, curled up in a dry corner, looked at her hopefully. She shook her head. "No. I've got to find her. I've got to go."

She followed a well-worn path toward the edge of the cliff where Mariah had watched the storm, and from there she saw the wreck lying on the shoals. The relentless sea still pounded and tore at the wooden corpse, pulling it, bit by bit, beneath the waves. Tangled spars, sails, and rope washed up in the heavy, breaking surf, and wreckage littered the beach in both directions. Human wreckage, twisted and grotesque, wove through the scene like a blood-red thread in a sand-colored fabric.

Thankful caught her breath, and clapped her hands over her nose and mouth as hot bile rose in her throat. She had never before seen so much death, but she watched, repulsed yet absorbed by the scene below, unable to close her eyes.

On the crowded beach were the villagers who had come to pick through the remains of the wreck. People she had known all her life stepped over the bodies, pushing them aside to help themselves to anything that might have use or value. Some went through the clothing of the dead sailors, and others hacked off the fingers and ears of the dead men to get at their rings and earrings. One woman, a neighbor who sat in the next pew at church and had been to quilting bees with Thankful's mother, braced her foot on the chest of a dead man and yanked hard at his necklaces. The beads scattered, and the woman dropped to her knees, frantically scrambling to collect them all.

From her vantage point high above the disaster, Thankful watched the tragedy unfolding in dark fascination, until she saw her father walking among the bodies. She dropped quickly to the ground and, lying on her stomach, peered over the edge of the cliff. He walked through the wreckage, and stopping at each corpse, noted something in a little book. Justice Doane was with him, as were some of the men who'd come to the house earlier that morning, and they directed each body to be laid out on a section of beach they'd cleared for that purpose. No one paid attention to the violation of the dead. Her eyes were riveted on her father as he performed his grim task, and when he paused to absently scan the beach, she ducked out of sight.

But where was Mariah? Had Sam been aboard this wreck? Was she looking for him? Thankful lay on the damp sand overwhelmed by the terrible activity on the beach, and wondered what to do. Uncomfortable and chilly, she pulled her cloak tightly about her and noticed how much of the cliff had been eaten away by the sea during the storm. She wriggled closer to the edge and looked down. Beneath her, the sand, mixed with grass and shrubs from above and seaweed and wreckage from below, was smoothed out by the receding tide, which made little rivulets on its way back to sea. She saw a bit of fabric—another body: a dead sailor's coat. But the bright, multi-colored cloth held her eye. "Her shawl! Oh, my God! Mariah!" She scrambled to her feet, and slipping and sliding along the path down to the beach, sprinted across the sand.

The shawl had gotten tangled with seaweed and debris, and frantically digging in the sand, Thankful pulled it free. She pushed and tugged at bits of wreckage, searching wildly about for signs of her friend.

A light rain started to fall and gusts of wind blew sharply as she looked across the wide beach. I can do this, she thought desperately. God help me be strong—I can do this! If Mariah is here, then she's searching for Sam. If I want to find her, I'll have to look for him, too.

She clutched Mariah's shawl and walked into the nightmarish scene. What she had once witnessed from a safe distance was now at arm's length. Bodies, gray and pale, sprawled about her: crumpled and mangled; wet from the sea; wet from the rain; draped in seaweed; wrapped in ship's line; half buried in sand; caught beneath wreckage. Dead eyes watched her. Open mouths twisted into hideous, toothless grins, smiled at her. Broken limbs, bent at wild angles, beckoned to her. Smashed skulls, headless bodies, and torn limbs vied for her attention. Ears and fingers lay scattered in the sand like carrion picked clean and tossed aside by human scavengers.

Suddenly lightheaded, Thankful swayed on her feet and clutched her stomach. Nausea crept into her throat and she vomited. She staggered to the wet sand and scooped up some water to rinse her face. A corpse washed up at her feet, its arms and legs waving a death's greeting in the churning surf. She closed her eyes, and swallowed, then turned to walk up the beach, forcing herself to go on.

A group of women she knew, including the one who'd grabbed the necklace, stood laughing and talking together, comparing their takings. It's like shopping on market day, Thankful thought. They're enjoying this—having a good time. They don't even care.

She stumbled over a piece of flotsam and unexpectedly saw Josiah. The old man was sitting in the sand, staring out to sea, his arms resting on bent knees.

"Josiah!" She knelt next to him and shook his arm. "Where's Mariah? Have you seen Mariah?"

He looked at her with blank eyes. "It's my old friend—it's Bill."

"Bill? Old Bill?" She looked at the dead man beside Josiah. Old Bill had washed up on the beach and lay on his front, his legs splayed and his arms twisted beneath him. His head had rotated on his broken neck so that he stared grotesquely up at Thankful over his left shoulder, and his bottom jaw slid sideways out of alignment, monstrous and unnatural. His thin white hair had grown long during his time away, and spread out beneath his head like the points of a star.

"Josiah! If this is Old Bill, then— Is this Sam's ship?" She shook him again roughly. "Is this Sam's ship?"

Josiah looked into her frightened, worried face, and noticed Mariah's shawl. "That's hers. Where's she? Where's Mariah?"

"That's what I've been asking you! She must be hunting for Sam! You have to help me find her!" She stood, tugging at his shirt. "Now! Come!"

He got up, and together they walked along the beach calling for Mariah. Josiah moved wreckage, and looking into the faces of the dead, they searched for Sam.

"Thankful Knowles!"

Dazed and overwhelmed, she stared down into the face of a mutilated corpse as if it were he who had called her name.

"Thankful!"

It was her father's tired, cross voice, and she turned to face him.

"Papa."

"Child! What in God's name are you doing here?"

She closed her eyes, her head throbbing with dull pain. How can I answer him? she wondered. I've kept secrets and lied to him for so long. "We're looking for Mariah," she said, holding up the shawl. "I've been to her cabin and she's not there. We thought she'd be here, searching for Sam. We can't find her, and we've been up and down the beach." She glanced around as she spoke.

Knowles stared at her, stunned in his disbelief. "You've been to Lucifer Land? My God, daughter, you— And who is 'we'? Barrett! What have you to do with—"

"Don't see her," Josiah said, coming up behind Thankful. "Maybe she walked up the beach a ways."

"Then let's go." She turned to walk off with Josiah, but her father grabbed her arm.

"Thankful! Stop where you are! You will stay right here and—"

"And what?" She jerked her arm out of his grasp and flashed mutinous eyes at him. "And what? I know everything about Mariah and Sam. I always have! I helped her every time I could. You don't know anything about them. Nothing. I heard the words you preached and the prayers you made, and I know the pain you caused! You should be ashamed before God!" She turned to Doane. "And you! Do you know what your justice did to her? Do you even care?" Her angry, accusatory words took in all the men standing with them. "You're the ones who were wrong! All of you! Josiah and I—we're her friends, and Sam's, too. This is Sam's ship that's wrecked, did you know that? He came back for her, just like she knew he would. Now she's missing, and we're going to find her!"

John Knowles spoke in quiet, even tones, his voice grave. "Go home, Thankful. Go home now. We'll deal with this later."

She regarded him calmly. "No." Then she turned away with Josiah, and they walked north along the shore.

After a while, Josiah said, "Goin' to be a might ticklish in your house tonight, then, eh?"

Thankful trudged along at his side, grim and determined, Mariah's shawl tied around her slim waist. "I really don't care."

They walked for a few more miles, and then headed back to Mariah's cabin.

"This wreck'll be washin' up on the beach for weeks t' come," Josiah observed.

"I'm sorry about your friend," Thankful said.

"If the stories about Sam're true, then Old Bill were probably a happy man. Up until this end, anyways."

Mariah was not at the cabin. Josiah rounded up the goat and tied a rope about her neck. Thankful put Ruth in Mariah's basket, then spotted one of the combs. "I'll give this to her mother." They stood outside the little cabin. "You don't think she'll ever come back, do you?" she asked. "Do you think she's dead?"

"Can't say. More'n likely they both are. But things have a way o' comin' out different'n you think they will. So, you can't never say." Josiah walked her home. "You goin' t' be all right in there?"

She sighed. "I expect so. It can't be much worse than everything else that's happened today. You've been a good friend to Sam and Mariah—and me, too. Thank you." She kissed him lightly on the cheek.

"Well," he said, blushing. "Well. Then. G'night." And he tipped his hat and walked off with Naomi in tow.

2

At the tavern, Israel stumped around in an unusually bad humor. He had gone to the beach early that morning, poked about in the flotsam, and had come away with the disturbing rumor that the wreck was Sam's ship. If this were true, then his plans for cashing in on Sam's success were as dashed as the ship itself. His dark mood lasted for days.

Some of the truth came out with the swift capture and arrest of nine pirates who had survived the storm. Seven were from the *Mary Anne*, and two, miraculously, from the *Whydah* herself. Of those two, one was John Julian.

The nine pirates had been kept overnight in Josiah's jail before being taken to Boston for trial. They told him stories that made him almost wish he had gone with Sam on that voyage south after all. But he reflected on what had happened to Old Bill and what was going to happen to these nine captives. "I'm poor an' alive," he was glad to say. "Can't argue with that, eh?"

The irony of the events that took place during the storm did not go unnoticed by the locals. In the tavern one night, Josiah, Will and Susannah, and Nate Pound talked of Mariah's banishment, her faith in Sam's promise, and the storm.

"He come back for her. She always said he would." Josiah held a clay pipe in his hand and broke off the end of the long stem before putting it to his mouth and lighting it from the burning rush Will held. "Aye," he puffed, "aye. Thanks. Too bad about the storm though, else it might've worked out for them."

"Some reckons 'twas the A'mighty handin' down his vengeance against the outlaws," Will said sitting down. The taproom was finally empty of all but the four friends who lingered at a table over their tankards of ale. "An' others is sayin' how 'twas Mariah herself, hopin' t' kill Sam, that brung the storm by playin' dice with the devil. Talkin' o' vengeance."

"Stuff an' nonsense," Susannah said crossly. "Nobody makes weather in a witches' cauldron."

"Aye," Nate said. "Weather comes from where it comes from an' no place other."

They were all silent for a moment. Then Josiah said: "Still, 'tis a puzzlement, ain't it? Where'd she get to? An' how 'bout that wreck comin' right on her front step, so t' speak? Sam was that close t' droppin' anchor, weren't he? Headed for here, I expect, an' Israel's smugglin' business."

"An' poor, sweet, Mariah sufferin' the way she done the whole time out there, waitin' an' waitin'," Susannah said. "Why, I could hardly believe her wantin' to stay in Lucifer Land after all she'd been through. She could've waited here for Sam."

Samson came to Josiah, and whining softly, put his chin on the old man's bony knee. "You miss her, too, eh?" He ruffled the big dog's black fur. "You know," he said, taking a long pull on his pipe, "if the Lord's hand was in it, you could say everythin' she done, an' everythin' Sam done, up t' the time of the wreck, come t' that end for a purpose. Now, Sam's a pirate, an' a mighty successful one, supposin'. An' she's brought t' bed with his child, though they ain't took vows, an' the baby dies. S'pose the A'mighty wants t' make a point t' each o' them 'bout payin' for their sins. Sam's ship goes down an' he loses his biggest prize—Mariah—just as he's close enough t' grab her. Then, at the same time, after Mariah's survived all year out there, she misses her footin' on those damned cliffs, an' over she goes, just as Sam's passin' her front door."

"But why'd the A'mighty want t' do it like that, for?" Will asked.

Josiah shrugged. "How the hell do I know? I wouldn't've done it that way."

"I suppose there ain't no question o' her goin' over them cliffs," Susannah said. "An' why'd she want to go out into the storm? Not like she could've seen Sam's ship—or even known it was there."

Josiah shrugged again, and wiped away a tear with his thumb. "No. John Knowles' girl found her shawl on the beach, an' we looked an' looked. Been a week, but she ain't come back." He chuckled. "Give her pa a earful, young Thankful did. An' Doane, too. Right there in front o' everyone. Feisty little thing."

"Who's t' say Mariah's dead? Or Sam?" Nate asked after a while. "His body ain't washed up that I heard of, leastways. Who's t' say they ain't together, them two?"

"Well, if you ain't the one for romantic thinkin'," laughed Susannah. "No wonder you got a new babe every year." Nate drank from his tankard to hide his blush. "Mariah always talked o' Sam tellin' her stories o' his sailin' days. Palm trees, an' all." Susannah sighed. "She'd've gone with him, if she could."

"There's no doubt 'twas Sam's ship, then, eh?" Will asked.

"None," Nate said. "Not with Old Bill an' John Julian aboard. John say anythin' much in the jail?"

"Aye, he talked plenty. I told you most o' what he said, 'bout Paul an' the treasure an' all." Josiah watched the smoke curl up from his pipe. "But what I ain't told you is the name o' that ship. *Whydah*, she was called. African name meanin' paradise bird or somethin' like that." He puffed on his pipe for a while. "Well, the ship's gone, an' the plunder them pirate's had is gone, too. They'll be no more news o' her. 'Tis a shame. John says she was a bonny boat."

3

Thankful never saw Mariah again. She kept the shawl, and washed and wore it, despite her father's objections, at her own wedding the following spring. Shortly before she was to leave with her husband for their new home, she walked fearlessly out to Lucifer Land. The cabin had been picked clean by locals who risked their immortal souls for a souvenir of the witch-girl, but no one had taken the bucket Mariah had carried to the brook so many times. Thankful stooped to pick it up and thought of all her friend had endured there alone. "Please, God," she murmured, "please let her know happiness now. Let them, all three, be together."

She stopped at the cemetery to visit Samuel's small grave. "Your mother loved you and your papa very much," she said softly. "And I miss her, because I love her, too. Goodbye, little one."

✠ ✠ ✠

No one ever knew what happened to Sam and Mariah. Did the sea reach out and pull them into its depths, where they lie together with his golden ship, the *Whydah*? Sam kept his promise and came back for her. When he called, did Mariah freely go to him?

The stories of divine retribution eventually faded away, but the tales of Mariah's pact with the devil took on a life of their own. Like all negative yarns, they grew bold in plot and detail, linking her with the sea and Sam's pirate band. Some would call her the Sea Witch of Billingsgate. People would swear they'd seen Sam, years later, a wandering recluse with money to spend, searching for Mariah. Others claimed to have seen them at her cabin counting treasure, or fighting tooth and claw as she tried to stop him from taking the gold from her. When the wind blew up the cliff and across the moor, it was said to be the sound of Mariah mourning for her dead baby and lost lover. When storms came and the wind howled, folks said it was Mariah screaming and cursing Sam to eternal damnation for having abandoned her to that lonely place.

For years after that April storm, the lure of pirate gold brought attempts to recover the wealth, but the sea, too cold, and with currents too strong, held its prize in a tight grip. The *Whydah* lay quietly in the darkness on the ocean floor, her bell and cannons buried in the shifting sand along with her treasure—and her secrets.

Epilogue

OVER THE YEARS, CAPE CODDERS HAD BECOME VERY EFFICIENT AT picking through the debris from ships wrecked on their shores. Anything of value washed up after the storm of April 26, 1717, was gone by the time Captain Cyprian Southack got to Eastham. Southack was a man who liked things neat and tidy, and he vented his frustration both in his journal and in letters to Samuel Shute, the colonial governor of Massachusetts. He arrived at the scene on May 3, a week late, but the locals had gotten there first.

British law claimed pirate property for the Crown. Governor Shute, wanting to salvage what was left of the *Whydah* as soon as possible, appointed Southack, an expert salvor and cartographer who had chartered the Cape waters, to do the job. Determined to accomplish his mission, Southack packed up and made the trip from Boston to Cape Cod.

From the beginning, everything conspired to go wrong as he doggedly pursued his goal. The weather was still foul, and rough seas prevented on-site salvage. The ship was unstable—what was left of her was slipping off the sandbar into water so deep and cold that even in fair weather no diver could get to her. And then, of course, there were the locals.

Captain Southack took up his royal authority, and with his assistants, conducted a house-to-house search for the *Whydah's* confiscated debris. The locals, allowing the king's men to come into their homes, took part in the farce by heartily denying having been to the beach since the day of the storm. He came up empty-handed. It was unbelievable that so much salvage could disappear so thoroughly. In personal debt, and with goods from the *Whydah* that would net the Crown less than £300 on the auction block, Southack gave up. He left Cape Cod on May 13 an exasperated man, and went back to map-making.

✠ ✠ ✠

Of the146 men aboard the *Whydah* when she wrecked, 130 were pirates, and sixteen were their prisoners, including the officers and seamen of the *Mary Anne,* the *Anne,* and the *Fisher.* Over the next few weeks, 102 bodies washed up along the beach for miles in either direction bringing the total of men accounted for to 104, including the two survivors. It's easy to assume that the remaining forty-two men, including Sam, lie buried with their ship. But no one will ever know for certain. And no one will ever know all their names.

The two known survivors from the *Whydah*, John Julian and Thomas Davis, along with John Brown and the prize crew of pirates put aboard the *Mary Anne*: Simon von Vorst, Thomas Baker, Thomas South, Hendrick Quintor, Peter Cornelius Hoof, and John Shuan—were all arrested on April 27, 1717. After a short stay in a local jail, they were brought over land to Boston to await their trial.

The two *Whydah* survivors were never tried. Thomas Davis, a Welsh carpenter, convinced the court that he had been impressed into the pirate crew because of his skills and was acquitted. John Julian, once owned by Israel Cole, was again sold into slavery, and on March 22, 1733, was hanged for the murder of a Mr. John Rogers. It was common for the unclaimed bodies of executed prisoners to be given to medical students for dissection, and according to an article in *The Boston Newsletter*, on March 30, 1733 John's corpse was used for this purpose. The article goes on to tell us that, "The Bones are preserv'd in order to be fram'd into a Skeleton". This may be the source of the idea that his skeleton is in the collection of the *Warren Anatomical Museum* at Harvard Medical School, in Cambridge, Massachusetts. Current research at the museum says this is untrue, and that neither the skeleton, nor the bag made from the skin of a pirate, also in the collection, are believed to belong to John Julian.

On October 18, 1717, in a Boston courtroom, John Brown and his prize crew of six from the *Mary Anne* were tried together for the crime of piracy on the high seas. The trial, which ended on October 30, was sensational news, and was attended by a standing-room-only crowd. The evidence and testimony of the pirates and their victims became one of the prime sources for information about Samuel Bellamy's career. Thomas South, one of Brown's prize crew, was declared innocent of all charges after the court found that he, too, had been forced to join the pirates. The remaining six were condemned to die.

During their wait for execution, they were visited in their cells by the great theologian and pastor of Boston's North Church, the Reverend Mr. Cotton Mather. He heard their confessions and worked hard to save their souls. These sessions were recounted in the sermons he preached and in a pamphlet he wrote called *The End of Piracy*.

Cotton Mather accompanied the pirates to the scaffold when they were hanged in Charlestown on November 15, 1717. The execution drew a large audience that watched in eager anticipation as the condemned men climbed to the platform. One or two of them spoke to the crowd, warning of the consequences of falling into the hands of outlaws and leading a wicked life. The mob listened in silence to the solemn words, but cheered as the pirates, convulsed in ghastly death dances, strangled in the ropes. Mather was secure about the positive, far-reaching effect of the trial, and in his written account of the execution pronounced, "Behold, reader, the end of piracy!" But Cotton Mather was wrong.

In an attempt to stop the scourge of piracy, King George I of England issued a general pardon in early 1718, an Act of Grace available to any pirate willing to lay down his arms and swear allegiance to the Crown. While many pirates took the king's pardon, many did not, and despite the work of Cotton Mather, King George, and many others since their time, piracy still exists today.

Appendix
Some Evidence, Good Guesses, and Loose Ends

AMONG THE REAL PEOPLE IN MASTER OF THE SWEET TRADE whose lives were documented after the wreck, are Palgrave "Paul" Williams and Israel Cole. Paul left Block Island aboard the *Marianne,* and planning to meet up with Sam, headed for Maine less than a week after the storm. Somewhere along the way, he learned about the wreck of the *Whydah.* After leaving Maine, he put into Provincetown Harbor and very likely visited the tavern on Great Island. Nearly a year after the wreck, he took the king's pardon, but eventually fell back into his old habits serving as either captain or officer on a number of pirate ships over the next five years. He is thought to have died in Rhode Island, possibly under an assumed name, some time during the 1730s.

Israel Cole had inherited less than £50 from his father, but at his own death reportedly left behind £10,000. Details of Israel's life are sketchy at best, but the money came from someplace, and living a hardscrabble life on the outer Cape in the early 1700s would not yield such a fortune. A mocking little poem by Benjamin Franklin that appeared in the *New England Courant* in 1724, at the time of Israel's death, not only questions the origin of his fortune, but also suggests he would spend eternity in "some black dark Hole" paying for his illgotten gains.

Some of the pirates Sam sailed with were famous in their own right and had long careers. While many of their personal histories remain unknown, the information accepted as truth often varies from source to source. It is believed that Henry Jennings and his crew surrendered in Bermuda and took the king's pardon there. In 1718, Benjamin Hornigold surrendered to Woodes Rogers a former privateer who had been appointed governor of the Bahamas, then set off in pursuit of pirates himself. His ship hit a hidden reef off Mexico in 1719, and all hands were lost. Oliver "La Buze" Levasseur is thought to have left the Caribbean, possibly in the company of Paul Williams, for the Red Sea and Madagascar. It is believed he was hanged in the 1730s. The details in MASTER OF THE SWEET TRADE about Levasseur's background, personality, and clothing are all fiction.

The ferocious "Blackbeard", whose real name was Edward Teach, did indeed sail with Hornigold and Sam. In 1718, he engaged in battle with the British Navy and was killed by a young officer, Lieutenant Robert Maynard, who displayed the pirate's decapitated head on a pike at the bow of his sloop.

It is known that the *Fisher*, riding out the storm with the *Anne*, was severely damaged and was abandoned the next day. Richard Noland—Sam's quartermaster—and nineteen other pirates sailed the *Anne* to Maine where she, too, was left behind. They made their way back to the Bahamas where they took the king's pardon in 1718.

2

In Sam's time, part of the area now known as Wellfleet was called Billingsgate, and the land bridge that now connects Great Island to Wellfleet did not exist. The tavern, often called "Higgin's Tavern", which was a thriving business, remained in operation until the 1740s, but by 1800 the island was deforested and deserted. There has been archeological work on the site, and artifacts have been found. You can still visit the remains of the tavern foundation and see the place where the real Susannah Brown very likely served Sam Bellamy tankards of ale.

Very little is known about Sam's personal life. That he was born in February, in 1689, is an educated guess based on his having been baptized in March of the same year, soon after the death of his mother. His family came from Hittisleigh, Devonshire, England, which supports the legends that say he was from the "West Country", where Devon is located. His parents are Stephen and Elizabeth Paine Bellamy—the Paines being the family connection he is believed to have had with Israel Cole. It is also thought that he was a baby when his newly widowed father brought his six children to live in Plymouth, where he would have gotten his first taste of the sea. The details in the book about the Bellamy family and their involvement in the ropewalk are fiction.

It is worth pointing out that, in a time period when most children in his economic and social class were under-educated—if they went to school at all—it is very likely Sam received some book learning. His continual re-election as captain suggests that at least minimal reading and writing were among the skills he had to offer, as well as possible military experience. He was certainly a natural leader with a likeable, charismatic personality, who inspired trust and loyalty in his crew.

For nearly 300 years, everything known about Mariah Hallett has come from rich Cape Cod folklore. There is no genealogical evidence to prove she ever existed, though Hallett is an old Cape name. She is often called Goody Hallett, "goody" being a shortened form of the antiquated term "goodwife" that was once used as a title for married women. The legends about her are varied and fanciful, and the theme of witchcraft runs through many of them. Seamen claim to have seen her, or her familiars, a goat and a cat, riding porpoises in the wake of their ship, and others believe she plays dice with the devil for their souls. Some say she bowls with the devil in an area of Wellfleet known as "Hallett's Meadow," using balls and pins made from the skulls and bones of seamen. One story says she lived in a whistling whale and wore red shoes. In MASTER OF THE SWEET TRADE, the details about Mariah and her family are fiction.

✠ ✠ ✠

The wreck of the *Whydah* is still considered one of the worst to have occurred on the backside of the Cape—the graveyard of the Atlantic. Over the years, approximately 3,000 ships have been lost along these thirty or so miles of the eastern shore of Cape Cod. Wellfleet's Great Beach, stretching from Newcomb Hollow in the north to Marconi Beach in the south, has seen many disasters like the one in this book. In 1914, shipping was rerouted through the newly opened Cape Cod Canal and away from the hidden shoals in this treacherous stretch of ocean.

The Cape Cod National Seashore (CCNS) protects more than 43,500 acres of land, wetlands, dunes, and beaches from development and misuse, and encompasses most of the Atlantic and Bay coasts from Eastham to Provincetown. I have placed Lucifer Land in the CCNS near the Marconi Station, in Wellfleet, and you can walk along the cliff, just as the exiled Mariah did while she waited for Sam. If you walk south along the beach and stand with your back to the water tower, looking out to sea, you will be in a direct line with the debris site of the wreck that is still explored every summer by the diving crew of *The Whydah Project*. Walking on the wide beach, you can imagine the terrible disaster Thankful saw when she looked down from the cliff on the morning after the storm.

This is a rough, windswept moor. If you visit on a gray, rainy day, the atmosphere is as easy to feel as the salty mist on your skin, and you will understand why some folks still believe Mariah haunts this coast.

Folklore and legend is abundant on the Cape, and its history is much older than the days of Sam Bellamy. Its deep maritime tradition is clear in everyday life, as well as in the stories that have been told for centuries. But it doesn't matter what tales you hear or read, the land and sea are filled with the ghosts of the people who have lived and worked on this "narrow land."

3

It was Cape Cod folklore that sparked the imagination of the young Barry Clifford nearly 240 years after the wreck of the *Whydah.* Growing up on the Cape, he'd heard the legends about Sam and Mariah, and knew them all by heart. His uncle, Bill Carr, a master storyteller, had spun captivating yarns of pirates and pirate loot, reminding him that "gold don't float!" Barry knew the *Whydah* and her treasure were still there, waiting for him.

In the 1970s, Barry owned a Cape Cod marine salvage company and while researching a diving job came across Captain Southack's journal and maps. In his hands, finally, was the dream come true—a "map" to Sam Bellamy's treasure ship.

His search began and consumed his life. In 1984, Barry and his team of divers, working off the coast of Wellfleet, Massachusetts, on Cape Cod, found a cannon and some pieces-of-eight. They continued to recover coins, jewelry, weapons, and gold bars for more than a year, but nothing to prove these things had come from the *Whydah.* Then, in 1985, the long-hoped-for proof was found when the ship's bell was brought into sunlight for the first time in more than two-and-a-half centuries. On it were the words: "THE ✠ WHYDAH ✠ GALLY ✠ 1716." Without this discovery, there would have been no way to conclusively identify the find. At last the parts of the ship on which Sam had lived, along with ordinary, everyday objects he might have used, were finally authenticated. The old legends tingled with life.

Barry's discovery led to questions, not only about Sam Bellamy, but about pirates in general. The people looking for answers work at the *Expedition Whydah Sea Lab and Learning Center* in Provincetown,

Massachusetts, on Cape Cod. In the museum are displays of modern diving equipment and framed newspaper articles that document the discovery of the wreck and the ongoing exploration. The historic wreck of the *Whydah* and its aftermath—the arrest, trial, and execution of the "Bellamy six"—is also documented in reproductions of primary sources (official court documents) and broad sheets (newspapers) from 1717.

The dive team continues to bring up more artifacts from the debris site every summer, and many of these items from the *Whydah* are on exhibit. Everyday items, relics, coins, and the beautiful golden jewelry of the Akan people from West Africa that became part of the pirate's treasure; cannons and weapons, the gibbet, and the iron shackles and restraints used on the African captives from the *Whydah's* days as a slaver, all serve to tell the human story of greed and desire, success and loss, misery and death in graphic detail.

Among the many other objects on display from the *Whydah* is her bell. Preserved in a Plexiglas cube filled with seawater, the words inscribed on her bronze sides can still be read.

An important result of careful research is a timeline describing Sam's whereabouts, on a nearly month-to-month basis, covering the time of his probable arrival on Cape Cod in early 1715, to the big storm on April 26, 1717. This research produced the names of historical people and pirates Sam knew, as well as those who knew of him. Testimony from the pirates' trial in October, 1717 provides new insight and some details of life in a pirate crew.

There is also a list of about thirty-three pirates who served with Sam as crew or officers on one ship or another. Sam, Paul, John "Jack" Lambert, Fletcher, Noland, and Burke are on that list, as well as the three pirate friends in this book: David "Davy" Turner, William "Old Bill" Lee, and John Julian. Also on the list are Hendrick Quintor and Jean Taffier. Quintor was of African heritage, born in Amsterdam, and was believed to have sailed with Levasseur before joining Sam. There is no evidence that he was ship's cook. Taffier, a gunner, is thought to have been among the pirates Sam and Paul rescued near St. Croix, and retired from piracy in the 1720s. He did not die in the wreck of the *Whydah,* but is believed to have been with Paul Williams aboard the *Marianne* at the time of the storm. The details in this book about Taffier's life are fiction.

The *Project Whydah* lab staff "dives" into the past, researching the recovered treasures to find new information about the lives of seamen and pirates of the early eighteenth century. Their work testifies not only to the ageless hunt for gold, but also to the twenty-first century hunt for history.

4

In MASTER OF THE SWEET TRADE, as in other works of historical fiction, the conversations are made up. There are, however, parts of the story that sound real but are not, and should be mentioned. In the chapter titled "The Free Prince and the *Whydah*" Sam reads a passage from the ship's log written by Lawrence Prince, who was a real person and captain of the *Whydah* when Sam seized her in February, 1717. The actual log no longer exists, and I invented the words he reads.

In "The Jail", two of the characters, Joseph Doane and Samuel Treat, who were real people, discuss a newspaper article that tells of Sam's life as a pirate. *The Boston Newsletter* was the first regularly published newspaper in the American colonies, with the first edition coming off the press on April 17, 1704. The article about Sam, however, is fiction. At Mariah's hearing, farther along in the same chapter, Justice Doane reads an indictment (the charges against her) and concludes with a summation and sentencing. These words are invented, also.

In the "Free Prince and the *Whydah*" is a shortened version of the "free prince" speech which comes from *A General History of the Robberies and Murders of the Most Notorious Pyrates,* written by Captain

Charles Johnson. Scholars believe this is the pen name of Daniel Defoe, the author of *Robinson Crusoe.* The "free prince" speech is reproduced in many legends and stories about Sam, and did much to establish his "Robin Hood-like" character. I borrowed it, condensed it, modernized the language, and Sam says these words to Captain Prince—instead of Captain Beer, his captive in Defoe's original story. The "advantage" speech that Sam delivers to Robert Ingols in "The Storm at Sea" comes from the same source.

A General History, published in two volumes between 1724 and 1728, is a collection of biographies of contemporary pirates and was offered to the public as fact. To augment his extensive research, Defoe invented a lot of what he wrote, embellishing the real biographies and concocting others. Over the years, Defoe's book became a primary resource and reference tool for the authors of swashbuckling adventure classics such as *Treasure Island* by Robert Louis Stevenson, the *Captain Blood* books by Rafael Sabatini, and *The Book of Pirates* by Howard Pyle, to name but a few. It is also the source of much of the pirate mythology the *Whydah Project* and other researchers work hard to disprove. Experts now believe "walking the plank", for example, is a literary invention.

The quotation from the Church of England's *Book of Common Prayer* in "The Storm at Sea" chapter is real and comes from a version of the book the young prisoner would have known. Biblical verses quoted in the book come from the King James Version. "Thou shalt not suffer a witch to live" is Exodus 22:18; "Whither thou goest I shall go; where thou lodgest I shall lodge", Ruth 1:16; and "Blessed are the merciful, for they shall obtain mercy", Matthew 5:7.

5

The hard, brutal life that Sam, Paul, their friends, and crew lived is softened by the passing of nearly 300 years. From this great distance, and the safety of an armchair, we can read about their world and view it as a romance or adventure on the high seas. Pirates can become heroes, and we can sympathize with their plight. It's easy to forget that in Sam's day piracy was a capital crime.

There is very little difference between the pirates of history (including the "Golden Age of Piracy", approximately 1680-1725) and the pirates who stalk shipping today. The commission of their crimes and their outlaw reasoning follow similar patterns, and the resulting outrage and struggle to suppress the criminal activity have the same urgency. Despite the major differences of advanced technology and the super-sized ships upon which modern pirates prey, one thing remains the same: a pirate ship sailing away from the scene of the crime leaves no footprints and is hard to find.

The International Maritime Bureau has established a Pirate Reporting Center in Kuala Lumpur, Malaysia that tracks pirate activity and offers warnings and assistance to masters of merchant vessels. Visit www.marisec.org/piracy/index.htm for an interesting look at modern piracy and the efforts to stop it.

Today, historical pirates are a fun part of our culture. We venerate this group of criminals with books, stories, magazines, block buster movies, costumes for children for all ages and adults, trinkets, toys, games, Web sites, camps, and museums, and we consume and visit them with pleasure. People take part in historical pirate re-enactments, pirate entertainments, and pirate fantasies. "Distance lends enchantment" is the old saying, and perhaps that's why we can imagine ourselves in the bow of the *Whydah* with Sam Bellamy and, just for a few moments, turn our faces to the wind and our eyes to the ever-moving horizon.

Cast of Real Characters

THE FOLLOWING REAL-LIFE PEOPLE ARE PART OF OUR HISTORY. While some are very famous, most are ordinary people whose names are linked to the historical events in this book. I told their stories my way, and without them MASTER OF THE SWEET TRADE would have been very different.

Thomas Baker
Samuel Bellamy
Stephen and Elizabeth Bellamy
John Brown
William and Susannah Brown
Jeremy Burke
Israel Cole
Thomas Davis
Joseph Doane
John Fletcher
Walter Hamilton
Peter Cornelius Hoof
Benjamin Hornigold

Francis Hume
Robert Ingols
Henry Jennings
John Julian
John Knowles
Thankful Knowles
John "Jack" Lambert
William "Old Bill" Lee
Oliver "La Buze" Levasseur
Cotton Mather
Richard Noland
Lawrence Prince
Hendrick Quintor
John Shaun
Samuel Shute
Thomas South
Cyprian Southack
Jean Taffier
Edward "Blackbeard" Teach
Samuel Treat
David "Davy" Turner
Palgrave "Paul" Williams
Simon von Vorst

The Articles

A SPECIAL MENTION MUST BE MADE OF *THE ARTICLES*: THE SET OF rules most pirate crews used to govern their lives aboard ship. In Sam Bellamy's time, laws were particularly hard on the poor. Anyone, including a starving child, might have been hanged for stealing a bit of bread. The men who became pirates were frequent victims of the abuse of power on land and especially at sea.

The articles were unusually democratic for their time. They protected the pirates from each other, distributed the loot fairly, kept all the power out of one man's hands, and put a sense of order in a disorderly world. In *A General History of the Robberies and Murders of the Most Notorious Pyrates* by Captain Charles Johnson (Daniel Defoe), there is a list of the articles voted on by members of Bartholomew Roberts' crew. Sam's crew adopted a version of the articles, and the short list that follows, paraphrased from *A General History*, would be familiar to them. The language has been modernized.

1. Every man will obey civil command.
2. Every man who signs the articles will have a vote in important matters. Those who do not sign have no vote.

3. Captain and officers will be elected at the beginning of each voyage or when the ship's company sees fit.
4. The captain's power is absolute in time of battle, giving chase, or foul weather. In all other matters, he is governed by the vote of the majority.
5. The quartermaster will have charge of the common stock (the treasury) until the time comes for a share-out. He will keep a book listing each man's share, and each man may borrow against his share at any time.
6. The captain and quartermaster each receive two shares; the sailing master, bosun, and gunner receive one and a half shares each; other officers, one and a quarter shares; the rest of the ship's company, one share each.
7. Each man is to keep his weapons clean and fit for service.
8. No woman or boy is to be brought aboard ship.
9. No married man is to be forced into service.
10. If any man defrauds the company, deserts the ship in time of battle, or strikes or abuses another member of the company, he will be punished by whipping, marooning, or death as the majority sees fit.
11. All lights will be put out at eight o'clock p.m. Smoking will be allowed only in the open.
12. If any man becomes ill or receives a severe injury and is put ashore, he will be given proportionate compensation out of the common stock for his survival.
13. Musicians are to have rest on the Sabbath (Sunday).
14. No man is to play at cards or dice for money.

A Recipe for Ship's Biscuits

ABOARD SHIP, GOOD FOOD WAS HARD TO COME BY. EVEN WHEN A ship was well-provisioned with enough water and non-perishable food to last for a long voyage, it was hard to keep food and water from spoiling, or, of course, running out. A ship might stop at ports-of-call along the way and pick up new provisions. At sea, sailors collected rainwater, fished, shot birds, or caught sea turtles, a favorite and nutritious meal. One necessary staple (basic food) on board every ship, whether naval, merchant, or pirate, was the ship's (or sea) biscuit. In MASTER OF THE SWEET TRADE, John Julian eats one in the chapter "Pirates", and Mariah puts them in her soup in the chapter "Winter".

This dry, hard, unleavened (made without yeast or baking powder) bread has been around in one form or another for thousands of years. When properly made and stored, these biscuits will last for a very long time, which is why they were common aboard ship. Armies ate them for the same reason, and they were first called "hardtack" during the American Civil War.

A common problem aboard ship was keeping the biscuits (and

often everything else) dry. Mold could be caused by wet weather, improper storage, or being stored too soon after baking, and they had to be thrown out. Very often the biscuits were infested with weevils. When a sailor dunked one in his coffee, the weevils floated to the top, and he'd skim them off before drinking.

This is a basic recipe for ship's biscuits. There are others, but they are all more or less the same. They don't sound very tasty, but hungry people have been known to eat just about anything.

Preheat oven to 425 degrees.

Mix together thoroughly: 5 cups of flour, 1 cup of water, and 1 tablespoon of salt. Knead the dough and flatten or roll until it is ½ inch thick. Cut into 3"x3" squares, and poke a series of holes in the center (use a toothpick or a fork) so it looks like a cracker. Bake until dry and lightly browned.

After baking, turn the oven off and open the door, leaving the biscuits to dry out as the oven cools down. Or turn the oven temperature down to 200 degrees and bake them again for an additional half hour. The point is to get all the moisture out of the biscuits and make sure they're thoroughly dry before storing them for your long sea voyage. The holes help dry them out, too. (That's why there are holes in crackers.)

If you look in a cookbook at regular biscuit recipes, there won't be much difference. Add butter and baking powder to the ship's biscuit recipe (but don't double bake) to make light, fluffy biscuits. Adding sugar makes scones. If a pirate (or anyone else in the early eighteenth century) was lucky enough to get sugar, honey, or butter, he'd spread it on top of his ship's biscuit as a treat—after knocking out the weevils.

There are lots of recipes for twice-baked breads that make dry, cruchy treats. These tasty breads are made in many flavors, and are fun to dunk, too. In Germany there's *Zwieback* (which means twicebaked), and in Italy, *biscotti* (biscuits.)

Places to Visit

HERE IS A LIST OF THE PLACES YOU CAN VISIT ON CAPE COD, Massachusetts, that are either mentioned in MASTER OF THE SWEET TRADE, or have historical or local relevance.

**Expedition Whydah Sea Lab and Learning Center*
16 MacMillan Wharf, Provincetown
www.whydah.com

*Great Island Trail (off of Chequesett Neck Road, Wellfleet)
An eight-mile round-trip hike takes you passed the remains of the tavern foundation.

*Marconi Wireless Station, Wellfleet
In the Cape Cod National Seashore, off Route 6
The shoreline has eroded about 300 feet since the early 1700s and nothing remains from Sam's day. If you look out to sea from the water tower, you will be in a direct line with the debris site of the *Whydah* wreck.

*Marconi Beach, Wellfleet
One of the beaches in the Cape Cod National Seashore

*Coast Guard Heritage Museum (at the Trayser) 508-362-8521

3353 Main Street (Route 6A), Barnstable Village
In addition to the collection of art and memorabilia commemorating the heritage of life-savers and surfmen of Cape Cod, the U.S. Coast Guard in war and peace, and much more, there is a late-seventeenth century gaol (jail) on the property. This is not its original location, but it has always been in Barnstable. It is just possible, though no one knows for sure, that the nine pirates who survived the April 26, 1717 storm, including John Julian, were imprisoned in this building on their way over-land to Boston and their trial. At this writing, the gaol is being restored and is closed to visitors—but it's still there. (Please note: this is not Josiah's jail in MASTER OF THE SWEET TRADE.)

*The Cape Cod National Seashore Salt Pond Visitor's Center
508-255-3421
Eastham, off Route 6
www.nps.gov/caco

*Wellfleet Chamber of Commerce 508-349-2510
www.wellfleetchamber.com

Here are some off-Cape day trips you might enjoy:

*New England Pirate Museum 978-741-2800
274 Derby Street, Salem, MA 01970
www.piratemuseum.com

*Salem Wax Museum of Witches and Seamen 978-740-2929
288 Derby Street, Salem, MA 01970
www.salemwaxmuseum.com

*Mystic Seaport 860-527-5315
75 Greenmanville Avenue, PO Box 6000, Mystic, CT 06355-0990
www.mysticseaport.org

And so forth:

*"International Talk like a Pirate Day" is every September 19.

*There are many "pirate" Web sites available, but a*vast, parents!* These can be treacherous waters. Do not rely on dead reckoning, but study your charts and lay a true course first. (Not every Web site is appropriate for young eyes. Know what your kids are looking at, *please.*) One Web site with accurate historical information for re-enctors is: www.gentlemenoffortune.com.

Glossary

ABSOLUMENT: French; "absolutely."
AFT, STERN: the back part of a ship or boat. Also the usual location of the helm and the mizzenmast.
ALORS: French; "then."
AMIDSHIPS: the middle of a ship, either between fore and aft or from side to side.
APPRENTICE: a person learning a craft under a skilled worker. An apprentice in the 1700s was usually a boy, sixteen years or younger.
ATHWART: crossways; parallel to the beam (width) of a ship.
AUSTERE: simple, bleak or bare; no frills.
BACKGAMMON: a game played with checker-like pieces on a board with the moves determined by a throw of dice.
BALLAST: stones, or other heavy matter, placed in the bottom of a ship to help keep her stable.
BANSHEE: in Irish and Scottish folklore, a frightening female spirit. They appear suddenly, and the loud, continuous weeping and wailing warns a family that one of them will soon die.
BARBARY COAST: from the 14th to the late-18th centuries, the European name for the coastal areas of Northwest Africa: Algiers,

Tunis, and Tripoli, where piracy was treated as a state business. The term came from "Berber", the name of the original inhabitants. It also referred to the region's "barbarous" pirates.

BAR SHOT: small, iron projectiles that resemble dumbbells, fired at a fleeing ship to slow her down by snarling her rigging and tearing her her sails. Pirates seldom fired cannon balls (round shot) at a ship they wanted to rob, but might fire them at the hull of a naval vessel in order to sink her or at least stop her from pursuing them.

BEAM: the widest part of a vessel.

BELAY: 1. to make fast a rope by winding it around a belaying pin or cleat. 2. An order to stop what one is doing.

BELAYING PIN: one of many wooden 'pins' (about eighteen inches long and an inch and a half to two inches in diameter) that fit into a rack inside the deck rail, two racks for each mast, one on each side of the ship. There are also "pinracks" around each mast. A rope (running rigging) is wound around the pin in a figure eight to stop (belay) it from moving and hold it in place.

BILE: a bitter, acidy fluid, yellow, green, or brown in appearance that aids in the digestion of fats, and is often vomited when the stomach is empty.

BILGE-WATER: water that tends to collect in the bilge (the very bottom of a ship) under the lowest deck, where it becomes stagnant and foul.

BLACK FLAG: See: JOLLY ROGER.

BLOCK AND TACKLE, DEAD EYE: various mechanical devices combining ropes and pulleys for hauling and lifting. A dead eye is a certain kind of pulley, made of wood, and is quite heavy.

BON DIEU: French; "Good God."

BONNE DAGUE, LA: French; "the good dagger."

BOSUN: (pronounced: *bo*-sun; properly spelled boatswain): 1. The officer responsible for the small boats, rigging, and maintenance aboard ship. The "foreman" of the crew. 2. Historically, also in charge of delivering punishment.

BOSUN'S CHAIR: a thick slab of wood fitted with rope running through holes at either end like a child's swing. It makes a seat for a sailor to be hoisted aloft.
BOUND (GIRL): an indentured (female) servant. A man or woman who is bound by a contract to work as a servant for a definite period of time, commonly five or seven years. The contract states that the servant works for another person without pay in exchange for free passage to another country. When the set period of time is over, the person is released from the "indenture" and is free to build his or her own life. This was very common in Colonial America.
BOW: (rhymes with cow): the front part of a ship or boat.
BOWSPRIT: a spar projecting from the bow of a sailing vessel, to which the headsails are secured.
BRACE: two of a kind; for example, a brace of pistols is two pistols.
BREECHES: trousers that stop just below the knee and are commonly edged with a band of fabric. The band may be fastened with a buckle or button.
BRIG: a two-masted vessel, square-rigged with a gaff mainsail.
BROACH: in stormy seas, being turned broadside (sideways) to the waves. The best position for a ship to ride out a storm is head on (into the wind). If she broaches, she may roll over.
BROADSIDE: 1. when a ship is sideways to something, like a wharf or another ship. 2. Also, when the port or starboard gun batteries all fire at once, a ship is said to be "giving a broadside."
BULKHEAD: a wall aboard a ship dividing space into compartments or cabins.
BULWARK: the sides of a ship extending above the upper deck, providing protection from the sea and preventing people and things from going overboard; also deck rail.
CASSANDRA: from Greek mythology, a Trojan prophetess whose predictions were never believed. Someone who constantly predicts bad news is often referred to as "a Cassandra".
C'EST BON: French; "that's good."

C'EST LA GUERRE: French; "that's war."
C'EST MAGNIFIQUE: French; "that's magnificent."
CABIN BOY: a boy, usually ten or twelve years old, working as a servant aboard ship; usually serving the captain and officers.
CANNY: shrewd, sharp-witted, crafty.
CAPSTAN: a vertical winch used to haul in heavy loads like the anchor.
CAREEN: 1. to put a ship or boat on the beach to scrape its hull clean of marine life. 2. To rush.
CARTOGRAPHER: a person who makes maps.
CAULK: to stop up holes and make something watertight, like a ship or boat.
CHANDLERY: a shop that deals with provisions and supplies for ships. The person who owns the shop is called a chandler.
CHASUBLE: the outer vestment a priest wears at mass.
CLICK (TO A PONY): a signal for a horse or pony to go. A person makes the sound with the tongue and cheek.
CLUB-HAULING: a method of going about (turning around) and heading into the wind to avoid broaching. Certain sails are arranged so the ship loses speed, and the anchor is let go as she turns into the wind. When the sails catch the wind, the anchor cable is cut.
COLIC: in humans and animals, a sharp, sudden abdominal pain usually caused by trapped gases in the intestines. It's particularly dangerous in horses. When the animal instinctively tries to lie down and roll, looking for comfort, its intestines may become twisted, causing a far more serious problem.
COLORS: a national flag. Pirates flew a country's flag as a disguise in order to appear harmless.
COMMISSION: the right of any naval or military officer to hold his rank. A wealthy man whose commission was purchased for him held a rank without having earned it.
CONDESCENSION: the act of talking down to a person, or to be patronizing.

CONSORT, (TO SAIL IN): sailing together in a group; in association with another ship.
CORSAIRE: French; "pirate."
COURSE: 1. the plotted direction in which a ship is headed. 2. Also, the lower, and largest, square sail on either the fore or main mast, for example: the "main course."
CROWN: sovereign power; the monarch or his/her representative.
CUTLASS: a heavy sword with a slightly curved and sharpened blade having a basket-like guard to protect the hand. Ideal for cutting, slashing, and hacking an opponent.
DAFT: silly.
DAVY JONES: sailor's slang for the bottom of the ocean. When a sailor dies and is buried at sea, he is said to go to "Davy Jones' Locker."
DEPOSE: to remove an official or leader from office by overthrowing him/her.
DRAUGHTS: (pronounced: drafts): the game of checkers.
EIGHT-POUNDERS: a cannon that fires 'round shot' (cannon balls) weighing eight pounds each.
ELDER: a church official.
EXECUTION DOCK: a special place for the execution of pirates in a section of London called Wapping, on the bank of the River Thames, not too far from the Tower of London. A pirate was hanged near the low water mark of the river for two reasons: 1. it was near the water, symbolizing the "scene" of his crime, and 2. it represented the jurisdiction of the Admiralty, the naval office in England responsible for punishing pirates. The body was left "hanging in chains" until it rotted. Captain William Kidd was hanged at Wapping in 1701. (See GIBBET.)
FAMILIARS: a witch's companions; spirits in the form of animals, usually a cat or goat that would attend, serve, or guard the witch.
FIRST MATE: on a merchantman, the first officer next in line after the captain. On a pirate ship, this is the quartermaster. A mate is also

the first assistant to an officer: bosun's mate, gunner's mate, carpenter's mate, etc.
FLAX: a plant with fibers that are spun into linen threads.
FLOTSAM: goods lost in a shipwreck or gone overboard and later found at sea or washed ashore.
FO'C'SLE: (pronounced: *fok*-sel; properly spelled forecastle): a structure on the main deck between the foremast and the bow; also the below-deck area between the foremast and the bow. The crew's quarters, generally on a merchant ship. A pirate crew was much larger than a merchant crew, and the men slept anywhere they could, even on deck, in the open.
FORE: another word for the front part of a ship or boat.
FORELOCK: a lock of hair growing from the hairline above the forehead. In the days when a man tipped or removed his hat as a demonstration of respect, he would touch his forelock if hatless.
FOREMAST HAND: an ordinary seaman. The term refers to the fact that the crew sleeps in the area of the ship in front of the foremast. (See FO'C'SLE.)
GAIT: a manner of walking.
GALLY, GALLEY: a ship built for sail, but that could be rowed with long oars called sweeps; also, a ship's kitchen.
GANT de CUIR, LES: French; "the leather gloves."
GENERAL COURT: the governing body of the Massachusetts Bay Colony, which was centered in the Boston and Salem areas. The first meeting in 1631 was small, but eventually two delegates were elected from each town. By 1641, the colony had its first code of laws and elected government officials. It was an early example of a successful representative democracy, and is now the Legislature of the Commonwealth of Massachusetts.
GIBBET: (pronounced: *ji*-bet): 1. a gallows. Also a somewhat human shaped iron cage in which the dead body of an executed criminal was displayed until it rotted. 2. A judgment imposed to deter crime. Dead pirates would often be left hanging in a gibbet at the low-water mark

in Wapping, England until their bodies had been submerged three times by the incoming tide of the River Thames. Also known as "hanging in chains." (See EXECUTION DOCK.)

GLASS: a telescope. Also an hour glass.

GRAPNEL IRONS: a small anchor-like tool with four hooked arms used to seize and drag something.

GREAT CABIN: the captain's area, aft.

GREAT ROOM: the largest or main room of a house or tavern.

GUNPORTS: openings in a ship's side for the muzzle of a cannon, often with a hinged door that could be closed to help keep out water.

GUNWALE: (pronounced: *gun*-ul): the upper edge of the side (bulwark) of a ship or boat.

HARE: to run very fast (like a rabbit).

HAWK: to peddle (sell) goods in the streets.

HEAVE TO: stop. Trim the sails so as to keep a vessel almost stationary. The term is used in emergency situations or imminent danger.

HEEL: when a ship leans very far to one side or the other while under sail.

HELLFIRE AND BRIMSTONE: a dynamic form of religious speaking or writing meant to frighten the listener or reader into submission by threatening them with the fires of hell.

HELM, HELMSMAN: 1. the steering apparatus connected to the rudder, the wheel or the tiller; 2. the man at the wheel or tiller.

HOLYSTONE: 1. a brick-like block of sandstone; 2. to scrub a wet deck using the stone, often with sand as an additional abrasive.

HOMESPUN: a coarse linen or wool fabric woven at home; used for clothing and household needs.

HULL: the structural frame and planking forming the body of a ship.

IMPRESS: to force someone into service aboard ship. Until the early 19th century, the British Navy sent "press gangs" ashore to increase the crew by [often forcefully] recruiting men and boys and rowing them out to the waiting warship. The gangs looked for experienced seamen or someone with a special skill. Impressments also happened in the merchant service, but to a lesser extent.

INDENTURED SERVANT: See BOUND (GIRL).

INDICTMENT: the criminal charge, or charges, against a person.

JABOT: French; a fabric ruffle worn down the front of a shirt (or of a blouse or dress).

JONAH: anyone thought to bring misfortune, disaster, or simple bad luck. Jonah is a character in the Old Testament.

JOINER: a carpenter who specializes in interior woodwork.

JOLLY BOAT: a small boat carried aboard ship for utility work.

JOLLY ROGER: a pirate's black flag with a design in white symbolizing death. A standard design was a skull above a pair of crossed bones, but there were many variations, for each crew wanted something different by which they could be identified. Sam Bellamy's black flag was described by an eyewitness as a "death's head with bones across". Edward "Blackbeard" Teach used a flag with a skeleton holding an hour glass and a spear pointing to a bleeding heart. The Jolly Roger didn't necessarily mean death, but it was a fear tactic, warning a captain to give up and cooperate before it was too late. Some pirate crews flew a solid red flag when they meant death.

KISS THE GUNNER'S DAUGHTER: to be tied to the barrel of a cannon and flogged.

KNELL: the slow tolling of a bell, as in a funeral.

LAMBING: overseeing the healthy birth of lambs in the springtime.

LARBOARD: the old-fashioned word for port.

LAY TO: stop. Trim the sails with intent to stop and wait.

LE ROI DE FRANCE: French; "the king of France."

LEE SIDE: the side of a ship or building that is sheltered from the wind. (See WEATHER SIDE.)

LETTER OF MARQUE: a governmental license given to a privateer allowing certain acts of piracy against an enemy in the name of that government, usually when at war. Any plunder is given to the licensing government and shared, in part, with the privateer.

MAELSTROM: a violent whirlpool.
MAINMAST: the middle mast on a ship with three masts, usually the tallest. The first is the foremast and the third one is the mizzen, the shortest. There is no mizzen on a two masted vessel.
MAMAN: French; "Mom."
MARLINSPIKE: a pointed, tapered iron spike used to open the strands of a rope when splicing.
MERCHANTMAN: a ship used for commerce.
MESS: 1. a group of people who usually eat together; 2. the place where meals are regularly served.
MODE: French; "in current fashion."
MON AMI, MES AMIS: French; "my friend, my friends."
MON DIEU: French; "my God."
MOONCUSSING: the method by which "land pirates", working only on dark, moonless nights, sent out false signals to ships at sea. The captains were lured into thinking the passage was safe, and when the ships crashed on the shore they were looted by the gangs. They were called mooncussers because they cursed the revealing light of the moon.
MOSES' LAW: thirty-nine lashes with a whip as punishment. This phrase is traditionally associated with the Old Testament, where it is suggested the forty lashes would kill someone—and thirty-nine wouldn't. The thirty-nine strokes with a whip are, in actuality, more than enough to cause someone to pass out or die.
N'EST-CE PAS: French; "isn't it so?"
OAKUM: 1. loosely twisted hemp fiber mixed with tar; 2. used to caulk ships.
OLD MAN: slang for captain.
OLD NICK: one of the many substitute names for the devil. Old Scratch, Lucifer, Prince of Darkness, and Satan are others.
ON THE ACCOUNT: term comes from the practice of a pirate drawing money against his share of the loot before a share-out. To "go on the account" is another way of saying "turn pirate".

ORDINARIES: public houses, taverns, or bars
OUI (pronounced: *we*): French; "yes."
PAINTER: the rope at the bow of a small boat for tying it to something.
PATE: an old-fashioned word for the top of the head.
PIECES-OF-EIGHT: silver coins; one eighth of a Spanish reale; equal to one peso.
PINK: a ship with a rounded bow and a small high stern.
POOP DECK: the raised deck in the stern of a ship; usually reserved for officers. (Often confused with the quarter deck, which is not raised.)
PORRINGER: a one handled metal bowl or cup used to serve porridge. Cooked oatmeal is a kind of porridge.
PORT: the left-hand side of any vessel. Historically: larboard.
POULTICE: a warm, moist substance spread on a cloth and applied to sooth an aching or inflamed body part.
POURQUOI: French; "why."
POWDER MONKEY: aboard a naval ship, a young boy who brings supplies from the powder magazine (a storage area) to the gun crew when firing cannon.
PRIVATEER: an armed private ship licensed by a government to attack enemy shipping. The license given to the captain, called a "Letter of Marque", was issued only during war.
PRIVY: an outhouse (toilet); from the word private.
PRIZE CREW: the members of a pirate crew put aboard the "prize" (captured ship) to command and sail her.
PURITANS: members of a strict 16th and 17th century Protestant group which opposed, and wanted to "purify", the ceremonies and government of the Church of England.
QUAFF: to drink deeply.
QUARTER DECK: a section of the main deck, generally from the mainmast aft to the stern. Usually reserved for officers. (See POOP DECK.)

QUARTERMASTER: a pirate officer in close command with the captain. Very often the best educated aboard ship, with many clerical-like responsibilities, including handling the loot, both cash and saleable goods, supervising the share-outs, and acting in interest of the crew.

QUAYSIDE: (pronounced: *kee*-side): at the side of a wharf or dock.

RATLINE: (pronounced: *rat*-lin): the small ropes that cross the shrouds and provide steps for climbing the masts to the yards and tops.

RIGGING: a collective term for all the wires and ropes aboard a ship used to stay the masts (standing rigging) and work the yards and sails (running rigging.) Standing rigging is fixed; running rigging is movable. (See SHROUDS).

ROPE, LINE: the same thing, except rope is generally thicker. Rope and line do many jobs aboard ship, and are used most importantly for the rigging. All ropes have names. A "hawser" for example, is a very thick rope, around four or five inches in diameter, used for securing a ship alongside a dock, for towing, or for securing an anchor.

ROW: (rhymes with cow): a loud fight or argument.

S'IL VOUS PLAÎT: French; "if you please."

SAILING MASTER: historical term for navigator.

SALEM WITCH TRIALS: In Salem, Massachusetts, 1692, the sensational arrests, trials, and executions (by hanging and pressing to death) of twenty men and women for the alleged practice of witchcraft in a time when belief in the devil was more literal than it is today. The girls who brought the accusations against their friends and neighbors roused the villagers into a fearful, hysterical uproar. Several years later, town officials, in shame and sorrow, offered restitution to the families of the condemned. By the early 18th century, all but six of the wrongly convicted had been exonerated. In 1957, the General Court passed an act formally pronouncing the innocence of five women and one man. Some modern investigators believe that a certain mold growing on rye, a grain used for bread, may have caused

hallucinations in some of the girls who ate it.
SALVOR: a person engaged in marine salvaging (recovering property from a wreck).
SCUPPERS: holes cut in the bulwark at deck level allowing water to escape from the deck.
SEA LAWYER: 1. a person who knows all the rules, regulations, and rights, or acts as if he does; 2. also a person who is more likely to question orders than carry them out.
SEA SMOKE: old-fashioned sailor's slang for fog.
SETTLE: a wooden bench with arms and a high back, often with a storage space under a hinged seat. If the settle faced the fireplace, the high back would hold the heat from the fire and, at the same time, protect the person sitting on it from drafts. Settles were not upholstered.
SHARE, SHARE-OUT: an equal portion of pirate loot; the time when the shares are distributed, at a council, often ashore. Each man comes forward to receive his share when his name is called.
SHIP'S COMPANY: a collective term for all the people aboard ship, including officers and crew.
SHIP'S LOG: a daily record kept by the captain.
SHOALS: any place where water becomes suddenly shallow, endangering navigation; a submerged sand bar.
SHROUD: a cloth covering a dead body.
SHROUDS: standing rigging. A permanent set of tar-covered ropes stretching from both sides of the deck rail to the head (top) of the lower section of all masts, where there is a platform named for the mast, for example, "foremast top". From there, a second set of shrouds, the "topmast shrouds", go up to the masthead, the very top of the mast. The shrouds support the mast and are used as rope ladders to go aloft (climb up) to the masts and yards and come down again. A man might be sent to the "mainmast top" as a lookout; also as punishment, often in bad weather.
SHUTTLES: in weaving, the wooden tools for holding lengths of the

weft thread as it passes horizontally back and forth, over and under the warp threads to form the fabric.

SKELETON CREW: the smallest number of the crew to do the job; the "bare bones."

SLAVER: a ship built or used exclusively for the slave trade. The *Whydah* was a slaver.

SLIP HIS CABLE: old-fashioned sailor's slang for "he's dead".

SLOOP: a single-mast vessel designed to move cleanly and quickly through the water; very popular with pirates.

SLUSH ICE: the thin ice that forms first as a surface freezes.

SNOW: a two-mast vessel similar to a "brig."

SPILL THE WIND: a method used to make a sail ineffective by causing it to lose its wind (go flat). In MASTER OF THE SWEET TRADE, Sam symbolically "spills the wind" from Jennings' "sails" by making off with the treasure aboard the S*te. Marie*. Hornigold does it by seizing the *Marianne* before Jennings.

SPLICING LINE: to untwist the strands of one end of two separate ropes, then interweave the ends to form a longer rope.

STARBOARD: the right-hand side of any vessel.

STEP THE MAST: when the lower end of a mast is placed into a hollow receptacle at the bottom of a boat so the mast will stand upright.

STUNSAILS (pronounced: *stun*-s'ls): narrow sails that extend beyond the outer edges of square sails. Used in light winds to enlarge the sail area and increase speed. Also called "studding sails."

SWEET TRADE: a description of piracy: Sweet (an attractive) Trade (way of life).

SWIVEL GUN: a small cannon-like gun mounted in a yoke on the deck rail, making it easy to swing around to aim at a target. Deck cannons didn't have that mobility.

TACK: any change in direction of a vessel in order to take advantage of the wind.

TANKARD: a large drinking cup (a stein) with a handle, made of

earthenware (clay) or pewter, often with a hinged lid.
TAPROOM: a bar where beer is "tapped" from (drawn out of) a barrel.
THE ODYSSEY: an ancient Greek epic (a long narrative poem) by Homer about Odysseus, the hero of the Trojan War, and his ten-year journey to return home.
THEOLOGIAN: a person who studies God and religious beliefs.
TOUJOURS: French; "always."
TOLL: slow, regular ringing of a bell, as in a funeral; also KNELL.
TOPGALLANT SAIL: (pronounced: t'*gan*-sel): the third sail above the deck on any mast.
TOPMAN: selected seaman assigned to the top of a mast to work the upper sails.
TRIM THE SAILS: to position sails to the best advantage.
VOILÀ TOUT: French; "that's all."
WAKE: the disturbed pattern of water left in the track of a vessel underway.
WAR OF SPANISH SUCCESSION: 1701-1714. Several European countries combined forces to prevent the unification of Spain and France under a single monarch. The Treaties of Utrecht (1713) and Rastatt (1714) maintained the balance of power. Known as Queen Anne's War in the English colonies, it was a major reason for the increase in the pirate population. Left high and dry by the ungrateful nations they served, many men turned to piracy as a way out of the desperate situations in which they found themselves not only during the war, but when it ended.
WARP THREADS: in weaving, the threads that are put onto a loom first to form the length of a fabric.
WATCH: a system for dividing time and the crew for the purpose of working the ship. 1. Every twenty-four hour day is divided into seven parts, four hours each, except for the dog watches, which are two hours each. (See the section titles in the Table of Contents for the names of the watch periods.) The ship's bell is rung eight times to

mark every watch change, for example, at twelve noon when the Forenoon Watch ends and the Afternoon Watch begins. The bell rings again at each half hour for the length of the watch: one bell at 12:30, two bells at 1:00, three bells at 1:30, four bells at 2:00, and so on, until eight bells ring again at 4:00 and the First Dog Watch begins. The pattern is repeated continually. On board a ship, it is a way to tell time. A half-hour glass (see GLASS) is used to measure the divisions of time. 2. The division of the crew into working and resting halves. The "watch on deck" works, while the "watch below" rests.

WATER BREAKING: when the amniotic sac, which holds an unborn baby and the fluids surrounding it, ruptures. It signals the onset of birth.

WEATHER SIDE: the side of a ship or building on which the winds blows. (See LEE SIDE.)

WEATHERLY AND STIFF: when a ship's sails are being used to the best advantage in sailing close to the wind, and when a ship's not easily heeled over. In MASTER OF THE SWEET TRADE, when Josiah tells Sam that Mariah is "weatherly and stiff ", he means she is strong and dependable and won't be easily "knocked over" by the ordinary hardships in life.

WEFT THREADS: the crosswise threads that form the width of a fabric. The threads are wrapped around the shuttles and woven under and over the warp threads.

WORSTED: firmly textured, tightly twisted woolen yarn made from long fibers.

About the Author

Elizabeth Moisan, a native New Yorker, has worked professionally as an artist since graduating from Parsons School of Design in 1970. In addition to a forty-plus year career as a designer in the home-furnishings industry, she has done illustration, set design, and taken on watercolor and portrait commissions. She is an Arts and Letters member of the Cape Cod Branch of the *National League of American Pen Women*; the founding host of *A Book in the Hand* and *Shelf Space*, two literary programs; the facilitator of a writing group; and founder and member of *Just Plain Folk*, a folk music group that performs locally.

A 13th generation Mayflower descendant, she lives on Cape Cod—a place with very deep family roots—a short distance from the setting of her book. ***Master of the Sweet Trade*** is her debut novel.

Please visit: www.elizabethmoisan-books.jimdo.com for more information, and links to see her art work. You may contact her using the form on her web site, or visit the ***Master of the Sweet Trade*** Facebook page.

Made in the USA
Middletown, DE
30 July 2016